THE HEIR'S

BETRAYAL

The Fallen Heir

Book Two

Rachel Hetrick

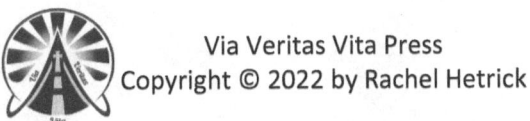

Via Veritas Vita Press

First printed in the United States of America in April 2022.

Cover Design by MiblArt
Editor: Enchanted Inc. Publishing

ISBN 978-1-953139-08-5 (paperback)
ISBN 978-1-953139-09-2 (ebook)

Published by Via Veritas Vita Press
Website: www.rachelhetrickwrites.com

First Edition
10 9 8 7 6 5 4 3 2 1

For my Dad,

Your support has been

nonstop, and for that, I am

so grateful. Thank you so much

for everything you've done for me!

I love you!

SIGN UP FOR MY AUTHOR NEWSLETTER

Enjoy interactive maps, short stories, and other exclusives from this series by subscribing to my newsletter and visiting my website at:

www.rachelhetrickwrites.com

A Map By Mellacross

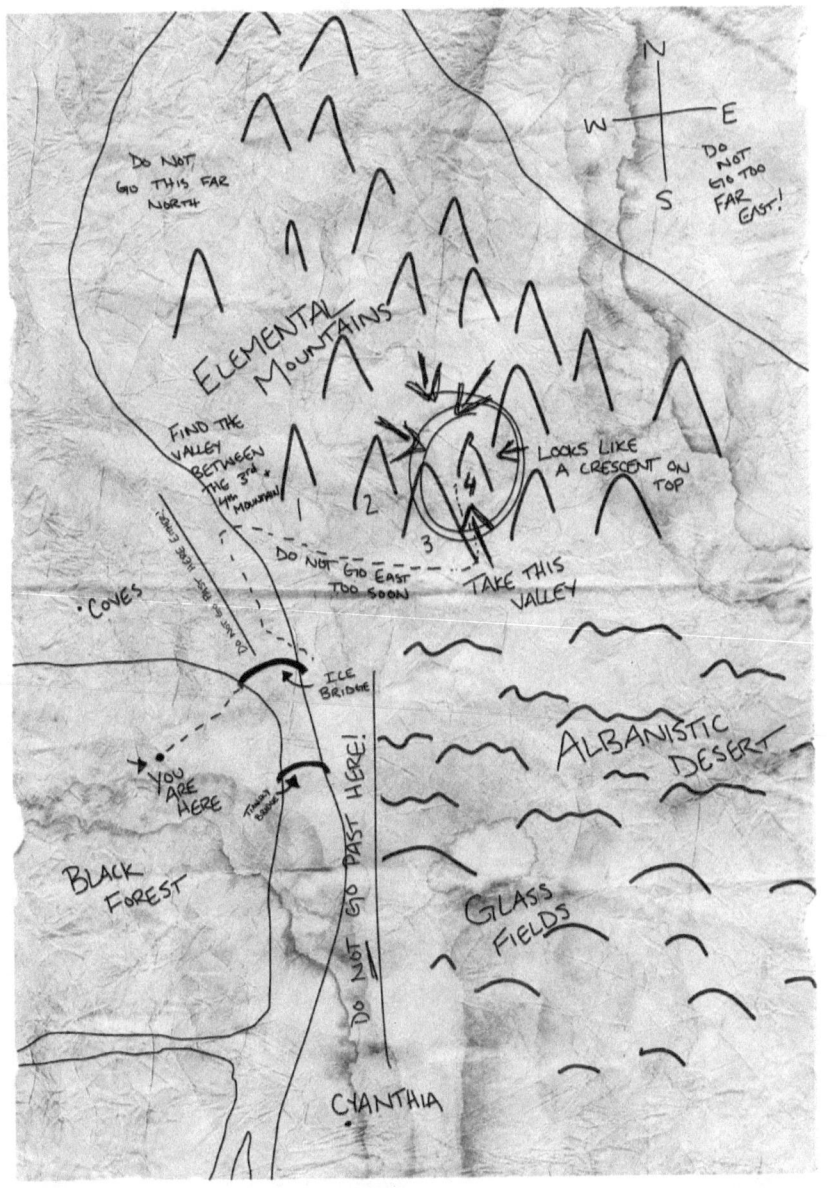

Prologue

Something was wrong. Terribly, horribly wrong. Diomedes's bare feet pounded on the cold brick as he sprinted to the throne room, a single flower in his tiny fist. The royal guards stepped out of his way, and somewhere in the back of his mind he heard them calling out questions, but the words rang hollow and empty in the young prince's mind.

"Your Highness." A guard stood outside the throne room doors, and he stopped Diomedes with an outstretched hand. "What's the matter?"

"I need to see my father," Diomedes replied, trying in vain to push past the strong arm blocking his path. "It's an emergency," he enunciated, hoping to sound commanding.

"With all due respect, Prince Diomedes, the king is dealing with the events of last night. He's too busy to—"

"Let me in," Diomedes said, grunting as the guard all but restrained him. "Let me in!"

A familiar voice echoed down the long hallway, and Diomedes tensed. He didn't, however, stop straining against the guard.

"Your Highness, calm yourself." A man in a white tunic and green cloak stopped a few feet from the grand doors to the throne room. "You're doing yourself a disservice by throwing a tantrum. You'll never gain what you desire by acting like a child. I thought I'd taught you better than that."

Diomedes shoved away from the guard, biting his tongue so he would not point out that he was, in fact, a child. His tutor stared down his wide nose at Diomedes, his bushy eyebrows furrowing in the middle.

"I need to speak to my father," Diomedes said, glaring up at him.

His tutor's sour face did not change, at least not right away. But the longer he stared at Diomedes, the softer his gaze became. Did he know? Had he already heard what had happened to Diomedes's mother the previous night?

With a sigh and pursed lips, Diomedes's tutor nodded toward the two guards. "Open the doors for the young prince."

"But, sir, the king—"

"Now," the tutor ordered, waving his hand off to the side. The wrinkles around his neck deepened as he tilted his chin down. Addressing Diomedes, he said, "I expect to see you in the third floor library in twenty minutes. Do not be late."

For the first time since he had been introduced to his tutor, Diomedes did not hate the man. He nodded, spitting out a quick word of thanks before entering the throne room through the doors the guards had opened for him.

As soon as he crossed into the throne room, however, Diomedes's drive faded. He paused near the doors as they closed behind him. His hands dropped to his sides, one still gripping the flower.

"Son, what are you doing in here?" King Butch stared down at Diomedes from his throne, his eyes narrowing. On his fair hair rested a thick band of silver with jewels of green and blue spaced evenly around it.

The king was not alone in the room, and Diomedes recognized one of the other two men as a marshal. He wore the royal guard uniform, except his collar was royal blue: the marking of a leader.

The second man in the room was dressed like a member of King Butch's council—high-collared robe and all—but Diomedes did not know him.

Diomedes's stomach clenched when his gaze found the empty throne next to his father's. With the torrential storm crashing in his skull, he barely remembered to bow before stepping any farther into the room. It was a quick bow, and when he looked up, his father's brow had creased even more.

"Why are they taking Mother's things?" Diomedes asked, noting the way the adults exchanged glances at his question. "Where are they taking them?"

King Butch closed his eyes, releasing a deep sigh. "Gentlemen, we will finish this discussion later."

"Of course, Your Majesty," the marshal said, saluting as he backed toward the doors. As he passed Diomedes, his eyes softened and his chin tilted down.

For some reason, the marshal's expression made Diomedes stand taller, lifting his shoulders back. He kept eye contact with the marshal until the man had passed him.

The council member, on the other hand, paid no heed to Diomedes as he left.

When silence swept around Diomedes, he turned his attention to his father, stepping closer to the center of the room. For a mere second, his eyes drifted upward, following the long strips of maroon curtains that fell like waterfalls from the vaulted ceiling. A scene of purple flowers and a meadow spread over the bricks above Diomedes.

"Come here, Dio." King Butch's voice was gentle, his gaze soft.

Knowing his obedience was the fastest way to receive his sought-after answers, Diomedes walked to the foot of the stairs leading up to the thrones. His father leaned to one side, resting his elbow on the arm of the elaborate chair.

"How are you, my boy? I know last night was probably scary and confusing."

Diomedes lifted his chin. "Why are the servants clearing out Mother's room? Where'd she go?"

King Butch rubbed the bridge of his nose with two fingers, another long exhale slipping from his lips. "Dio, I know this has to be hard for you, but your mother . . . is gone."

"Why? When is she coming back? I saw her in my room, and the guards—"

"She's not coming back, Son. She . . . she—" King Butch cleared his throat, running his fingers over his mouth. "She loved you very much, Dio, but she's gone."

"Why? I don't understand. Why isn't she coming back?" Diomedes's voice rose, and he held out the flower, which had already begun to wilt since he had taken it from a vase in his mother's room. "Why are they taking her things?"

"Dio," King Butch said, adjusting his collar, "I don't understand why she left either. I don't." The king massaged his temple. Dark circles had gathered beneath his eyes, and he slouched more than normal. "Come here," King Butch said, waving his hand as he motioned Diomedes forward.

When Diomedes reached him, King Butch lifted him onto his knee. His father's embrace was warm, and it would've been comforting under any other circumstances. But with his mother's absence on his mind, Diomedes fidgeted, his spirit unsettled.

"I'm sorry this has happened, Dio. I really am. I can't pretend to understand what's going on. I'm confused too. You aren't alone in this. Your mother, she . . . she made a decision. One that affects us both. But in moments like these, you and I must acknowledge the tragedy and, in time, move forward."

"What?" Diomedes stared up at his father, his mouth partially open.

King Butch's eyes softened. "Dio, this is hard, and I don't have all the answers. I'm hurting and lost too."

"But Mother is—"

"Your mother made a choice. You'll have a choice to make some day too. I promise we will make it through this together."

The doors to the throne room cracked open, and both father and son looked up. Diomedes recognized the blond woman who walked in. She had been in the castle and had spent plenty of time around his father. Evangeline—*Miss* Evangeline; his tutor had corrected him every time.

"I'm sorry for interrupting," she said, her voice delicate as she glanced between the king and the prince. Her arm was in a sling, and she rubbed the fabric strap repetitively. "But it's important."

Diomedes looked up to his father's face, expecting him to send her away as he had the marshal and council member, but a frown crossed Diomedes's face as his father lowered him to the floor, sighing.

"I'm sorry, Dio, but I need to speak with her."

"But—"

"I'm sorry, Son. You need to leave."

Chapter One

Diomedes Maudit ducked out of the way a moment before a bottle exploded into pieces against the wall next to his head. He narrowed his eyes as he scanned the dimly lit room to see which drunken patron of the tavern had thrown it; however, in the tightly packed crowd, it proved to be an impossible task.

The room appeared to swirl as it descended further into mayhem. Across the sea of fists and flying bottles, Armannii Ovair's silver eyes glinted as he let go of the man he'd been holding in a headlock. The man's unconscious body collapsed to the sticky floor. Armannii dodged a barstool hurtling toward him, frowning in the direction it had come from. His eyes met Diomedes's, but the elf shifted his attention soon after.

A roar distracted Diomedes from his friend, and he stumbled backward against the bar as a man twice his size rammed into him.

"You're mine, Princeling." The man slurred his words, his breath making Diomedes's skin crawl.

He caught the man's fist before it even came close to his face, but he struggled against the man's weight. The edge of the counter dug into Diomedes's spine, and he ground his teeth together.

Jabbing his knee upward, Diomedes spun underneath the man's arms as his attacker collapsed in pain, smacking his head against the bar. The man didn't get up again.

Cracking his neck side to side, Diomedes glanced around for any more physical threats. Out of the corner of his eye, he saw a woman with long black hair dance out of the way of a lanky man. Blanndynne held a grin on her dark red lips as she landed a kick to the man's backside, sending him flying into a nearby post.

A small smile crossed Diomedes's lips as he watched her, but it fell away just as quickly when six men dressed in royal guard uniforms burst through the tavern door. As they scanned the room, their eyes locked on Diomedes.

He glared at them, his bruised hands balling up into fists. Of course they had found him. Of course it had been wishful thinking that his father would give up the search since he'd been gone two months. And of course they were already halfway across the room.

"Time to go," Armannii said as he appeared next to Diomedes. It was no surprise the elf had navigated the chaos with little to no problem; however, his lip was bleeding, and a knuckle-shaped red mark was showing on his cheek.

"It would appear so," Diomedes replied. He hoped some riled-up patron would distract the guards and make it difficult for them to reach him across the room. Well, that, and he hoped to make it to the door before they realized he was going for it.

"I'll get B if you think you can make it outside by yourself," Armannii shouted over the noise.

"I think I can manage," Diomedes said, using the large man who had attacked him as a stepping stool to get onto the counter. He sprinted across the glass-strewn surface, leaping over the hands snaking out to catch his ankles. Using a ceiling beam, he swung down, landing in the middle of the fray.

Diomedes gritted his teeth as he entered the free-for-all. Elbows caught him in the shoulders and ribs, but he gave as well as he got. Most people around him were already caught up in some sort of brawl, but twice someone lunged for him.

The first time, he caught the man under the chin, knocking him backward with a swift uppercut. However, the second time, a burly woman came from behind and wrapped her arms around him, pinning his arms to his sides. He grunted as she lifted him off his feet and squeezed the air out of his lungs.

"That reward is *mine*," she said, her voice like footsteps on gravel.

"Doubt it," Diomedes coughed out before slamming his head backward.

The woman cried out when his skull connected with her nose. She dropped him instantly, tripping backward as the rowdy crowd swallowed her.

Diomedes rubbed the back of his head as he shoved his way to the front of the room. The door—now hanging by one hinge—came into view at the same time as one of the royal guards. Diomedes gave the rest of the area a once-over to assure himself there was only one nearby.

"You're coming back to the castle with us, Your Highness," the guard said, drawing his sword.

Snorting, Diomedes pressed his thin lips into a sneer. "I'm still 'Your Highness,' am I? I would've thought my father had taken care of that by now." He had refrained from unsheathing his sword in the tavern, content to fight hand to hand. However, he was not naive enough to think the guard wouldn't use his weapon to coerce him into submission, so he drew his sword and matched the guard's stance, enjoying the way the hilt fit perfectly in his hand.

"It's imperative you come with us." The guard took a step toward Diomedes, who stood his ground.

"Is it now? And why is that?" Diomedes tilted his head. Only ten feet stood between him and the exit. "Is my father in a listening mood?"

The guard didn't respond.

"No? In that case, I think I'll pass." Diomedes raised his sword to counter the guard's first swing. The clank of metal against metal faded into the noise in the tavern, and while half the men in the pub wanted to sell him over to his father for the monetary reward, he had no desire to accidentally injure the disorderly patrons. Thankfully, fewer people collected near the door, allowing Diomedes and the guard a wide berth to swing their swords.

With each attack and parry, Diomedes forced the man where he wanted him to go. His body moved with a mind of its own, having been trained in combat from a young age. This freed his mind to focus all thoughts on escaping. Every step Diomedes took pushed his opponent farther from the exit as he circled closer.

Even when the guard caught the edge of Diomedes's arm with the tip of his blade, Diomedes remained in control. Hot air hissed out through his teeth, and the guard paused for a brief moment.

"Your Highness, I—"

The pain from his bleeding bicep was a small price to pay, and Diomedes smirked as he brought his sword down, cutting off the guard's words and slicing his leg. The man's eyes widened, and he let out a howl. Diomedes drew toward the exit as the guard crumpled down to clutch his bleeding thigh.

"You might want to find a healer for that," Diomedes said, a smug grin on his lips. He sheathed his sword, then gripped his bloody sleeve. "It looks like it hurts."

Without another word, he disappeared into the darkness of the Black Forest.

"Well, that was another waste of time," Armannii said as he closed the front door to the house they'd been staying in. It was tucked into the northern part of the Black Forest.

"I take it you didn't find what you were looking for?" Diomedes's friend Camile said from behind a counter. She was busy cutting up vegetables for a soup that already had Diomedes's stomach rumbling in anticipation.

"We didn't," Diomedes said as he tossed his bag on a short table near a sofa. "But I don't know why you're complaining about a bar fight. Weren't you born in the middle of one?" Diomedes asked Armannii, snorting when the elf rolled his eyes at the joke.

"Can I help with anything?" Blanndynne asked Camile as Theo, Camile's son, came running out from one of the back rooms.

"Could you check on Maisy? She's supposed to be napping in the far back bedroom." Camile thanked Blanndynne when the genie left the kitchen.

"What's wrong with your eye?" Theo asked as Armannii scooped him up. The elf flinched when Theo poked his swollen cheek, but a smirk rested on Armannii's lips.

"I fought off a bear."

"Really?" The boy's voice rose in awe.

"No," Diomedes said, chuckling. He thanked Camile when she handed him a cloth soaked in cool water, and he passed it to Armannii. "He just didn't duck out of the way of a fist."

"To be fair, I dodged the first one. It was the second one that got me," Armannii said as he put Theo down and started to nurse his swollen eye. He stopped when Diomedes winced as he pulled at the fabric of his bloody sleeve. "Let me."

Diomedes sat down at Camile's dining table, and Theo sat across from him. The young boy watched with wide eyes as Armannii pulled back Diomedes's sleeve.

"How'd you get that?" Theo asked, drawing his mother's attention.

"Theo, go get the box of bandages out of your father's and my room." While strict, her voice was gentle, and her son didn't argue.

"Thank you for letting us stay with you—ow!" Diomedes hissed through his teeth when Armannii poked the torn skin. He smacked Armannii upside the head. "Watch it. That hurts."

"That's what happens when you run into another man's sword. Don't be a baby," Armannii said, rubbing the side of his head where Diomedes had hit him.

"You're welcome," Camile said, drawing Diomedes's attention away from the sting in his arm. "We're lucky to have found this place as quickly as we did after fleeing Cyanthia. Forrest and I were delighted when Armannii sent word that you needed a place to stay. It's the least we can do after what you did for us . . . for Forrest." She paused, a crease furrowing her brow, but only for a second. Camile placed a smile on her lips when she glanced at Diomedes, who was watching her with a steady gaze. "And besides, Forrest has appreciated your help the last couple of days, and Theo loves having the two of you around."

"Thanks, kid," Armannii said when Theo came back with a box of bandages.

"Do you have a plan of where to look next? Or are you just going to keep getting into pub brawls?" Camile asked, changing the subject. She crossed the room to the table with a bowl of freshly washed and cut carrots. Theo grabbed one right away, and Camile stroked his curly black hair as she watched Armannii fix up Diomedes's arm.

"As much as I enjoy the pub scene, I hope that's not in our future again any time soon," Armannii muttered, using the wet cloth meant for his swollen cheek to wipe the skin around Diomedes's injury.

"I've seen you get into brawls for no reason at all. I don't see what the issue is," Diomedes said, clenching his jaw when Armannii tightened a fabric bandage around his arm. He said a word of thanks when he finished, rolling down the sleeve of his black tunic.

11

"I don't have a problem with it. But this was the third one in two weeks, and we still haven't gotten any useful information," Armannii said while wiping his hands on his trousers. "I go into fights I know I can win. That's the issue."

"We did win."

"Not quite," Armannii said, shaking his head. "We didn't get arrested, nor did we die; I'll give you that. But we left, which is as good as losing. And on top of that, we haven't made any progress."

Blanndynne came back to the main room with Camile's two-year-old daughter, Maisy, on her hip and joined them at the table. "She was already awake when I went in. And as for the bar fight, I, for one, thought it was entertaining," she said, shrugging. "Whether it produced the information we've been looking for or not. Good way to practice fighting."

"Did you hit anyone?" Theo asked, and Camile snorted, making him sit down when he got too excited and stood up on his chair.

"Go put your shoes on," Camile said before Blanndynne could answer his question. "We're going to the market to pick up your father in a few minutes."

"But—"

"Now," Camile said, only grinning after he'd left the room. "Would one of you mind accompanying me to the market? I'm sure it would be fine, but there were rumors of bandits nearby, and—"

"Of course," Armannii said, standing up. "I'll go."

"Thank you," Camile said, patting Armannii on the arm before taking Maisy from Blanndynne. "Keep an eye on the soup while I'm gone, would you?"

Blanndynne and Diomedes nodded. In a matter of minutes, Armannii had grabbed his quiver and bow and followed Camile, Theo, and Maisy out the front door.

"It really is kind of them to let us stay here," Blanndynne said, rising from the table to go stir the soup.

Diomedes nodded, running a hand through his hair. He was in desperate need of a bath but didn't feel like filling the tub in the bathroom.

"I thought it would be today," he muttered, rubbing his temples. The minute Camile and the children left, it felt like Diomedes could slouch. It had been luck—well, luck and Armannii's connections in the Black Forest—that had led them to their old friend's doorstep. He was appreciative of them opening their home to them, especially knowing the threat of danger it could offer if a royal guard were to find out they were not only hiding an escaped fugitive—Forrest—but also harboring Diomedes. However, he couldn't help but wish for some time alone. He wanted time to think, to sort out his priorities and remind himself why he wasn't home in the castle, where time alone was common, as were baths.

"Hey," Blanndynne said, and he glanced up to see her staring. "You didn't answer my question."

"Sorry, distracted. What question?"

"I asked if you wanted to see what I've been practicing now that Armannii's gone." Her ruby lips spread into a smile.

"You mean with the—"

"Yeah." She nodded. "Care to be my puppet?" A glint of something, maybe eagerness, flashed in her eyes.

"I mean, I want to see. But does it have to be me?"

"Do you see anyone else around?"

Diomedes pressed his lips together. The last thing he wanted was to lose control over his own mind, but an air of curiosity lingered. Would she be strong enough to enchant him if he was fighting her tooth and nail? It was worth finding out. "Let's see what you've got."

Chapter Two

She was beautiful. Stunning. Her eyes were a dark swirling vortex of the deepest blue he had ever seen, almost to the point of being black. He could've gotten lost in them—wanted to get lost in them. Her scent was rich as honey, drawing him closer every time she walked by.

"Make sure you hang them straight, otherwise they'll dry with wrinkles." Her voice was a melody sung by the birds.

Diomedes watched her soft lips form the words and nodded before she had even finished speaking. With his mind focused on Blanndynne, his hands moved automatically, scrubbing each article of her clothing before hanging it over a rack to dry. He smoothed out any wrinkle he found. It had to be perfect—perfect for her.

He couldn't help but think how helpful she had been over the last two months since she'd rescued him from the castle. Her bravery had been awe-inspiring. No one was like her—no one even compared. How could he have been so lucky as to have found her? Doing her laundry was the least he could do to say thanks. He wanted to do more. To please her. To make her smile. Anything to light up those eyes.

It wasn't until he was dumping the dirty water outside that he questioned the grandiose image of Blanndynne in his head. A fog began to disperse, and his mind started to think for itself once more.

Frowning, Diomedes bit his cheek as he emptied the last of the water into the puddle he had created. His boots were completely soaked on the inside. He shook his head, muttering under his breath.

"Your laundry?" he growled when he entered the house again. "You made me wash your clothes?" He tossed the bucket to her, glaring when she caught it and laughed. She jumped off the counter and placed it in the corner, where he vaguely remembered grabbing it from. Diomedes's memories from the last twenty minutes were shrouded in a hazy mist.

"Hey," she said, putting her hands up, "you agreed to it."

"I agreed to see if you had improved in enchanting, not to do your laundry." Diomedes crossed his arms over his chest only to find that he had been so bewitched that he'd forgotten to roll up his sleeves, which were now soaking wet. He grunted.

Blanndynne shrugged. "Well, we decided it wasn't wise to try on the children, so I can't practice on Theo or Maisy. I've only tried it on Camile once, and Armannii almost caught me. *And* Armannii has been training me to fight, so my clothes have been disgusting. I need more people to practice on, and I was running out of cleanish options to wear. What did you expect? Besides, it's not every day you get the prince of Phildeterre to wash your tunics." She raised an eyebrow as a grin spread across her mouth. "But it lasted longer, didn't it?"

Diomedes tilted his head, clenching his jaw to prevent a smirk from arising. "I suppose it did. But it faded as soon as I left the house."

"I noticed. I could feel it weakening when you shut the door. The proximity part is the hardest."

"It was better though. You're right." He glanced up at her.

It *had* been stronger.

That much had been clear. She was a beautiful woman, but the thoughts that had flashed through his mind while he was under her enchantment—namely her hypnotic eyes and entrancing features—were nothing close to the ones he had every day.

"What?" she asked when he continued to stare at her.

"Nothing," he said, cracking a few of his fingers. "I'm going to go change my shirt. Thanks for the sopping-wet sleeves, by the way." Diomedes left the living room and shut the door to the small room he and Armannii shared.

It was a stable compared to the lavish castle in which he had grown up. A cold trickle of air constantly seeped through the cracks in the outer walls, though Forrest had tried to cover some of them with a few boards. A dark water stain tinged the corner of the ceiling over Armannii's cot.

But it was still better than the alternative.

Prison.

Banishment.

Maybe worse.

Diomedes sucked in a breath when his wet sleeve caught on the bandage covering his arm. It throbbed as he unstuck it and pulled the tunic off the rest of the way. Still holding the tunic, he glanced down at his injury. The bandage had slipped, revealing pink skin tinged with blood.

Tossing the tunic on his cot, Diomedes focused on his arm. He grimaced. His fingers were far less nimble than Armannii's, but after a minute of fiddling, he fixed it.

The cot creaked as he sat down and grabbed his bag from the floor. After riffling through it for a new tunic, he paused. Paper rustled, and he pulled out an old piece of parchment. His mother's scrawling handwriting filled the page, and he rubbed his hand over his stubbly chin as he scanned it.

Twenty-three years had come and gone, and with them every accurate memory he had of his mother's voice. He couldn't remember the sound or even the cadence. Instead, he heard his own voice reading her words.

Diomedes, my love.

If it were not for you, my son, I would fear the future. I have seen the damage your ancestors have caused, and even now I can see how important it is that you make your own way.

Do not fall into the same pattern as them, hating that which you do not understand. Magic can be a beautiful thing. There are men who cannot see that beauty, and instead they seek to destroy the unknown. This is foolishness.

But even now, my sweet, you are wise. I can see the same spark of curiosity in you that I feel burning within myself. Do not try to dampen it because it makes you different than those who have gone before you.

You will make a great king someday, my son. I love you, Dio, and I always will.

Diomedes folded the letter and tucked it back into the bag. His mother's words left him shivering, as if they'd sucked all the heat from his body. He knew what she was referring to now, though he wondered if she had known the true accuracy of her words. His ancestors, specifically his great-grandfather, King Kylian, had been more corrupt than the world would admit. The darkness in Kylian's heart had led him to murder his own child and lead the country into a century-long war.

Yes. His mother had been correct, and it was her words that had guided him when she herself could not.

When he thought about it, the boy who had lost his mother all those years ago seemed like an entirely different person. He could remember sitting at his window seat waiting for his mother to come back, but it was almost as if he were seeing it through someone else's eyes—a child's eyes.

But she had left for a noble reason—the same reason he himself had left the castle two months earlier. They had both left to stop the war, and Diomedes was determined to succeed where his mother had failed.

Diomedes eventually went out to grab a snack—Camile had stocked up on oranges just for him—and he caught Blanndynne frowning at a wall while brushing her hair in a mindless way.

"You all right?" Diomedes asked, joining her at the table. He leaned back in his chair and began peeling the orange.

Blanndynne didn't respond right away. She continued brushing the same part of her hair over and over again until Diomedes waved his hand in front of her face.

"Sorry?" she said, blinking a few times. The brush in her hand disappeared as she turned to face him.

"What was that?" Diomedes asked, catching a drop of juice before it rolled off the palm of his hand.

"I was thinking about Elias."

"Who?" Diomedes raised an eyebrow.

"Not this again. It wasn't funny the first, second, or third time, and it's not funny now. It will never *be* funny. You know 'who.' Kylian's brother." She straightened up, her eyes narrowing at him.

"Kylian was an only child."

"Fine, play this game." Blanndynne rolled her eyes, and her jaw clenched. "Just don't do it around me." She stood up to leave, but Diomedes pushed his chair back and stood, catching her arm in his grip. The partially peeled orange dripped juice from his other hand.

"I'm not playing a game," Diomedes said, his voice low. "I don't know who that is." He let go of her, and they both sat back down.

Blanndynne shook her head. "Diomedes, I don't want—"

"Listen, I don't know why you're upset, but—"

"Upset?" Blanndynne said, her eyes widening. "Of course I'm upset. You and Armannii keep acting exactly like you did when I first told you about Elias, and I'm tired of it."

"I'm not trying to hurt you. I just—" Diomedes took a deep breath, trying to keep his tone level in the hopes that it would help Blanndynne stay calm or at least not break his eardrum with the pitch he knew she was capable of reaching when angry. "I just don't know anyone by that name, let alone an ancestor of mine."

Blanndynne crossed her arms over her chest, and her frown deepened. "You've done this too many times. I don't believe you. How could you not remember him?"

"I don't know, but maybe you could help jog my memory." He finished peeling the orange and started eating it.

"I'm not doing this," Blanndynne said, trying to walk away again, but Diomedes jumped to his feet and stepped in front of her. "Move."

"Blanndynne, look at me. Do I look like I'm lying?" He held his hands out in exasperation. "I'm just as confused as you. If you've told me about this person, I should remember, right? Maybe something happened to make me forget. But—"

"It's Armannii too," Blanndynne spat. "Both of you have apparently made some sort of pact to make me miserable by acting like you've forgotten my last master over and over again."

"Why would we do that? That doesn't sound like either of us. We joke, but not about something that clearly means a lot to you." Diomedes's mind was already processing what she'd said. "Last master? You mean before we found you?"

"You're telling me you really don't remember?" Blanndynne's words had venom behind them, but her face softened when Diomedes nodded. "I don't understand why—"

"Me neither," Diomedes said, leading her back to the table. She didn't resist. "Why does this person have you so upset? What did he do?"

"You don't remember going to the royal catacombs to look for his grave? How could you forget that?"

Diomedes's brows knitted together as he shook his head. "I remember going to look for Kylian's *daughter's* grave—for Raylee's grave—not his brother's." Diomedes ran his hand over the back of his neck. "You're serious?"

Blanndynne raised her hand to her face, rubbing her forehead as if the conversation were giving her a headache. "Elias was my last master before you broke my vessel and freed me. But it was Elias who was supposed to free me. He had promised me he'd do it, exchanging his third wish to give me my life back. He knew he couldn't use the third wish and keep his promise to me because he'd already used his first two wishes. He knew he'd lose his ability to free me, to break my vessel, as soon as he made the third wish. He promised me he'd . . ."

"He lied." Diomedes's voice was gentle. He leaned forward, resting his elbows on the table. He finished off the orange, wiping his mouth with the back of his hand while what felt like a permanent frown cemented further on his face. How could he have forgotten one of his ancestors? And not just any ancestor— Kylian's brother.

When she spoke again, her voice was a whisper. "He lied. He promised to free me, to break the vessel. But he betrayed me."

Diomedes tried to find some memory of Blanndynne talking to him about Elias—some tiny mention of his name—but found none. "I'm sorry. I'm sorry you went through that, and I'm sorry I don't remember anything about him. At all."

Blanndynne tucked her hair behind her ears. "You really don't remember . . ." Her voice trailed off again.

"I don't." Diomedes sat up straighter, smoothing the fabric of his trousers down with both hands. "This isn't easy for you, I can tell. But what all did you tell me about him before?" Diomedes asked, trying to add a casual air to his voice, but it wasn't as effective as he'd hoped. "Please."

It took a while for Blanndynne to start, but she eventually began to tell him about Elias, his great-grandfather's older brother. However, the more she told him, the more confusion filled Diomedes's mind. How could he have forgotten such important information about his ancestry? How could he have forgotten that Kylian was never supposed to be king, that he had not been the heir? How had he forgotten Elias's three wishes for health, knowledge, and favor?

Diomedes wrung his hands in his lap as Blanndynne spoke, his heart racing the longer he sat still. It didn't make sense. How could someone forget an entire person in only a few weeks?

It was another hour before Armannii, Camile, Forrest, and the children returned. Blanndynne had long since finished explaining what she'd apparently already told Diomedes about Elias by the time Forrest's family and the elf walked into the house. When Armannii closed the door, he had a wide grin on his face. He tossed his bag onto the floor and leaned his bow and quiver against the wall.

Diomedes lifted an eyebrow, looking up from the knife he was sharpening. He'd taken it from a man who'd tried to mug him, and while it wasn't his nicest weapon, he'd grown rather attached to it. "Why do you look like you fell into a fortune?"

"Fresh air will do that to ya." Armannii patted Diomedes's shoulder as he passed, and Diomedes flinched.

"What'd you do to him?" Diomedes directed the question to Camile and Forrest. He shifted, cocking his head to the side as he watched the elf. "I haven't seen him this happy since he cheated a guy out of his coin purse with a staring contest."

"That was fun," Armannii said, swooping Theo up in his arms. "But no amount of free money can make me this happy."

"I'd disagree, but that's neither here nor there," Diomedes said, glancing to Forrest for answers when Camile left the room with Maisy. "What's with him?"

Forrest was emptying two cloth bags of produce onto the kitchen counter, a smile on his face. When Armannii and Diomedes had freed him from the castle dungeon, he had not looked nearly as healthy as he did now. His violet eyes glistened.

"Ovair overheard a few men at the market talking about you. And—"

"There's someone northeast of here who might have some information for us. Apparently, word has spread that the crown prince of Phildeterre"—Armannii changed his voice to sound formal when he spoke Diomedes's title—"is searching for anyone who might have information on the sorceress." Armannii paused, holding Theo upside down, and grinned at Diomedes, leaving the little boy in gales of laughter. "I'm sure your father is well pleased. I say we leave in the morning."

"No!" Theo said when Armannii flipped him back up. "Stay!"

Armannii chuckled, lifting Theo so he sat up on his shoulders. "I'll be back eventually, kid. Besides, when we leave, you'll get your room back."

"It's your room now. Stay!" Theo said, pouting.

Diomedes lost interest in the child and the man-child, and he focused on the good news Armannii had brought. He let his mind do something he hadn't allowed it to do since the second time a lead had ended in the middle of nowhere. He allowed hope to trickle in.

Maybe this time the lead would go somewhere useful.

Maybe this time he would step onto the trail that would take him where he longed to go—that would take him to his deepest desire.

Maybe this time he would find the object.

He would gain magic.

He would end the war.

Chapter Three

Diomedes missed Camile and Forrest's house almost as soon as Armannii found them a place to stay farther north. While their friends' house may have had cold drafts and stained ceilings, it hadn't been nearly as bad as the spider-infested nightmare to which Armannii had led them. Cobwebs clung to corners and to the sides of the cracked windows. Every floorboard squeaked or creaked, and a musty odor lingered in every room. The shack had only one bedroom, and while there was a cot, Diomedes decided before it even came time to rest that he would elect to sleep on the floor. The mattress on the cot was stained in multiple places and smelled like something had died inside it.

Even though he had *opted* to sleep on the floor, Diomedes still woke up crabby and sore. It took him several seconds of staring at the mildew-covered ceiling to remember where he was, and that didn't help his attitude.

Armannii and Blanndynne were already awake, and they glanced up when he walked into the living room. The elf sat in the corner on the floor; there were only two chairs, and one was occupied by Blanndynne, while the other was missing a fourth leg.

"Looks like it didn't work," Armannii said, a grin on his lips as he shifted on the floor.

"What?" Diomedes muttered, going for his canteen, which he'd left on a small table the night before.

"The beauty sleep."

Instead of responding, Diomedes rolled his eyes and took a swig of water. "Think the pub is open yet?"

"Probably. It's not far. But we should decide what we're going to do before we go in this time," Armannii said, picking through his quiver. He pulled out one arrow tipped in silver and one that appeared to be gold and laid them to the side. Most of his arrows were made from a dark metal Diomedes couldn't recognize at first glance.

"It's best if we split up in the pub. The guards will be looking for all three of us, and we're less likely to be noticed alone," Diomedes said, putting the canteen back down on the table before joining the two of them. He leaned against the wall and pulled his knife out—not to examine it like Armannii was doing, but to clean the dirt from beneath his fingernails.

"I'll get a game going if you think it'll help." Armannii glanced up, a twinkle of mischief in his silver eyes.

"Can you look out for possible informants while arm wrestling sweaty men?" Blanndynne asked, an eyebrow raised. She had been braiding her hair back in two tight braids and was just finishing the second half of her hair.

"Women sometimes take me up on it too," Armannii said, pointing an arrow at her before sticking it back in the quiver. "And yes, I can multitask."

Diomedes cleared his throat. "Do we have any idea who we're looking for?"

"Besides the fact that it's a guy, nope," Armannii said, standing as he put on his quiver. "So keep an eye out."

"All right." Diomedes put his knife away, glancing between the two of them. "Lead the way."

The pub, like almost every other one Diomedes had been to with Armannii, was terribly lit and smelled as if it hadn't ever been cleaned. Diomedes's boots clung to the sticky floor as he made his way to an empty table at the back of the room. Armannii was already drawing a crowd where he sat at the front, challenging a man twice his size to an arm wrestling contest. He wore a knit cap to hide his elf ears, but his silver gaze wasn't something easily hidden. Still, it was easier for him to pass as human than it was for others Diomedes had met, like Tilly, the harpy. Though he'd only seen her in the safety of her home, he was sure she'd have more issues hiding her feathery exterior and giant wings than Armannii did his ears and eyes.

Two tables away, Blanndynne sat with her back against the wall, sipping something from a metal cup. Her dark gaze scanned the room, pausing only a second longer on Diomedes than everyone else.

Diomedes watched the patrons in the pub; it wasn't as full as other pubs they'd been to, likely because it was still early. Most of the inhabitants were huddled around Armannii, who grinned while the man he'd just defeated emptied his coin purse onto the table. Diomedes raised his hand over his mouth to cover his snicker, and while he hoped they would find answers to questions he'd had for months, he was grateful they wouldn't walk away empty-handed. He ordered a drink and waited.

Movement to his right caught Diomedes's attention, and he watched a man with spindly legs sit down at the table next to him. His knees almost reached the underside of the table, and he looked like he was sitting at a table for children.

When the man nodded to Diomedes, he copied the stranger. "New?"

Diomedes grinned. "That obvious?"

The man nodded. "Relocating or just passing through?"

"The latter," Diomedes said, then thanked the barkeep when he walked over and handed him his drink. Diomedes handed the barkeep a few bronze coins, nodding as the man thanked him and went back to the counter.

"Probably wise," the man said, a grin passing over his lips. "There've been a series of raids by the royal guards recently. They're searching everywhere for the prince."

"Right," Diomedes said, trying to hide that he'd nearly choked on his drink. "They were in the village I just passed through too."

"Sticking their noses where they don't belong if you ask me. If the prince wants to run amok, I say let 'im. Probably do the kid some good."

Diomedes chuckled, raising his cup toward the man. "I couldn't agree more."

The man nodded, and neither spoke after. For what felt like two hours, Diomedes watched patrons come in and out. None of them seemed to notice him, and the longer he sat, the more he felt the hope of getting worthwhile information dripping out of him. He finished his drink, leaning back against the chair. Already, his mind was moving to what they'd do when they returned to the broken-down shack, lacking the answers they'd entered the pub to find. Maybe they could go back to Forrest and Camile's. It'd at least be more comfortable there.

Sighing, he rubbed the back of his neck. Diomedes could feel the strain of the many miles they'd traversed over the last few weeks. It combined with the weight of a seemingly never-ending search for information on the one thing that could help him end the war on magic. After a while, his eyelids got heavy, and he blinked a few times to wake up.

Diomedes stared at the options around the room, but none of the men stood out to him as someone who might hold the information he was looking for. Five men stood around Armannii as he took on opponent after opponent. Besides the barkeep and the man at the table next to Diomedes, the only other person in the pub was a woman with the hood of her cloak pulled down over her face. She sat across the room from him, and while he couldn't see her eyes, it felt like she was watching him.

Diomedes lifted his empty cup, pretending to take a sip as he peeked over the rim at the woman. Something about her didn't seem to fit with the scene around him. Her posture was too rigid. Worse yet, something about her was familiar. A flash of gold within her hood reflected in the lantern above her table. She was wearing jewelry. It was yet another thing out of place—just as it had been when he'd noticed her at the last two pubs.

The hair on the back of Diomedes's neck stood on end, and he glanced over at Blanndynne. She was focused on Armannii, her back to Diomedes.

Was she following them? It couldn't be a coincidence; they were at least half a day's walk north of the last pub. If the woman had recognized him, she could very well have called the royal guards before she'd taken her seat to watch Diomedes.

Heeding the warning in his gut, Diomedes rubbed his face, using the motion to cover his mouth with his hand as he spoke in a whisper.

"Armannii, hit the table twice if you can hear me."

Not a second later, Armannii slammed the table two times with his fist, spitting out a joke that made the onlookers burst into roars of laughter.

"The woman across the room was at the last two pubs. She's watching me. I'm going to leave. If she follows, give me two minutes, then come find me. I'll head toward the shack."

Armannii didn't respond, but Diomedes had faith he had heard. Diomedes stood up. He didn't look at the woman as he left, but he couldn't shake the sensation that she was watching him.

The pub was relatively close to the shack, and after putting on the pair of glasses Armannii had inscribed with a sight rune, he regained his bearings. Diomedes set off, his body on full alert. He kept his hand on the hilt of his sword, ready to draw it in a second if he sensed he was being followed.

But as he got closer to the shack and still hadn't heard any unnatural disturbances amongst the trees, he started to question if he had just been paranoid. It made sense after the disaster of the last pub. But he'd been all but sure he'd seen her before. Maybe it was just a coincidence. And while he tried to reassure himself that it was better safe than sorry, he couldn't help but kick himself for getting spooked by a single person.

"Why'd you leave?"

Blanndynne shrieked when Diomedes spun around with his sword aimed at her face.

Diomedes let out the breath he'd inhaled, glaring at her. "I could've taken your head off."

"Would've hurt, but I'd have been fine eventually." She lowered herself to the forest floor, above which she'd been floating. That explained why he hadn't heard her sneak up on him.

Diomedes scoffed, putting his sword away. "I thought I'd been recognized. Or followed. I thought the woman in the pub looked familiar, like she'd followed us all the way from Forrest and Camile's. Told Armannii, but I couldn't tell you without defeating the purpose of us splitting up."

"Right. Well, I didn't notice her. But I got distracted. Did you see Armannii beat the man twice his size?" Blanndynne asked as they continued walking in the direction of the shack.

They passed several broken-down structures Diomedes had used as landmarks, and Diomedes listened to the noises of the forest beneath the sound of Blanndynne going on about Armannii's arm wrestling match.

"Have you?" Blanndynne asked, waiting by the front door of the shack while Diomedes scanned their surroundings one last time.

"Have I what?" He pulled off and folded his glasses as he entered the shack, Blanndynne following behind him.

"Won a match against Armannii."

"Arm wrestling? No," Diomedes said, tossing his bag on a table, making it shake. "He's tried to teach me how to win, but I can't get the hang of it."

"That's because you don't want to practice," Armannii said, grinning when it was clear he'd startled them with his entrance. The door hadn't even creaked like it had for the two of them.

"Well?" Diomedes said as Armannii closed the door behind him.

The elf continued to wear a huge smile on his face. "I would say that was fairly successful for only an hour or two. Restocked our coin purses, and—"

Armannii held up one finger, tilting his head to the side as his smile grew wider. With a dramatic flourish, he opened the door he'd just passed through.

The woman from the pub stumbled through the door as soon as it opened, but she righted herself quickly. Diomedes freed his sword, gripping it with white knuckles at the sudden intrusion. Stepping back, Diomedes aimed the tip of his blade at the stranger while Armannii shut the door behind her.

"Didi, B, I'd like you to meet the stranger who stalked us all the way from the pub. Sorry, love, can't do a better introduction without a name." Armannii crossed his arms over his chest as he leaned against the only exit, a smirk still perched on his mouth.

"Could've used a warning," Diomedes grumbled. He could almost hear his own pulse pounding in his ears. His body vibrated, and his stomach tightened. "Or at least some indication that I was right." He flicked his glare to Armannii for half a second before returning it to the stranger.

Blanndynne raised an eyebrow as she glanced from Armannii to the girl. "Who are you?" she asked, tilting her head to the side.

The girl straightened up, removing the hood of her cloak. She had dark brown hair braided down her back and at least a dozen golden hoops pierced through both of her ears. Her copper skin shimmered in the light from the runes Armannii had written on the ceiling before they'd left for the pub. The stranger narrowed her eyes as she scanned the room. She was shorter than Blanndynne, but not by much.

It was by no means bright in the small shack, but there was enough light for Diomedes to recognize the amulet the girl wore around her neck. It was in the shape of a sun, and in the center were the three moons of Phildeterre in different phases: one full, one half, and the last a crescent. The three moons were offset from one another, and beneath them was a silhouette of mountains.

"Go on, sweetheart. Tell us why you followed us back here." Armannii gave a satisfied smile and slouched his shoulders.

"I'm not anyone's 'sweetheart.' Especially not yours," the young woman said through clenched teeth. Lifting her chin, she turned her focus to Diomedes. "My name is Amira, and I am the daughter of—"

"Raidah." Diomedes lowered his sword, nodding. "I know who you are. Not sure why you thought stalking us was the right decision though."

It was Armannii's turn to raise an eyebrow. "Well now, I guess I should've put on my clean tunic. I didn't know we'd have almost-royalty here."

"Your Highness," Amira said, ignoring Armannii, "my mother sent me to find you. She's informed me that you're in search of information—information she has."

Blanndynne's eyebrows were still furrowed. "And you know we've been searching for this information because?"

"Well, you haven't exactly been subtle about it." Amira glanced at Blanndynne. "Word has spread from those you've questioned over the last two months."

"All the way up to the northern part of the kingdom, apparently," Armannii muttered. His grin had faded, and like Blanndynne, he watched the stranger with a new air of caution. "Why did mother dearest send her daughter to find us here? Why not send a servant, or better yet, a messenger?"

Amira kept her back to Armannii. "If what she said about you is true, Your Highness, then it was of utmost importance that the invitation to meet with her be delivered quickly, efficiently, and by someone you would hopefully recognize."

Diomedes put his sword away and crossed his arms over his chest. "Meet with her? Why not send the information with you?"

"My mother wants to meet with you."

"Because?"

"*Because* you are the son of the northern kingdom's rival. She needs to know she can trust you before she hands over the information."

"The northern kingdom doesn't exist anymore, love. Not since King Valryn's reign," Armannii said, and for the first time, Amira turned around.

Her hands clenched into fists as she took a few menacing steps in the elf's direction. "You are not part of this conversation. Neither of you." She swiveled to nod at Blanndynne. "This is between the prince and me."

"It's actually not," Diomedes said, noting the smug grin on Armannii's face. "They're just as much a part of this as I am."

"Sorry to disappoint, sweetheart." Armannii stepped forward, tucking his hands into his pockets. "Didi, B, and I are a package deal."

Amira lifted her chin, her eyes narrowing on Diomedes. "I suggest you let me speak to you alone, *Your Highness*."

"Or?" Diomedes asked, raising an eyebrow.

"I'll leave."

Armannii glanced at the front door behind him. "Out what door?"

Amira had turned back to face Diomedes, and she responded to Armannii without looking at him. "The one behind you."

"I'd like to see you try to—"

"That's enough," Diomedes said, nodding to Armannii. Shifting his gaze back to Amira, he frowned. "If your mother wants to meet with me, who are you to stand in the way of that?"

She matched his stance, crossing her arms over her chest. "I hold just as much political standing as my mother."

"I'm not arguing that," Diomedes said, shrugging. "However, you're lacking in one area." He paused, cocking his head. "Information."

"As soon as I have a moment to talk to you *alone*," she said, glaring over her shoulder at Armannii, "I'll take you right to her."

"You're a stranger," Blanndynne said, her hands on her hips. "You can't expect us to leave you alone with the prince of Phildeterre."

"B has a point. You could be dangerous." Armannii shrugged. "I doubt it, but anything's possible out here." The smirk on his lips seemed to infuriate Amira more.

"Your choice," she said, her attention back on Diomedes. "You and I chat, or I leave and tell my mother you are no longer interested."

Diomedes ground his teeth. His blood boiled at the thought of being manipulated. But when he glanced up at Armannii, he made his decision.

The object he was after was too important. Besides, he could protect himself from the stranger if need be.

"Go for a walk. Keep an eye out for royal guards," Diomedes said, shifting his gaze between Armannii and Blanndynne.

Armannii raised his chin. "But—"

"Now," he said, waving a hand with a sigh. "I'll speak with Amira alone."

Armannii's eyes widened. "But we—"

"*Alone.*"

Blanndynne strode across the room, avoiding eye contact with Diomedes. She grabbed Armannii around the upper arm and led him out of the shack. The whole building shivered when she slammed the door.

"Thank you," Amira said as she spun back around to face Diomedes.

He leaned against the edge of the table and shook his head. "It wasn't for your sake. Where's your mother? Is she nearby?"

Amira unfastened her cloak and draped it over the back of one of the chairs. She was wearing a dyed crimson leather corset over a cream colored tunic with billowing sleeves. Her trousers barely peeked out from her boots, which went all the way up her legs. The hilt of the dagger strapped to her thigh glimmered in the light; however, that wasn't her only weapon.

The cloak had covered the battle-ax strapped to her back. It made a clunking noise as she unstrapped it and placed it on the table.

Diomedes watched her, impatience driving him to tap his fingers on the wood.

"Amira," he said as his hands gripped the table, "tell me where your mother is."

"You said you know who I am." Amira sat down across the table from him, her posture straight. "But we've never met. Tell me what you know about me."

Diomedes narrowed his eyes and had to force his muscles to relax before he pulled something. "Tell me where your mother is."

"I will." Amira tilted her head, and a smile spread over her lips. "But first, answer a few of my questions."

Diomedes took a deep breath as he straightened his shoulders. He reached for the nearby chair, but remembering its missing fourth leg, decided to forgo sitting on it. He licked his lips, not taking his eyes off Amira. After another moment of silence, Diomedes snorted. "All right."

"Good. Then—"

"If"—Diomedes held up his pointer finger—"you answer my questions as well." He raised an eyebrow as he waited for her response.

Amira's lips parted slightly. "Sounds fair to me. How do you know about my family?"

"Tutoring." Diomedes leaned back against the wall. "My tutor spent plenty of time on my grandfather's 'success' in uniting the five kingdoms." He rolled his eyes. "Your mother was next in line for the throne of Byshan, which means your family line was removed from the glamorous life of ruling because of his actions. You and your younger brother were born into a normal family— high class, albeit, but not royal. You should be the princess of Byshan, but alas, you aren't."

"Fair enough," Amira said, nodding, although the mention of Diomedes's grandfather, King Valryn, had her wrinkling her nose. "Ask your first question."

"How about the same question? What do you know about me?" He smirked.

"I know plenty, Your Highne—"

"Diomedes."

"All right, *Diomedes*," Amira said, raising an eyebrow. "I know you are firstborn to King Butch and his first wife. I know you're currently the most wanted person in all of Phildeterre. I know you don't want to be found by your father. I know that—"

"Do you know why?"

"Excuse me?"

Diomedes crossed his arms over his chest. "Do you know why I don't want my father's men to find me?"

"No, not really. But I assume it has something to do with your stance on magic."

"Which is?"

"You oppose your father's view that it is untrustworthy and, at worst, evil."

He chuckled, shaking his head. "That's a light way of putting it." Diomedes pushed off the wall, leaning forward to place both hands on the table as he bent toward her. She copied him, leaning forward in her chair.

"Oh?"

"Magic isn't evil. In its truest form, it's power. That's what my father doesn't understand. Magic can be used for good."

"You believe that?"

"I believe magic is the key to ending the war." Diomedes leaned back again, though he kept his back off the wall, choosing to stand straight.

"That's another thing I know about you. Or it's something I've heard." She continued to lean forward and rested her chin on one hand. "You want to end the war."

Diomedes nodded. "Yet another reason I can't let my father find me."

Amira's eyebrows met in the middle, and she pursed her lips. "Because you oppose the war?"

"That, and I seem to be the only one in the royal family trying to end it." He bit the inside of his cheek and squinted at the wall behind Amira's head. "When I left two months ago"—Diomedes rubbed the side of his cheek, inwardly cringing at the stubble that had sprouted—"I committed treason—in my father's eyes, at least. And if I were ever to return, I'd be punished for my crimes."

"How?"

"However my father and his band of fools saw fit." He clenched his jaw. "Could be lifetime imprisonment, banishment, or if it was a bad day, maybe death, though my friend Armannii seems to think that's a bit extreme."

Amira didn't respond, but she did sit up straighter.

Diomedes continued in the absence of conversation. "But whatever the punishment, it will surely come with being disinherited."

"Which means your sister will take the throne when the time comes." Amira glanced down at the table, her eyes scanning it as if words were scrawled there. "What is her stance on the war?"

"If I had to give it my best guess?" Diomedes waited for Amira to nod. "She'll choose my father's way of ending the war, which could take another hundred years. She means well, but she lacks a sense of urgency."

"Which is why you need to stop the war."

"Right." Diomedes nodded.

"Well then, I suppose we should go see my mother."

Diomedes pressed his lips together, a grin spreading as he nodded. "I suppose we should."

Chapter Four

Although he was eager to meet Amira's mother—and more importantly, get pointed in the right direction—Diomedes waited for Armannii and Blanndynne to come back from wherever they had gone. He stood next to the table with Amira, making small talk until he heard the doorknob squeak.

"So," Armannii said as he stuck his head into the room, "are B and I allowed to join the adults now?"

Diomedes waved him in, rolling his eyes. "We're finished."

"Great. Could I have a word with you?" Armannii put his hands on his hips, nodding at the door he had just walked through.

Sighing, Diomedes nodded, and Armannii led him out after Blanndynne had walked through the door. "We'll be back," Armannii said over his shoulder.

As soon as the door shut behind them, Diomedes shivered. The temperature had dropped outside since they'd returned from the pub. "If this is about me agreeing to talk to Amira alone, I hope you realize she wasn't going to give me the information if—"

"I know," Armannii said, stepping back from Diomedes with his arms crossed over his chest.

"Good, then what—"

"How do you know we can trust her? How do you even know she is who she says she is?" Armannii's stance was wide, and even in the low light Diomedes could tell his entire demeanor had changed in a second. The elf glared at the door behind Diomedes.

"I've seen portraits of her and her family from when she was younger. And besides that, she's wearing her family's crest."

"That doesn't mean you can trust her. Or her mother."

Diomedes rubbed his brow, sticking one hand in his pocket. "Look, the sorceress spent plenty of time in the northern parts of Phildeterre. It's reasonable that Amira's mother came into contact with her."

"Reasonable, yes, but worth risking your life?" Armannii shook his head.

"Yes," Diomedes said without hesitation. "This war is bigger than just one life, Armannii. We have to do what it takes."

"So this isn't about some object an untrustworthy little man said would give you magic?"

Diomedes tensed. "You're the one who introduced me to that 'untrustworthy little man,' if you remember. And Otto unintentionally gave us the backup plan we didn't know we needed."

"And then tried to have me arrested and you held for ransom." Armannii sighed, scratching his head. "It's not that I'm not with you. I am. But Otto never does anything 'unintentionally.' I just . . . I don't like it."

It wasn't the first time Armannii had voiced his suspicion about the object in the last two months. He'd brought it up on more than one occasion since they'd failed to end the war using the truth of its evil beginnings. Diomedes knew it wouldn't be the last.

Still, he took a deep breath to calm himself before addressing his friend. "I hear what you're saying. I do."

Armannii remained silent, his gaze downcast. The wind whistled around them, and Diomedes wished he had grabbed his cloak on the way out. Even distracted by the cold, though, he could tell something else was nagging at his friend's mind.

"There's something else, isn't there?" Diomedes asked, sticking both hands in his pockets in the hopes that they might warm up.

"It doesn't matter."

"Talk."

Armannii's eyebrows knitted together, and he bit the inside of his cheek. Multiple times he opened his mouth as if to respond, but no words came out.

"Armannii."

"It's just . . . that's the second time you've told me to leave during a vital conversation."

"What are you—"

"In the Dark," Armannii said, running his hands over his face. "You did the same thing with Otto."

Diomedes nodded, taking a hand out of his warm pocket to rub his shoulder. "I did, and I'm sorry. I'm just trying to find this object so I can do what I've promised so many people—what I've promised *myself*—I would do. This war has to end, and . . . I can't fail again."

"Then let me help," Armannii said, his voice louder than before. "You know I'm here for you. But I can't help if I don't know what's going on."

Diomedes tilted his head down. "I'm grateful. It's just . . . I'm responsible, or my bloodline is. It's my great-grandfather's fault the war started in the first place. This country, these people, they're depending on me to end the war. They all know that my father isn't going to do anything. It falls on me; that responsibility is *mine*."

Armannii shook his head, a sad look in his silver eyes. "It's like you told Amira; B and I are with you. You don't have to trudge around carrying the weight of the world." He stepped forward to place a hand on Diomedes's shoulder. "If you would just look up, you would see others like B and I who want to help carry it. Let us help. We want to see you succeed as much as you do."

A lightness filled Diomedes at Armannii's words, and he nodded. "Thank you."

"You're welcome, Princeling." Armannii grinned at him as he removed his hand from Diomedes's shoulder. "What's the plan?"

"We're going to meet Raidah."

Armannii's eyebrows rose. "Seriously? That journey will take days with you on foot. Even with a horse, it would take too long. And it's dangerous to go—"

"We need answers, and Raidah has them, apparently. Besides, Amira said she's not up north at the moment. She's nearby, and Amira will take us to her."

"Doesn't that seem a little too convenient?"

"Could be."

"You think it's a trap? I don't mean to be negative, but have you considered that Raidah might be working with your father? I mean, I know I said he wouldn't kill you, but I doubt he'd shed any tears at my funeral. Or B's. There's a pretty hefty reward on our heads at the moment. You sure you want to risk it?"

Diomedes paused, biting his lower lip. The thought hadn't occurred to him. That in itself should've been alarming. How could he have not considered the threat of being turned over for some prize? He was being sloppy. Desperate.

And if he wasn't careful, it was going to get him killed.

"Fair point," Diomedes said, rolling his shoulders back. "You're a good judge of character. You talk to Amira. See if you can figure out whether she's doing this for a reward."

"All right. But I get the feeling she doesn't like me much."

"You did insult her by pointing out she isn't royalty anymore," Diomedes said, a grin on his lips.

"Truth hurts."

"See if you can get a feel for her on the way to Raidah's. Trap or not, we'll go into it prepared for all outcomes."

"Your mother is staying at an inn?" Diomedes asked, pulling back the hood of his cloak to glance at Amira. They stood in the middle of a large village hidden north of the shack. It had taken some convincing, but he'd managed to get Armannii and Blanndynne to agree to abandoning the terrible shack in the hopes that there would be a more comfortable place to stay the night.

A tavern would do nicely; that was, if he could get Armannii to use some of the money he'd earned at the pub to pay for a room. Diomedes pushed his pair of sight rune–inscribed glasses farther up the bridge of his nose.

"What? Did you expect her to stay in a broken-down shack as well?" Amira scoffed, not even bothering to cast her gaze at Diomedes. "We may not be royalty because of your grandfather, but we are not going to grovel in the mud like you."

Instead of responding, Diomedes forced himself to take a few deep breaths. With each one he took, his fist—which was clasped over the hilt of his sword—relaxed.

They stood outside the entrance to Minngoon Inn. The words on the sign glowed a warm orange, and the closer they got, the better Diomedes understood the hidden rune magic that made them glow. The letters were carved out of a piece of solid wood that lay on top of an inner piece upon which a light rune had been carved. The light from the rune made the cut-out letters glow in the low light of the Black Forest. It was a risky sign, especially to have in a village that was not warded to make it a safe haven to those with magic.

"Are you coming or not?" Amira asked, already halfway through the door. She had paused to look back at Diomedes. Blanndynne and Armannii, who had been walking behind them a ways, sauntered up beside him.

"Of course," Diomedes said, following her into the building.

Unlike other inns and taverns he had been to, the ground level did not have a pub or a place serving food. Instead, the entrance room had a counter pushed to the left side. The surface had been carved from the same dark wood that made up the building. A man with a trimmed beard and a jagged scar above his brow greeted them.

Amira nodded at him, though Diomedes averted his gaze as he passed. As Amira led Diomedes, Blanndynne, and Armannii up a set of stairs at the back of the room, Diomedes tightened his grip on the hilt of his sword beneath his cloak just in case they were ambushed.

But as they made their way down a narrow hall, it seemed more and more like Amira had been telling the truth. Armannii had questioned her during the first half of their journey to meet Raidah. Diomedes had not had time to confer with his friend regarding whether or not the young woman had been lying.

"Wait here," Amira said as she paused outside one of the doors lining the hallway. "I'll go in and announce your presence, and someone will come fetch you." She didn't give them any chance to respond as she opened the door and closed it behind her.

Before Diomedes could ask, Armannii was already whispering his observations. "Well, as far as I can tell, she's telling the truth."

"Good," Diomedes said.

"Or she's the best liar I've ever met. That could also be the case." Armannii shrugged and readjusted his grip on his bow.

Diomedes pressed his lips together. "Either way, we go in there prepared for anything."

Blanndynne glanced at the closed door behind Diomedes. "And how exactly are we supposed to act around this girl's mother?"

"Treat her as though she's royalty unless she requests otherwise," Diomedes said, straightening the black vest over his tunic. He had only packed one vest when leaving the castle, but this was the first time he'd worn it. After two months of only wearing tunics, he fidgeted with the vest. It felt too formal, like he was about to go in for one of the council meetings he so dreaded.

"And that means?" Armannii drew out the last word.

"The opposite of how you treat me," Diomedes muttered as the door opened.

A young man, probably in his teen years, stepped out and bowed. "My name is Al, and my mother will see you now." His tone was curt, and he stared at Diomedes like he was someone not to be trusted. His hard expression didn't change when Diomedes thanked him with a genial smile. Al had the same dark hair as Amira, though it was cut short.

Diomedes inclined his head, walking through the door the young man held open for them. Though he had introduced himself as Al, Diomedes knew from his tutoring that he was Amira's younger brother, Alphaeus, second in line to a throne that no longer existed. If Diomedes remembered correctly, Al had been born around the same time his half sister, Ellayne, had been. That would make Al around the age of eighteen.

As soon as Diomedes stepped into the room, he stopped recounting his geography and cultural lessons. Cinnamon incense filled the air past the point of being pleasant. It overwhelmed Diomedes's nose, but he refrained from cringing.

"Prince Diomedes Maudit, thank you for coming."

It took him a second to find the person who had spoken because there were at least nine other people in the room, five of which were female like the voice. But after a quick scan, his gaze landed on Raidah.

The would-be queen stood at the center of the room near the back. Seeing her elegant red-and-gold wrap dress made Diomedes feel better about wearing his vest, though he wished he'd had the chance to bathe beforehand. Numerous golden bracelets jangled on her wrists as she held out her hand. He stepped forward and bowed as he took her hand in his, pressing his lips lightly against her knuckles.

"I was delighted to hear your invitation, and from your daughter no less." He straightened up as he let her hand go. "May I introduce my companions, Armannii Ovair and Blanndynne Serpenni." Diomedes gestured behind him and was pleased to see Armannii following his lead, bowing to Raidah. Blanndynne curtsied, and since she had reminded him of her history with the Maudit line, Diomedes was not surprised to see that her execution was flawless.

There were no windows. Lanterns cast in iron were spaced evenly along the walls, and they lit up Raidah from behind, making every piece of gold on her sparkle, from the pins in her hair to the shimmering lace of her hem.

Amira looked absolutely plain standing to the right side of her mother.

Of course, that had probably been her intent when she'd departed to find him. She'd likely tried to be inconspicuous, and an outfit like her mother's would've stuck out like a beggar at a royal ball. The golden hoops in her ears had not aided her mission to go unnoticed, at least not in the pubs to which she'd followed them.

Al wore a golden vest with a red shirt beneath it. Diomedes noticed that the boy's eyebrow was pierced, a golden rod going straight through it. He wore several golden rings, which he fidgeted with while he stood to the other side of Raidah.

While growing up in the castle, Diomedes had rarely dressed as lavishly as these would-be royals. The servants scattered around the room also wore the deep red of Raidah and her children.

After inclining her head at Armannii and Blanndynne, Raidah returned her focus to Diomedes. "As I'm sure Amira told you, I have been informed of your position on the war, and I want to offer my services to your mission. However, I ask that you and I speak alone. You never know who might be listening."

Though he was not watching Armannii, Diomedes was sure the elf was trying to get his attention, especially after Armannii had told him about wanting to be part of the private conversations. But Armannii's hearing was impeccable. The elf would be able to listen to the conversation, and that provided more reassurance to Diomedes as he offered his most cordial smile to Raidah.

"I would be honored."

Chapter Five

Inside the main foyer were three doors branching off into separate rooms. Raidah led Diomedes toward the one in the middle, leaving Armannii and Blanndynne behind. Diomedes glanced over his shoulder as he left. Armannii nodded curtly, apparently not pleased at being left behind but not fighting it either. Blanndynne, however, was too busy speaking to Amira in a hushed voice.

"Your Highness? This way," Raidah said, drawing Diomedes's attention. One of the servants stepped forward and closed the door, separating Diomedes and Raidah from everyone else. "Please make yourself comfortable."

The room held a recamier, and a chaise lounge faced it perpendicularly. Raidah went to the chaise lounge, sweeping her skirt to the side as she sat down.

"Have a seat, Your Highness," she said, nodding toward the backless sofa.

"Please, call me Diomedes." He sat down, leaning against the scrolling edge. His gaze wandered around the room. It was not unlike the first, with iron lanterns casting a warm glow around them. There were a few paintings hanging on the walls, and he recognized the Cyanthian castle in the horizon of one of them.

"It's well-kept for an inn, wouldn't you agree?" Raidah asked, following his gaze to the painting. "Quite suitable for people like us."

"Of course," Diomedes said, turning his attention back to her. "The best inn I've seen in the Black Forest."

Raidah raised an eyebrow but did not respond to his comment. Something about the way she lifted her chin left him feeling like he had when he was a child in the presence of some important lord or lady his parents were hosting: insignificant and unimportant.

He cleared his throat in the hopes that it would also clear the feeling. It didn't. "So, your daughter tells me you have information I've been in search of."

"I'd like to determine where your loyalties lie before I tell you what I know," Raidah said, adjusting the wide strip of fabric that had fallen crooked on her shoulder.

"Of course." Diomedes waved his hand, motioning for her to continue.

"How much do you know about my family, Your Highness?"

Diomedes snorted as he rubbed his chin. "Your daughter asked a very similar question."

"I'm sure she did. She's wise. Enlighten me as to your response."

He tilted his head, thinking through each word before he opened his mouth to speak. "You and your family were cheated out of ruling the northern kingdom of Byshan when my grandfather combined the five kingdoms into one." Diomedes watched for any reaction from Raidah, but her facial expressions remained carved in marble.

"And what is your opinion on your grandfather's actions?"

Diomedes scoffed, his gaze traveling to the floor. "He was a fool to create a civil war during the Split of Phildeterre. War within war. He was selfish. His desire was only to gain more territory and influence." Diomedes shook his head, his speech stilted.

Despite having had a plethora of tutors, all of whom had taught about his ancestor's great victories in shaping the country, Diomedes had managed to emerge with a mind of his own. Even though he only had three of his mother's letters, her encouragement to remain his own person had developed in him a deep stubbornness that had kept him from falling prey to the propaganda, at least until he'd met Armannii and been shown the realities outside the castle walls. The elf had helped cement Diomedes's pushback against what he had been taught.

He knew, probably better than the common man, how twisted his grandfather and great-grandfather had been, how the latter had begun the war because of his fear of magic and how the former had seized control of the broken country when it was at its weakest and most fragile. It made his skin crawl knowing he was related to them.

Raidah must've seen the vexation written in bold letters across his face. "I believe we share the same sentiment, Your Highness."

Diomedes looked up from where he had been subconsciously tracing the lines in the floor while fuming over his ancestry.

"And I believe we are on the same side in regard to the war," Raidah continued, watching each of Diomedes's movements down the bridge of her nose. "You favor the side of magic?"

"Yes," he said, nodding. While he was able to keep his features neutral, his muscles tightened and his stomach flipped at the mention of magic, at the mere thought of it. "As I told your daughter, magic is power. It could be beneficial in rebuilding Phildeterre."

"Your father would never hear of it."

"That's true, but my father will not reign forever. And as I'm sure you're aware, I'm next in line for the throne." He restrained his facial expressions, keeping them from revealing that he wasn't being completely honest. In all reality, his father had most likely drafted up disinheritance papers to remove him from the line of succession. But as far as Diomedes knew, that information was not public yet. The thought had him tightening his hands into fists. The longer they searched for an object that would give him magic and the ability to end the war, the more time they wasted and the more time his father had to announce he'd been disinherited. That would make taking the throne that much more difficult.

Raidah did not question his statement about inheriting the crown. "And how will you rule differently from your ancestors?"

Sitting straighter, Diomedes lifted his chin. He had a feeling he was nearing the end of Raidah's test, and she had saved her most important questions for last.

"I have every intention of bringing magic back to Phildeterre, of giving people with that gift their rightful place in society. That, of course, means the Split of Phildeterre will be over. No more war between those with and without magic."

Raidah arched an eyebrow. "Is that all?"

Her challenge had caught him off guard, and he struggled to swallow. Of all the times he'd imagined taking the throne, the problem of a country that had banned magic versus a country filled with magic had always been his top priority—so much so that he had neglected to consider what other changes he would make to Phildeterre. Somewhere in the back of his mind, he knew what Raidah wanted him to say—that he would reinstate the division of kingdoms and place her and her family back within the world of royalty. However, as Diomedes clenched his jaw, he knew that item was not high on his list of priorities.

So, with as charming a smile as he could muster, he continued. "Of course not. That is only the beginning. Phildeterre will undergo a world of change when I succeed my father; however, it will all take time." Diomedes repeated the phrase he had cringed at every time his father had used it on him. Naturally, things took time, just not as much as King Butch took. His father did things slowly. Diomedes would not.

With a fixed look of concentration, Raidah gave a brief nod. "Obviously."

Diomedes continued to smile, knowing it would get him further than his typical frown. "Now that I've answered your questions, if you would share with me what you know, I would greatly appreciate it." He sat up straighter, feeling the confidence he had lacked from the beginning of the conversation. He knew he had passed her test, and by the slight grin on her face, Raidah knew it too.

"Of course, Your Highness. But please forgive me, as what I know requires context." She waited until he nodded to continue. "As you may know, I was once married. My husband was a brave man—a man of honor. He was not from a noble line, but that did not matter to me, nor to my parents, thankfully. He was proud of his heritage, and his wisdom and determination won not only my heart, but also those of my family members.

"We married quite a few years after King Valryn destroyed our royal line. The Split was heating up again after a few years of relatively few casualties because of a new opposition to your father. Now, you must understand, Your Highness, that my family and many in the north have resented the royal lineage of Cyanthia for quite some time. Your grandfather caused a great deal of hardship in the north. Because of the hurt and damage done, we in the north began offering the Elemental Mountains as a safe haven for those with magic. It was our way of standing up against your grandfather as well as your father. So when Emmalee—you probably know her as the sorceress—came to the north in search of allies to fight against your father, my husband and I were more than willing to help.

"I myself hosted many of her commanding officers and footmen while my husband served as one of her captains. The sorceress kept only a small group of people close to her, and my husband and I were honored to be a part of that. Well," she said, pausing as she glanced to the side, "my husband died fighting for her—for our kingdom. I continued to help, but it lessened in the absence of my husband." Raidah glanced at Diomedes, her eyebrows furrowed but every other feature remained neutral.

"I'm sorry for your loss, Raidah," Diomedes said, acknowledging the pain in her voice. He had never been in love. He couldn't begin to imagine what it was like to lose that.

"I do not tell you this so you will pity me." Raidah sat up straighter, once again adjusting the strap of her dress. "As I said, my husband and I belonged to Emmalee's inmost group. There were a few others, though we rarely met one another. Emmalee did not want us to be in contact for fear that her enemies would use us collectively as a way to access her. There was, however, one particular woman whom my husband and I met on multiple occasions—the sorceress's dragon whisperer."

Diomedes's ears perked up. Since he had first realized his father kept a secret library in his office full of books about magic, he had spent most of his time researching dragons. The enormous fire-breathing reptiles had captured his attention when his mother had flown off on one the night she'd left him and his father. His curiosity still piqued whenever they were mentioned. To his knowledge, there were no more dragons left, the last having died during the siege on the Elemental Mountains that killed the sorceress.

"As interesting as that information is, I don't see how it's imperative that I know this," Diomedes said, shaking off the curiosity that had sprouted at the mention of his favorite creature. He was beginning to wonder if he was wasting his time and if the information she was giving him was about to be as useful as all of the information he had gathered in the last two months—that was, completely and utterly fruitless.

Raidah narrowed her eyes at him. "I have heard, Your Highness, that you are searching for an object that will give you great power."

"Yes," Diomedes said, nodding. "That's true."

"Well, while I don't know explicitly where this object is—or even *what* it is—I do know someone who would have a better idea."

"I know where the object is. It's in the Elemental Mountains where the sorceress left it. But what I don't know, Raidah, is how to get to it." He felt the urge to glare but forced himself to take a breath before he accidentally offended his only chance at information thus far.

Raidah cocked her head to the side, clearly enjoying the impatience scrawled over Diomedes's face. "The dragon whisperer walked away from the final battle in the mountains, unlike many of our fallen comrades. She has not been seen since, but she would know where the sorceress died and therefore where this object ended up."

The information he had been waiting for was almost within reach. "And where exactly is she?" Diomedes asked, leaning forward.

A smirk crossed her lips. "Emmalee knew you'd come. I don't know how, but she did."

Her words caught him off guard. "What do you mean?"

"A little while before she died, Emmalee gave me specific instructions. She told me you would follow in your mother's footsteps and that I should be prepared to help you when the time came." Raidah chuckled. "I didn't believe her, of course. I'd forgotten she'd even mentioned it until I received word that the prince of Phildeterre had left his father's side."

"You knew my mother?"

Raidah nodded. "I met Queen Lenora on a few occasions. You're very much like her."

Diomedes shifted in his seat, unsure how to react. "And the sorceress expected all of this?"

"I'm sure it's played out differently than she thought it would, but yes. She was a wise and cunning woman, and she left something for you." Raidah gestured toward the table beside Diomedes. A box—small enough to fit inside his hand—sat on a pile of four books.

He raised an eyebrow, waiting for her to confirm that he was supposed to look inside. The lid to the box creaked as he opened it and glanced inside. A tiny rectangular mirror about an inch long reflected light back up at him.

"Not really my style," Diomedes said, pulling it out of the box. A golden chain was connected to it, making the mirror wearable as a necklace.

"Emmalee said it might be useful to you."

Diomedes ran his thumb over the mirror. It was reflective only on one side. The back was a matte gray.

"I will give you the dragon whisperer's last known location, but I want to say something else first."

As he tucked the mirror into his pocket, Diomedes had a feeling he knew what she was going to say—some request to be given back the royal lineage of Byshan when he became king, or something similar.

"If and when the time comes for you to publicly oppose your father and his council and you go to end the war, you will have allies in the north if need be. We would like to see the end of the Split as much as you, and we understand that in order for that to happen, we may need to fight again. When that day comes, we will stand by you."

Diomedes's mouth almost fell open, but he caught himself before it happened. Still, his eyes widened. "I-I appreciate the support, Raidah." His hands tightened in his lap as he tried to level his reaction. "That's some of the best news I've heard today, besides the possibility of finding the object I've been looking for these past two months."

"I'm pleased to be of service. Now, the dragon whisperer."

Chapter Six

By the time Raidah and Diomedes walked out of the back room, the only people left in the main foyer were Amira, Al, Blanndynne, and one of the servants. The first person Diomedes wanted to talk to had not been waiting outside for him.

"Where's Armannii?" Diomedes asked as Blanndynne rose from a chair.

"He left. Didn't say where he was going," Blanndynne said to Diomedes before nodding at Raidah and smiling at her. "I was just speaking to your daughter about how lovely I find your dress."

Diomedes inclined his head to Raidah and the others before leaving the room. He rubbed the back of his neck, listening for signs of Armannii in the empty halls of the inn. He had expected the elf to be sitting outside after the conversation with Raidah, ready to talk about everything he'd overheard. Diomedes curbed his annoyance by clenching his jaw.

Tracing his way back to the lobby, he left the building, scanning the surroundings before his eyes landed on another glowing sign. He sighed. Diomedes shoved his hands into his pockets as he crossed the street to a pub—his best guess as to where the elf had gone.

Like many of the pubs they had entered over the years of knowing each other, it reeked of sweat and sour old fruit, likely from the numerous spilled drinks and messes. With a quick scan of the dark room, Diomedes found Armannii.

The elf sat at a table with three other men and one woman, and each one of them held a few cards in their hands. Diomedes couldn't tell from this distance which hustle his friend was running, but it was clear he was winning—not because Armannii was smiling, but because every other person at the table was glaring at him.

Although he wanted to speak to his friend, Diomedes didn't interrupt the game. Instead, he took a seat at a table nearby. He crossed his arms over his chest and leaned back in the chair as he watched the card game play out.

At one point, the woman leaned over and whispered something to Armannii with a smirk on her lips. The elf glanced sideways at her before wiggling his eyebrows. A second later, whatever card he had placed on the table left her scowling at him.

Diomedes snorted, casting his gaze around the room to keep an eye out for any threats. They were far enough north that he doubted they'd see much in the way of royal guards, but he was pretty sure there would be people who would try to return him to his father if they recognized him. However, no one seemed to notice him, and he returned his focus to the card game.

One of Armannii's opponents slammed his cards down before shoving his chair away from the table and standing up. With one last glare at Armannii, he stormed past Diomedes, who avoided eye contact. No need to start a fight. The man's clenched fists had seemed a little too eager to meet a stranger's nose.

Armannii was lucky it hadn't been his.

The competitors left the table one by one until it was just Armannii and the woman sitting next to him. With the ambient noise in the pub, Diomedes couldn't hear or begin to decipher what words they were exchanging. However, the woman continued to get redder in the cheeks, her eyebrows furrowing into a deep canyon every time Armannii laid a card on the table.

Tilting his head to the side, Armannii raised an eyebrow as he gazed over his remaining cards. With an extra flourish, he picked one out of the middle, tossing a grin at his opponent as he placed it down with careful precision. The woman's eyes widened, and with a screech of frustration, she slammed her cards on the table with a bang.

"You cheat!" Her shriek echoed around the room, and it was clear she had successfully grabbed the attention of everyone in the pub. "You had to be cheating."

Armannii chuckled, a smirk on his lips as he tucked the last of the gambled coin purses into a bag. "Far from it, love. I just know how to play." He winked at her, but when he scanned the room and his gaze landed on Diomedes, he lifted his chin. His jaw set, and Diomedes watched as his fists tightened on the strap of the bag.

"Thanks for the game," Armannii said to the woman, who looked like she was only a few seconds from flipping the table. The elf moved his gaze away from Diomedes, focusing instead on the door that led outside.

Rising to his feet, Diomedes followed Armannii out of the pub, waiting until they were alone in an alley before speaking.

"So I finally get the chance to learn more about what we've been searching for, and you run off to a pub?" Diomedes kept his hands in his pockets, but his shoulders rolled back as he cocked his head to the side. "Seriously?"

"What?" Armannii flung an arm out to the side. "It's not like I got an invitation to sit in during your conversation. What'd you expect me to do? Sit outside, sip tea, and twiddle my thumbs?"

Diomedes blinked a few times, his forehead wrinkling as he stared at Armannii in the dim light from the street. "No, I figured you'd eavesdrop. You've had no issue doing that in the past."

"Did you think to check the walls? As soon as that door shut, I couldn't hear a thing."

"I . . . I didn't."

Armannii's tone, which had been bitter a second earlier, softened. "It was probably runed."

"Silencing rune," Diomedes muttered, running his hand through his hair. "I'm sorry. I didn't even think to check. I was so sure you were going to be able to listen in. I-I was counting on it actually."

"What did she have to say?" Armannii asked, crossing his arms.

Diomedes sighed, glancing over his shoulder toward the main street. "She doesn't know exactly where it is."

"Great."

"But," Diomedes said, pulling the small mirror out of his pocket, "she gave me this. Told me the sorceress herself left it for me. Something about it helping along my journey. And Raidah gave me directions to find someone who might be able to steer us to the object in the mountains. I'll tell you more, but I want to tell Blanndynne at the same time. So . . ." He nodded toward the street, and Armannii nodded.

"After you."

"So I'm guessing now you want to go find this dragon whisperer?" Armannii scratched his chin. He held in his hands the instructions Raidah had given Diomedes to find the dragon whisperer. According to the parchment, they needed to head even farther north and at least half a day of walking to the west.

After they'd returned to the inn, Armannii had rented a room at Diomedes's request. They sat around a small table between the beds, of which there were four. Diomedes leaned forward, rubbing his face with his hands.

"It's the first lead we've had," Diomedes replied, sighing as he glanced up at them. Their room was not as extravagant as

Raidah's had been, but it beat sleeping in the broken-down shack they'd left. He was thankful to not have to worry about swallowing a spider in his sleep.

Blanndynne nodded. "I think it's a good idea. It sounds like Raidah gave you enough information to actually find this person."

"Then again, it also sounds like the dragon whisperer may not even be alive," Armannii muttered, folding the instructions and handing them back to Diomedes. "What?" he asked when they glared at him. "You're the one who said this person was never seen again."

Diomedes rubbed the bridge of his nose between two fingers, exhaling as he did so. "We should get some rest and then at least go check out the dragon whisperer. If she isn't there or can't help, at least we've checked."

Armannii raised an eyebrow, glancing back and forth between Diomedes and Blanndynne. "All right. If you're serious, let's do it. But do me a favor and don't get your hopes up."

"Believe me," Diomedes muttered, "that's not a problem."

Chapter Seven

Someone in the room above theirs woke Diomedes up. For a while, all he did was lie in the bed, his mind drifting back to the conversation with Raidah from the day before. She had written out a series of instructions for how to find the dragon whisperer, and a part of Diomedes wanted to pull them out of his bag and examine them. At least then he'd be doing something productive rather than staring at the black ceiling. But instead, he lay there and fantasized about what it would be like to meet the dragon whisperer, or better yet, to meet a dragon.

The image of his mother escaping the castle via his room filled his head. He'd been four and hadn't quite understood what was happening. It wasn't until he was older that he'd discovered the beast his mother had flown away on was a dragon. That was when the obsession had started . . .

After what felt like hours of staring at the wall across from him, Diomedes sat up when someone knocked on the door. Armannii mumbled something but didn't make any movements indicating he was interested in getting up. The knock woke Blanndynne, but when he glanced at her, she shrugged.

Rolling his eyes, Diomedes stood up and shuffled across the room, attaching the knife he slept with under his pillow to his belt. His gaze roamed over his sword, and for half a second he considered arming himself with a more significant weapon. With the amount of people searching for him, it probably would've been a good idea. But he didn't pick it up. Instead, he stifled a yawn as he reached for the door.

"Took you long enough," Amira said when he cracked it open. Glancing behind her, Diomedes scanned the empty hallway before stepping out and closing the door behind him.

"Does your mother need to speak with me again?" Diomedes asked, running a hand through his hair.

Amira gave him a once-over before shaking her head. "It's the middle of the day. Did you just wake up?"

"I've been up for a while. What do you want?" Diomedes asked, recognizing his rude tone after he'd spoken the words. She seemed to notice it too because she stuck her chin out and crossed her arms over her chest.

"My mother sent me to tell you we're departing for home soon. She wanted me to give you this," she said, reaching into her pocket and pulling out a piece of parchment. "It's a map of how to find our home," Amira added before she handed it to Diomedes.

He thanked her, his attention on the map. "I appreciate it." When Diomedes looked up, she nodded. He offered her a smile. "And I'd appreciate it if you'd thank your mother again for her insight."

"So she told you what you wanted to know?"

Diomedes tilted his head, pressing his lips together as he folded the map and stuck it in his pocket. "In a way. It wasn't handed to me on a plate, so to speak, but it seems to be more of a lead than I've had before."

"Well," she said, taking a step back, "I wish you luck. Hopefully you'll be successful in your plans to end the war. And when you do, maybe I can help you rebuild the country."

"Thank you, Amira," he said, bowing his head. "Safe journeys."

She disappeared down the hall, and Diomedes returned to the room to find Armannii sitting up in bed, rubbing his eyes with the palms of his hands.

"About time you got up," Diomedes said, crossing the room to his bag. He transferred the map into it, putting it between the instructions for how to find the dragon whisperer and his mother's letters.

"Didn't know we were in a rush," Armannii mumbled as he staggered out of bed and toward his bag on the other side of the room. It was still strange to see his friend without some sort of vest or jerkin. He looked younger with just the forest-green tunic.

Blanndynne still sat in bed, and it was no surprise to Diomedes that she was fixing her hair, this time pulling it up into a high ponytail.

"I need a few more supplies from town," Blanndynne said when she'd finished her hair. "Anything you two need while I'm out?"

"Food," Armannii said, straightening his leather vest. "We're out of dried meat. And maybe something for breakfast."

Blanndynne nodded before walking out the door, leaving Armannii and Diomedes to pack up.

"So Raidah gave you a map to her home?" Armannii asked, his back to Diomedes.

"She offered her services should we ever be in need of them." Diomedes didn't react to the fact that Armannii had eavesdropped.

"Remind me again, how are you planning to end the war when we return?" Armannii asked, pausing what he was doing so his shoulders went rigid.

Diomedes also stopped moving, using most of his focus to find an answer to his friend's question. "If, or rather when, we find the object, I'll have magic. Then I'll end the war."

"I'm sorry to be the bearer of bad news, but you're missing a step or two there, Didi." Armannii turned around to face him. His brow was furrowed, which was uncommon. "Maybe you'll have magic, but have you thought through how you're going to return to Cyanthia? Or how you're going to take the throne? I mean, your father is still running the country, and I doubt he's going to step down willingly. What's your plan for when you come face-to-face with him? He is your father, after all. Your family."

"I can't figure out what the middle steps will be until I have magic." The mere thought sent his heart racing adding to his rising level of stress.

"So there's no plan?" Armannii asked, putting his hands in his pockets.

"The plan is to go find this dragon whisperer, then go from there with what we gain from that." Diomedes straightened up, challenging Armannii to ask further questions. He didn't.

"All right. I'm with you," Armannii said, turning back to his bag. "I want to see this war ended too. You're not going to do this alone. I won't let you. You'd end up dead. Or worse. Then who would go pubhopping with me?" Though his voice held a joking tone, something heavier lay beneath it: concern, and knowing Armannii, Diomedes knew it was concern for him. Their blood was different, but they were brothers, and Armannii treated him as such, teasing whenever possible and protecting Diomedes when the world sought to tear him down. While the elf's questions were irksome, his loyalty made up for it.

They fell into silence.

It hadn't taken them long to pack up what little they carried, and both their bags sat near the door, along with Armannii's bow and quiver. Blanndynne kept all of her things in what Diomedes referred to as her magic hidden storage room, which meant there wasn't anything of hers to pack up.

After they'd finished packing, Diomedes sat back on his bed, staring at the parchment with the instructions to find the dragon whisperer while Armannii sharpened a few of his arrows. He had a variety, some tipped with silver, others wood, and some brass or various other metals.

Diomedes, having read the instructions a few times, let his eyes glaze over as he watched Armannii work. It was only when the elf's ears perked up that Diomedes snapped out of his daze.

"What?" Diomedes asked when Armannii shot to his feet.

"B is coming, and she's running," Armannii said, racing to the other side of the room to put the rest of the arrows back in his quiver. He slung it over his shoulder at the same time Diomedes shoved the paper into his pocket and drew his sword.

Blanndynne burst through the door, panting and clutching her side. "Guards," she said, her voice shaking. "I didn't know they had followed me until a minute ago."

Armannii pulled out an arrow as Diomedes helped Blanndynne into the room and closed the door behind her.

"Are you hurt?" Armannii asked, his silver gaze scanning Blanndynne. "B, are you—"

"I'm fine. I took a few of them out and put up a quick ward around the inn, but it won't last long." Sweat dripped down her forehead, and when she pushed her hair out of her face, it clung to her skin in wet strands. "We need to leave before—"

"It's too late," Armannii said, his eyes closing. "They're inside already. I can hear them searching the rooms on the bottom floor."

"How many?" Diomedes asked, handing his bag to Blanndynne so she could put it in her magic storeroom. He didn't want to have to worry about losing his belongings while fighting.

"Can't tell. Maybe ten?" Armannii said, glancing at Blanndynne for confirmation.

She nodded. "Something like that."

"All right. Armannii, see if you can—"

"They're on our floor," Armannii said, cutting Diomedes off. "Get ready to—"

The door slammed open.

Armannii aimed his bow at the first royal guard who entered the room.

"Your Highness." The royal guard inclined his head as he spoke, surprising Diomedes with his formality. The royal guard's attention, however, went to the immediate threat of the elf standing only a few feet away with his bow drawn.

"Daven," Diomedes said, drawing the man's attention away from Armannii. "I assume my father sent you?"

"Yes, Your Highness." Daven kept his hand on the hilt of his sword, but he had not yet drawn it. A flicker of hesitation crossed his brow as his gaze dropped to the weapon in Diomedes's hand. "He wants you to come back to Cyanthia."

"So I've heard." Diomedes tilted his chin upward. "And as I told the numerous other guards, that won't be happening. Not any time soon, at least."

"Sire, you understand," Daven said, holding up his hands. "We've been instructed to bring you in by any means necessary."

"Oh, I know. The men who found us at the last pub made that quite clear." Diomedes moved his sword to his injured arm, using his free hand to lift his sleeve where his bicep was still bandaged.

Four more guards filed in through the doorway, standing behind Daven. Some of them seemed more eager than Daven to force Diomedes back to the castle, having already pulled out their weapons. But Daven remained calm as he spoke.

"I know you have meant no ill will toward your father or any of his court members. You must have a reason for whatever this"— he gestured around the small room, which felt smaller when more guards filled the hallway outside—"is. But you need to come back with me."

Diomedes lowered his sword, cocking his head to the side as he stared down each of the royal guards, starting and ending with Daven. "Do I?" Diomedes took a step toward Armannii, who was doing what he could to block Blanndynne from the guard's view.

"How long have you known me, Daven? How long have any of you known me?" A smirk crossed Diomedes's lips. "In all those years, have I ever turned down a chance to practice?"

"Your Highness—"

"Let me put it this way. You beat me, beat all three of us, and then you can bring me back to my father with my tail tucked between my legs. But when we win, you give my father a message for me."

"What message?" Daven's eyebrows creased.

Diomedes raised his sword again. "I'll tell you when I'm finished."

Daven straightened up, rolling his shoulders back and puffing out his chest. He bore the mark of a captain—a red collar on his royal guard uniform—and as many captains as Diomedes had known, none of them had worn it more proudly than Daven. The red in the collar matched the captain's hair, which he brushed aside. Diomedes had fought him on many occasions and was not surprised when Daven drew his sword in one swift motion.

"If that's what you wish." He nodded toward Diomedes.

There was no way to tell how many royal guards waited outside for them, but the moment Daven charged, the only thing Diomedes could focus on was the battle in front of him. He ducked out of the way of Daven's sword.

To the right of Diomedes, Armannii shot his arrow, landing it in the thigh of one of the guards. But there were too many in too close a space, and Armannii quickly switched to his sword. The elf moved toward two guards behind the captain. Before Diomedes could see if Blanndynne had recovered and was ready to fight, he returned his focus to Daven.

Diomedes leapt to the side, moving out of the way of Daven's reach. However, that left him pressed up against a wall with nowhere to go. Lifting his sword, he blocked Daven's weapon as it slashed the air toward his side. He took a step forward and caught Daven's chin with his elbow, forcing his opponent backward.

It was almost too difficult to keep track of his friends as he fought Daven, but he still tried. Armannii grunted when two new guards shoved him against the wall, and he ducked out of the way of a sword. He evaded and took down those two as he had the first.

Three more guards entered the fray, and they managed to push Armannii out of the room and into the hallway. Diomedes lost sight of him, hoping the elf's superior fighting skills would keep him alive.

Out of the corner of his eye, Diomedes watched Blanndynne pull throwing-knives from within her vest. Two of the guards went down before they'd even taken a full step toward her. However, one continued to charge Blanndynne, and she stepped out of the way, catching the man's hand between her arm and her side.

Crack.

Diomedes didn't flinch when Blanndynne snapped the guard's arm, and he raised an eyebrow at the screech of pain the guard made as he fell to the ground, clutching his broken arm tightly.

By the time Diomedes refocused on Daven, the captain was already swinging his sword. Grunting, Diomedes caught the weapon with his, but Daven pressed forward until Diomedes's shoes slid backward. Hands shaking, Diomedes struggled against Daven. He had no choice but to straighten up as soon as his back smacked against the wall. Daven had him pinned, and not by chance. Though they stood at the same height, Daven was all muscle, and Diomedes was not. He had been in a similar position multiple times while training with Daven and some of the larger guards.

"You must return to the castle, Your Highness," Daven said through gritted teeth.

Diomedes winced as Daven leaned into him, and he could barely keep his grip on his weapon, which was the only thing keeping Daven's sword from cutting him in two. Still, he glared back at Daven.

Instead of responding, Diomedes focused all his efforts on the muscles keeping Daven from winning. Armannii had not yet returned to the room, and he wondered how many guards were out in the hallway. They were outnumbered in what felt like a ten-to-one fight. There were far more than just ten guards, and as more kept spilling in, Diomedes began to question if they'd be able to get out.

Blanndynne grunted when a guard tripped her, and out of the corner of his eye, Diomedes watched a guard raise his sword. It wasn't a jade weapon, so it wouldn't kill her, but it would hurt.

"Blanndynne, focus," Diomedes spat out, and the second she met his intense stare, he could tell by the look in her eyes that she understood.

"Stop," Blanndynne said, her voice smooth even as the guard moved to strike.

The man froze.

When another guard started toward her, she turned her attention on him. "You too." Power radiated from her voice, and as she rose to her feet, she enchanted the three other guards in the room—all except for Daven.

The captain made a mistake the moment he took his attention off Diomedes and focused on the strange way his men were acting.

Diomedes took advantage, catching Daven in the gut with his knee. The captain dropped his sword, clutching his stomach. He was unable to protect his face as Diomedes swung his fist, catching Daven in the jaw. Daven hit the ground with a thud.

"Take care of them," Diomedes said to Blanndynne, who had sweat dripping down the sides of her face.

She nodded, and when she spoke next, all five of them dropped to the floor.

"Your Highness," Daven said, trying to get up despite the fact that his men lay unconscious around him. "You have to come back to the castle."

"Oh, I'll come back." Diomedes sheathed his sword, a grin on his lips. "But only when I decide the time is right, and now is not that time." He punched Daven one more time just as the man was about to rise to his feet. Diomedes stepped over the captain's crumpled body, brushing his overgrown hair out of his face. "Make

sure my father knows that the next time he sees me, he'd better be ready. I'm ending this war, one way or another."

"You're sure you're reading those instructions right?" Armannii asked, readjusting his bag. Diomedes had been surprised when he'd exited the room in the inn and found that the elf had taken out all of the guards not only on their floor but on the lower floor as well. They'd made it out of the village just as more guards were arriving.

The trio had been traveling for what felt like hours. It probably had been hours. Diomedes couldn't tell. The dark canopy of the Black Forest barely allowed in light when it was noon and the sun was high in the sky, let alone when the three moons were full and at their peak.

"Yes. Why?" Diomedes didn't bother looking back, knowing Armannii was rolling his eyes.

"Because I'm pretty sure we passed that tree about twenty minutes ago." Armannii paused, sticking his hands in his pockets and nodding toward a tree next to him. "In fact, I'm positive we passed it because you tripped on this root." He removed a hand from his pocket and pointed toward the ground in front of him.

Diomedes's bruised shin throbbed for a second, but he ignored it. "Then you try leading."

"Thought you'd never ask." Armannii took the instructions from him, patting Diomedes on the shoulder as he passed. After a single glance, Armannii led them in the opposite direction Diomedes had been taking them.

Tightening his lips into a straight line, Diomedes didn't argue as he followed the elf. Though he wouldn't admit it, he felt less stressed with Armannii leading, a sense of direction not being one of his natural gifts.

While his eyes focused on the ground, scanning for rogue tree roots, his mind wandered. The confrontation with Daven had left him sorting through old memories, particularly memories of training with the royal guards. However, it had stirred up others as well.

As he traveled, his mind wandered to other training sessions—those with his sister, Ellayne, while they were growing up. He couldn't remember the last time they had actually sparred; it certainly hadn't happened within the last year or two. However, he couldn't help but linger over the memories.

"You're not thinking," he had said to her, earning himself a glare.

"Oh, because you can suddenly read my thoughts now?" Ellayne flicked her blond ponytail over her shoulder. She crossed her arms over her chest.

Diomedes almost grinned, but he refrained as he lowered the training staff to the ground. "If you'd been concentrating, you would've noticed that I was heavily relying on my left foot. You could've used it against me, and you would've still had a weapon in your hand." He narrowed his eyes at her. "Instead, your staff is halfway across the training room, and—"

"I get it." She huffed as she crossed the brick floor to collect her staff. Ellayne muttered something else under her breath, but she was too far away for Diomedes to hear whatever insult she had retorted with. "Let's go again."

He had always given her credit. No matter how many times he'd knocked her on her rear, she'd never quit. She must've been fourteen or fifteen in the memory, and though he'd never admit it to her face, he had been impressed with how many of the royal guards she had disarmed even at that age.

However, she had not managed to get the upper hand on Diomedes—not that day, at least. Diomedes continued to follow Armannii through the Black Forest, and a slight smile crossed his lips. He pictured his sister's glower when she'd pushed herself up to sitting from the floor after he'd once again beaten her. Not for the first time, he wished he had brought Ellayne with him.

Armannii's voice made Diomedes look up from the ground, his smirk quickly disappearing into a neutral expression. "I didn't take you for the type of person who enjoyed waltzing through the Black Forest."

Diomedes raised an eyebrow but didn't respond. There was no need to encourage the elf's comments. He knew Armannii would continue whether he spoke or not.

"Glad to see it brings a smile to that horribly dreary face of yours." Armannii grinned as he turned back around, barely flinching as he darted out of the way of a tree in his immediate path.

"How much farther?" Blanndynne asked from behind Diomedes. "If it's more than another hour, I'm going to need a break."

"Shouldn't be much longer, you know, now that we're going in the right direction." Armannii's shoulders shook as he chuckled to himself.

Diomedes clenched his jaw.

"I thought genies didn't get as tired as humans. Why are you so exhausted?" Armannii asked when Blanndynne trailed behind.

Blanndynne glanced at Diomedes for just a second. He knew why. Enchantment—ensnaring the mind—took about as much energy as flying. It drained her. But given Armannii's negative reaction to Blanndynne's history with enchantment, neither one admitted the truth.

"I told you," Blanndynne said, glaring at Armannii. "I had to fight off the other guards while Diomedes fought the captain."

"You don't get that tired in our training sessions," Armannii argued, pausing as he placed his hands on his hips.

"You're just one person."

"Mm-hmm," Armannii said, a glint flashing in his silver eyes. "One person who took out the rest of the royal guards single-handedly."

"Whatever. I'm tired, but I'll live." Blanndynne adjusted the clasp on her cloak.

"Just keep going," Diomedes muttered, thankful when Armannii continued leading. The sooner they found the dragon whisperer, the sooner he'd find the magical object and end the war. A little thought tickled the back of his mind. *If it works.*

Those three little words caused him to hesitate for a second, and Blanndynne noticed.

"What?" Her voice came out weary.

He shook his head. "Nothing. It's fine."

But the thought remained there. If the object didn't work—didn't give Diomedes the power he needed to oppose his father and the council—there was no alternate plan.

Then again, if they did find it, there was every possibility that it would work. Diomedes stuck his tongue in the back of his cheek as a small grin crossed his mouth. He would successfully do something no one thought possible. He, a man born from a magicless line, would gain magic. The thought sent a thrilling chill down his spine, and he straightened his shoulders.

To have magic. The thought filled him with an excitement he hadn't experienced in a long time. He tried to picture the look on his father's face when he returned, storming into the council meeting with all the power he would ever need to end the war. The mere thought took away the aches and pains from all the walking, fights, and lack of sleep, and each step he took brought him closer to the realization of that dream.

Chapter Eight

After walking for another twenty minutes, Armannii stopped in front of a landmark Raidah had mentioned in the instructions. Three trunks grew together into one twisting monster of a tree. In the middle of the trunks was a structure made out of the same wood as the bark. A door at least eight feet tall sat at the center, and around the rim was a crack leaking the slightest amount of light.

"This definitely has to be it, right?" Armannii asked, putting his hands on his hips as he looked the gigantic structure up and down twice. "I've been all over the Black Forest, and I've never seen something like this."

"It matches Raidah's description," Diomedes said, his fingers grazing the hilt of his sword. Something about the place left a knot in his stomach, but he couldn't place his finger on why.

"Should we knock?" Blanndynne said. "Or—"

"We knock," Diomedes said. He nodded toward Armannii, who shrugged before walking up to the door.

Raising his bow, Armannii tapped on the door. The sound was hollow, echoing amongst the trees. Diomedes strained his hearing, trying to listen for any sign of life on the other side of the door. After a few seconds of silence, Diomedes nodded toward Armannii.

"Again."

Armannii switched to his fist and pounded on the door; the result was the same.

With a frown, Diomedes stepped up next to him and slammed his palm on the wood.

"Open up," he ordered, raising his voice. The door shook as he struck it again.

"I don't think anyone's home," Armannii said after another second. "I can't hear any movement on the other side. Should we—"

Before Armannii could finish his sentence, Diomedes tried the doorknob.

"Locked." Diomedes punched the door, pressing his lips together as he let out a forced laugh. "Figures. We get this close, and it's another dead end." He kicked the nearest root, grimacing when his toe crunched inside his boot.

"Move," Armannii said. The elf nodded toward Diomedes, who stepped back.

Armannii pulled his rune pen out of his vest and twirled it between his fingers. As he got closer to the door, he tilted his head to both sides, eliciting an audible crack each time. Armannii moved the pen over the door, and a light blue line followed his motions. After a second, he tucked the pen away and tried the knob again. This time it twisted, and the door creaked open.

"After you, Your Royal Pain," Armannii said, swinging the door open and gesturing to Diomedes. His grin would've annoyed Diomedes if he hadn't just opened the door. "You're welcome," Armannii muttered after Diomedes entered the home.

The light from inside the home made Diomedes's eyes water, and he quickly removed the glasses bearing the sight rune. He tucked them into his pocket for the next time they were needed. Diomedes blinked as his eyes started to adjust, and it was a few seconds before he was able to make out the blurry shadows of furniture.

Blanndynne crossed the entry room, which held a small two-person couch, a sitting table, and a rickety rocking chair. She pushed open a door, revealing a bedroom with minimal decorations: a cot, a shelf with about nine or ten books, and a trunk. The kitchen consisted of a few counters and cupboards, and it was connected to the main room that Armannii and Diomedes remained in.

"Not much, is it?" Diomedes turned his nose up when he noticed a hole at the foot of a nearby wall, probably made by a rodent of some sort.

"Still a step up from the shack before the inn," Armannii said, brushing off the couch before sitting down. He crossed one leg over the other and laced his fingers behind his head as he leaned back. "At least there's furniture here."

"And another bedroom off of this one. But no dragon whisperer," Blanndynne said as she reentered the main room. "Which is kind of the entire reason we're here. So what now?"

Diomedes frowned at a bowl on the counter. He nodded toward it, waiting for the other two to notice what he'd seen.

Armannii sat up straighter, tilting his head. "Whoever lives here has been home recently."

Blanndynne crossed the room to the bowl and picked up the bread Diomedes had noticed. "Still fresh."

"So we wait."

Diomedes ran his fingers through his hair for what felt like the fiftieth time since they had entered the house. With an absence of conversation, the room had fallen into a repetitive cycle of creaks and groans. The house spoke for itself amidst the silence.

Picking at the fraying ends of the couch arm, Diomedes almost jumped when Armannii straightened up next to him.

"Someone's coming," he whispered. He stood up, and the other two followed his motion.

Diomedes reached for his sword but hesitated. If they were going to get information out of whoever walked through that door, it was likely better to start with a pleasant conversation rather than an ambush.

Armannii and Blanndynne watched him, their gazes tracking as he let his hand fall to his side without the blade.

"We try to talk first," he muttered. "If we don't get what we need from there, we'll move on to different measures."

Blanndynne nodded, leaning back against the counter. "Have fun explaining how we're here. I'm sure the owner of this place will be thrilled at our trespassing and forced entry."

Diomedes ignored her, his attention on the door. Having heard shuffling from the other side, he guessed the occupant was searching for a key. Diomedes rolled his shoulders back, bracing for the first interaction with the stranger. His stomach tightened, and another impulse to reach for the hilt of his sword tempted him. His fingers twitched.

The door opened, creaking as it had when they had first entered.

A man walked through the door and froze as soon as his gaze landed on Diomedes. He was shorter than Diomedes, closer to Blanndynne's height, though that could've been because he had a hunch in his shoulders. His fair hair was scraggly, like it hadn't seen a brush or a bath in a long time. He wore a brown cloak with holes near the hem, and in his arms were bags with produce and other food items. His eyes reflected bright green in the light of the lamp. For a second, Diomedes thought there was something almost reptilian to them.

"Who are you? What are you doing in m-my house?" The man's voice was high-pitched, like he hadn't yet reached adulthood, but the scruff on the lower half of his face told a different story; some strands were already graying.

"Where's the dragon whisperer?" Diomedes asked, intentionally ignoring the man's question. "I was told she lived here."

The man shook his head over and over again. "No, no, no. I, but, you—" He froze, his eyes widening. "You're him, aren't you? The one the voice told me about in my dreams. You're him!" His voice trembled.

"Do you know me?" Diomedes waited for the man to respond, but he simply shook his head. "My name is Diomedes. I'm—"

"The prince? She never said it would be—but you shouldn't be here. What if—what if they find you? I could be arrested—persecuted for harboring you. It would be a disaster, no, a tragedy. I—"

"That's enough. Help him with the bags." Diomedes held up a hand, motioning for Blanndynne to take the bags the man was gripping with white knuckles.

The man took a step back, but Blanndynne held up her hands to show she had no intention of hurting him. He clutched the bags tighter but loosened them after a few seconds and handed them to Blanndynne. He rubbed his hands together repeatedly, switching his worried gaze between all three of the intruders every few seconds.

"I apologize for ambushing you like this. We came looking for the dragon whisperer who allied herself with the sorceress. I believe she has information I've been searching for." Diomedes dipped his head in a brief nod, the way he had seen his father greet strangers. "How about we have a seat?" He gestured toward the rocking chair, and after a few seconds, the man nodded and shuffled across the room. He sat down with a huff.

Armannii crossed the room to close the door, which the man had left open. Instead of returning to the couch where Diomedes sat, he remained standing near the exit. The man continued to flit his trembling gaze between the three strangers. His hands shook as he crossed them in his lap, and he bounced his legs up and down.

"What's your name?" Diomedes asked, tilting his head as he rubbed his chin. He briefly glanced over his shoulder when an apple fell out of one of the bags Blanndynne was arranging on the counters behind him. But he returned his attention to the man as soon as he started speaking.

"Mellacross. Ian Mellacross, Your Highness," the man said, speaking quickly. He inclined his head in Diomedes's direction. "I never would've thought, I mean, how is it that I—I'd get a chance to meet royalty. Well, I mean, a second time."

Diomedes raised an eyebrow. "Oh? Who else have you met?" Mellacross's comment had held enough intrigue that Diomedes couldn't resist asking the question.

"I, well, when I was younger, I met your mother, the late queen."

In less than a second, Diomedes's shoulders stiffened. Every muscle tightened to the point that he was almost in pain.

"Really?" Diomedes choked on the word. He leaned forward, as if that would make Mellacross's words clearer. "When?"

Mellacross nodded. "It was a long time ago. I was a child. Hardly a teenager. I think I must've been twelve at the time. Maybe thirteen. I don't know, I'm sorry. But when she joined the sorceress, I met her with my mother."

"Your mother? Was she the dragon whisperer?" Diomedes asked, using his energy to remain focused on why he was there. When Mellacross bobbed his head, Diomedes continued. "Where is she? I need to speak with her."

"She's gone," Mellacross said, his gaze lowering to the floor. "Died years ago, actually. Very sad."

"Oh." Diomedes couldn't bring himself to say more as his hopes at finding out more information on the object came crashing down. Again.

Armannii spoke next, and Mellacross shifted to face him. "You said a voice told you we were coming. What did you mean by that? What voice?"

Mellacross blinked, and just like earlier, his irises reflected a bright green before the pupils shifted into vertical slits. Diomedes rubbed the inner corner of his eye, blinking a few times to make sure he was actually seeing the man's eyes change. But just like that, Mellacross's eyes were hazel, the pupil round like any other human's.

"Voice? Oh, you mean *her* voice. I mean, well, it's hard, a little difficult, really, to explain. The voice, she, well, it's the sorceress's." Mellacross glanced at Diomedes, who frowned.

"She's dead," Diomedes said, scratching his chin. Mellacross nodded rapidly.

"I know. Everyone knows. It's common knowledge actually. That she's dead, I mean." Mellacross's words were quick and almost manic.

"So you're saying a dead woman spoke to you?" Diomedes raised an eyebrow, watching the man.

"Yes." Mellacross fidgeted again, crossing his arms over his chest briefly before smoothing out his pants. He went back to bouncing his legs soon after, moving the rocking chair with him. "My mother told me, before she died, of course, that the sorceress would contact me. Impossible, I thought. I didn't believe her. Why would I? Dead people can't talk. Right? Of course not. But about a month ago, I heard the sorceress's voice in my dream."

Armannii snorted but covered it with a cough when Mellacross sent a very unthreatening glare in his direction.

"It's true. My mother said the sorceress would contact me, and she did. Really. The sorceress told me that another person would come seeking to end the war. I didn't believe her either. Thought I was crazy." Mellacross ignored another snort from Armannii, or maybe he hadn't heard it because all of his attention rested on Diomedes. He stared at him with wide eyes. "It took twenty-two years for it to happen. Twenty-two years. But it happened. Just like she said. That's why you're here, right?" Mellacross asked Diomedes, his voice going up even higher at the end of his question. "To end the war?"

Diomedes inclined his head. Mellacross's personality was exhausting, and his speech was difficult to listen to, but Diomedes pasted a smile on his face nonetheless. "That's what my friends and I are doing. But we need some assistance." Diomedes found himself wanting to speak to Mellacross, who was clearly older than him, as if he were a child.

"And that's why you're here?" Mellacross flicked his gaze between the three. "But what can I do? I can't fight, and—"

"That's not what we need. Not at the moment at least," Diomedes said, raising his hand to stop Mellacross. "What we need is information on an object, one that belonged to the sorceress. I know that it's in the Elemental Mountains somewhere—at least, that's what I've been led to believe. But what I don't know is where exactly it is, which mountain specifically. There are too many caves to search in one lifetime. I—"

Mellacross cleared his throat. "You need to know where the sorceress left this object?"

"Yes." Diomedes pressed his lips together as he stared down his nose at Mellacross.

Running his fingers through his scruff, Mellacross frowned. "I, well, I guess I should apologize, as you've come all this way for nothing, I mean. I'm sorry. I never, I mean, when I was a boy, I never went to the caves with my mother. I couldn't begin to tell you where the final battle happened, let alone where to find what you're looking for." Mellacross wrung his hands, smoothing his trousers again afterward.

Time slowed down around Diomedes. Another dead end. He wanted to be alone, wanted to take his frustrations out in a loud and unbecoming manner. He wanted to shout and break things, to punch a wall or flip the furniture.

But he didn't.

The worst part was he could tell by the glances Armannii was sending him, all of which were laced with an air of seriousness, that the man was telling the truth. Armannii was good at reading people, and when the elf nodded and didn't argue with the dragon whisperer's son, Diomedes felt his stomach sink. Mellacross had spoken the truth.

And they were back to the beginning.

Sitting up straighter, Diomedes nodded, closing his eyes as he rubbed his aching temples. "Well then," he said as he stood, "I apologize for the intrusion." The weight of yet another failure bore down on Diomedes, and he felt his frustration rising up to combat it.

Armannii shifted, tilting his head as he glanced toward the back room. "How far is the nearest inn?"

Mellacross rose to his feet, then wrapped his arms around himself and rocked back and forth on his heels. "The village near here, it's small. I don't think, well, I'm pretty sure it doesn't have one. I-I haven't gone anywhere else in a long time. Too long to be away from home."

Diomedes exchanged glances with Armannii and Blanndynne. How long would they have to walk to get to a place where they could rest and Diomedes could try to come up with their next step? He was already tired, his feet were sore, and the emotional stress of their biggest lead ending in a dead end had him speaking before he had thought it through.

"My friends and I are tired from traveling. Do you think we might be able to—"

"No, no, no," Mellacross said, shaking his head before Diomedes could finish his request. He tapped his foot as he rubbed his hands up and down his arms as if he were fighting to stay warm. "What if the royal guards came? I-I would be arrested. Right? And then—"

"If it makes you feel any better," Armannii said, cutting in as he took a step toward Mellacross, "I know for a fact that we weren't followed. Listened for it myself." He turned his head so Mellacross could see his pointed ears.

"It would only be for a few hours," Blanndynne added, her voice gentle as she stepped forward. She offered Mellacross a genial smile, and it was only when her hand moved down by her hip—out of Armannii's line of sight—that Diomedes realized what she was doing. "What do you say, Ian?"

Mellacross stopped shaking, and he frowned before nodding slowly. "I-I suppose, I mean, it would be rude if I . . . okay. Please, stay and rest." His voice, though still hesitant, had slowed down.

Diomedes cast a quick glance at Armannii to see if he'd noticed what Blanndynne had done, but the elf just grinned and shrugged at Diomedes.

"Thanks, mate," Armannii said, and Diomedes agreed.

"I'll show you, I mean, if you follow me, the extra bedroom is this way." Mellacross nodded toward the back room.

Armannii followed Mellacross first, and Diomedes nodded to Blanndynne with approval before following the elf. Blanndynne smirked. Diomedes was impressed that the genie had managed to enchant Mellacross right under Armannii's nose.

Though spending more time with the dragon whisperer's son was far from what Diomedes desired, he was thankful he didn't have to walk endlessly to find a place to stay—at least not that night. It would be less irksome to plan their next steps after sleeping for a few hours and having something to eat.

Mellacross set up a collapsible cot in his bedroom, which was connected to another bedroom in the back. Both rooms already had one cot each. Mellacross insisted that the three intruders have the three beds and that he would sleep on the couch in the living room—likely under the deep suggestion from the genie controlling his thoughts and decisions. Diomedes—tired of traveling and being let down by vague or absent answers—did not argue. Without another word to anyone, he claimed one of the cots in the first bedroom and went to sleep.

Chapter Nine

Unaware of where he was or what time it was, Diomedes startled awake as soon as he recognized that the hand on his shoulder was real, not just part of the dream in which he was invested. He shot up in the cot, smacking his forehead on something. Or someone.

"Sh," Mellacross said, rubbing his head as he stepped back. "I didn't mean to startle you, Your Highness, but she told me to come get you."

"Blanndynne?" Diomedes asked, massaging his throbbing forehead. "What does she want?" He glanced toward the door to the back bedroom, where Blanndynne was supposed to be sleeping, but it was still closed. Had she sent Mellacross with a message? And how had she managed to keep a hold over the man for so long and with walls in between? "Why didn't she come wake me?" Armannii still slept on the cot in the corner. Diomedes squinted at Mellacross.

In the low light—the only source of which was in the main room—Mellacross's eyes flashed bright green, and he straightened up.

"Not your friend. The sorceress." His voice was not only monotonous but void of all hesitation and stutters. Though his gaze fell on Diomedes, it was as if his eyes saw right through him.

Diomedes pushed himself into a sitting position. The thin wool blanket he had covered himself with pooled in his lap as he tilted his head to the side. "Sorceress? She's spoken to you again?"

"Speaking. Now. She wants you to find it. She told me so."

Pushing his hair out of his face, Diomedes rubbed his eyes with the back of his hand. "Well, I need to know where she left it."

"She knows. And she will tell you." Mellacross nodded to the main room before turning to leave.

With a grunt, Diomedes reached under his pillow for the knife he had stashed there. Since leaving the castle, he always made sure the knife was under his head at night. He tucked it into his belt before following Mellacross into the living room. At least if it was a trap, Diomedes would have some sort of weapon to use against him.

"Sit," Mellacross said, his voice still void of any intonation. "She wants me to draw a map."

Diomedes gestured toward the table, holding back a yawn. A small part of him believed Mellacross was telling the truth, but a larger part of Diomedes figured the man had lost his mind. He was sure it was a possibility, living out in the Black Forest all alone.

Mellacross had already set up a piece of parchment and was bent over it, drawing. The hunch in his back became more pronounced, and Diomedes's eyes became unfocused as he stared at the way the fabric on the man's tunic tightened over his rounded shoulders.

"You must pay attention here," Mellacross said, pulling Diomedes's focus down to the map.

In the crude drawing, Diomedes could make out the Elemental Mountains taking up most of the top half of the map. It helped that Mellacross had labeled some of his drawing.

"It is important you don't venture too far east into the desert, as it is easy to get lost; the mountains are only visible a small percent of the time. And don't go too far west into the Cyro Sea or you might fall in. Stay along the coast and follow it up to the Elemental Mountains." Mellacross used the back of his pen to point as he explained.

Diomedes nodded to show he was listening, though his attention remained divided. While he knew it was easier to remain suspicious and skeptical of Mellacross's sudden usefulness, he couldn't stop the rise in hope he'd all but lost before they'd gone to sleep.

"Once you reach the mountains, follow the ridge east until you see the fourth mountain peak. It looks like a crescent moon at the very top. Take the valley between the third and fourth mountains. There should be a stream that leads up to a large waterfall. Go to the right of the waterfall and scale it all the way up. When you get to the top of the ledge where the water comes out from the side of the mountain, there will be a cave entrance hidden by hanging moss. That is your entrance into the cave system."

Diomedes straightened up, leaning forward so his elbows rested on his knees. His head was reeling with the information while at the same time trying to juxtapose the trembling little man with the confident and collected man before him. If he was telling the truth, then the sorceress really was the one speaking to Diomedes, and that alone was a thrilling concept. "*The* cave system?"

Mellacross nodded once more and went back to drawing. He continued to speak as he traced lines through the mountains. "She says there are many different paths in the system, and though she can steer you in the right direction, it is up to you to find the correct path."

"What's that supposed to mean?"

He did not answer. "Once you have found the room, you will need to descend further. What you seek lies in the deepest bowels of the mountain, in the belly of the beast, so to speak."

"And how will I know when I've found 'the room'?" Diomedes tried to restrain his frustration. Though he was receiving the answers he'd been searching for, they were more cryptic than he would've preferred.

"You will not stumble across the room. It may only be entered with intention."

Diomedes clasped his hands under his chin, digging his nails into the palms of his hands to remain calm. "And when I find the object? What do I do then? Can she tell me what it is?"

Mellacross stopped moving, his gaze transfixed on the map he'd drawn. "All in good time."

"All in good time?" Diomedes raised his voice. "If she wants me to find it, why keep it secret? How can she—"

"Wh-what's going on? What happened?" Mellacross scratched his head, glancing up at Diomedes and then down at the map. When he saw the pen in his own hand, his eyes widened. "Did I . . . did I draw this?"

Diomedes didn't answer, turning instead to kick the nearest thing, which happened to be a doorframe. "Why can't I just get a straight answer?" he muttered as Armannii and Blanndynne filed through the doorway.

"What's with the temper?" Armannii asked, squinting in the light. His vest was crooked, and he straightened it as he walked into the main room.

"And the scribbles?" Blanndynne added as she peered down at Mellacross's map. "Is that supposed to be Phildeterre?"

"Did I do that? Did I draw that?" Mellacross asked again, having stood up and backed away from the table. His eyes—hazel once more—were wide, and his hands shook as he pointed at the parchment. "When did I do that?"

Diomedes held up his hands, silencing the room. "Sit down," he ordered, and apart from Armannii's skeptical look, everyone complied without further questioning. "Mellacross woke me. Said something about the sorceress talking to him again, and he came out here and started drawing the map. Apparently, the sorceress was giving directions for how to find the object. Really obscure directions, but still."

Armannii, who sat on the couch next to Blanndynne, picked up the map and skimmed over it. "So it's in the Elemental Mountains. We already knew that. How is this—"

"The cave entrance is between the third and fourth mountains in from the Cyro Sea. The fourth mountain is the one with the cave system, and it looks like it has a crescent moon at the top. We're supposed to follow a valley up to a waterfall and then climb up to the right of the waterfall to a cliff, where the cave entrance should be covered in moss."

"Should be?" Blanndynne asked, leaning over Armannii to look at the map. "That's a little—"

"Vague. I'm well aware," Diomedes said, frowning. "Unfortunately, the sorceress left when I started asking for more directions."

"Left?" Mellacross said, his voice weak. "What do you mean?"

"Figures," Armannii mumbled, handing the map to Blanndynne before standing up. "All right. Ten minutes?"

Diomedes couldn't help but grin. When he'd all but given up hope, the answer he'd been waiting for had been placed in his lap. "Ten minutes."

Armannii shoved his hands into his pockets and glanced at Mellacross. "You okay there, mate?"

"I don't—did I—she's never . . . I mean, she hasn't ever spoken through me, ju-just to me. But she, the sorceress, she spoke to you?" Mellacross asked, scratching the back of his head as everyone turned to look at him. He sat in the rocking chair.

"In a way, yes. She spoke through you and drew that map." Diomedes nodded and crossed his hands behind his back.

"I didn't know . . . and then she was gone." He tossed a hesitant glance at the map, rubbing his hands together in his lap. Mellacross continued to mutter incomplete thoughts under his breath, and Diomedes turned his attention to the elf.

"I'll grab my things, and we can go," Armannii said as he left the room. Blanndynne laid the map back on the table and followed Armannii.

It only took Diomedes a few seconds to grab his bag and his belt with the sword attached. Diomedes folded the map, placing it in his bag, which he tossed on the ground in the main room. Glancing at Mellacross—who was still in the rocking chair—Diomedes put his sword and sheath on.

"May I ask you a question?" Diomedes asked, tightening the belt and resting his hands on his hips when he had finished.

"Me? Why? I mean, of course, Your Highness." Mellacross nodded. He continued to flick his eyes to the ground every couple seconds, but it seemed like he was trying to force his attention to stay on Diomedes.

"Do you have your mother's power? I mean, would you be a dragon whisperer if there were still any dragons?" Diomedes cringed inwardly when he realized he'd copied the man's speech pattern.

Mellacross froze, his hands tightening on the arms of the rocking chair. "Why? What do you know? Are you—do you—"

"I'm just curious." Diomedes held his hands out in a nonthreatening gesture. He waited until Mellacross took a deep breath, then continued. "Have you ever met a dragon?" Diomedes thought he heard Armannii chuckle in the back room, but he ignored it.

Since he had been a little boy, Diomedes had imagined seeing a dragon. To ride on its back. After years of remembering the night his mother left, he'd pondered what it'd felt like, and now he wondered if it had been Mellacross's mother's dragon.

Mellacross stiffened again. "I—well—yes."

"And?" Diomedes asked, raising an eyebrow. "What was it like? Could you speak to it? Control it?"

"Terrifying," Mellacross muttered. A tremor spread through his body, and he wrung his hands nervously in his lap. "Horrifying. It was huge, and it reeked of blood, smoke, and death. Its teeth— they were the length of my arms, and there were rows and rows and rows of them. And the way it growled. It wanted to, I mean, if it had had the chance, it would've killed me. Burned me alive."

Diomedes sat down on the couch across from Mellacross, trying to remember the drawings of dragons he had seen in the books he'd read in his father's office. "Did you fly on it? I mean, did your mother let you—"

"Oh, no. No, no, no." Mellacross shook his head. "I hate heights. Hate them. I would never—could never. No." The man struggled to swallow.

Frowning, Diomedes cocked his head to the side. "But your mother was a dragon whisperer. Wouldn't that get passed down to you? It is inherited . . ." He pictured Mellacross's eyes shifting to the brilliant green with vertical slits for pupils. He must've inherited it.

"No, no, no. I mean, yes. I can talk to them. But no. I'm not . . . I'm not like her. Not like my mother. Sh-she was brave. I-I can't. I wouldn't be around the dragons. No. I couldn't." He started rocking in the chair.

"You're scared of them." Diomedes didn't need Mellacross to respond; the answer was as clear as the glass in the Glass Fields of Phildeterre.

"I-I, well, yes. I suppose I am. But it doesn't matter. My mother's dragon is gone. Dead. And its baby—it's not my problem."

"Baby?" Diomedes's ears perked up. "I didn't know there were any dragons left. Where is it?"

Mellacross ran his hand across his mouth, still shaking his head. "It's not my problem. Not my problem."

Diomedes glanced behind him as Blanndynne and Armannii entered the room.

"Ready?" Armannii asked, his bow slung across his shoulder.

With one last look at Mellacross, who seemed to be declining into some sort of panic attack, Diomedes nodded.

"Let's go."

"We can't just leave him like this," Blanndynne said, her brow creasing as she frowned at Mellacross.

"Fair enough," Armannii said, and he put his bag down, riffling through it until he pulled out his canteen. "I'm assuming there's water nearby?" He directed the question to Mellacross, who lifted a shaking hand and pointed to the left.

"Th-there's a stream over that way." He lowered his hand into his lap and continued to rock back and forth.

"I'll refill our water," Armannii said, holding out his hand for Blanndynne and Diomedes to give him their canteens. "I'll be back soon."

Diomedes and Blanndynne waited until he had been gone for a few minutes before talking.

"Let's see it," Diomedes said, a smirk on his lips as he crossed his arms over his chest and watched Blanndynne.

"See wh—" Mellacross relaxed as soon as Blanndynne turned her attention on him. She raised her hand, palm out, toward the dragon whisperer's son.

"You're getting faster." Diomedes tilted his head, squinting at Mellacross's eyes. They weren't as cloudy as he'd expected them to be. "And better," he added. "I can barely tell he's under. And Armannii didn't even notice last night."

"Thanks," Blanndynne said, and she nodded toward the back room. "Go to bed, Ian."

"And maybe make sure he doesn't remember . . . this." Diomedes gestured toward her, and she chuckled.

"He won't remember a thing."

"You're sure this is a good idea?" Blanndynne asked, pulling the hood of her cloak farther down to hide her face. "If we're seen—"

"Don't be seen," Armannii mumbled as he continued toward the main street of the town. They'd spent an entire day walking north after Armannii had returned, and Diomedes had been getting ready to cut his feet off when they came to the edge of the town. Each step brought them closer to the Cyro Sea, and the temperature seemed to be dropping consistently. "I want to make sure the northern ice bridge is open to get to the coast of the Cyro Sea, otherwise we'll need to head south to the Tiansky bridge and—"

"That would take an extra day and a half just to—"

"Which is why I'm checking. It would be even more obnoxious to get to the northern ice bridge, realize it's closed, and have to backtrack. May as well find out now," Armannii said, cutting Diomedes's complaint off. "Besides, we need to get warmer clothing anyway, or we're going to freeze to death. We're going to have to stop and sleep near the sea either way, and it's going to be cold."

"All right. Just keep your hoods pulled down and hope the ice bridge is open," Diomedes muttered, lowering his voice when they neared a woman with a basket of bread.

"Let's hope." Armannii walked in front of the other two. "Stay quiet and stick next to me. And if you venture off like you did last time, B, we're leaving without you. Got it?" He ventured a glance over his shoulder.

"Uh-huh," Blanndynne said, a smile on her lips. And Diomedes knew why. Armannii's eyes had shifted to gold. "I'm sure you'd leave me, liar." She wiggled her eyebrows, and he rolled his eyes as he continued down the street.

Underneath his cloak, Diomedes gripped the hilt of his sword, ready to pull it out at a moment's notice. But there was no need as Armannii led them toward a shop with a sign that read "Winter Wear."

Anywhere else not near the Cyro Sea, a shop that sold purely cold-weather clothing would've gone out of business during the warmer seasons. However, the need to stay warm was clearly a year-long struggle, as those around them pulled scarves and hats tighter around them every time the wind blew.

"I'll go ask about the ice bridge. Stay with her," Armannii said to Diomedes.

With a nod, Diomedes followed Armannii into the shop. Blanndynne came in behind him, and they separated from the elf to go in the opposite direction of the counter.

"You're sure Mellacross's map is reliable?" Blanndynne whispered as she picked up a wool tunic with long sleeves, examining it. "It seems like a substantial risk to go all the way up to the Elemental Mountains on the word of a man who doesn't have all of his wits about him."

Diomedes glanced over his shoulder to see Armannii talking to the young woman running the front counter. The elf was probably eavesdropping—not that it mattered. There were no other patrons in the shop, and the woman kept glancing around Armannii's shoulder to look at Blanndynne and Diomedes; Diomedes wasn't sure if it was because she suspected their true identities or if she thought they were about to steal. Either way, he was not fond of how much attention she was sending their way.

He turned back around and focused on the crate of warm socks in front of him. His toes already felt numb from the cold.

"Hey." Blanndynne nudged him with her shoulder, and he sighed.

"You weren't there. It was like Mellacross was someone completely different. He spoke like he had no control over himself. It was strange. I didn't believe him at first, but then he started talking about how to get into the caves. And you heard him the night before. He had no clue where to find the object. But when he woke me up . . . I don't know. It was different."

"If you say so," Blanndynne said, folding the long-sleeved tunic back up and placing it in the stack with the others.

Diomedes didn't feel like arguing and instead focused on finding a pair of socks that didn't look like they were made of wool dyed in some sort of bodily fluid. Just as he found a dark blue pair, Armannii walked up and placed a hand on his and Blanndynne's shoulders.

"I spoke with the clerk. It's all good news. The ice bridge is open, and there's an inn down the street we can stay in tonight. She recommended an extra pair of socks, a long-sleeved tunic, wool trousers, a hat, and gloves. Pick what you want and give them to me. I'll pay."

Blanndynne nodded, leaving them to find her size while Diomedes and Armannii stayed by the socks.

"She didn't recognize me, did she?" Diomedes whispered in a barely audible voice.

"No. Just thought you were a common thief. I gave her peace of mind." Armannii winked when Diomedes glanced sideways at him.

"Let's hurry and get out of here. The sooner we find the inn and sleep, the sooner we can wake up and head north. Then we'll be one step closer to—"

"Ending the war. I'm aware. But I don't want to freeze to death, so stock up." Armannii patted him on the shoulder before leaving to go look at the trousers.

Chapter Ten

iomedes gazed out over the vast frozen Cyro Sea. The sunlight bounced over the brilliant white ice with beautiful teal undertones. He had never been this far north before, had never seen the Cyro Sea in person. The closest he'd ever been were the books he'd skimmed through to please his tutor growing up. But to be here, to feel the sting of the wind as it bit his rosy cheeks and to smell the crisp air, was something completely different.

It was too bright though. After spending an extended amount of time in the Black Forest, reemerging into the parts of Phildeterre that the sun touched left him squinting with tears in his eyes. He wished there were some way to reverse the sight rune on his glasses so that he could block some of the sunlight, and he was half tempted to ask Armannii if there was such a rune.

They had stayed the night at the small inn in the village with the winter clothing store and then at a different inn near the Cyro Coves after another full day of walking north. Unfortunately, it had been foggy when they had left, so Diomedes had not had the chance to see the giant ice structures in the sea that served as homes to many of the sirens in Phildeterre, and by the time the fog cleared, they were too far northeast to hope to see them.

"Stay off the ice as much as you can," Armannii said, pointing to where a patch of ice sparkled bright blue.

Diomedes scanned the area around him, but the ground was a mixture of glistening snow and brilliant white sand, which had blown in from the east. "How are you supposed to be able to tell what's ice and what's sand?"

"Around here, it'll be fine, but the farther north we get, the thinner the ice is." Armannii pulled his emerald-green hat down to cover his pointed ears more.

"And we can't go farther east because?" Blanndynne asked, her voice muffled from the scarf around her neck.

"Mellacross said to follow the coastline." Diomedes nodded ahead of them. They walked along what would've been a beach had the water not been frozen for years. The sand and the ice had mixed, and it was difficult at times to determine if they were walking on solid ground or if they had wandered out too far onto the sea and were walking on a foot or two of ice separating them from the freezing water beneath. "Just watch where you step. I'm not in the mood for a swim."

"Especially not in this water," Blanndynne said. "It'll suck the air out of your lungs before you've even registered you're under."

"Speaking from experience, B?" Armannii asked, a smirk on his lips.

"Yes." Blanndynne's voice was flat as she scanned the horizon. "We better get moving. It'll be dark soon, and that's when it gets really cold."

Diomedes couldn't imagine the temperature dipping any further. It was already colder than the dead of winter in Cyanthia. Not being a fan of the cold, he tried to stay inside when that time of year came around.

He pulled his cloak tighter as he followed Armannii up the coastline. The wind whipped around them, kicking up frozen bits of ice and sand together. It stung any exposed skin. After about ten minutes, Diomedes had to pause to pull out one of his extra tunics, which he promptly wrapped around his neck and lower face. He pulled his knit hat down so the only exposed skin around his face was a thin slit for his eyes.

"When were you here last?" Armannii's question, which was directed at Blanndynne, came out jumbled and distorted by the wind even though they all walked close together.

Blanndynne glanced to the left, scanning the frozen landscape, with its jutting icebergs and cyan hue. "A long time ago. But nothing's changed."

"What, you mean it was a frigid wasteland then too?" Armannii bumped her with his shoulder, and she glanced sideways at him.

"Unfortunately."

"Why would you want to come to a place like this? It's not exactly where I'd choose to vacation." Armannii readjusted his bag.

Diomedes noticed that his own bag was causing his hip discomfort and moved it so it rested behind him. Thanks to the numerous layers of clothing, the strap was not cutting into his neck as it had earlier that day.

"I didn't choose to come here," Blanndynne said, her voice flat. "One of the people who found my vase had business out here, and"—her shoulders drooped—"I tried to run away."

Armannii didn't respond verbally, but his jaw clenched as he cast her a sidelong glance.

"He was one of the first few to control me."

Diomedes struggled to make out her words as they walked in front of him. She must've lowered her voice because Diomedes strained to hear the rest of her explanation. He picked up his pace to stay closer, and though faint, he heard her story.

"He was a terrible man. Greedy and selfish. But I suppose most of those who sought me out were. But the things he wished for . . ." She shuddered. "I didn't know how useless it was to run;

I'd never had the chance before. The other two men who had controlled me left me in my vase when they didn't have use of me. But this man, he let me stay out.

"One night, while we were staying in a village east of here, I waited until they had all fallen asleep. I ran. I didn't know where to go. I had only been in Phildeterre for a year or so, and it was the first time I had been north of the Glass Fields. The desert—it was endless. At least, it felt that way. It was a good thing I left at night because the heat of the day probably would've killed me. Well, it would've made it more difficult at least."

Diomedes recalled Mellacross's directions to stay away from the Albanistic Desert, and he glanced to the right. Somewhere over there—he couldn't see very far because a hill blocked his view— were the dunes with sand as white as the snow around them. He felt the tickle of curiosity itching in his mind. But he knew better.

Follow the directions.

Find the object.

End the war.

He tightened his jaw, turning to focus on the ground below him. The snow clung to his boots in clumps. But there were sections where the wind had carried the snow away, leaving only the teal-tinged ice. Those sections left him wary. There was no way to tell how thick the ice was, and Armannii's warning about thin ice had him on edge.

To distract himself, Diomedes focused on Armannii and Blanndynne's conversation as they made their way farther up the coast.

"I remember how quickly the temperature dropped the closer I got to the sea. Before long, I was a shivering mess. We'd been traveling in the desert, and all I had were sandals and warm-weather clothing. And it was the dead of night.

"I didn't stop. I was too scared of what my master would do to me if he caught me. That kept me going. I must've walked for three or four hours before I finally reached this horrible frozen shoreline. But just like now, it was hard to tell the shore from the ice. And with only the light of the three moons, two of which were only slivers, I accidentally started walking on the sea.

"I must've been farther north than we are because after a few minutes, I heard a sound like glass breaking. As soon as I saw the crack beneath my feet, I panicked. I started running back the way I had come, but it didn't matter. Within a second, I fell through the ice.

"It was like I forgot how to breathe the instant I felt the water around me. It took the air out of my lungs. I-I remember thrashing about, trying to find my way up to the surface, but I didn't come up where I fell in, and a thick slab of ice separated me from a breath of air. My whole body ached, and even in the short amount of time I was under, I could feel my control over it slipping away. It was so cold that it almost felt like I was on fire, like I was burning.

"And then I was back at the camp, soaking wet and shivering at the feet of my master. I didn't know that you could call a genie back by using their vessel. But that's what happened. When he saw I was gone, he called me back. After I returned, I remember wishing I had died here. It seemed like a better fate than being controlled for the rest of my life. And my master, he was furious. He . . ."

Her voice trailed off as she shivered. They had been walking for almost an entire day, and the sun was starting to lower toward the turquoise horizon. Patches of ice and snow farther out sparkled, glinting in the light.

Diomedes and Armannii remained silent for a while, leaving plenty of time for Blanndynne to finish if she so desired. But after a few more minutes of only the wind speaking, it was clear she was done.

"You're one of the few people I've heard of who took an unexpected swim in the Cyro Sea and came out alive," Armannii said, his voice light, though his back was tensed. "Do you think you actually would've died? I thought genies were a little more, I don't know, stubborn when it came to the whole dying thing."

Blanndynne cocked her head to the side, casting a furtive glance at Armannii and then Diomedes. "I'm not sure. And I'm not particularly eager to find out."

Armannii chuckled. "I wouldn't be either. Like I said, it's best we stay away from the thin ice."

Diomedes stared down at the ground again, watching where he stepped with careful eyes. After hearing Blanndynne's story, the last thing he wanted was to have the same experience.

"Little worried there, Didi?" Armannii teased when he looked over his shoulder.

"I think the word you're looking for is 'cautious,' " Diomedes retorted.

Armannii let out a laugh as he turned back around, but he stopped abruptly. "Spread out and get on your hands and knees," he barked.

Time slowed down as Diomedes heard what sounded like something fragile cracking and squeaking. One second Blanndynne was standing next to him, and the next she floated a few inches above the frozen ground while Armannii dropped to his hands and knees.

But it was too late for Diomedes to do the same.

The sound of thunder cracked, and the ground beneath his feet gave way. He plummeted into the water before he could make a single noise.

Blanndynne had been right. All of the air in his lungs disappeared, swallowed by the frigid water. He choked, thrashing about as he searched for the way up. But the frigid temperature tore his focus away, forcing him to agonize over the sting and ache the water sent through him.

His head hurt. Whether it was from air deprivation or the freezing temperature, he was not sure, nor did he care. He needed a way out. The palm of his hand slammed against the ice above him. There was no break for him to swim through.

Kicking as hard as he could, Diomedes pressed his shoulder into the ice blocking his freedom. His lungs burned; cried out in agony for a single breath. With each passing second, his brain felt fuzzier. He couldn't focus on anything but breaking through the ice. Any other distraction could cost him his life.

Diomedes cringed as he rammed into the ice again, but nothing changed—nothing except that he was getting sleepy. His arms and legs were numb, and while he mentally screamed at them to keep moving, they stopped. He floated, unable to move his limbs.

Darkness embraced him, luring him into giving it his last breath. With thoughts of the object, the war, and his desire to fight for those with magic all stolen by the sea, he gave up. He succumbed.

". . . not how you're going to die. Wake up." Someone slapped Diomedes across the cheek. It was enough to draw him out of the comfortable nothingness and into a world of frostbite and pain.

His chest felt like it was about to explode. Unable to control his body's reaction, he turned to the side and coughed out a small pond of salt water, which had been trapped inside him.

Armannii leaned back on his heels. He was kneeling next to Diomedes, and for a brief second, a look of absolute relief covered his face. His hair, like Diomedes's, was already solidifying as the water froze.

"Add that to the list of times I've saved your life," Armannii said, shivering as he thanked Blanndynne, who handed him his cloak. Instead of putting it on, he covered Diomedes with it.

"Wh-what happened? How did you—"

"Come to your rescue?" Armannii ran his fingers through his hair, shaking out what moisture he could before it all froze. "I found where you were trying to come up and broke the ice."

"And you ju-jumped in?" Diomedes pushed himself into a sitting position, wrapping Armannii's cloak tighter. His nose dripped, but it didn't get far before that too started to freeze.

"Not my smartest idea, I'll admit." Armannii shrugged, rubbing his hands over his arms to warm up.

"You're right," Diomedes said, narrowing his gaze at him.

"Strange way to say thank you," Armannii said, snorting. "But you're welcome nonetheless."

"You could've died."

"And you *would* have." The elf nodded his thanks to Blanndynne again when she handed him his bag and his weapon. He pulled out his rune pen and traced a few runes on the inside of his tunic. They glowed a warm red.

All Diomedes had to do was raise an eyebrow at Armannii, and the elf read his mind.

"Warmth. That way you can use my cloak." Armannii tucked the pen away and pulled out a second hat, handing it to Diomedes. When Diomedes didn't accept it, Armannii leaned forward and snatched the wet hat off of Diomedes's head. He forced the dry one on and sat back again.

"Didi, you're the crown prince of blah-blah-blah. You're the one who's going to end this war. We need you alive. And if that wasn't enough of a reason to jump in after you, you're also my friend. And that's the one and only time I'll ever admit that." Armannii crossed his arms over his chest, frowning at Diomedes.

Diomedes glanced at Blanndynne, who had worry written in big letters over her face, but her gaze didn't meet Diomedes's. She was too busy staring at his leg.

Armannii's gaze locked onto the pink water pooling around Diomedes's leg at the same time Diomedes felt the first wave of pain, though it was duller than he thought it would be, what with the sheer amount of blood.

"What in the—" Armannii leaned forward.

Diomedes hissed through his teeth when Armannii pulled back a tear in his pant leg to reveal a five-inch gash.

"Must've sliced it on the ice when he fell in," Blanndynne said, kneeling down on the other side of Diomedes. She furrowed her brow, glancing first at the injury and then over her shoulder. "We need to bandage it up fast and keep moving. I think there's a storm coming."

Diomedes followed her line of sight to a growing formation of gray clouds in the distance.

"Doesn't this day just keep getting more interesting?" Armannii muttered under his breath. He opened his bag and pulled out a wad of bandages. "Glad I keep these in stock. Figured you'd need them at some point. I think we should all appreciate my foresight."

"I'll appreciate whatever you want as soon as we get somewhere without the threat of imminent danger," Diomedes said, exhaling sharply when Armannii began to wrap the bandage around and around his leg. For the first time, Diomedes was grateful for the cold, assuming he had the low temperature to thank for the dulling of what was meant to be terrible pain.

"So never?" Armannii raised an eyebrow, making eye contact with Diomedes while his hands continued to work on the wound.

Diomedes chuckled darkly. "You said it, not me."

"We'll have to rewrap this when we have a moment, but in the meantime"—Armannii grunted as he stood up, offering a hand to help Diomedes to his feet—"this will have to do."

His leg throbbed at the sudden shift in position, but it wasn't unbearable.

"Can you walk?" Blanndynne asked, picking up Armannii's bag, bow, and quiver so the elf could focus on helping Diomedes.

"The answer is going to have to be yes, Didi," Armannii said, threading his arm behind Diomedes's back. "That storm is moving in this direction. Fast."

"Then yes." Diomedes gritted his teeth as he took his first step on his injured leg. Painful, yet doable. "Let's go."

Chapter Eleven

The wind howled, and having lost the tunic he'd been using to protect his face and neck when he fell in the sea, there was nothing Diomedes could do to stop the sting of the ice and sand. He cringed as another gale ambushed them.

"We need to move inland!" Blanndynne shouted over the sounds of the storm rushing around them. It kicked up snow and sand, pelting them from every direction as it swirled in a chaotic tumult.

"We can't!" Diomedes shook his head as he hollered back. "Mellacross said it's too easy to get lost in the desert."

"B is right." Armannii readjusted his grip under Diomedes's arm when they both slipped on the ice. "We're in for a lot worse if we stay out here in the middle of a storm. It's worth the risk, and we have maybe an hour before sundown. We need to find someplace east to hunker down."

"But—"

"Sorry, Diomedes," Blanndynne said as she started to walk to the east, away from the expansive frozen sea. "We don't have much of a choice."

Instead of arguing, he leaned on Armannii. They followed Blanndynne, and the farther they walked, the less snow there was. However, the amount of sand increased, making it more and more difficult to continue with an injured leg.

Diomedes's muscles ached, and he wanted nothing more than to lie down in the sand, cover his face with the cloak, and wait for the storm to blow over. But with Armannii starting to shiver next to him, Diomedes continued.

"B, do you know where the nearest town is?" Armannii shouted, his voice wavering in the wind.

"No, but I can try to fly ahead."

Armannii struggled to pull Diomedes up the bank of a hill, but the sand kept shifting beneath their feet. It felt like they were going nowhere.

"Go," Diomedes said, regretting opening his mouth as soon as he closed it on a mouthful of gritty sand.

Nodding, Armannii added, "We'll keep heading in this direction."

Blanndynne handed Armannii his bag back, but he shook his head when she tried to give him his bow and quiver.

"Why not?"

"Don't need it," Armannii said, and for the first time in what felt like years, Diomedes thought his friend sounded out of breath. "P-put it in your magic storage room. On loan. I'll take it back when I don't have to drag Prince Can't Carry His Own Weight across the Albanistic Desert."

Diomedes would've rolled his eyes if he hadn't been focusing so hard on keeping the sand out by squinting.

"I'll be back," she said before taking off into the air. In a second, she was out of sight, soaring over the ridge Armannii and Diomedes were still struggling up.

"You better," Armannii said under his breath. "Come on. We need to keep moving away from the sea. I don't know about you, but I don't exactly want to be skewered by a flying icicle."

"Right." Diomedes set his jaw, focusing only on the next step forward. He tried to keep his pace the same as Armannii's, but they ended up out of sync multiple times. Armannii would take one step, and with his aching leg, it would take Diomedes two just to keep up.

"I need to stop," Diomedes said when they reached the top of the next dune.

"We can't. Not with the storm—"

"You keep going." Diomedes let go of Armannii, collapsing to the ground as the sand slipped out from beneath his boots. "I'll—"

"Shut up and get up," Armannii snapped. He bent over and yanked Diomedes to his feet. "Stop being a royal prat and come on."

"Armannii," Diomedes said through a clenched jaw, "I can't keep up." But he let Armannii pull him to a standing position.

"Then we'll slow down. But you and I are going to make it out of this just fine. Someday we'll laugh about all the places we had to empty sand out of, and I'm sure the gash in your leg will make a lovely scar. Now shut it and let's go. It's downhill from here, so—"

Diomedes didn't get to hear the end of Armannii's sentence because a strong gust of wind caught them from behind. The sand moved beneath them, and before they could right themselves, they started tumbling down the other side of the dune they'd just climbed.

Squeezing his eyes shut, Diomedes couldn't tell which direction Armannii was rolling or if they were headed in the same direction. He was too concerned with the amount of sand flying around him. He tucked his arms and head in, doing what he could to protect his extremities as he rolled for what felt like an eternity.

His leg, which had been throbbing before he fell, felt like it was on fire by the time he skidded to a stop at the bottom of the sand dune. Carefully, so as not to get any sand in his eyes,

Diomedes sat up and ran his fingers through his hair, shaking out what felt like an entire beach worth of sand. He kept his eyes closed as he brushed off his hands, then went to clearing the sand off his face.

When he finally did open his eyes, he scanned the white valley in which he'd ended up. To his right, Armannii was shaking off his clothes, but he didn't seem to be injured.

"That was certainly a quicker way down than I was expecting, eh, Didi?" Armannii shouted over the wind; it was worse at the bottom. "You all right?"

"Fine!" Diomedes hollered, wincing as he forced himself to his feet. Because his clothes and hair were still damp from the sea, the sand clung to him like fruit flies to a melon; it didn't matter how much he shook his clothes or Armannii's cloak.

Armannii patted him once on the shoulder when he walked up. "I thought you were pale before, but with all this sand, you look like a ghost." He wiggled his eyebrows and flinched when sand fell in his eyes.

"Let's keep going," Diomedes said, adjusting the belt his sheath attached to, which had gotten twisted in the tumble.

"Do you still want me to help you, or—"

"No."

"Well then," Armannii said, turning his nose up with a grin. He spoke in a mocking tone, one he had used before to imitate some of the king's council members. "If you're too good for help."

"You just helped me off the side of a sand dune," Diomedes said, and anyone with normal hearing wouldn't have heard it, but Armannii, with his pointed ears, did.

"I think it was the other way around. Need I remind you that the charming nickname Didi stands for—"

"I know." Diomedes blinked a few times as the wind picked up. The lighthearted banter was easing the panic he had been feeling ever since falling into the sea.

Armannii nodded in the direction they had been heading. "Shall we?"

Diomedes wasn't sure how long he had been limping through the desert when Blanndynne finally found them. It was dark, both because it was fully night and because the clouds covered the moons that had risen, making them appear like dulled and blurry lights. But by the look of the largest blur, it was close to the middle of the night. He squinted up through the light rune glasses at Blanndynne as she landed in front of them.

Sweat covered her brow, along with a fine layer of sand. She panted, which wasn't a surprise given how much effort it took for her to fly; especially through the strong winds.

"I'm impressed you actually landed and didn't just collapse," Armannii said. "You've been gone for hours." He offered her his arm to lean on, and she took it as she nodded. She looked tired enough that the gusts of wind from the storm might blow her over. "That's the longest you've flown, isn't it?"

"I-I had to stop multiple times. I got lost trying to find you. But there's an abandoned town not far from here, we just need to—"

"Keep going," Diomedes said, finishing her statement. "Lead the way." The grit that entered his mouth scratched, and he tried to get rid of what he could by running his tongue along his teeth. He and Armannii had stopped multiple times as well, but the longer they waited, the worse the storm got.

Before they started off again, Diomedes returned Armannii's cloak to him. Though the temperature had only risen a few degrees since they'd entered the desert, Diomedes wasn't shivering nearly as much as he had been when he'd first come out of the sea. Armannii, on the other hand, was.

"You're sure?" Armannii asked, hesitating to take the cloak Diomedes was handing to him. "I'm fine without it."

Diomedes raised an eyebrow. "You're not a good liar. The heat runes are fading, aren't they?"

Armannii fluttered his eyelashes, smirking as he took the cloak. "What could've possibly given it away?" he asked, shaking the cloak to remove the layer of sand that laced the outside. "These runes don't last long, and I'd redraw them, but they can be a bit fickle, causing fires and whatnot." He wrapped his cloak around himself, still grinning as his eye color went back to normal. "You going to be okay, B? Or do you need a minute to rest?"

Blanndynne glanced behind them, and Diomedes followed her gaze. Though it was difficult to tell the dark of the storm from the general darkness, there was an ominous look about the sky behind them.

"We need shelter before this gets worse," she said, returning her attention to them.

"Worse?" Diomedes blinked when a gust of wind blew a cloud of sand at him. "Seriously?"

"This is just the beginning," Blanndynne said, repeating it twice before Diomedes could make out her words.

One by one, they made their way up and over the sand dunes. It was slow progress, but when they crested the top of one of the last dunes, Diomedes finally saw what Blanndynne had referred to as a town. It was nothing more than a few destroyed buildings. None of them looked like they had all four walls and a roof. Some only had two walls left standing. Some only one.

"This is it?" he shouted, and Blanndynne glanced back at him. Her hair was a rat's nest, knotted in such a way that Diomedes doubted she'd ever untangle it, even with her powerful magic.

"It's the closest place I could find," she replied, pulling her cloak tighter around her chin.

"Beggars can't be choosers, Didi," Armannii said, and he followed Blanndynne as she trudged down the dune.

Diomedes's leg was stiff, and it ached like someone had taken a blacksmith's hammer to it. But it didn't stop him as he made his way toward the sad excuse for a town.

"At least find one with a roof," he said as they entered what had once been the main street. It wasn't paved. Perfectly white sand covered it like the rest of the desert. But the buildings must've been built on some sort of foundation because the sand didn't seem to be moving out from under them despite the strong winds. Instead, it piled up against the remaining walls, leaving drifts as tall as the buildings themselves in some cases.

"This way," Blanndynne said, waving them toward one with three walls and part of a roof still remaining.

The door to the building slammed open and closed with every gust, and Diomedes caught it with his hand before it could plow into him on the way in.

"How do we stop the wind from coming in the missing wall?" Diomedes asked, thankful that he didn't have to yell anymore. His throat was raw, and he thanked Armannii when he handed him a canteen with water in it.

"We don't." Blanndynne swept some of the sand on the floor to the side. "Oh, this is ridiculous," she finally said when more sand blew in and replaced what she'd just moved. With a flick of her wrist, she created her own breeze, and Diomedes covered his eyes with his arm as she blew the sand out through the broken wall.

When he moved his arm and saw what she'd uncovered, he let out a laugh that surprised even him.

"Genius," he said as he bent over and helped Armannii pull up the hidden hatch in the floor. It was stuck at first, but with a few extra tugs, the square door opened, and a wave of musty air filled the space. Diomedes coughed, moving his hand back and forth in the hopes that it would purify the air.

"Perfect for a sandstorm." Armannii brushed his hands together, but in Diomedes's opinion, it didn't matter what they did. He knew they'd be clearing sand off of themselves for weeks to come. His hair felt as crispy as the fried dough the castle's chef used to make for dessert on special occasions.

"I suppose I'm first then," Armannii said, already starting down the ladder.

Diomedes waited for Armannii to call back up, which he did after he reached the bottom.

"It's an old storeroom," Armannii said as Diomedes descended.

A few old crates, which had large cracks and holes in them, were stacked against the far wall. The paint on the labels was worn and faded, and Armannii was already lifting the lids to see what was in them.

"Looks like bags of wheat, maybe some other grain. Must've been a bakery or something."

"Or something," Blanndynne repeated under her breath as she joined them. "Draw a light rune over there," she said, nodding toward the wall where the ladder was. "Then we'll close the hatch and wait this out."

Armannii closed the lid of the crate and pulled out his rune pen. Sand rained down on him as he drew on the wall. After a few seconds, the light from the rune filled the small storage house, and Diomedes climbed halfway up the ladder to close the hatch.

"Now let's just hope the sand doesn't cover us so we can't get out," Armannii said, a grin on his face as he sat on one of the sturdier crates.

"Yeah, because our hope is what controls the storm," Diomedes muttered as he sat down against the wall. His leg ached, and in that moment, he almost wanted a long hot bath more than anything else.

More than finding the object.

More than gaining magic.

More than ending the war.

Almost. But not quite.

Chapter Twelve

Armannii had dozed off in the corner after rewrapping Diomedes's leg and the bandage around his bicep, both of which had been filled with gritty sand. The storm continued to blow over the top of them, but the storeroom, which had been constructed with stone bricks rather than sandstone bricks, remained intact. Still, Diomedes could hear the faint moaning of the wind above them.

At least an hour had passed, and Blanndynne still sat next to the ladder working on her tangled mess of hair with a brush. She would flinch or wince every few seconds, and Diomedes didn't blame her.

His own hair was knotted and had somehow bonded to the remainder of desert left in it. He had dried enough that he was able to brush off the sand that had clung to his damp clothes, but it felt like whatever he did, he couldn't get all the sand off his skin.

The worst part had been when Armannii was cleaning up Diomedes's injured leg. Apparently, the bandages had not prevented sand from entering the wound, which had made the process of cleaning it all the more painful.

"Do you have any water in your canteen?" Diomedes asked Blanndynne.

She shook her head. "You?"

Diomedes tipped his empty container upside down to answer her question.

"Guess that's the next thing to be concerned about, huh?" Blanndynne furrowed her brow when the brush caught in her hair again.

"Seems like it." Diomedes leaned his head back against the wall as he watched her. "There must be a well or something around here, right? I mean, whoever lived here before would've needed to quench their thirst as much as us."

"Stands to reason," Blanndynne said, shrugging. "Otherwise Armannii or I will have to find water using speed runes or flying."

Diomedes's jaw tightened. Of course he'd be of no use. Not only did he have an injured leg, but he had no magic that could transport him at a quicker pace; he didn't even have a horse.

"What?" Blanndynne asked, staring at him with an eyebrow raised. "Why do you look like you just stepped in dung?"

"Doesn't matter," Diomedes said, pushing himself up so he wasn't slouching as much. "What's important is that we keep going as soon as we are able."

"Right," Blanndynne said, though she was still frowning at him. "But that's not it. What's wrong?"

Diomedes searched for an excuse but came back empty-handed. "I'm just eager to find the object."

Blanndynne paused in the middle of working out a knot and looked up at him. "Really? Why would that cause you to make that face?"

He shrugged, though the answer was clear. The object would put him on even terrain with her and Armannii. It would give him magic. It would give him power.

"I'm annoyed we're off course from finding it. And I know the storm was unexpected, but it sent us off the path the sorceress laid out. I suppose I'm eager to get back on it."

"And we will. I'm sure the storm is already subsiding as we speak." Blanndynne offered him a small smile, but Diomedes could clearly hear another gust of wind above. "Then we'll get back to finding the object so you can end the war."

He nodded, but his brow creased. "You think I'll be able to do it? End the war?"

"Course I do. And if it's not with this object we're looking for, it will be with something else." She tilted her head as she watched him. "Diomedes, you freed me. I suppose in my mind, there's nothing you can't do."

"Oh?" He scratched his chin, grinning at the ground.

"It's true," she said, leaning forward to rest her chin on her hand. "And I'm not the only one who believes it. Armannii does. Camile and Forrest. And Raidah definitely sounded like she was behind you."

Diomedes nodded as Blanndynne listed off the names. He had rarely questioned Armannii's position, and it was good to hear Blanndynne's, but the more names she listed off, the more a sort of confidence grew in him. However, the weight of what he was planning—finding an object that would give him magic, something that was impossible by all standards—seemed to balance out the positive emotions, leaving him questioning how he should be feeling in the first place.

"This is just a small setback." She resumed brushing her hair as Diomedes nodded slowly.

"You're right."

With the lack of conversation and having walked for more than his fair share of hours the day before, Diomedes fell asleep. It was far from restful, and in one of the dreams he was helpless to do anything as a storm whisked him off the balcony of his room in the Cyanthian castle and carried him out into a familiar-looking hedge maze. Diomedes wandered around for what felt like hours, making wrong turns and reaching dead ends. Just as he turned a corner and noticed a light, Blanndynne woke him up.

"What?" Diomedes asked, his voice gravely and his throat sore. More so than before, he wished his canteen were full of water. It didn't help that he'd ended up slouching over on his injured arm, and a crick in his neck threatened to give him a headache before he was even fully awake.

"I think we should check outside," she said, both to Diomedes and to Armannii, who stirred in the corner.

Armannii leaned back and stretched as he yawned. "It sounds like the storm is about over. The wind has died down at least." He licked his chapped lips and glanced at them. "Either of you know how long I was out?"

"No idea. Kind of hard to tell down here," Blanndynne said. She had managed to free her hair from most of the knots and had braided it into a crown around her head.

Armannii rubbed his cheek with the palm of his hand and sat up straighter. Reaching into his bag, he pulled out his canteen, the sight of which left Diomedes trying to swallow. However, his throat felt too dry to do so.

After trying to drink out of it, Armannii frowned. When he looked at Diomedes and Blanndynne, both of whom were watching him, he grimaced.

"Mine's not the only empty one, is it?" He sighed as he put it back in his bag.

Diomedes shook his head. "We should search the town for a well or something."

"Right," Armannii said, groaning as he pushed himself to his feet.

Holding back his own grunt, Diomedes also stood. His leg was sore after so much exercise and then sitting still for too long. Leaning against the wall, he stretched it only to find that the rest of him was sore as well.

"I'll check to make sure the storm is over first," Armannii said, already halfway up the ladder. "B, I'd move if I were you. I have a feeling we're going to have a bit of sand come down on us when I open this thing."

She scrambled out of the way, and Armannii turned his head to the side as he pushed on the hatch. It didn't budge. He frowned as he looked up at it.

"I guess my comment about being buried alive may have actually come to fruition." Armannii turned his head to the side again as he heaved his shoulder into the hatch. White sand slipped through the cracks, but the hatch still didn't open all the way. "Give me a hand, Didi."

Although the ladder was not built for two fully grown men, Diomedes joined him. There was barely enough room for them both to have a single foot on a rung at the same time, and Diomedes clasped the side of the ladder with one hand while he pressed the other against the hatch.

"On three," he said, nodding at Armannii. "One, two, three." He shoved his hand against the square door and had to look away as sand poured down on them. He held his breath; he didn't want sand in his lungs any more than he wanted it in his eyes.

Armannii coughed next to him, but it turned into a laugh. "It's a good thing you moved, B." He peered up at the sky through the broken-down building. "Storm's over, and by the look of the clear sky, we were down here for a full day." Armannii pointed to the largest moon, which was right where it had appeared to be when Blanndynne had found them the night before. "I'm going to go take a look around. I'll be back in a minute." He climbed the rest of the ladder, sitting at the top and brushing his hands off before he got all the way out and closed the hatch again.

Diomedes shook his head, running his fingers through his hair as he tried to get the sand out of it. "He didn't take his bag," Diomedes said, nodding toward the corner Armannii had fallen asleep in.

"He's not going to have much luck getting any water back," Blanndynne added, pursing her lips. "It's hard to believe we spent a full day down here."

Nodding, Diomedes sat on a crate. He pressed his hand over his mouth, stifling a yawn.

"How long do you think he'll be?" Blanndynne asked, glancing up at the hatch.

"No idea," Diomedes said, shrugging. "He'll be back soon, I'm—"

Before Diomedes could finish his sentence, Armannii opened the hatch and scrambled back down the ladder.

"We need to leave. Now."

Chapter Thirteen

Armannii raced to the corner and grabbed his bag before answering any of Diomedes's or Blanndynne's questions. He gripped the strap with a white-knuckled hand, putting it over his shoulder.

"Sand crawlers," Armannii said, and something about his wide eyes left Diomedes shuddering. "There were at least ten of them surrounding the building."

"If there were that many, then there must be a hive here. I didn't realize we'd traveled south. I didn't know. I—" Blanndynne glanced from Diomedes to Armannii, her eyes wide. Armannii's bow and quiver appeared in her hand, and he thanked her when she handed them to him.

"Of course you didn't," Armannii said, glancing up at the hatch before turning his attention to his bow and quiver. "You were flying in the middle of a storm. Besides, they're farther north than I would've guessed they'd be. I didn't think they crossed into Byshan territory."

"Still, I'm sorry." Blanndynne pulled a few throwing-knives from thin air and tucked them into her vest.

Diomedes had read about sand crawlers during his tutoring; he'd even seen the outer skeleton of a dead one. However, he had never come into contact with a live crawler. The beetle-like creatures were hard to kill because their bones were on the outside. A layer of spikes lined their backs, and each one had a tail ending in a stinger that could grow to over eight inches long. One sting from them and most people were dead within twenty-four hours.

It didn't help that they used their four front legs to burrow beneath the sand, often traveling unnoticed by passersby until night descended and it was too late.

"If there's a hive, that would explain why the town is completely destroyed." Diomedes adjusted his sheath around his waist, wondering how much damage the blade would do against the sand crawlers. "Why can't we just wait to leave until the sun comes up and they go under?" It was a reasonable question, but Armannii shook his head.

"I think the storm kept them unaware of our presence when we arrived because it was vibrating the ground, messing with their senses and whatnot. But they know we're here now, and a few layers of stone"—he tapped the cellar wall—"won't hold them for long. We need to get out of here fast," Armannii said, glancing down at Diomedes's hand on the hilt of the sword. "That means we don't engage. B, how rested are you? Think you can carry Didi out of here? I'll use speed runes to—"

"I can try," Blanndynne said, casting her gaze toward Diomedes. "But I don't know how long I can fly. I haven't fully recovered from finding this place."

"Here," Armannii said, crossing the room. "Give me your wrist." He held his rune pen out. "It'll help concentrate your power for a little while. Do what you can, B. You'll both be safer if you're off the ground." When he finished with her wrist, the rune glowed bright teal before fading. He then bent over and traced the rune for speed on his boots. To Diomedes, who had seen the elf draw the rune many times before, it kind of looked like a spiral with a tail.

"What about you though?" Blanndynne asked, her brows cinching. "They're fast, especially when they're tunneling beneath the sand."

"They're fast, I'm faster." Armannii stood and faced her. "I'll go first and lead them away from here. Give me thirty seconds, and then come up and take off. Head north, and we'll meet up near where the sea, desert, and mountains meet. Hopefully the crawlers will stop following when we get far enough north."

"Either that or the sun will come up," Blanndynne said, and Armannii nodded.

"Ready?" he asked, one foot on the ladder. Armannii waited for them to confirm before he clenched his jaw. "Remember, thirty seconds."

He lifted the hatch and disappeared, closing it behind him. For a second, Diomedes thought he could hear Armannii making a commotion as he tried to pull the attention of the sand crawlers away from the building. But then it was gone.

Blanndynne and Diomedes waited in silence until Blanndynne said, "That's thirty. Think it's enough?"

"Let's go," Diomedes said, starting up the ladder with his rune-inscribed glasses in one hand. He wanted to be prepared to put them on as soon as they were outside. "Ready?"

When she nodded, Diomedes opened the hatch and pulled himself out. He put on the glasses. With a quick survey of the building, he didn't spot any sand crawlers within. Blanndynne climbed up the ladder, and he offered her a hand, pulling her out of the hole. It strained his injured arm, and he clamped his jaw to keep from making any noise. Diomedes held a finger to his lips, motioning for Blanndynne to remain silent, which she did.

As quietly as they could, they closed the hatch and ventured toward the missing wall. With the light of the three moons, Diomedes could make out a few of the remaining walls of destroyed buildings. But it was silent. Not a sand crawler in sight.

Diomedes motioned for Blanndynne to follow him as he stepped out of the building. The desert was too silent. Even the wind seemed to be holding its breath.

Hiss.

The first crawler attacked. It came from beneath the ground, leaping toward Diomedes, who didn't have enough time to react.

Blanndynne grabbed his arm, yanking him out of the path of the white beetle, which landed in the building they'd just left. Diomedes didn't have time to thank her as another one sprouted up beside them, this time aiming for Blanndynne.

Drawing his sword, Diomedes caught the side of the crawler, which was at least two feet long and a foot and a half tall. Its stinger bent backward over its body like a scorpion, and it came an inch away from Blanndynne's arm before Diomedes knocked it away.

"Up," Blanndynne said, no longer keeping quiet.

Diomedes didn't argue, knowing the one he had just hit was a third of the size of a full-grown sand crawler. He kept his sword in his hand as Blanndynne floated up and looped her arms underneath his armpits. The sand near them began to swell just as Blanndynne lifted him into the air.

The crawler's stinger scraped the underside of Diomedes's boot when they were seven feet in the air, but it didn't break the sole. The crawler, which was bigger than the first two they'd seen, fell back to the ground, where it quickly reburied itself in the sand.

"Good timing," Diomedes said, his whole body shaking with adrenaline as they soared higher. The light of the moons cast shadows over the white terrain, and if he squinted, he could see the ground moving with the sand crawlers beneath it. "But I have bad news," he said, watching the sand shift under them. "They're tracking us."

"How?" Blanndynne asked, her voice rising in pitch. "We're in the air. The ground I get, but we're flying. We can't possibly be creating enough vibrations to tell them where we are."

"I don't know," Diomedes said, shaking his head. "But they're definitely following us."

"How far will they travel from the hive?"

"No idea, but we're ahead of them for now. If you just keep— wait! Stop!"

Blanndynne froze in midair, causing Diomedes's lower body to swing forward with leftover momentum. "What? What is it?"

Diomedes pointed to a figure in the sand. "Armannii," he said, his voice shaking. The elf was facedown in the sand, surrounded by crawlers.

And he wasn't moving.

Without another word, Blanndynne flew toward Armannii, but she stayed about ten feet above the ground.

"You have to get him out of here," Diomedes said, his mind spinning for a solution. It was hard to think after seeing a spot on the back of Armannii's tunic begin to bloom with darkness.

"But—"

"Drop me off over there." Diomedes pointed to a spot void—at the moment—of crawlers. "Grab him and get him somewhere safe. Once you do that, come back for me. I'll move north."

"Diomedes, I—"

"Now, Blanndynne. Before the rest of them arrive."

Blanndynne soared to the location Diomedes had directed her to and placed him on the ground.

"Go," he said, his jaw set as he adjusted his grip on his sword. "Go!"

Diomedes watched as she flew back toward Armannii. "Hey!" he shouted, stomping his good leg in the sand. Diomedes whistled through his teeth and swished his sword in a figure eight, trying to work out the nerves flooding through him before the first crawler reached him. He was unsuccessful.

The sand in front of him bulged, and he moved to the right as a sand crawler the size of a small dog lunged at him. As he moved, he raised his sword, catching the end of its tail with the blade. It hissed as the barbed end fell off in a different direction.

Before he could readjust his feet in the sand, two more emerged and leapt toward him from opposite directions. Diomedes ducked, feeling the air around him stir, moving the hair on the back of his head.

A crawler that came up to Diomedes's knees hissed as he separated the stinger from its body after the barbed end got stuck in his bag. In a brief second, he glanced over his shoulder to see if Blanndynne had successfully taken Armannii out of the circling crawlers. He couldn't see either of them, and he didn't have long to look before another crawler thudded into his back.

Diomedes cringed as it dug its spiked feet into his skin. He moved out of the way of another while trying to reach back and remove the one clinging to him. He wondered why he hadn't been stung yet but found the answer to that when he finally managed to rip the crawler—and some of his skin—off his back. It was one of the beetles he'd cut the stinger off of.

He used the crawler in his hand as a shield when another leapt toward his face. The one he held screeched as the other's stinger entered its underside. When the crawler that had jumped at him landed on the ground, it didn't scurry away like the others had. Instead, it paused, turning in one direction and then in the other.

Diomedes didn't notice until a few more seconds had passed without another crawler trying to kill him. He tossed the one in his hand onto the ground. It was twitching and making a strange spitting sound.

Holding his sword with both hands, Diomedes spun in a circle, waiting for the next attack, but it didn't come. The crawlers surrounded the beetle that had stung one of its own. He watched as it turned in circles, almost as if it was scanning its surroundings. It was chittering, and the others were making similar noises back at it.

As quietly as he could, Diomedes stepped away from the crawler with all the attention on it. None of the others seemed to pay any attention to him. Instead, their focus was on the traitor.

Diomedes held his breath when the first crawler attacked the betrayer. The creature cried out, and soon twenty other crawlers were on top of it.

It was his chance.

Sprinting, Diomedes only looked back once to make sure he wasn't being followed, but what he saw made him skid to a stop.

He was not being followed.

Instead, there was a pile of sand crawlers that must've been twenty feet tall. They wriggled all over one another, and from a distance, in the low light it looked like a sand dune was moving, living, breathing.

Diomedes stuck his sword in his sheath and kept going, not looking back again until he couldn't run anymore. He leaned over, pressing his hands into his knees as he tried to catch his breath. His lungs burned, and his injured leg screamed in pain.

But he hadn't been stung.

That, at least, was a plus.

He wiped the back of his hand over his forehead, removing a layer of sweat from the exertion. Diomedes had all but forgotten the stinger protruding from his bag. His mind instantly went to Armannii. A cure. The elf needed a cure. As with many venomous creatures, the only way to combat the poison was to use it in the healing process. Diomedes carefully wrapped the stinger in one of the winter hats—he didn't want to accidentally prick himself on it on the off chance it might still be dangerous—and placed it at the bottom of his bag. He clenched his jaw. He needed to find Blanndynne, and more importantly, he needed to find Armannii before his twenty-four-hour window was up.

As he turned to the right, he noticed the horizon lightening from deep blue to pale pink. He'd be safe from any remaining crawlers soon, as they only came out at night. But with a quick scan of his surroundings, a heavier weight bore down on him. He was alone. Blanndynne and Armannii were nowhere in sight.

The sun began to ascend, and Diomedes felt the first wave of panic rising in him. He knew he needed to keep traveling north while the temperatures were still tolerable, especially with no water. And though the rising sun did help him find his sense of direction, it also brought with it new concerns. The Albanistic

Desert was known for being deadly during the night, with creatures like the sand crawlers skittering around in the south, but even worse during the day, with the blazing sun and nowhere to seek shelter from it except underground.

Sighing, Diomedes pulled the sleeves of his winter tunic down, knowing it would be worth it in the long run to not have a blistering sunburn. He wrapped his scarf around his face. When he'd covered most of his skin, he resumed his journey north through the white sand.

With every passing hour, the dry air around him got warmer. He couldn't stop the sweat from dripping off him as the sun rose higher and higher in the sky.

To keep himself distracted, he practiced in his head what he would say to his father when he returned to Cyanthia, when he returned with an object that could give him magic. Diomedes pictured his father, who was taller and more muscular than he was. In fact, most of their likeness was in their eyes. His father's were a lighter shade of heather gray than Diomedes's, but it was similar——more similar than his mother's eyes. Diomedes remembered how dark they had been. Despite the short time she had been in his life, it felt like her eyes had shown him more kindness. More understanding. More love.

Diomedes gripped the strap of his bag until his knuckles turned white. The thought of his mother brought something else to mind, and he paused, kneeling in the sand as he searched through his bag.

He found what he was looking for, and to his disappointment—though not to his surprise—he pulled out the wrinkled, smudged, and completely unreadable letters his mother had left him. Diomedes's hadn't even considered the damage his swim in the sea had done to his belongings because all his focus had been on either the storm, his injured leg, or finding the object. His face scrunched up as he tried to smooth out one of the letters over his trousers, but the parchment ripped in the middle.

With an exasperated sigh, Diomedes put the letters back in the bag. He knew he had more important things to worry about, like the lack of water in his canteen. Yet the loss of his mother's words bore down on him, making it feel like each step was more difficult than the last. Or maybe that was the dehydration.

His throat was just as dry as the air he breathed in. Each breath became more labored, and after another half hour, his lips were chapped and bleeding. The sun burned him, reflecting off the pure white sand and onto any skin he hadn't protected. He tried covering himself with his cloak but couldn't stand the extra heat it added.

The sand began to rise in temperature, and when his boots sank deep enough into the sand that it spilled inside, it felt like fire against his legs. Even the breeze that blew through the desert was almost unbearable, carrying with it hot air and fiery sand that bit at him.

Diomedes coughed, trying to use what little saliva he had left to wet his lips and throat. He supposed that if he tried to speak, his voice would be hoarse, or maybe he wouldn't be able to talk. He didn't try.

How long had he been walking? How many sand dunes had he crossed over? Was he even heading in the right direction?

Mirages tricked his eyes every time he looked up. He saw his sister on more than one occasion, and she beckoned him to the left or the right. But he didn't go off course. The sight of Ellayne, with her long blond hair and wide smile, made Diomedes wonder what she would've done in the desert if she had been in his position.

He snorted.

She'd be dead.

There was no way his little sister could survive the trials he had been through over the last few months. It required too much out-of-the-box thinking, and that, he knew from experience, was not one of Ellayne's specialties.

In the mirages, he also saw Raylee, the daughter of King Kylian, the daughter the king had sent assassins after. When she had spoken to Diomedes in death, the truths she had revealed to him about the start of the war—the war he was trying to end—had fanned the fire under him. As he walked through the desert, he saw Raylee calling out to him. She urged him to keep going. To keep fighting.

And then he saw his mother. The sight of her, or at least how he remembered her the night, caused him to falter. How many times had he wished to see her one more time? How many times had he dreamt that he'd wake up a child again and have her come into his room to wake him up? How many times had he passed her room, a room now occupied by Ellayne's mother, and hoped for a glimpse of his mother reading a book or writing at her desk? How many times?

Diomedes kept his eyes locked on his mother. Her dark hair floated in the arid breeze. Her dark purple dress billowed. Her thin lips pulled into a smile that softened her angled features. He couldn't—wouldn't—look away.

And then he was in front of her.

With a shaky hand, he reached out to touch her. He just wanted to feel her arms wrap around him. But as soon as his fingertips neared her cheek, she vanished.

He collapsed to his knees.

The sun.

The heat.

The grief.

Diomedes cringed as the heat from the sand transferred through his trousers and burned his knees. He wasn't sure how long or far he'd traveled, if he'd made any dent in the Albanistic Desert at all. But he couldn't go any farther. Not with an empty canteen and no break from the rays of sunlight.

He bent over, his forehead nearly touching the sand as he wrapped his arms around himself. A raspy chuckle came out of him when he realized the irony of his situation. About twenty-four hours earlier, he had almost died in the exact opposite conditions. His laugh turned into a cough, which then ruptured into a wheeze.

How long would it take him to die? He assumed it would be longer than drowning. In that moment, he would've done anything to be back in the sea. At least it would've been quicker. Less drawn out. Less—

"Finally, I found you."

Chapter Fourteen

It had to be another mirage. Why wouldn't it be? His mind was trying to get him to keep going. To live. To survive. But he couldn't. The rest of him had given up. Despite how real her voice sounded, Diomedes did not look up when Blanndynne spoke. It was a trick. It had to be.

"Diomedes? Hey."

He startled, falling back on his behind when a hand touched his shoulder. With the sun directly overhead—he wasn't sure when that had happened—he had to hold up his hand to block it out so he could see her. She was there, actually standing in front of him.

"For a second I thought I was too late." Blanndynne knelt down next to him and shoved something into his hand. Something cool. Something that sloshed with liquid. "Drink." She guided his hand with the canteen up to his cracked lips, and he had to force his lungs to breathe after he'd gulped down as much water as he could in one breath.

He gasped when he finished it off, and his eyes widened when she handed him another one. "Thank you," he rasped after he had finished that one too.

"I found help, a town, and . . ." She trailed off, leaving the sentence unfinished. "Well, it's best that you see for yourself." She took the two empty canteens. In the blink of an eye, they vanished and were replaced with a new one.

Diomedes took it but did not drink it right away. The water he had already drunk was not sitting well in his stomach, and he winced.

"Where?" His voice was still hoarse, but his throat didn't hurt nearly as much as it had the first time he'd spoken.

"Not far. I'll carry you as long as I can, but I've been flying most of the day trying to find you, and the rune Armannii drew to help me wore off half an hour ago. So I'll—"

He shook his head. In the confusion of his dehydration, he hadn't noticed how exhausted she looked. Though the heat from the desert played a large part in the sweat dripping off her, he was sure exerting herself by flying as much as she had added to the rest of it. Dark circles drooped beneath her eyes, and she, like him, was panting. She wore a scarf that wrapped around the top of her head all the way around her neck and covered her shoulders.

"I can walk. Save your strength." He took her outstretched hand, rising to his feet. "Is Armannii—"

"He's alive." Her gaze dropped to the ground. "There's someone—" Her jaw tightened, and she glanced away for a second. "You'll meet him. Armannii is being taken care of, but he has a fever. The crawler stung him near enough to his spine that the poison spread faster than normal."

Diomedes's stomach, which was full of water that sloshed when he walked next to Blanndynne, felt nauseated. He frowned, blinking a few times as he tried to process what she was saying.

"I have a stinger from one of the crawlers. It could be used in a cure."

"You have it with you?" she asked, her voice rising.

"Yes." Diomedes started to go through his bag, but Blanndynne shook her head.

"Then I'll fly you there." Blanndynne held up a finger to stop Diomedes from interrupting her when he opened his mouth. "Don't waste time arguing."

"Right." He wasn't going to argue. If anything, he was willing to send her with the stinger if she thought it would help. But another part of him didn't want to be left alone in the blazing sun again. His throat was getting dry from talking and from the hot air around them.

"Ready?" she asked, lifting into the air. She floated around behind him, gripping him under the arms when he nodded.

He had thought the movement of flying would help cool him down, but the air was too hot to be anything but uncomfortable. In order to save the water in the canteen he held—he wasn't sure how many more Blanndynne had placed in her magic storeroom—he didn't try to speak while they flew over the dunes.

Blanndynne picked up on his silence. They did not speak until they reached a small structure. In the distance, other similar structures peeked out of the sand. They were partially underground by the looks of it, though it may have been because the sand had drifted over the sides.

The building they landed by was similar to the one they had taken shelter in during the storm. It was made from white sandstone, and it remained completely intact.

"Inside?" Diomedes asked Blanndynne, waiting for her to finish drinking from the canteen he'd handed her.

"This way," she said, motioning for him to follow her.

Diomedes held his breath as Blanndynne led him toward the front door. There were no windows from what he could see— probably because a sandstorm like the one they'd experienced would take out any window it met.

"Hold on," Blanndynne said, placing a hand in front of Diomedes. "Before we go in, I need to tell you something." Though she was clearly winded, something about her posture was rigid, and she eyed the door like a monster might leap out at any second.

"Whatever it is needs to wait," Diomedes said, pushing past her to knock on the door. His concern for Armannii outweighed the curiosity created by Blanndynne's words.

"It's about the man who—"

The door opened before Blanndynne could finish. A man with shaggy sandy-blond hair opened the door. He appeared to be in his early to midthirties, and the sun had tanned his skin several shades darker than what Diomedes assumed it was naturally. Around the man's chin grew a scraggly beard, which he reached up and smoothed at the sight of the two strangers at his door.

"I didn't expect you to return, let alone with the person you went searching for." His voice was orotund, and Diomedes took a half step back. He had not expected such a formal tone from someone who looked like he had spent his life under a rock. Or a sand dune.

Next to Diomedes, Blanndynne lifted her chin, her shoulders rolling back. "Well, we're here," she said, her tone crisp as she stepped forward. Blanndynne entered the house when the man backed away, leaving the door open for them.

The entry room was lit with lanterns hanging in each corner. Diomedes briefly glanced at the man, noting his white tunic and matching trousers. But when Diomedes caught sight of his friend lying on a cot, his attention rested solely on the elf.

"How is he?" Blanndynne asked, unwrapping the scarf from her head as she approached Armannii. She stroked the elf's light brown hair back from his forehead, which was beading with sweat.

The closer Diomedes got to his friend, the worse Armannii appeared. His skin was ashen and nearly the color of the stranger's tunic. But worse than that, a sickly green color showed beneath his skin, and by the spindly lines sprouting from around his back and up his neck, it appeared that the hue was traveling through his veins. Deep black circles surrounded Armannii's closed eyes, and his whole body trembled, though he appeared to be sleeping. Or unconscious.

"He's gotten worse," the man said, his voice matter-of-fact as he joined them next to the cot. The man turned his attention to Armannii and lifted one of the elf's hands for Blanndynne and Diomedes to see. His fingers were turning gray, starting at his fingernails. "His limbs are slowly entering paralysis. He'll be dead within the hour. You came just in time to say goodbye."

"What?" Blanndynne shrieked, spinning away from Armannii to face the man. "You said you were going to work on the cure."

"I did. I pulled all the ingredients together except for one. Unfortunately, there isn't time to go find it."

"I have it," Diomedes said, his words clipped. Both Blanndynne and the stranger stared at him. "At least, if it's what I think it is, I do."

"The stinger?" Blanndynne asked, watching Diomedes as he fished through his bag. "Is that what you need?" She directed the question to the man.

"Venom from a crawler, yes." The man, who was also watching Diomedes, stood with his hands clasped behind his back, and something about his stance was familiar. He kept his posture straight, his chin raised.

"It's here somewhere. I know it is," Diomedes muttered. Frustrated that he hadn't yet found what he was searching for, he tossed his bag on the ground and rummaged through it. For a second, he panicked, wondering if he had dropped the key to saving his friend while wandering around in the desert. But he found it soon after. Diomedes carefully unwrapped the stinger he had cut off and handed it to the stranger. "Will this work? There has to be some poison still in it."

The man held the stinger closer to his face, examining it. "How fresh is it?"

"Fresh," Diomedes said, narrowing his eyes at the man. Diomedes sighed. "I cut it off one of the crawlers that attacked us last night. Can you use it or not?"

"There should be enough poison left to extract, but—"

"Then do it." Diomedes closed his bag and stood back up.

"But," the man continued, a sour look crossing his face, "there's no promise it will work."

Diomedes lifted his chin, and before Blanndynne could stop him, he stepped forward and clenched the man's tunic in his hand. They stood at about the same height.

"Do it. Now," Diomedes said, glaring at the man with as much vehemence as he could muster in his exhausted state.

The stranger nodded, though something in his eye made Diomedes question whether he was intimidated or just eager to get away from him. Maybe both. He left the room with the stinger, and Diomedes let out a long sigh as he took the chair sitting next to Armannii. After he sat down, he ran his fingers through his hair, flinching when they got stuck in the knotted mess.

"You do want him to help Armannii, right?" Blanndynne asked as she absentmindedly straightened a wrinkle in Armannii's tunic. It was only then that Diomedes noticed the leather vest the elf normally wore was lying at the foot of the cot.

"Of course I do. Why would—"

"Threatening him probably isn't the wisest idea," she said, glancing at Diomedes. Blanndynne's scarf hung loosely around her shoulders. Every few seconds, she glanced up at the door the man had disappeared through, a distant look in her eyes.

Diomedes didn't respond. He turned his full attention to Armannii. It was strange to see him so pale. In the time they'd been there, his tremors had gotten worse. The longer he stared, the more it was as if he wasn't truly seeing, and his mind wandered.

Armannii had rarely ever been sick in the time that Diomedes had known him. But Diomedes did remember one time from a few years earlier when Armannii had gotten sick enough for Diomedes to notice.

They were supposed to meet and visit one of their favorite taverns, but after waiting an hour for Armannii to arrive, Diomedes gave up and went back to the castle. His friend moved frequently enough that it would've been too difficult to find where he had been staying, so he shrugged it off and figured Armannii had run into trouble; it seemed to be his special talent.

But when Armannii found him a week later, he had not been able to lie his way out of what had really happened. Diomedes remembered Armannii telling him that he had been too sick to get out of bed, sick enough that he hadn't been able to keep anything down. Knowing the elf's healthy record made it almost difficult to believe, but his silver eyes had spoken the truth.

What Diomedes wouldn't give to see his friend open his eyes and tell him that it was going be okay. To know that he was going to make it through this. It felt wrong to see him so sickly—so close to death.

Diomedes didn't want to think what it would be like if the cure failed, if he lost his closest friend. In many ways, Armannii was closer to him than his own blood. Well, besides Ellayne.

If Armannii died, he'd lose more than a friend.

He'd lose his older brother.

"How long does it take to make this cure?" Diomedes muttered, glancing in the direction the stranger had gone. He felt like he couldn't sit still, and he tapped the edge of the chair with his thumb.

"Don't know," Blanndynne said, stroking Armannii's hand. "But if you need something to get your mind off all of this, there's a well between a few houses farther into town. It's in a covered building. You drank quite a bit of water on the way here. Do you want—"

"Yes." Diomedes held out his hand.

Blanndynne pulled the empty canteens out of thin air, and after pulling his winter tunic out of his bag to make room for the canteens, Diomedes stood up.

"I'll be back. If something happens—"

"I'll come find you."

"No," Diomedes said, gripping the strap of his bag as he shook his head. "Stay here with Armannii. Do what you have to for him. If something happens to him, don't leave him alone." He left after she nodded.

The light difference walking outside had Diomedes blinking back tears, and after the door shut behind him, he stood still for a few seconds until his eyes adjusted.

When he could finally see, he followed what must've qualified as a road into town. Unsure where exactly the well was, Diomedes paused to look between every building.

He finally found the well, though he had initially passed it. The building, which was a quarter of the size of the other houses, was made of the same white sandstone. As soon as he walked in, though, he could feel the change in the air. The space inside the small room was cool and refreshing, unlike the arid desert outside.

Diomedes leaned over the edge of the well, trying to see the water at the bottom, but it was too dark. He wondered how deep they had needed to dig before they'd reached water this far into the desert. The room was only lit with a single lantern by the entrance, but it was enough to illuminate the rope and pulley system rigged to the ceiling.

With many cranks of a winch, a bucket full of water appeared from the rim of the well. Diomedes reached over, pulling it toward him. He used it to refill two and a half canteens but had to lower it down to fill the rest of the third.

Part of him wanted to use what was left of the water to rinse off, but a small voice in the back of his mind reminded him that water was likely a scarce resource in the town. If Mellacross's directions were accurate, he'd be near a river as soon as they could get out of the desert and into the mountains; however, that depended on how soon Armannii recovered. If he recovered. Diomedes quickly dismissed the unwelcome thought, though it did motivate him to return to his friend.

It struck Diomedes as interesting that he hadn't even bothered to ask the man's name, nor had the stranger offered it. Blanndynne's comment when they'd first arrived returned to the front of his mind. She had wanted to tell him something, possibly something about the stranger taking care of his best friend. Diomedes made a note to ask about it when he returned.

On the way back to the man's home, Diomedes readjusted his grip on the bag—now made heavier with the additional water weight—and observed the emptiness of the town. Not a single person walked the streets like him, and Diomedes frowned. The man couldn't be the only inhabitant.

Not in a town of this size.

Something about it sent chills down Diomedes's sweaty back.

Chapter Fifteen

There you are," Blanndynne said from in front of him. She had somehow made it to where he stood staring at the town without him noticing. She had a crease in her brow as she frowned.

"What are you doing here? You weren't supposed to leave him. Is he—"

"He's okay. E—the stranger. He sent me to tell you the cure is done." Blanndynne nodded toward the stranger's house, which sat by itself on the very outskirts of town. She was clearly waiting for him to follow, but Diomedes stayed where he was. "What is it?" she asked, glancing in the direction Diomedes was staring.

"Where is everyone?" Diomedes asked, nodding toward the empty streets.

"The people here sleep during the day. It's too hot for them to get any work done, so they wake up at sunset and go to sleep at dawn." She tugged on his arm as he scanned the buildings. "Come on."

Blanndynne led him through the sand. When she closed the door behind them, Diomedes dropped his bag near the wall and crossed to the cot.

The man looked up from the only chair in the room, which sat at Armannii's feet. He was mixing an orange-tinged paste in a bowl, but he paused when Diomedes approached.

"It's ready?" Diomedes asked, nodding toward the mixture. "It'll cure him?"

"That is the hope, but I can't guarantee the results. Turn him over so I can see his wound." The man waited as Diomedes and Blanndynne worked together to turn Armannii onto his stomach.

A large crimson stain covered the center of Armannii's back and the cot beneath him, and it reminded Diomedes of the targets he had used during his combat training growing up. The darkest stains were near the center, where there was a gaping hole not only in Armannii's tunic but also in his punctured skin.

The crawler's stinger had gone in at least two inches, and the skin around the wound was blackened and withered.

"Remove the tunic," the man ordered, still mixing the salve with a bristly brush.

Realizing how difficult it would be to maneuver Armannii to take the tunic off over his head, Diomedes grunted as he pulled a knife out. With two slashes, Armannii's tunic no longer stood in the man's way, nor did it inhibit Diomedes's view of the decay on his friend's back.

Though most of the withered skin was focused near the puncture wound, which still continued to ooze dark blood and opaque green liquid with the consistency of melted sugar, the rest of his back was growing darker and more lifeless by the minute.

"The movement has aggravated the infection," the man said as he stepped near where Diomedes knelt.

"That fast?" Diomedes asked, his voice cracking.

"It's a vicious poison. Move aside." Taking the brush out of the mixture, the man began painting Armannii's back with it. It wasn't until he was applying it that Diomedes cringed back from the smell that was coming from the wound and the various liquids leaking out of it, or possibly from the cure. Maybe even a combination. Either way, it smelled as if someone's stomach had been sliced open; at least, that was what Diomedes thought it would smell like. The acidity made Diomedes's eyes water, and he covered his mouth and nose with the back of his hand.

Armannii did not move even after the salve bowl was empty, the contents spread over his back. Blanndynne leaned against the wall near Armannii's head, her eyes wide as she glanced back and forth from the elf to the stranger.

"Well?" she asked, her voice abrupt. "How long will this take? When will we know if it's working?"

"I suppose when the elf tells us. Or doesn't," the man said, crossing his arms over his chest. "Now, if you'll excuse me, I'm going to salvage what little sleep I can while the sun is still out."

"Wait," Diomedes said, standing up to face him. Though the man's aloof personality was grating against Diomedes's patience, his training from his tutors demanded that he give thanks where it was due. "Thank you for helping him. And I don't even know your name. I'm—I'm Didi," Diomedes said, choking on the nickname Armannii had given him. He held out his hand to shake the stranger's, but the man put both hands behind his back, standing up straighter. "Who are you?" Diomedes matched the man's posture when he raised an eyebrow at him. Blanndynne shifted against the wall, and when Diomedes glanced at her, she was fidgeting with the edge of her belt.

"I believe you'll get a clearer answer from her," the man said before departing into the room at the back. In the silence he left behind, the click of a lock turning could be heard.

Diomedes frowned in the direction the man had gone. "What's that supposed to mean?" He turned back to Blanndynne, crossing his arms over his chest. "Who is he?"

Blanndynne tucked a strand of hair behind her ear as she nodded. "It's Elias, Kylian's brother."

"What?" Diomedes did everything he could to keep his jaw from dropping. His head whipped around to look at the bedroom door. Blanndynne had straightened up when he turned back to face her. "That's impossible. It's been nearly a century since—"

"I know, but it's him," Blanndynne said, her voice more emphatic. "Try to imagine my shock when the first door I knocked on was opened by my final master." She spat the last few words, her voice a harsh whisper. She flicked her gaze to the door. It remained closed. Her jaw tightened, and she clenched her hands into fists.

"Did he recognize you?" Diomedes asked, sitting down in the chair next to the cot. He rubbed the back of his neck, trying to find a reasonable explanation for how his great-grandfather's brother could possibly be in the next room. He came up with nothing.

"No." Blanndynne shook her head vigorously, a glare in her eyes. "He didn't. It was like I was a complete stranger. And what was worse was that he seemed surprised that *I* knew who *he* was."

"You're sure it's him?"

"What, do you think I'm just going to forget what the man who betrayed me looks like?" Blanndynne asked him in a hoarse whisper. "Of course it's him. He's exactly how I remember. Look." She unclenched her fists, frowning at her right hand as she lifted it toward him, palm out.

Diomedes's eyes widened when a misty haze appeared above it. Just as he was about to ask what she was doing, images of the stranger started materializing within the cloud. He looked younger, and his hair was shorter, but his face was the same. In the memories—at least, that was what Diomedes assumed they were—the man wore similar formal attire to what Diomedes had hanging up in his wardrobe in Cyanthia. A little outdated, but clearly royal.

"This guy is tanner and a bit older but definitely the same person," Diomedes muttered, running his hand over the lower part of his mouth. "How is he even alive?" Diomedes refrained from asking about when she'd learned to show her memories, focusing instead on the larger matter.

"I don't know. When he opened the door, I froze. It was like seeing a ghost. I just—"

"Why wouldn't he remember you?" Diomedes asked, cutting her off.

"I don't know the answer to that either." Blanndynne ran the end of her scarf through her fingers, her focus on her hands instead of Diomedes. "But that's not all. He's . . . he's different. I mean, he reacted when I said his name, but he's not the same."

"And you haven't asked him what happened?"

"I've been a little preoccupied," Blanndynne said, her voice curt as she gestured toward Armannii.

Diomedes glanced at the elf, nodding slowly. "You're right. I'm sorry." He rubbed his thumb along his jaw, flicking his gaze to her. "Are you okay?"

Blanndynne pressed her lips together, frowning. It was several seconds before she responded. "The last time I saw him, I was devastated. He . . . he lied to me." Her voice was soft as she lifted her gaze to the door behind Diomedes. It sounded like she had more to say, but she didn't continue right away

"And now?" he asked.

"I can barely stand being in the same room as him. But his was the first house I came to, and he knew instantly what had happened to Armannii, and—"

"You did what was best for him," Diomedes assured her. "With how standoffish Elias is, I'm surprised he offered to help."

"He didn't do it for free," Blanndynne muttered. "He made me promise I'd tell him how I know him."

"And?"

"And what? I'll tell him the kind of cheating traitor he is as soon as Armannii is healthy."

Diomedes pressed his lips together, frowning. "You're not curious as to how he and I are standing in the same house? I mean, he's got to be—"

"Old. Yeah. But he doesn't look it." Blanndynne sighed, biting on the side of her nail. After a second, she lowered her head. "I'm sorry. I just want to get Armannii better and get out of here."

Diomedes didn't respond, letting her process in the silence of the room. His head ached, and he wasn't sure if it was from the information that his ancestor was in the next room, or all of the time in the sun, or his lack of sleep. Either way, he was finding it more and more difficult to keep his eyes open.

"You rest," Blanndynne said after a while. "I'll keep an eye on Armannii."

"No," Diomedes said, a yawn forming at the back of his throat. "I'm fine." As he spoke, his eyelids felt heavier than the bricks that made up the house.

Blanndynne didn't argue. And she didn't have to. After a few minutes of silence, Diomedes slouched in the chair, dead asleep.

Eventually, Blanndynne rustled his shoulder. He startled awake, using the heel of his hand to rub the sleep out of his eyes as quickly as he could.

"What is it? Is he—"

"He hasn't moved," Blanndynne said, standing up straight. She stretched her arms out to the sides, opening her mouth in a yawn. "But he's still breathing. I guess that's a good sign."

"How long has it been?"

"Four, maybe five hours." She ran her hands down the front of her tunic, smoothing out the wrinkles. "Elias just left to get some food, and I'm getting hungry." She spoke the man's name as if it were bitter on her tongue. "We could use a restock in our supplies, and since Armannii is normally the one to do that—"

"I'll go, unless you think it's wiser for you to go. There's a better chance people might recognize me." In all reality, he had no desire to go outside. The idea of being in the home without other people to have to speak to sent pleasant chills up Diomedes's arms. The ability to be alone was still one of the biggest things he missed about living in the castle—that and consistent bathing.

"I can go if you don't want to," Blanndynne said, glancing between Armannii and Diomedes.

"Good." Diomedes rose to his feet, cringing when he moved his injured leg. "I'll stay here and keep an eye on him."

Blanndynne snorted. "I guess that settles it then. You could've just said you didn't want to go."

Diomedes shrugged. "You picked up on it just fine."

"I'll be back soon," she said, wrapping the scarf around her head before leaving.

He nodded, offering her what little smile he could muster as she left the house. The sun had taken most of his energy, but being around people could easily do the same thing. As much as he appreciated her and Armannii, it felt like a breath of fresh air being in a room in silence; he could feel his energy levels rising second by second.

And with those energy levels came a renewed sense of determination. As he watched Armannii, he urged his friend to heal quickly. Diomedes had no desire to leave him behind, yet a small thought grew. If leaving Armannii in the town so he could heal meant Diomedes could end the war sooner, wasn't that what his friend would want?

Diomedes weighed the question in his mind, but the answer wasn't as black-and-white as he desired. After years of friendship, Diomedes knew his friend thrived on adventure and adrenaline. How annoyed—how devastated—would Armannii be if Diomedes left to go to the Elemental Mountains alone? Would he be angry? Or would he be grateful?

He knew that many others would be thankful he had taken the initiative. Diomedes scratched his chin, lost in thoughts of people joining him as he returned to the castle to end the Split of Phildeterre once and for all—something many before him had tried to do—and the honor they would pour out. He grinned. It would go down in history. He would be remembered for centuries as the man who had ended the war that split the country in two.

Distracted by the images flashing through his mind, Diomedes didn't notice the green ooze leaking out of Armannii's wound until it dripped onto the cot and then onto the ground where he was staring.

Diomedes shot to his feet, his mind emptying of all its previous thoughts as concern for his friend replaced it.

"Armannii? Hey!" Diomedes scanned the room for something to clean the mess with but stopped when he heard a whimper come from the cot. "Hey, Armannii. Hey." He moved around to where Armannii's head rested.

Though the elf hadn't opened his eyes, his face had creased into a frown, and his brow was sweating more than it had earlier.

"No," Armannii moaned, his lips barely moving. "No, no."

"Hey, it's okay. You were stung. You're going to be okay." Diomedes ran the back of his hand across Armannii's forehead like he remembered the royal healer doing to him when he had been sick. Armannii's skin felt like a fire burned beneath it.

Panicking, Diomedes grabbed one of the canteens he had refilled as well as one of the winter socks he hadn't used. He emptied some of the water onto the wool and began dabbing at Armannii's face.

"Kit," Armannii said, his voice weak. His eyelids trembled as his eyes moved underneath frantically.

"Wake up," Diomedes said, pouring more water over the sock. "Come on," he muttered under his breath.

The more Diomedes patted Armannii's face, the more his friend groaned. With each passing second, Armannii became more and more unsettled.

"Kit, no," Armannii said louder than before. The next time he spoke, he was shouting. "Kit!"

"Armannii. Wake up." Diomedes swallowed back as much of his rising panic as he could, but the mix of the acidic odors coming from the wound and the liquid oozing out of it left his head reeling.

With a moan, Armannii flipped his head to the other side so he faced away from Diomedes. It was more movement than Diomedes had seen, and that filled him with the slightest bit of hope.

Standing up, Diomedes raced over to a small counter against the opposite wall and started opening the cabinets below it. When he found what he was searching for—a kitchen rag—Diomedes rushed over to Armannii and began soaking up the putrid mess on his back.

Diomedes tried to hold his breath, wrinkling his nose as his hands were soon covered in the liquid. But his actions were not in vain. After he had removed most of the mess, Armannii calmed down.

Exhaling, Diomedes plopped the wet rag on the ground near the foot of the cot and returned to dabbing Armannii's face with the damp sock. He expected Armannii to wake up completely, especially since he'd returned to a regular breathing pattern, but he didn't.

Half an hour later, Blanndynne came back. "What happened?" She took one glance at Diomedes sitting against the wall near Armannii's head and the stained mess on the side of the cot from where the liquid had run over Armannii's back and off the edge.

"Don't know," Diomedes replied, pushing against the floor as he stood up. He gestured toward Armannii. "A little while ago, he started talking, but he was still unconscious." He went on to explain where the mess had come from, watching Blanndynne's dark eyes widen as he spoke.

Blanndynne set a bag of supplies on the floor near Diomedes's belongings. Standing over Armannii, she bent down and picked up the wet sock.

"I was using it to cool him down," Diomedes said, nodding toward the open canteen at the foot of the cot.

Blanndynne didn't say anything. Instead, she poured more water onto it and started blotting the back of Armannii's neck.

"Where's Elias? When is he coming back?" Diomedes asked, glancing from his friends to the door. He refrained from rubbing his temples because his hands were still covered in he-didn't-know-what. "I bet he would have a better idea of what's going on here."

"Don't know. I didn't see him while I was out." She rested the sock across the center of Armannii's broad shoulders at the top of his spine. When Blanndynne turned to look at Diomedes, her brow was drawn. "What do we do if he doesn't wake up soon?"

Diomedes bit the inside of his cheek. "I've given it some thought."

"And?"

"And you should stay here with him while I continue north."

"No," Blanndynne said, shaking her head, her attention still on Armannii. "It's too dangerous. It's ridiculous."

"More dangerous than strolling through a sand crawler–infested desert? Or taking a quick dive in the frozen sea?" Diomedes leaned back against the wall. "I have to keep going. There are too many people depending on me."

"Armannii is depending on you!" Blanndynne's voice went up, and Diomedes startled at the anger in it. However, he remained outwardly calm.

"The best thing I can do is leave him here with you to get better. Besides, he'd want me to keep going. He knows how important it is that I end the Split. He'd understand."

Blanndynne shook her head. "He'd be furious if he woke up and found that you'd gone without him. Besides, you can't leave me here with Elias. I can't—I *won't* stay here with that man."

Diomedes, feeling restless, started pacing. "I know, but Armannii is . . . The best thing for him is to get better."

"Take me with you. Diomedes, I want to go with you." Blanndynne spoke in a lower voice, her eyes searching his face as she stood up and stopped him in his tracks. "I want to help you end this war."

"It's just—"

"Please," she said, raising her chin. "Let me go with you. Please. I can't stay here with Elias. Seeing his face reminds me of what it felt like to be a slave. I need to leave. I can't stay." Her voice was frantic. She grabbed Diomedes by the hands, not minding the dried mess from Armannii's back. She clung to them like she was going to be yanked away at any second, like he was her lifeline. "Diomedes, you have to let me go with you. I can't feel powerless again."

Diomedes sighed. In his mind, it would be foolish not to take her with him. Her powers had only continued to grow. But at the same time, Armannii would be safest if she stayed with him to make sure he had what he needed. "I'll think about it. And you aren't powerless." He pulled his hands out of hers, and she backed away, taking her spot by Armannii's head again.

"I know that. And I know I'm free. But seeing him, it's like I'm reliving the pain of his betrayal every time." Blanndynne rubbed her eyebrow, leaning forward and placing her head in her hands.

"You're more than free, Blanndynne. You're learning to take control. He has no power over you. No one does."

Blanndynne's attention was on Armannii, and instead of responding to what Diomedes had said, she froze. Crouching over, Blanndynne picked up one of Armannii's hands, careful not to bend his arm the wrong way.

"Look," she said, holding out his hand, which was twice the size of hers, for Diomedes to see. "It's not gray anymore."

The previous conversation abandoned, Diomedes frowned as he stared at the coloring on the ends of Armannii's fingers. She was right. His skin, though still pale, carried with it a peachy tone it hadn't had before.

"What about his face?" Diomedes asked. "Any color in his cheeks?"

Blanndynne leaned over Armannii, trying to get a better look since he was still facing the wall. "I think, well, maybe there's a bit more color." She stood straight, glancing at Diomedes. "Do you think it's working? The cure?"

"He's not dead, so something happened." He sat back down in the chair. "Elias didn't exactly explain what the process would be after he put whatever that stuff was on his back."

"Maybe what happened while I was gone was his body getting rid of the venom or poison or whatever that was killing him. Maybe all he needs now is to heal."

"Could be," Diomedes said, nodding. He ran his hands over his trousers, smoothing them out, but regretted it when flecks of dried poison or whatever he'd mopped up came off on them.

"I wish I knew the healing rune," Blanndynne said, though her voice was soft enough that Diomedes wasn't sure she was speaking to him or anyone but herself.

"Maybe someone else around here knows it," Diomedes said.

Blanndynne shook her head. "That could get us into trouble. As much as I hate saying this, we need to find Elias. Out of the three of us, he at least knew what he was doing. If you still don't want to leave the house, I'll—"

"I'll go," Diomedes said, shaking off the panic he'd felt when Armannii had gone into a fit. He hid his trembling hands in his pockets. "There's probably more you can do for him if something happens."

Blanndynne didn't hide the relief on her face, and she nodded. "You're probably right." She paused. "And thank you."

Diomedes inclined his head as he cleared his throat. "Did he say where he was going?" Not that Diomedes knew the location of anything except the well.

"No, but the market is at the center of town. He might be there."

"All right," Diomedes said. "I'll find him." He leaned over his bag, leaving all but one of the canteens on the floor so he didn't have to carry the extra weight. He slung the bag over his shoulder.

"Oh," Blanndynne said, turning to face him. She had taken his place in the chair, scooting it closer so she could hold Armannii's hand. "The market is underground. You go in through the building with double doors and follow the staircase. There were tons of people going in and coming out when I went. You won't miss it."

"Underground, huh?" Diomedes let half a grin slip. "I suppose it's the safest place in the desert," he said in a softer voice as he left.

Chapter Sixteen

refreshing breeze blew past Diomedes as he opened the door. The sun had set, and the town was lit up by torches mounted on every building he passed. It seemed to lighten the sky directly above the town with an amber light.

People wove in and out of buildings, none of them giving Diomedes a second look. Like Raidah, her children, and her servants, most of the inhabitants had a golden glow to their skin, likely from living in the desert.

After a quick stop at the well, which he had to wait in line for this time, Diomedes had washed his hands and was ready to find Elias.

Diomedes pulled up the hood of his cloak, still not wanting to risk being noticed. He followed a young couple who were holding hands as they strolled between the buildings, oblivious to everyone and everything except each other. However, after a few more seconds of avoiding their heels, Diomedes slipped around them and returned to his faster pace of walking.

He kept his eye out for a building with double doors, and he almost missed it because the doors, which opened inward, were propped open. He paused as he passed in front of the small building, and an older lady with bright white hair muttered for him to move when he stopped in front of her.

"Sorry," Diomedes said, nodding toward her. "Is this the way to the market?"

The woman nodded and scampered down the stairs as if she weren't at least well into her eighties.

Glancing back once, Diomedes followed the woman down the stairs. People filed in after him, and two children raced down the steps, darting in and out of the traffic going up as well as down. A woman—Diomedes assumed she was their mother—wore a scarf over her hair like the one Blanndynne had donned earlier and held on to it as she chased after them, hollering at them to come back.

The sounds of voices speaking over one another got louder with every step down until it all became a hum. Every once in a while, Diomedes caught a fragment of a conversation or the sound of a merchant shouting about their daily deals, but mostly the voices were indiscernible.

The farther Diomedes went down, the stranger the scents floating up and tickling his nose were. A mixture of spices wove in with a sweeter smell, one similar to how the Cyanthian castle kitchen had smelled when the chef was making pastries. Following those was an overbearing musky scent, probably from the incense booth near where the staircase let out.

Diomedes's nose crinkled as the musk overtook all the other scents. When he passed by the first merchant watching him from a booth, Diomedes's eyes widened at the sight of the market.

The ceiling, which was three stories tall, was lit up with lanterns made with every metal Diomedes could think of, as well as some others he didn't recognize. Booths lined the walls of the room, which could've fit at least three of his father's throne rooms back-to-back. People passed by, some with clearer intentions than others, who walked about with a casual air.

He stepped away from the middle of the room, where most of the foot traffic was, so he could take a moment to think. How in the world was he going to track Elias down in the chaos around him?

"Looking for something in particular?" a woman asked, tapping him on the shoulder.

He spun around, his attention shifting to the woman. "Someone, actually." Diomedes flicked his gaze around, trying to see if anyone else was paying attention. As much as he desired to venture into the market and haggle, the image of Armannii lying injured on the cot kept him present. "The man who lives on the edge of town. Elias?"

The woman, who had a birthmark on half of her face, shook her head. "Sorry. Don't know him. But maybe you're interested in buying a new tunic?"

Diomedes bit the inside of his cheek as he scanned the crowd, not fully listening as she started to list off the other products she sold. "I'm sorry, not interested."

He didn't wait to hear her response as he continued through the crowd of people. His injured leg ached as he walked, stiff from all the time he'd spent sitting. It also didn't help that there was probably more sand within the bandage.

A group of women near him giggled, all covered in similar scarves to the one that Blanndynne had donned in the desert. He let them pass by, searching for any sign of Elias's sandy hair or white tunic. Unfortunately, white seemed to be the overwhelming color of choice for most of the residents. It made Diomedes stand out with his charcoal-gray tunic, which he'd rolled up at the sleeves.

Every once in a while, he thought he saw the back of Elias's head, but each time the man turned around or Diomedes glanced back after passing by, it wasn't him. Frustrated, Diomedes clenched his hands into fists, one by his side and the other around the strap of his bag. He had no doubt that a marketplace as large as this would be prime hunting territory for pickpockets.

"Interested in a pair of sandals?" a merchant nearby asked, stepping in front of Diomedes.

"No. Have you seen—" He stopped when he noticed a familiar face a few booths over. "Excuse me," Diomedes said as he left the sandal merchant and pushed through the crowd. Though people moved in front of and around him, Diomedes kept his gaze locked on Elias, who appeared to be in an intense discussion with a merchant.

Diomedes stayed a distance away, stepping back where the flow of traffic wasn't as heavy. He watched, waiting for Elias to leave. But the conversation continued. With all of the ambient noise and people doing business around him, Diomedes couldn't hear a word they were saying. He thought of Armannii, wishing he had the elf's incredible hearing, though he knew his friend would not enjoy the crowded space because of how overwhelming it was to his senses.

Since he couldn't eavesdrop, Diomedes tried to read the body language of the two men. Elias spoke with his hands, gesturing every few seconds either to the merchant or to the inside of the booth behind him. Elias shook his head vigorously, a scowl on his lips. The merchant matched Elias's sour expression with one of his own, slapping his hand on the table multiple times. The men stared intensely at each other, like one of them was about to rip the other's head off at the flip of a coin.

Eventually, Elias clenched his hands into his fists, raised his shoulders up, and stomped away in the opposite direction of Diomedes, who followed behind. Quickening his steps, Diomedes caught up to Elias and grabbed him by the upper arm.

"I apologize," Diomedes said, bowing his head when Elias turned a wrathful glare in his direction. "But I need you to come back with me."

Elias wrinkled his face, staring Diomedes up and down before looking around at the crowd of people. He frowned. "Why?"

"It's not a 'why' kind of question," Diomedes said, lowering his voice as much as he could in the noisy marketplace. "And besides, you know why."

Instead of agreeing, as Diomedes had expected him to, Elias shook his head. "No."

"Excuse me?" Diomedes took a step back as though the man had slapped him. "Why not?"

"My business here is not finished," the man said, casting a dirty look toward the booth he'd just left.

Diomedes glanced at it too, but he could already feel his anger coming to a boil. Diomedes stepped nearer to Elias, leaning in and speaking in a low growl. "My friend is lying on a cot in your house dying, and I need your help to save his life. I'm sorry if I don't care about your shopping list right now."

"You don't understand. That man cheated me."

"No," Diomedes said, gripping the hilt of the knife on his belt, "*you* don't understand. I'm not asking. You're coming back with me, or—"

"Or what?" Elias asked, straightening up and glaring Diomedes dead in the eye. He gestured to where Diomedes's hand held his knife. "You'll stab me in the middle of this crowd?"

"My friend is dying." Diomedes forced his hand to move away from his weapon, clenching it behind his back as he did when he addressed his father. He gritted his teeth before he spoke again. "Will you *please* come back and help him?"

Elias stared down his nose at Diomedes, and for the first time, Diomedes could see the family resemblance: the stubbornness in his eyes, the tension in his jaw, and the look of disdain written in large letters over his face.

"No," Elias finally said, his attention back on the merchant, who had turned his back. "This is too important," he muttered.

"How could whatever this is be more important than saving a life?" Diomedes asked, dumbfounded.

"I am saving a life." Elias glanced back at Diomedes, who was frowning. "Mine."

"What?" The word came out clipped, and Diomedes folded his arms over his chest.

Elias grunted. With a glance around to make sure no one was looking, he pulled up the sleeve of his tunic. A darkness was spreading through the man's veins, leaving his skin tinged with an unnatural blackness, like charcoal. Even Armannii's back hadn't looked that bad.

"What is—"

"It's an effect of whatever curse was laid on me." Elias rolled his sleeve down and cleared his throat.

"A curse?" Diomedes raised an eyebrow, glancing up from Elias's arm to see if anyone was watching.

"That's my guess," Elias said as he narrowed his eyes at the merchant, who was successfully making a sale. "I heard of a book that might give me some answers, and I sought out that man to find it for me. I was supposed to pay five gold for it, but when he sent word that he had the book, he doubled the price. I can't afford that. How am I supposed to—"

Tired of listening to his ancestor whine, his mind still on Armannii lying sick on the cot, Diomedes waved his hand to the side and cut Elias off. "What's the book called?"

Elias's jaw dropped. "You'll help?"

"As soon as I get the book, you return with me to heal my friend," Diomedes said. While haggling with merchants was typically one of his favorite pastimes, the threat of Armannii's life hung over him, removing any entertainment Diomedes might've found in that moment. Unlike many times before, Diomedes was determined to make the process quick and to the point. Then he could get Elias to help Armannii.

"*Curses and Spells of the Ancients.*"

"All right," Diomedes said, cracking a few of his fingers. "But you need to return to the house with me whether I'm successful or not. Understood?"

A sour look crossed Elias's face, but he eventually nodded. "Fine."

Diomedes said nothing else as he turned. Taking a deep breath, he walked over to the merchant Elias had been speaking to. He must've been in his mid to late seventies because his beard, which went halfway down his round belly, was white. His bushy eyebrows rose, and he met Diomedes with a wide toothy grin.

"What can I interest you with, boy?" He spoke with a jolly voice. "I have—"

"I'm looking for a particular type of book," Diomedes said before the man could begin to list off the various products he carried. From the looks of his booth, he was a procurer of rare objects since there were no more than a few of the same in what Diomedes would consider a category. On the table in front of him, Diomedes spotted a silver bracelet that reminded him of the one his stepmother never took off. His gaze traveled to a shelf at the back that had a few books between a stack of unique bowls—in that none of them were the same—and a small statue of a monkey. "I was told you're the best option in this part of Phildeterre."

Flattery had gotten him quite far in past, and it seemed to be doing the trick once again.

"Of course. What kind of book are you looking for?"

"One on curses," Diomedes said with as casual an air as he could manage. He kept his peripheral sight on the man as he picked up a small dragon figurine carved out of a bluish stone.

"Curses?"

"Mm-hmm," Diomedes said, putting the dragon back down and making full eye contact with the merchant.

The old man's brow furrowed, and he glanced around the marketplace as if to search for anyone who might be eavesdropping, or maybe he was looking for Elias. Either way, he eventually turned back to Diomedes with a skeptical look in his eyes.

"Well?" Diomedes asked, tapping his hand on the table. "Do you have any? Or should I seek someone else out?"

"I might have something," the man said, lowering his voice. "But I'm curious as to what you want with a book that would have you arrested in a heartbeat."

"Call it personal curiosity," Diomedes said, his lips pulling up in a smirk. He reached into his bag and pulled out his coin purse, which was still somehow damp from his unexpected swim in the Cyro Sea.

"Okay," the old man said, a sly grin crossing his face as well. "I'll grab what I have, and you can decide which ones suit your purposes best." He walked over to the shelf with the books, but instead of pulling any of them off the shelf, he opened a crate beside it and grabbed three books. When he returned to Diomedes, he placed all three of them on the table before him. "Have a look." The old man stepped back, crossing his arms over his round torso.

Diomedes nodded once to him before stepping forward. Instantly, his gaze landed on the book titled *Curses and Spells of the Ancients*, but in order to convince the merchant that his story was true and keep the old man from suspecting that he was working with Elias, Diomedes didn't look at it for too long. He let his eyes wander over the covers of the other two, one of which had been worn so much that the only way Diomedes could read the title was to open the first couple of pages.

"Careful," the merchant said, nodding toward the book Diomedes was flipping through. "The woman I retrieved that from said a spell was laid on it. Wasn't specific, but said it was rather nasty."

Diomedes pressed his lips together and moved on to the book he actually wanted. However, he gave it about as much attention as he had the first, and then the same for the third.

"Well?" the merchant asked, tilting his head to try to catch Diomedes's eye. "What do you think?"

"They're all quite interesting, but I'm afraid I only have enough for one. That being said"—Diomedes pointed to the book

Elias had requested—"This one. How much?" he asked, shaking his coin purse so it jingled in his hand.

"Twelve gold," the man said, stroking his beard. "I should charge twice that, but you seem like you'll put it to better use than other people."

Diomedes suspected the rise in price had to do with the sudden interest in the book. He tried to keep his facial expression even as he shook his head. "That's too high. It's a book, not a new bed. I'm sure you've got a better offer in you." Diomedes crossed his arms over his chest, matching the old man.

"It's an illegal book on curses, boy. Do you know what I had to go through to get this?" The old man's voice was a harsh, angry whisper, but he rolled his shoulders back and cleared his throat. "What are you willing to offer?"

Diomedes glanced down at the book, wondering how far he could push the man before he got as outraged as he had with Elias. It wasn't that he didn't have the gold for the man—he did—but something, maybe his pride, wouldn't let him pay it.

"Three. Maybe three and five silver." Diomedes shrugged, amused but unwilling to show it when the man stepped back and put his hands on his hips.

"You're kidding, right? This is a joke. Three? Really? I'll lower it to ten, but no more."

Rubbing his jaw, Diomedes leaned on his back foot. "Four."

"No."

"Unfortunate," Diomedes said, turning to walk away. He could almost predict the merchant's response, counting down in his head until the man called him back.

"All right. Come back, come back," the man called, and like many times before, Diomedes erased the satisfaction from his face before turning around. "Eight. For you, I'll do eight."

"No, but thanks," Diomedes said. "I'll find what I want somewhere else."

"Wait!" the old man sputtered. "Wait. Five. I was going to sell it to someone else for five."

Diomedes forced a contemplative look across his face. "You were going to sell it for five yet charge me more than twice that? I don't think so." He turned to leave again, but the merchant stopped him once more.

"Four and a half. And the dragon statue you were looking at."

"Fine," Diomedes said, hiding the wide grin that threatened to cross his face. He took the book when the man handed it to him and snorted as he put the dragon statue, which was half the size of a small apple, in his bag alongside the book.

The old man watched as Diomedes pulled out five gold and handed it to him. When the man disappeared to get the change, Diomedes slipped into the crowd. The man had earned the five gold, and just as he had done many times, he left having paid more than was agreed upon.

Diomedes walked back to where he had left Elias and found him leaning against one of the stone columns keeping the ceiling up.

"Well? Did you get it?" Elias straightened up when Diomedes came around the corner.

"I did." Diomedes opened the bag for Elias to look inside.

"How did you—"

"Doesn't matter. It's time for you to keep your end of the deal." Diomedes nodded toward the other end of the grand room, where people were still coming and departing from the marketplace.

"How is your friend?" Elias asked when they started toward the exit, making sure to avoid the booth where Diomedes had gotten the book.

"He woke up. Well, sort of. He started to shout, and the wound was leaking this green—"

"So the cure is working. Why do you need me?"

"He won't wake up. You need to come check on him to make sure everything is working correctly." Diomedes cast a sideways glance at a few people watching the two of them. He clutched his bag closer, ducking his head down.

"All right," Elias said without saying anything else.

Chapter Seventeen

What's so special about this book?" Diomedes asked when they reached the top of the stairs and entered the sandy streets of the town. Diomedes didn't expect the man to answer, given how little he'd spoken with him.

"Every other book I've read on the topic has referenced this one. It's old. One of the oldest." Elias's voice was tight as he led the way toward his home, which was good since Diomedes's sense of direction was disoriented after coming out of the underground marketplace.

"Doesn't look it."

"Magic." Elias's voice remained flat.

"Of course," Diomedes said after a few empty seconds had passed.

"I don't know what curse I'm under," Elias said, pausing in the sandy street. "I'm hoping this book will give me some insight."

Diomedes stopped walking too. "When were you cursed?" he asked, still frowning at the man's arm despite it being covered.

"Don't know. Can't remember. But I'm hoping your friend will shed some light."

Diomedes raised an eyebrow, wondering if Elias had picked up on Blanndynne's vehemence toward him. "What makes you think she knows anything?"

"She knew my name. Even I don't remember my name when the curse restarts. Nobody remembers me." His voice was low as he watched a family with three little children pass by. They almost reminded Diomedes of Camile and Forrest's children.

"Then how do you know your name? And what do you mean restarts?"

Elias rolled up his other sleeve, and Diomedes tried not to stare too intensely at the scar that spelled out Elias's name.

"Did you do that?" Diomedes asked, glancing up at Elias's face.

"Don't know that either. Every thirty days or so, I wake up in my bed, and for a few minutes, I know nothing. Not my identity, nor how I got here. Then things begin to trickle back, but there are still holes in my memory. I don't know where I'm from, nor who I really am."

"Interesting."

"What do you know?" Elias asked, squinting at him in the low light. "You're acting too calm about my curse, like you know something."

Diomedes tilted his head. "I don't know anything about your curse. I'm simply intrigued. I've never heard of anything like it." Diomedes had more questions, but he decided to put them off until they returned to the house and checked on Armannii. "I'm sure if you help Armannii, Blanndynne will tell you exactly what she knows. But only after Armannii is okay."

"Spoken like a true royal."

His words had Diomedes scanning around them to make sure no one had heard. There were only a few people still wandering between the buildings, and it didn't appear that anyone had overheard Elias's comment.

"How do you know who I am?" Diomedes asked when they got closer to his house and farther out of the town.

"I've studied you and your family. I read a lot." Elias tapped his temple. "Everything I've ever read stays up here."

Diomedes didn't say anything else as they walked the rest of the distance to the house. Instead, he split his attention between watching where he was going and staring at the stars above them as he remembered what Blanndynne had told him about Elias's wishes. He'd wished for health, knowledge, and favor. Maybe the wishes were still protecting him despite whatever curse had been put on him.

Even with the three moons—two of which were half full—lighting the sky and the ambient light from the town, the stars stood out like crystals in a sea of darkness. They hypnotized Diomedes, and Elias had to grunt at him when he continued past the front door.

"Careful," Elias said as he opened the door. "Your eyes might lead you off the edge of the world." He didn't bother to hold the door for Diomedes, who caught it as it began to close.

"How is he?" Diomedes asked as he removed his bag. He dumped it by the canteens and strode over to the cot.

Blanndynne yawned as she straightened up in the chair. "He hasn't moved a muscle."

"Hasn't said anything else?" Diomedes asked, cocking his head to get a better look at Armannii's face, still turned away from the rest of the room.

"No."

Elias had gone straight to his back room and emerged again with a pot of something. When he turned the container upside down over Armannii's back, a blob of a pitch-black jelly plopped down with a loud smack.

Diomedes bit his cheek, and even though Armannii didn't react, somewhere in the back of Diomedes's mind, he knew it must've been painful; the jelly had landed right in the center of his back near the wound.

"Careful," Diomedes said, flashing a quick glance at his friend.

"You asked for my help," Elias said, pushing the black blob toward the puncture hole.

Blanndynne leaned forward in the chair, trying to see around Elias, who stood in her way. "What's that supposed to do?"

With a sigh, he turned to face Blanndynne. "The salve I put on him earlier has done the job of drawing out most of the poison, but not all of it. As long as there's some venom still running through his body, he will remain unconscious."

"Why didn't the cure work all the way?" Diomedes asked, frowning as the jelly began flattening out over the wound.

"There could be a couple of reasons," Elias said, nodding for Blanndynne to stand up, and after a quick thank-you, he took the chair and sat down. "The first and most likely is that there wasn't enough original poison in the cure. The stinger you gave me had what I thought would be a satisfactory amount of venom, but it appears I was mistaken. Or it could be that your elf friend is holding on to the hallucination induced by the crawler's venom."

"From the sound of his distress earlier, that's less likely," Diomedes murmured, thinking of Armannii's panic as the poison drained out of his back.

"That's my thought as well. This handy little jelly will expel the rest of it, along with any other toxins in your friend's system."

"How?" Blanndynne asked again, eyeing the jelly as it began to pulse. Her eyebrows pinched together.

"It sucks it right up. Absorbs it."

"Why couldn't you have just used that from the beginning?" Diomedes asked.

"If your friend had just been stung, I probably could've used it. But after the poison spreads to a certain point, the jelly is ineffective until the poison is drawn back to the surface again, as the cure has done."

Diomedes ran his hand along the back of his neck, rolling it from side to side. The strain of walking as much as they had and carrying the bag had left his muscles tight and aching. At the thought of his aches and pains, his leg began to throb again.

An idea crossed Diomedes's mind, and he glanced at Elias. "I tore up my leg the other day. Do you think you could take a look at it?"

"Do I look like a healer?" Elias sighed, then nodded. "Sit down." He switched places with Diomedes, and within fifteen minutes, he had cleaned out the gash and rewrapped it.

"Thank you," Diomedes said, standing up. Even just replacing the bandages had helped the throbbing tremendously.

"Mm-hmm," Elias muttered, returning to the chair. He ran his hand over his trousers multiple times while watching the black jelly continue to pulsate over Armannii's wound.

"You're sure this will help him?" Diomedes asked after a few minutes.

"It should."

Glancing over at Blanndynne, Diomedes sighed. "You should tell Blanndynne about the darkness in your arm," Diomedes said, not making eye contact as he spoke. His eyes were focused on Armannii too.

"What?" Blanndynne asked, but Diomedes didn't answer the question.

Elias didn't speak right away. Eventually, he rubbed the bridge of his nose and spoke. "I believe I'm cursed."

Blanndynne glanced to Diomedes, but he simply nodded.

"Show her," Diomedes said, moving to the head of the cot, where he leaned against the wall.

When Elias pulled back his sleeve to reveal the growing darkness, Blanndynne wrinkled her nose.

"What is this?" Blanndynne asked, taking a step toward him, though he retracted his arm when she reached for it. She didn't step any farther, crossing her arms over her chest.

"I don't know," Elias said, sliding the sleeve down. "But I'm hoping to find out soon." He pointed to the bag, and without needing to be told, Diomedes pulled out the book and handed it to him. "I want to know what you know about me." He spoke to Blanndynne, though he glanced at Diomedes once.

Blanndynne shook her head. "Not until he's awake and well," she said, pointing at Armannii. "That was the deal."

While Blanndynne and Elias went back and forth arguing, Diomedes reached into his bag, fishing around until he found what he was looking for. He clasped the tiny blue-and-gold fragment in his fist, stepping between Blanndynne and Elias.

"Diomedes, tell him that—" Blanndynne stopped talking when Diomedes grabbed her hand and placed the fragment he'd kept from her vessel on her palm. She looked up at him with wide eyes, but her fist tightened around it.

"Tell him," Diomedes said, his voice low as he leaned down and whispered in her ear. "You're in control." He stepped back, returning to his place against the wall, ready to watch the action unfold.

Elias was frowning, his gaze switching between Blanndynne and Diomedes. "What was that?"

"Doesn't matter," Blanndynne said, her hand still clasping the fragment tight enough to make her knuckles white. "Sit down. I'll tell you what I know." She glanced over her shoulder at Diomedes, who nodded in approval.

"What's in your—"

"Your name is Elias Maudit," Blanndynne said, cutting him off with sharp words. She must've moved the piece of her vessel to her magic storehouse because when she put her hands on her hips, the fragment was nowhere to be seen.

"Maudit? As in—"

"Yes. Your younger brother was Kylian. You were supposed to be the heir, but you were sick and fell behind your brother in schooling and in physical stature. When you were in your twenties, you sent your men out to search for something to help you. They found a genie, and after hearing your story, the genie granted your first wish for health."

Elias rubbed the side of his face, shaking his head. "Wait, slow down." His voice trembled, and when Blanndynne glanced back at Diomedes, there was the slightest hint of smugness in her smile.

She was taking control of the situation, and Elias's emotions were almost completely at her disposal, as if she had enchanted him. It wasn't exactly what Diomedes had expected, but after hearing the story of the heir's traitorous behavior toward his friend, he didn't mind it either.

"I'm royalty?" Elias shifted his bewildered gaze to Diomedes, who nodded. "But how are we—I mean, if Kylian was actually my brother . . . that was nearly a century ago. I should be—"

"Dead," Blanndynne snapped. "That's what I thought. Where was I?" She tapped her chin before nodding. "Right, your second wish. After the genie generously gave you your health, you realized how far you'd fallen behind in your studies and tutoring. Your next wish was for the chance to catch up and surpass your brother, so the genie gave you the ability to retain every word you've ever read. And then—"

"How did you know that?" Elias asked, taking a shaky breath. "How did you know I could—"

Blanndynne spoke over him, continuing before he could finish his question. "By that time, you and the genie had grown close; you even considered her a friend and confidante. She trusted you enough to tell you what she desired most: to be free. And do you know what you told her?" Blanndynne didn't pause to let him answer. Her voice was rising, and Diomedes prepared for her to unleash her anger on the man who'd betrayed her. "You promised her—no—you *swore* to her that you'd free her instead of using your third wish. You knew that if you used that wish, you'd lose the power you had to free her, confining her back to a life of slavery. You were royalty. All you had to do was exchange your third wish for her freedom and break the vessel."

Elias squirmed in his chair, but every time he opened his mouth to speak, Blanndynne cut him off. It was clear by the way the man was acting that he had figured out who the genie in the story was and that he was now at her mercy.

Mercy that seemed to be wearing thin.

"You betrayed her. Instead of freeing her, you used your third wish. A wish for favor over the people. And she had no choice but to grant it. She had no power to say no. No control." Blanndynne took a deep breath and rolled her shoulders back, lifting her chin. "You betrayed me. You locked me away in my vessel for a century, and there was nothing I could do about it. You lied to me, Elias. You stole a hundred years of my life. I missed an entire war—a mass murder of my people—because you were a selfish, insecure little man. I don't know why I ever trusted you, and to this day, *you* are my biggest regret." Blanndynne towered over Elias, who shrank back in the chair at her words.

"I don't—I don't remember," Elias said, his voice shaking as he squeezed his eyes shut.

Clearing his throat, Diomedes caught Blanndynne's attention. He nodded toward the front door. He didn't need words to tell her to cool off. By the way she stormed out, she obviously wanted to put space between her and Elias.

After the door shut, Diomedes tilted his head, watching Elias mumble to himself.

"I don't remember. I don't . . ." He looked up at Diomedes with wide eyes. "I-I don't remember."

"Yeah," Diomedes said, nodding. "You've made that pretty clear."

"You knew?" Elias asked, but there was no accusation behind his words.

"She told me."

Elias was silent for a moment before standing. "I need to write this down." He left the room and returned with a journal and a pen. "I need to write it down before I reset, otherwise I'll never remember," Elias muttered, sitting back in the chair.

Diomedes puzzled over Elias's words, but he supposed it made sense. Despite the clear memory damage the mystery curse did to Elias, and possibly to other people, the second wish for knowledge must've counteracted part of the effects. At least, that's what Diomedes felt he could safely assume, knowing he and Armannii had forgotten Elias multiple times since Blanndynne had first told them. Just when Diomedes began to question why Blanndynne could still remember Elias, the man spoke again, though he was mumbling.

"If I don't write all of this down and reread it, I will forget it when the curse resets me." Elias scribbled, and he paused every couple sentences to reread what he'd written.

The room fell into silence, and Diomedes slid down the wall near the head of the cot. Though he had taken a nap earlier, his eyelids got heavier and heavier. At some point, Elias put the journal aside, stood up, and scooped the black jelly back into the pot.

Armannii still had not moved.

"I need some time alone. Your friend should wake up within the hour. If he doesn't, knock on my door," Elias said.

Diomedes nodded, holding back a yawn as his ancestor went to the back room. He wanted to fall asleep almost as much as he wanted to bathe. But he didn't. He stood up and crossed to the chair, hoping it would help him stay alert enough to watch for any signs of Armannii waking up.

A while later, Blanndynne walked back in, her cheeks and nose red. She crossed the room and sat down near Armannii's head. Diomedes didn't speak first, waiting for her to open the conversation.

"He's in the back room?" she asked, her voice flat at the mention of Elias. Diomedes nodded. "Good. I don't want to see him, at least not right away."

"Understandable," Diomedes said, shrugging. "How do you feel?"

"Angry. Hurt. But at the same time . . ." Her voice drifted off as she gazed at a point on the wall across from her. "Relieved. I've waited a long time to—well, I never thought I'd get the chance to—I'm glad you made me do that." Blanndynne flicked her gaze to Diomedes, a small grin on her face. "I felt . . . in control."

"Good," Diomedes said, a smirk on his lips. "I was hoping you would."

Blanndynne moved her hand, and the piece of her vessel appeared in her fingers. "I didn't know you kept a piece," she said, rubbing her thumb over it.

Diomedes chuckled. "Don't remember why, but I'm glad I did."

"I am too." Blanndynne clutched the shard in her hand, and it disappeared again. She sighed, her brows knitting together when she looked back at Diomedes.

"What?" he asked, raising an eyebrow.

"You just . . ." Her sigh turned into a short laugh. "You've given me more than anyone ever has. I feel powerful around you. It's addictive."

"I can understand that," he said, thinking of the intoxicating way magic called to him. "And I'm proud of you."

A groan came from the head of the cot. Diomedes straightened, and Blanndynne scrambled to her knees.

"Armannii?" she said, her voice filled with a hesitancy Diomedes had never heard before. Blanndynne placed a hand on his bare shoulder, rubbing it in gentle circles.

"B? What happened?" Armannii rasped. His voice was muffled, but the sound of it had Diomedes jumping to his feet.

"You got stung, you idiot," Diomedes said as he crossed the room to see Armannii's face.

Armannii shifted, turning so he was facing them, though he still lay on his stomach. "I'm the idiot? That's a rare occurrence. You must be basking in this." His voice was weak, but the small smile across his pale lips sent a waterfall of relief through Diomedes.

"Believe me, that's the last thing I'm doing. How do you feel?" Diomedes crossed his arms over his chest.

"You know that time we were at that tavern near the boulder field in the eastern part of the Black Forest, and that guy tried to lift a rock the size of a small kid but ended up stuck underneath?"

"That good, huh?"

"Try fifty boulders, and you might be getting toward how I'm feeling." Armannii tried to push himself up, but he hissed and collapsed back down.

Blanndynne sat back on her heels. "I flew you to this town and then went back for—"

"You left him in the desert with the crawlers?" Armannii's face and voice both darkened as he looked at Blanndynne.

"She did what I asked her to do," Diomedes said, drawing Armannii's ire away from Blanndynne. "You should thank her. She saved your life. And if you hadn't noticed, I'm not the one on a cot with a sting wound." He moved his hands to his hips, and Armannii exhaled loudly.

"At least we're back to normal."

"Meaning?" Blanndynne asked, tucking a stray hair behind her ear.

"Didi is back to being the idiot out of the three of us."

Diomedes rolled his eyes and shrugged. "If this is what happens when you're the idiot, then I think we're better off with it being someone else."

"Fair point," Armannii said. "Now one of you needs to get my rune pen out of my vest so we can get going."

"Blanndynne doesn't know the healing rune, and I'm sure I don't need to point out why I can't help with that."

Armannii snorted. "Ironically, I think you'd be better at runes than B. But I'm not asking either of you to draw the healing rune. I'll do it myself."

"No offense, but you can't even sit up." Diomedes shook his head. "How in the world do you think you're going to be able to—"

"Shut up, give me my pen, and I'll show you," Armannii growled. He glared at Diomedes until he moved to get the pen. "Thank you." The words carried every bit of bite the elf seemed to be able to muster as Diomedes placed the rune pen in Armannii's wiggling fingers.

"Now what?" Diomedes asked, crossing his arms as he leaned against the wall.

"Now I just have to . . ." Armannii's voice trailed off as he rocked to one side, wincing. Since Diomedes had sliced Armannii's tunic down the back, it fell forward and off the side of his shoulder when he moved. "Which one of you do I have to thank for this?"

Diomedes snorted. "Get on with healing yourself already."

"So it was you?"

Shrugging, Diomedes suppressed a grin as he watched Armannii switch the pen to his right hand. Still on his stomach, he reached up as far across his body as he could and pressed the pen into his left shoulder. But he paused.

"Now's the part where you actually draw the rune," Diomedes said.

Armannii closed his eyes, his face scrunching in what must've been concentration. "I don't want to accidentally draw it backward. Give me a second." He furrowed his eyebrows further as he began moving the pen over his shoulder. The lines he drew glowed a faint red and grew brighter the more strokes he drew. A bead of sweat blossomed on his temple, and he clenched his jaw.

"Are you—"

171

"Fine," Armannii spat, interrupting Blanndynne before she could finish her question. "I'm fine. I just forgot how much this thing burns," he said through gritted teeth. With a loud exhale, he lowered the pen and rested his head on the thin pillow.

Armannii didn't open his eyes, but Diomedes didn't need to see the gold in them to know he was lying. Every muscle in his body had tensed, and he gripped the pen tight enough that Diomedes thought he might snap it in two.

"Give it to me," Diomedes said, prying the pen out of his fingers. He looked at Blanndynne. "Get him some water."

She moved to the canteens as Armannii dug his fingers into the mattress beneath him. He clawed at it, and if he hadn't been clamping his mouth shut, Diomedes had a feeling his friend would've been screaming. Armannii's face was red, and just like when he had been unconscious and under the effects of the crawler poison, he was drenched in sweat.

The only thing Diomedes and Blanndynne could do was watch as Armannii suffered on the cot. But the longer they stood there, the more Diomedes turned his attention to the wound on Armannii's back. It began to close. After minutes of Armannii grunting and hissing, he began to quiet down, and a new layer of pink skin covered the puncture wound.

"As useful as it is," Armannii said, out of breath, "that has to be one of my least favorite runes." With a cringe, he pushed himself up until he was sitting. He placed a hand to his head, running his fingers through his hair and then over his face.

Blanndynne handed him the canteen she'd been holding, and he thanked her before downing the whole thing.

"Ah," he said, panting. "It's good to be alive." He grinned up at them as he swung his legs over the side of the cot. "When do we leave?"

"Seriously?" Blanndynne asked, her voice rising as she took the empty canteen. "You just came back from the brink of death. You need to rest and—"

"I'm good," Armannii said, dismissing her comment with a wave. "I've been lying in bed for—how long have I been in bed?"

"I'm guessing somewhere around twenty-four hours." Diomedes shrugged when Blanndynne glared at him. "What? He asked."

"And you make it sound like you weren't worried the whole time," she retorted.

"Aw, Didi, were you worried about me?" Armannii asked, a glint in his eye as he raised his hand to his chest. "I'm touched."

"Shut up," Diomedes said, sitting in the chair. "If you say you're ready to go, then I say we leave."

"Great, I'll just change and—"

"When it's night again," Diomedes added. "We don't want to travel during the day. Believe me."

"What time is it now?" Armannii asked, rolling his neck in small circles as he spoke.

"Early morning, I'd guess. It'll be better to wait until dusk." Diomedes glanced at Blanndynne.

"Thank you," she mouthed, but he didn't do anything to give away that he wasn't being completely truthful. It was probably past midnight, but Diomedes wasn't sure.

Though he was thankful Armannii was okay and eager to keep going, he could also tell that both he and Blanndynne needed to sleep in more than single-hour increments.

"All right," Armannii said with a deep sigh. "Then I guess you can tell me how you got out of a nest of crawlers alive and on foot with no speed runes."

"Isn't it obvious?" Diomedes said, raising an eyebrow at the confused look crossing Armannii's face. "I used my sword."

Armannii snickered. "And I'm sure you weren't nervous at all."

"Not a bit." Diomedes grinned.

"Liar," Armannii said as he ran his hand over the back of his neck. "But I'll hand it to you. What you did is impressive."

"Blanndynne's the one who has been flying everywhere," Diomedes said, tilting his head toward the genie. She blushed, smoothing out her tunic.

"And you came back from the dead," Blanndynne added.

"So what you're saying is"—Armannii raised an eyebrow, a broad smile crossing his face—"we're all incredible."

Chapter Eighteen

Diomedes startled awake when Blanndynne tapped him on the shoulder. Her hair was frizzy on one side, and she ran her fingers through it to smooth it down as she nodded toward Elias, who must've just emerged from the back room.

"What?" Diomedes asked, his voice quiet despite his racing heart. He glanced over at Armannii, who—despite protesting profusely about going back to bed—was sound asleep. He had tried to get Diomedes to take the cot, but Diomedes had refused. As uncomfortable as the floor was, there were still enough stains from Armannii's blood and the poisonous ooze on the thin mattress that he preferred the floor.

"He wants to talk to you," Blanndynne said, her voice a low whisper, though it didn't hide the irritation in her voice.

Diomedes scratched the side of his face and nodded. He used the wall to push himself to his feet, then crossed the room and stood beside Elias.

"I wanted to thank you," Diomedes said, his voice gravelly from just waking up. "He woke up a little while ago."

Elias ventured a glance at Armannii, then returned his gaze to Diomedes. "One of you used a healing rune," he said, surprising Diomedes.

"Well, yes." Diomedes rubbed the back of his neck. "He did."

"He needs to be careful. The wound may be fused, but there may still be adverse effects from both the venom and the injury. I've read of it leading to terrible nightmares and—"

"I'll keep an eye on him," Diomedes said. "Have you had a chance to read through the book on curses yet?" Diomedes couldn't help it as his curiosity crept in.

"I've spent some time reading it, but there are many curses listed. It'll take me a while to read through all of it," Elias said, casting a hesitant glance at Blanndynne.

She was all but ignoring him, her attention on Armannii. It was probably for the best.

"Well, I hope you find the answers you're looking for," Diomedes said.

"I do too. I'm going to go sleep for a few hours. Wake me before you leave." He returned to his room. In the split second the door was open, Diomedes could make out writing all over the wall—not on paper, but the wall itself.

Diomedes walked back to the head of the cot and sat down on the floor, which was still warm from where he'd been lying.

"I think he's scared of you," Diomedes said, a slight grin on his lips.

Blanndynne snorted. Her gaze remained focused on Armannii, who breathed steadily as he slept. She didn't engage Diomedes on the topic, and Diomedes respected her unspoken desire.

Though a fresh layer of skin covered the wound, Armannii still slept on his stomach. Diomedes watched his friend's back rise and fall with each breath and felt his own eyes getting heavy again.

"What time do you think it is?" Blanndynne asked, breaking the hypnotic trance Armannii's breathing had pulled Diomedes into.

"Don't know. But I do know a quick way to find out," Diomedes said, rubbing his eyes with the palms of his hands.

Blanndynne took the hint and stood up. When she opened the front door, a warm wind blew in, and Diomedes wondered how Armannii hadn't woken up. She shut it before the temperature outside could influence the cool inside.

"Early morning," she said as she sat back down. "At least, that's my guess. The sky is still a little pink."

Diomedes pushed his hair out of his face. "So we've got some more time to rest. Take advantage of it. We leave at sundown."

Several hours later, Diomedes woke up to find Armannii digging around in his bag. His ripped tunic lay in a crumpled pile on the floor, and he had yet to find a new one. Blanndynne was nowhere to be seen, but Diomedes didn't have to ask where she was because a few of the canteens were also missing.

"When'd she leave for the well?" Diomedes asked, stretching his sore back.

Armannii glanced at the empty chair before going back to rummaging around in his bag. "She just stepped out. I told her she'd wake you when she left. I was right." He snorted.

Diomedes caught sight of a triangle—a dull arrowhead—hanging from a twine cord around Armannii's neck. He had made note of the necklace before but had never asked about it. Armannii had always kept it tucked in his tunic, away from prying eyes.

"What?" Armannii asked, and Diomedes glanced up to notice him staring.

"Never pegged you as a jewelry type," Diomedes said, nodding toward the necklace.

Armannii's jaw tightened, but he forced a smile. "What, you're the only man who can wear a necklace?" he asked, referencing the royal medallion Diomedes had tucked under the neckline of his own tunic.

After a few more seconds, Armannii finally pulled out a dark green tunic. He shook it out and, with a grumpy look at its wrinkled state, put it on.

"How's your back?" Diomedes asked, noting that his friend had not winced while putting the shirt on. A good sign.

"You slept on the floor. How's yours?" Armannii said, fixing his hair. He nodded toward his vest, which lay near Diomedes. "It's better." Armannii caught the vest when Diomedes tossed it to him.

"And you're sure you want to come? You could stay here a little longer and—"

"Not an option," Armannii said, rising to his feet.

"Fair enough," Diomedes said, joining him. As he gathered up his bag and put his sword and sheath back on, he watched his friend out of the corner of his eye.

Armannii moved slower than he normally did, but he didn't complain. His bow and quiver rested against the wall near the door, and he ran his fingers over the bow. "It's a good thing she grabbed these," he said, his voice soft, almost pensive. He reached up with his other hand and ran his fingers over the string holding the arrowhead around his neck.

Diomedes paused, watching him. "Can I ask you a question?"

"Sure, but it'll cost you a . . ." Whatever joke Armannii had been about to crack faded away, as did his smile, when he turned and noticed Diomedes, whose face was serious. "What?"

"Who's Kit?" Diomedes asked, his voice low. He studied Armannii's reaction, noting the way his friend struggled to swallow.

"You heard me when I was—" Armannii paused, nodding toward the cot. "Right? You heard me when I was crying out. I know you were here. It's like I could tell what was going on in reality, but I couldn't reach it."

"I did, but you weren't exactly speaking in full sentences."

Armannii looked down, his eyebrows knitting together. "The venom, or maybe it was whatever you used to cure me, had a strange effect. I relived things . . . saw people I know to be . . ." His voice trailed off.

"Dead?" Diomedes leaned forward against the chair, resting his hands on the back of it.

Armannii cleared his throat, his eyes still on the ground. "Yes. And . . . I was in the Dark."

Diomedes moved around to sit in the chair. While he rarely pushed Armannii to open up—a favor Armannii returned—Diomedes couldn't help the curiosity creeping through him.

Armannii pursed his lips. "The woman I cared about died. I wasn't there to stop it, didn't actually see it happen. Just saw the . . . *her* body after. But in my head, while I was hallucinating, it was like all I could see was her death, or I guess how my mind pictured it had happened."

Diomedes leaned forward, resting his elbows on his legs as he clasped his fingers under his chin. "Kit?"

"Kit." Armannii's voice was a whisper. He rubbed the back of his head. "She shouldn't have died." Armannii finally looked up from the ground, meeting Diomedes's gaze. "I think you would've liked her. She . . . she was a lot like you. Stubborn, but for the right reasons. A pure heart. She wanted to make the world better, whether it was just for her and her brother or for the rest of the people in the Dark."

"Sounds like we would've gotten along," Diomedes agreed, rubbing the side of his jaw with his thumb. "I'm sorry she's gone."

"Mm-hmm," Armannii said, turning his back to Diomedes.

Unsure what to say next, Diomedes stayed quiet as he stood up again. Thankfully, the silence, which felt more awkward with every passing second, was broken when Blanndynne walked in from outside.

"Glad you're up and about," Blanndynne said to them. "Sun is about to go down."

"Good," Armannii said, straightening his shoulders.

Having known him for years, Diomedes could see the walls around Armannii stacking back up as if he had never mentioned Kit in the first place.

"We'll leave in a few minutes then?" Diomedes asked, and they nodded. "I'll tell Elias."

"Elias?" Armannii raised an eyebrow, pausing as he unscrewed the canteen Blanndynne had just handed him. "Who?"

"You tell him. I'll wait outside." She glared at Elias's door before leaving.

"Was it something I said?" Armannii asked, scratching his head when he turned his attention from the front door to Diomedes.

Diomedes shook his head. "Not really." He took a deep breath, wondering how best to tell Armannii that his ancestor was sleeping in the next room. "The man who saved you just so happens to be Blanndynne's last master." Diomedes held up a finger to stop Armannii from interrupting. "It gets more complicated than that."

"Course it does," Armannii muttered, taking another swig from the canteen. "Go on."

"He's also Kylian's older brother, and nobody remembers him, most likely because of a curse laid on him."

Armannii frowned. "When did we enter into some sort of fairy tale?"

"And he also looks like he's in his thirties. Oh, and apparently Blanndynne has told us about him multiple times and we keep forgetting."

"This just keeps getting better." Armannii glanced at the front door. "Why does this make B so upset? I mean, besides the fact that we keep forgetting."

"Elias was supposed to free her, but he went back on his word and betrayed her trust. He's the reason she was in the vessel for a century." Diomedes leaned against the wall.

"So her anger is justified," Armannii said, and Diomedes nodded.

"Just a bit," Diomedes said, pushing off the wall and crossing the room to Elias's door. "But he did save your life, so I'm not completely against the guy."

"I suppose that means I can't be either." Armannii adjusted his tunic as Diomedes knocked on the door.

"That's up to you." Diomedes stepped back, waiting for Elias to emerge. It took a minute, but his ancestor finally entered the main room.

"You seem to be doing well," Elias said, crossing his arms over his chest. "I'm Elias."

"Armannii," the elf said, his voice wary as he shook Elias's outstretched hand. "I suppose I have you to thank for the lack of death happening in my life."

Elias nodded. "That's one way to put it."

Armannii glanced from Diomedes to Elias, who stood side by side. "I guess I can see some sort of resemblance," Armannii said, narrowing his eyes as if he couldn't see. "But I kind of have to squint a bit."

"We wanted to thank you again before we left," Diomedes cut in before Armannii could make any more jokes.

"As overwhelming as it has been, you've given me answers I've been seeking for apparently a very long time. I'm sure she doesn't want to hear it from me, but I'm grateful to your friend for telling me who I am—where I came from," Elias said, stepping forward.

"She's outside already," Diomedes said, keeping his words clipped. When Elias turned to him, Diomedes held out his hand. "I wish you the best of luck in your research." His ancestor had a firmer handshake than he'd expected, and it reminded him of his father's. It was unsettling, and Diomedes pulled away as soon as he could.

"Thanks again, mate," Armannii said, giving Elias a two-finger salute as he backed toward the door. "Next time I get stung by one of those southern sand demons, I'll know where to go."

"I'd recommend not traveling through the southern desert. It's quite dangerous to travel in the desert at all, and—"

"Right, thanks," Armannii said, rolling his eyes as he left. "It was a joke," he muttered under his breath, though Diomedes doubted Elias had heard it.

Diomedes was the last out of the house, and he nodded once more to Elias before he shut the door and joined Blanndynne and Armannii at the edge of the house.

The arid wind whipped around them as they left the town. Though the sun was sinking behind the horizon, the heat of the day remained. It didn't take long before they were covered in sweat.

Armannii led the way, but he wasn't as difficult to keep up with as usual. Though he was good at hiding the strain he was going through, Diomedes could still see it.

Blanndynne kept her eye on Armannii, and Diomedes didn't blame her. It seemed they were both waiting for him to keel over.

But he kept going.

Diomedes let Blanndynne and Armannii walk ahead of him, and he allowed his mind to wander as Blanndynne answered more of Armannii's questions about Elias. It was expected, and maybe it was because of Armannii's uncharacteristically serious demeanor or the fact that he had almost died, but Blanndynne had more patience with him when he asked than she had when she'd told Diomedes about her past with Elias at Camile and Forrest's house.

The temperature dropped as the first moon popped over the opposite horizon, and Diomedes pulled his cloak tighter.

"It'll keep getting colder," Armannii said, pausing to catch his breath, yet another thing he hadn't done before the crawler attack. "We'll be out of the desert by the time the sun rises."

"Which means we'll have to walk all night," Diomedes said under his breath.

"And the mountains will be cooler," Armannii added, pulling out his canteen.

"Because goodness forbid Phildeterre have a place that isn't burning hot or freezing cold," Diomedes grumbled.

"Why do you think so many people live in the Black Forest?" Armannii said, shrugging. "Weather is pretty pleasant if you ask me."

Around the time the largest moon was in the middle of the sky, the dunes began to get smaller, and Diomedes's leg muscles were crying out in pain.

"Should I fly ahead and see how much farther it is?" Blanndynne asked, watching Armannii sip his water. For the second time that night, Armannii had been the one to ask for a break instead of Diomedes.

The elf shook his head. "We should be able to see the mountains in the distance once we get over these last few dunes. If it were day, we'd probably see them already."

Armannii was right. After climbing up five or six more dunes, they paused. The Elemental Mountains towered on the horizon, silhouetted by the light of the moons.

"I definitely thought we were closer," Diomedes muttered before heading down the dune.

They walked in silence for a while as the sandy ground beneath them shifted to sturdier dirt with dead plants sprouting out of it. Diomedes flinched when one of the bushes caught his hand within its thorny grasp. The brush grew denser as the mountains got closer.

They continued their trek, and with every passing hour, the sky got lighter and their destination got closer.

"Blanndynne, I need you to do me a favor," Diomedes said when the sun peeked over the horizon. They had paused near a grove of trees, and Blanndynne nodded for him to continue. "Follow Mellacross's map. He—or I guess the sorceress—gave specific instructions for how to approach the mountains. I need you to make sure we're approaching the right one."

"And the right one is . . . ?" She glanced up at the mountains. They were a wall in front of them, rising out of the ground and blocking most of their view.

"It's shaped like a crescent moon at the top. He said the entrance to the caves is between the third and fourth mountains in from the sea. I need you to fly west and make sure we head down the right valley."

"I could just run and—" Armannii started to say.

"No." Blanndynne stopped Armannii before he could reach into his vest for his rune pen. "I'll go. It'll be easier to see from the sky."

Armannii opened his mouth to argue, but he didn't have time before Blanndynne lifted off the ground.

"Fine," the elf mumbled, watching her disappear from sight. "We'll just set up camp then."

Although Diomedes didn't want to stop, at least not mentally, his aching body was grateful for the rest. When he looked at the mountains, excitement stirred within him. In another two days or so, they'd finally be at the cave entrance. At least, that was his hope.

Diomedes was doing his best to focus on anything but the slow passage of time when Blanndynne found them again. She landed on the ground in front of them, her face shiny from exertion. Besides the sweat and being slightly winded, she seemed to be handling the extended periods of flight better.

"We need to head more toward the west." She turned and pointed toward the mountains. "See the one that has a steep drop-off on the right side of the peak? That's the fifth mountain from the sea."

"You're sure?" Diomedes asked, shielding his eyes from the light of the rising sun. "It looks like it could be a crescent moon from a different angle."

Blanndynne shook her head. "The fourth mountain is hiding behind that one. You can't see it from the ground."

"Then I guess it's a good thing you went to go look," Armannii said, handing her a canteen.

"We'll head that way after we all rest up," Diomedes said, his attention on the mountains that would bring him one step closer to magic.

Chapter Nineteen

A day and a half of walking later, most of which had been spent going up and down foothills, Diomedes and Armannii stood waiting for Blanndynne to check their direction again. The brush they'd entered into the first day had turned into full woods, though they weren't nearly as congested as the Black Forest. It made navigation difficult. Multiple times a day, Blanndynne went up into the air to make sure they were headed for the correct valley.

When she returned with news that they were headed in the right direction, they waited for her to catch her breath before they continued. Eventually, they reached a spring that ran down and turned perpendicular to them.

"It runs into the sea," Blanndynne said as she nodded toward the crystal clear water. "I followed it partway when I flew over. From above, it looked like we need to stick to the right of it."

"Then to the right we go." Armannii held up his hand to stop them. "After I wash off. I've got enough filth on me to—"

"I don't need to hear the end of that sentence," Blanndynne said, her expression pinched as she shook her head. "Just go." She nodded toward the stream.

Diomedes joined Armannii, braving the cold runoff, though its temperature was nothing compared to his memory of the Cyro Sea. He was sure Armannii shared his sentiments. Despite the cold, it felt good to rinse the stubborn sand from his skin.

By the time they had cleared most of the sand from their bodies, Diomedes was shivering, eager to start moving again. Blanndynne sat on a boulder near the water, watching as they sloshed out of the stream.

"Better. Shall we?" Armannii pointed his bow to the right, gesturing for them to follow.

The trees grew denser the farther in they journeyed, but it was never enough to block out the sun like in the Black Forest. It was, however, an appreciated source of shade once Diomedes warmed up again.

"Really?" Armannii muttered when he took a step too near the spring and sank up to the rim of his boot in mud.

Diomedes snickered as he offered a hand to pull Armannii out. Unfortunately, when he grasped Armannii's wrist and tugged, Armannii's foot came out, but not the shoe.

"B, help me out?" Armannii asked, balancing on one foot while using Diomedes's arm to steady himself.

Blanndynne grinned as she floated above the mud and pulled his boot out without touching the ground. Half an inch of grime covered the boot, and before she handed it back to him, she flew to the river and let the water run over it.

"Thank you," Armannii said, still leaning on Diomedes as he put on his missing boot.

About halfway through the day, they paused underneath the shade of a few trees and had lunch, which Blanndynne had purchased from the underground market.

"Think we'll make it to the valley before nightfall?" Diomedes asked, rolling his shoulders after taking off his bag. He could feel the tension in his muscles with each movement, and the strain had created an ache that crept up his neck and was just beginning to cause a headache.

"Definitely." Armannii nodded, ripping a chunk of dried and seasoned meat from the piece he held. "If we keep going at this pace, we might even make it to the base of the waterfall."

A wave of excitement washed over Diomedes, but he refrained from letting it reach his face. If everything went well, he could be walking out of the caves the next day with the ability to end the war.

Blanndynne offered him an apple, and he took it, staring at his boots as he crunched down.

"What do you think is in the caves?" he asked, wiping a trail of juice from his mouth with the back of his sleeve. "Think it's anything like the maze in the Dark?"

"I have a feeling it'll be equally set with traps, if not worse." Armannii leaned back against the tree. There was still a trace of darkness underneath his eyes, but he hadn't complained about his weaker condition since they'd left the town.

"Hope not," Diomedes muttered. His mind brought up memories of bloodthirsty flying spiders and water enchanted with runes that were deadly to all nonmagic people. He didn't want to think about how it could get worse than what they'd seen there.

"It is the sorceress we're talking about. I'm sure she wasn't exactly keen on just anyone walking into her secret hidey-hole," Armannii said with a shrug.

"Yeah . . ." Diomedes's voice trailed off as he ate his apple.

Once they had eaten their fill, they continued their trek to the mountains. The valley—or canyon, rather—that wound between the third and fourth mountains narrowed the farther in they went. It was still uphill, and Diomedes's calves were shrieking in agony.

The sun had left the canyon when Armannii paused, tilting his head to the side. Blanndynne and Diomedes remained quiet, waiting to be told what the elf had heard. In the silence, the stream—which had grown and taken up more room in the canyon until they had no choice but to walk through it at times—trickled and mixed with a breeze rustling the leaves of the vegetation around them. The air was almost as fresh as it had been the few times Blanndynne had flown carrying Diomedes.

If Diomedes hadn't been as chock-full of anticipation to reach the caves as he was, it would've been peaceful.

"I hear water," Armannii said, turning back to them with a grin.

"Need I remind you that we're walking next to a stream?" Diomedes asked, nodding to the side at the clear waters.

"A *waterfall*, Didi," Armannii said, wiggling his eyebrows. "I think we're almost there."

Diomedes strained his ears, trying to hear what Armannii heard, but it was no use. He urged his aching muscles to move faster and tried to hide his frustration when his friends stopped to take in the beautiful views from the inside of the grayish-purple walls of rock. It wasn't until they'd followed the canyon around several more turns that Diomedes heard the waterfall. That spurred him on more than Armannii's mention of it. The closer they got, the more real it all became, and the faster Diomedes moved. The water level rose as they passed a few dams, and the roar grew louder with each step.

"That's more impressive than I thought it'd be!" Armannii shouted when they rounded the final corner. He craned his neck, looking toward the rim of the canyon, where water thundered down. The canyon opened up into a wide circle, and at the center towered a waterfall.

It must've been at least one hundred stories tall. It was hard to tell from the bottom, especially with the mist and droplets of water spraying in their faces. The breeze coming off the cliffside was frigid, and Diomedes rolled the sleeves of his tunic down to compensate. A large pool of clear water collected at the bottom and drained out through the stream they'd been following.

Blanndynne tugged her cloak tighter, and Diomedes watched his friends' reactions, amusement written across his face. Or maybe it was pride that they had reached one of the important landmarks Mellacross had pointed out.

"We're supposed to climb up this thing?" Armannii asked, his voice skeptical as he turned to glance at the wall to the right of the waterfall. It went straight up, and while there were cracks in the wall that were likely able to be climbed, one mistake would mean death. "I mean, I'm up for an adventure, but it might be our last . . ."

The sight of the waterfall sparked something inside Diomedes, and he tapped his foot, frowning. "Can you fly us up? That'll be the quickest way," he said, shouting over the thunder from the falls.

Blanndynne nodded. "Shouldn't be a problem."

"Good," Armannii said, finally taking his eyes away from the waterfall and cliffside to glance back at her. "Because there's no way he was making it up this cliff without help."

Diomedes rolled his eyes, but he didn't disagree. When Mellacross had mentioned scaling the side of a wet cliff, Diomedes had expected maybe a two- or three-hundred-foot waterfall, not fifteen hundred feet. That sounded to him like a quick way to die.

"Take him first." Armannii gestured to Diomedes.

Blanndynne gripped Diomedes under the arms like she had in the desert, and without so much as a warning, she soared into the sky. Diomedes's eyes widened, but he didn't say anything as they flew up the side of the cliff. A mixture of air and mist whipped around them, and goose bumps rose on his skin. After a few seconds, his feet landed on solid ground.

He stumbled when she put him down, but before he could go over the edge, Blanndynne caught his arm and yanked him back up. His stomach dropped. Her fingers tightened around his arm.

"Thanks." Diomedes took a deep breath, trying to ease the adrenaline the flight had sparked. It didn't seem like a wise idea to combine his shaky legs and a hundred-story fall, even if there was water at the bottom.

"I'm going down for him. Don't get too close to the edge. It seems slippery." With that said, Blanndynne dove off the edge.

Despite her warning, he took cautious steps and approached the cliff. Diomedes leaned over. He'd never been afraid of heights, but something about the fall straight down left him light-headed.

Below him, Armannii was an ant. Blanndynne landed next to him, and a second later they were soaring up the side of the cliff.

"Well that's a rush," Armannii said, a wide grin on his face as he landed next to Diomedes. He ran his fingers through his hair, his shoulders shaking as he let out a loud laugh. "Think you'd be able to catch me if I jumped off?"

"Let's not find out," Blanndynne said, fixing her wind-tousled hair. "Where do we go from here?"

Distracted by the waterfall and the drop, Diomedes had barely taken in the upper level of the cliff. It was flat for forty feet before the rock face continued to shoot up to the sky, forming the upper half of the mountain. The flat area was split in two by the thundering spring of water, which burst forth from a crevice in the mountain. On the opposite side of the stream of water, it looked as though a path led around the edge of the upper part of the mountain, though Diomedes couldn't see much more without risking his life on the edge of the cliff. Though the surroundings were primarily rock or water, there were some scrubby bushes growing near the cliffs in front of them.

Diomedes's curiosity drew him to a mossy section of the mountain to the right of the water source. The moss grew up the side of a wall of stone, and when he stepped closer, he tilted his head.

He withdrew his sword from his sheath, using it to poke at the moss. The blade went straight through. Diomedes pushed the green vegetation to the side, using his sword to widen a hole big enough for a person to walk through. Behind the moss was a dark tunnel that led down at a slant.

"Well, that answers that question," Armannii said, joining Diomedes at the mouth of the cave as he returned his sword to its sheath. "Who's first?"

Pulling out his rune-inscribed glasses, Diomedes walked through the entrance before anyone said anything else.

"Didi, wait," Armannii said.

Diomedes had gone a few paces when he noticed Armannii and Blanndynne weren't behind him. They stood at the mouth of the cave. Blanndynne lifted her hair off to the side so Armannii could draw the sight rune on her neck. When he'd finished drawing hers, she joined Diomedes inside the cave.

Unexpected annoyance turned Diomedes's stomach. When he tried to determine where it had come from, he realized it was because the moment he'd stepped foot in the cave, eagerness had been pulling him farther in. Stopping seemed almost impossible— and a waste of time. It was almost as if he felt the object calling out to him from the heart of the mountain. He wanted to find it. *Needed* to find it. Now.

Armannii blinked a few times once he'd finished his own sight rune. He tucked his rune pen into his vest and picked up his bow, which he'd leaned against the cave wall.

Diomedes tapped his foot, his arms crossed as he waited for Armannii to catch up. When Armannii started toward them, Diomedes turned and led the way.

"I guess we're following you then," Armannii mumbled from behind him.

The path was straight forward until they reached a point where the cave branched into two different directions. Diomedes paused, cocking his head to each side as he weighed the options. Somewhere in the back of his mind, an air of worry filled him. How many different paths were there? He tried to remember what the sorceress had said through Mellacross, but it felt like the conversation had happened years ago.

"You *do* know where we're going, right?" Armannii asked, not even trying to hide the skepticism in his voice.

"She said I'd know the way."

"How reassuring," Armannii said, and when Diomedes glanced sideways at him, the elf rolled his eyes.

"Mellacross was utterly vague," Diomedes said, gritting his teeth as he shook his head. "Can you send some light down each way? Maybe that'll help."

Blanndynne obliged, sending a stream of light down the right tunnel first and then the left. The paths looked identical.

"I'm glad that cleared things up." Armannii leaned against the tunnel wall, crossing his arms over his chest as he waited.

Diomedes ignored his friend, frowning in each direction. "Well, I suppose we can go down one, and if it doesn't lead anywhere, we can come back and try the other. Unless you have something useful to suggest?"

Armannii shook his head. "I've never been here either."

"Then we'll go right first. If it doesn't start descending down or ends in a dead end, we'll come back. Okay?"

"Lead the way, Didi." Armannii swung one arm to the side, gesturing toward Diomedes.

Chapter Twenty

At first, Diomedes thought he'd taken the wrong path, but after a few minutes, it began to slant downward. The walls were moist, and he did his best to avoid touching them or leaning against them because it was already much colder in the tunnels. He rubbed his hands together to warm them, but it didn't help as much as he'd hoped. In the end, he had to pull out a small stone with a light rune carved into it so he could see. Even with the rune glasses and Blanndynne carrying an orb of light above the palm of her hand, it was still hard to make out the path in front of him.

"Great," Diomedes muttered when he rounded a corner and came to another intersection of tunnels. This time, there were three.

"What—" Armannii asked as he came around the corner, but he paused. "Oh."

"Well, Mellacross did say there were multiple ways to get where we need to go. Maybe it doesn't matter as much which one we pick," Diomedes said, though even he didn't believe the words coming out of his mouth.

"Any suggestions?" Armannii asked, rubbing the back of his neck as he glanced back the way they'd come.

"We keep going," Diomedes said. His was voice a low mumble as he took the tunnel to the right and continued. Just like in the maze, Diomedes consistently chose the same direction so it would be easier to retrace his steps.

However, when narrow tunnels began branching off on different sides of the one they were in, Diomedes's stomach tightened. It only occurred to Diomedes to mark the way they'd come when it was too late. Still, if a tunnel ended in a dead end, Diomedes paused to mark its entrance with an X scratched into the stone with his knife. He'd need to sharpen it after they got out.

"What if the correct way is down one of these?" Armannii asked after a while, pausing to stick his head in one of the smaller branches. "There have been at least fifty."

"If we're going the wrong direction, we'll find out eventually," Blanndynne said, still in step behind Diomedes.

"This tunnel is still going down," Diomedes added. "If the aim is to get into the bowels of the cave system, my guess is that down is a good thing."

"Then there's also the fact that we haven't run into any traps yet." Armannii caught up to them in a few strides.

Diomedes considered his words. "Is that a complaint? Because I'm all right with the lack of deadly fauna and rune magic."

"I mean, it would make this place a little more interesting, don't you think?" Armannii asked.

"What, the stalactites, stalagmites, and endless tunnels aren't good enough for you?" Blanndynne retorted, and Diomedes glimpsed a smile on the elf's face when he looked over his shoulder.

"What can I say? I prefer caves with a bit more excitement."

"I'll take the boring caves over what we went through in the maze any day," Blanndynne said.

When they turned the next corner, the tunnel ended without warning. Diomedes grimaced before he turned around to face his companions.

"You were saying?" Armannii asked, raising an eyebrow.

Diomedes held his tongue as he pushed past Armannii, following the tunnel to the beginning, where he marked it. Another path branched off to the right. He glanced back at Armannii and Blanndynne, and they both shrugged.

Without a word, he took the path. It, however, held a dead end too. Each tunnel Diomedes chose either came to an abrupt stop or opened up into fifteen more tunnels. After a while, Diomedes felt like a pot of water on a hot stove—ready to boil over.

"This is endless," Diomedes muttered, resisting the urge to hit the wall of another dead end.

"And we've been doing it for the last hour at least." Armannii caught up to him, putting a hand on Diomedes's shoulder. "If we get lost in here, we don't have enough supplies to last more than a day or so. Maybe we should consider—"

"We're not giving up now," Diomedes said, knocking Armannii's hand off him. "Don't you see how close we are?"

"This is a dead end. And besides, I'm not saying we give up." Armannii put his hands on his hips. "I'm just suggesting we go back out, make camp, and see if we can't track down some sort of map. We know where the entrance is, and—"

"And we what? Go chasing after a map that might not even exist? How long do you think that would take?" Diomedes stopped and spun to face Armannii.

"It beats getting lost down here and dying of starvation."

"We're close," Diomedes said, clenching his hands into fists and gritting his teeth. "We just need to keep going."

"What do you think?" Armannii asked, glancing at Blanndynne.

"Maybe we should take a break," Blanndynne said, though she didn't seem tired in the least. "Have a snack or something. Then we can keep going."

Though he had no desire to stop, Diomedes nodded, rubbing the back of his neck as he dropped his bag on the cave floor.

Armannii and Blanndynne sat down too, and Blanndynne made a face when part of her leg ended up in a puddle. The tunnels were moist, and they'd passed sections with water streaming down the sides. Thankfully, this was not one of them.

Blanndynne left an orb of light hovering in the air above them, and Diomedes squinted up at it. How close was he to the object that could give him that kind of power? He turned his focus to finding his canteen in his bag instead of glowering at the light, knowing it would not go unnoticed by his companions.

He found the canteen, but when he pulled it out, a small chain with a rectangular object had tangled itself around the nozzle. The item clinked against the metal canteen, and Diomedes frowned. It took him a second to place the necklace.

"What's that?" Blanndynne asked, pausing as she readjusted the clasp of her cloak, which had rubbed against her collarbone and left a red mark.

"A gift from the sorceress," Diomedes said. He untangled the chain, holding it up to the light. All eyes fell on it. "Raidah said it would help me in my journey, but I guess I forgot about it."

"Think it can show us how to navigate these blasted tunnels?" Armannii asked, stretching his legs out in front of him. A grimace flickered over his face in the second he leaned against the wall, but it disappeared just as quickly.

Diomedes didn't respond, too busy examining the little rectangular mirror. It was a little less than half the length of his pinky finger. His tired appearance reflected back at him, and he adjusted his hair, watching his reflection do the same.

Except it didn't.

Diomedes blinked.

His reflection did not.

Diomedes frowned.

His reflection grinned.

"What is it?" Blanndynne asked, a hint of concern filling her voice. "What do you see?"

"Besides your own hideous reflection," Armannii teased, but the grin dropped from his face when Diomedes glanced up at him with wide eyes. "What?"

"The mirror. It . . . it's not me. I mean, it is. But it wasn't reflecting what I was doing." Diomedes handed Armannii the necklace when his friend held his hand out.

"Looks normal to me," Armannii said after a second of examining it.

"Me too," Blanndynne agreed, leaning over Armannii's shoulder to look at the mirror.

"Give it to me," Diomedes said, grasping the mirror when Armannii handed it back to him.

Diomedes stood up, holding the mirror closer to the light. He tilted it, his brow furrowing when his reflection nodded its head.

"What in the world?" he muttered, turning it the other direction. When he did so, the reflection shook his head. Diomedes glanced at the dead end the necklace was pointed toward. A whisper of an idea entered his mind, and he turned it back toward the open tunnel in the direction from which they'd come.

The reflection nodded again.

"I'll be back. Don't move," Diomedes muttered, grabbing his light rune stone and leaving down the tunnel. He ignored his friends' questions as he held the light out in front of him. The next split he reached, he held the light up to the mirror, pointing it in the direction of the new tunnel. The reflection shook its head. Diomedes directed the necklace down the main tunnel, and the reflection nodded.

After he checked several other tunnels, Diomedes returned with a grin on his face.

"Well?" Armannii asked. Both he and Blanndynne were already standing, clearly waiting for him to return.

"It's exactly what you wanted," Diomedes said, sticking his canteen back in his bag before returning it to his shoulder. "The reflection tells me where to go."

"How?" Blanndynne asked while Armannii raised an eyebrow.

"I don't know, magic?" Diomedes said, passing them. He held the necklace and light rune stone in front of him as before and led Blanndynne and Armannii down the tunnel.

"It doesn't look to me like it's changing," Armannii said from behind him. "What's it supposed to be doing?"

"You don't see my reflection nodding or shaking its head?" Diomedes asked, holding it up so Armannii could get an even clearer view of the reflection confirming they were going in the right direction.

"Nope. I see my handsome face when you hold it like that."

Diomedes's eyebrows creased, but he didn't add to the conversation as he kept following the mirror. In the back of his mind, he knew he should've questioned how the mirror worked. But in light of each step in what appeared to be the right direction—they hadn't hit any more dead ends—his mind could only think of one thing.

The object.

Gaining magic.

Power.

Chapter Twenty-One

The path curved, and the sight stopped Diomedes dead in his tracks. The skeletal remains of five bodies were strewn about the floor in front of them.

"Is this mess more to your taste?" Diomedes asked, turning around to glare at Armannii. "You wanted traps." He flung his arm out toward the skeletons.

"Much better," Armannii said with a forced grin, which he dropped as he stepped next to Diomedes. "But a better question is what should we be looking for so we don't end up like our friends over there. I don't know about you, but the whole lack of skin and muscle thing isn't really my style."

Diomedes scanned the floor, walls, and ceiling but didn't find anything that would indicate a lurking trap. His gaze fell on the bodies again, and something familiar caught his eye. "I think they've been here since the final siege on this place. They're all wearing royal guard uniforms." Diomedes tucked the necklace into his pocket and the rune stone into his bag; Blanndynne was lighting up the room with her magic, so there was no need for his anymore.

"You're right," Blanndynne said, her eyes narrowing on the nearest corpse. "And look at that skull." She pointed a finger, and a wisp of light followed it and hovered around the skeleton, casting it in a silvery glow.

"Is that a puncture wound?" Diomedes asked, squinting. From the vantage point at which he stood, he could just make out a dark hole in the crown of the skull.

"Like something stabbed him from the ceiling," Armannii said, his focus above them. "But I don't see anything that could've done that."

"They all have the same mark," Blanndynne said, guiding the light to each body by moving her fingers. "It has to be what killed them."

"But what triggered it?" Diomedes asked, his focus back on the floor. "A weighted stone maybe?"

"There's one way to find out." Armannii stepped next to him and held his bow out like a walking stick.

Before Diomedes or Blanndynne could stop him, he began tapping the ground in front of him, taking short steps. He kept his eye on the ceiling, but nothing shifted, moved, or creaked. When he'd passed the farthest skeleton, he turned around and shrugged.

"Maybe the trap can only be triggered once," he said.

"Do you want to go next? Or should I?" Diomedes glanced sideways at Blanndynne, who still stared at the nearest skull.

"I'll go," she said. "But I think I'll skip walking, just in case Armannii got lucky."

"I am pretty lucky," Armannii said from the other side, leaning down to rest both hands on the top of his bow as he grinned at them.

In a matter of seconds, Blanndynne stood next to him, and yet again, nothing had triggered.

"Didi, on the other hand . . ." Armannii's voice trailed off as he straightened up and nodded for Diomedes to cross.

Instead of giving his friend another reason to make fun of him, Diomedes stepped forward without hesitation. Nothing happened. At least, he didn't think it had.

But when he met Armannii's gaze, Diomedes's stomach sank. The elf's eyes were wide, staring at a place right above Diomedes's head.

Diomedes looked up. A spear had descended out of the ceiling and hovered an inch above his head. It wasn't connected to anything—simply floated in midair. It was metal, but a dark substance covered the end: dried blood.

When it didn't stab him right away, Diomedes choked over his nerves to ask, "What triggered it?"

"There," Blanndynne said, pointing to a glow coming from behind the nearest dead man. "It has to be a rune."

Armannii's eyes were locked on the spear, and it took Blanndynne smacking him on the arm to pull his attention from it. Even then, his gaze kept flicking from the spear to the purple glow.

"I can't tell what rune it is from here, and I don't want to risk—"

"Believe me," Diomedes said. "I don't want you to risk anything right now either. But can you think of any runes off the top of your head that could manage this?" He tried to keep his voice calm, but even he could hear a sliver of panic slipping in.

Armannii shook his head. "This is serious rune magic. I've never seen anything like it."

"What if I flew over there and—"

"I have a feeling that any movement I make, maybe even something that happens around me, is going to end poorly," Diomedes said, finding it difficult to swallow as he glanced up. Even with the cool air, his forehead was beginning to sweat, and his hands felt clammy as he wiped them on his trousers. The bridge of his nose underneath his sight rune–inscribed glasses was becoming slick too.

The glasses.

"I think I know what triggered it," Diomedes said, his voice low as he pushed the glasses farther up his nose. "Magic."

"You think?" Armannii asked, his voice filled with sarcasm as his focus once again locked on the spear.

"You're not getting it." Diomedes shook his head. "It's like the water in the maze. I think it triggered because I don't have magic."

"But why hasn't it struck you?" Blanndynne asked, pulling her ponytail around her shoulder to run her trembling fingers through it.

"I think whatever magic this is using is confused by the rune on my glasses. It can tell I don't have magic, but I'm also technically using magic."

"It was meant to keep your father and Evangeline out," Armannii said, nodding. "It makes sense. But shouldn't there be more bodies? Most of the royal guard don't have magic, if not all of them. Do you think they continued to pass through?"

"That's not as important right now," Blanndynne said, gesturing toward Diomedes.

"But it is." Armannii frowned at the tunnel. "They had to have gotten through to face the sorceress. How else would she have been defeated?"

"Again, I'm not seeing how that's more important than the spear over his head." Blanndynne's voice was cross.

"If we can figure out how they got past back then, we can get him through." Armannii spoke slowly, as if he were trying to explain it to a child. Blanndynne glared at him.

"Okay," Diomedes said, nodding. Silence fell around them as they began brainstorming ideas. With the spear hanging over his head, Diomedes struggled to sort through any idea that wasn't covered in a layer of panic. It left his thoughts jumbled and confused.

"What if you inscribe something else with a rune and give it to him?" Blanndynne suggested, but Armannii and Diomedes shook their heads at the same time.

"That won't show the trap that I have magic."

"Well, you don't have magic," Blanndynne said, crossing her arms over her chest. "Do either of *you* have any ideas?"

Armannii tilted his head to the side. Something between a frown and a grin sent mixed signals to Diomedes, who watched him.

"I may have an idea."

"What is it? I can't stand still forever." Diomedes couldn't help but glance up at the spear. It hadn't moved.

"If this thing wants to know you have magic, maybe we try to convince it fully." Armannii reached into his vest and pulled out his pen. "I'm not sure this will work, but"—he bent down and picked up a smooth rock, running his thumb over it—"you should write the light rune on here."

"It's not going to work. I don't have—"

"But she does," he said, making sure Diomedes was ready to catch when he tossed the stone to him, followed by the rune pen. "B, when he's finished tracing the rune, you light it up with your magic."

"I guess it's worth a shot." Diomedes stared down at the rock in his hand, twiddling the pen between his fingers. He tried to picture the rune he'd put away in his bag

"It looks like a sun," Armannii said, nodding for him to begin drawing.

"I know, I just don't know where to start."

"The middle, and make sure you go around twice before the five lines on the outside."

Diomedes sighed, sticking his tongue in his cheek as he began drawing, pulling what memories he could of all the times he'd seen Armannii draw it. Just as he'd expected, it didn't begin to glow as he drew it, but when he got to the end, Blanndynne pointed her finger at the rock.

The symbol began to lighten, and due to the new light, Diomedes had to squint when he tilted his chin up to check on the spear.

As before, it hovered there.

"It didn't—" Blanndynne started to say, but Armannii shushed her.

"Look." He motioned toward the rune behind the dead body, which had shifted from purple to yellow, and within another second, the glow disappeared completely.

And so did the spear.

"Come on." Armannii gestured for Diomedes to cross. "Before it changes its mind."

Diomedes jogged the rest of the way across, letting out a breath of relief when he'd reached Blanndynne's side.

"Huh," Armannii said, tucking his pen into his vest after Diomedes had handed it back to him. "I didn't actually think that would work."

"What?" Blanndynne and Diomedes said at the same time.

"Guess I am lucky."

Chapter Twenty-Two

The farther down they went, the more the temperature dropped. The air became even more saturated with moisture, leaving Blanndynne's teeth chattering behind Diomedes. No matter how many times he wiped his hands on his trousers, it felt like they were always clammy as he held the mirror out in front of him.

"Is it still working?" Armannii asked.

"Yes," Diomedes said, trying to keep his annoyance from dripping into his voice. It was the second time Armannii had asked since the spear room.

They walked in silence. Moisture dripped from the stalactites on the ceiling, and every once in a while droplets would land on Diomedes. He wiped a recent drop from his forehead, pausing in the middle of the motion when he rounded another corner.

"Another trap?" Blanndynne asked, stopping next to Diomedes in front of a stone wall with runes carved into it.

"No bodies." Diomedes glanced around after he'd said it to make sure it was true.

"Not a trap," Armannii said, pushing past Diomedes to get a better look. The tunnel had narrowed quite a bit the farther down they'd gone, and Diomedes shifted so Armannii could pass him. "A puzzle. Look." He ran his fingers along the lines of a few of the runes. "There are six of them, and they each represent an element."

Diomedes cocked his head, his gaze focused on the closest rune to him. "This one is light," he said, his brow furrowing.

"Right." Armannii nodded, stepping closer to look at the runes. He stood inches from the wall. "But I'm not sure what to do with them." Armannii sighed, sending a plume of dust out of the crevices in the wall.

One of the runes lit up.

"How did you—" Blanndynne started, but Armannii cut her off with a loud chuckle.

"It's the air rune," he said, his eyes gleaming in the glow of the new light.

Diomedes couldn't help but grin. "Genius."

"Why thank you," Armannii said, dipping into a bow.

"I meant the puzzle. We have to introduce the elements to the runes on the wall." Diomedes ran his fingers over the light rune. "Blanndynne?"

She stepped up, taking his place in front of the wall, and with a flick of her finger, she sent out a stream of light that flashed over all the runes. The light rune held on to the glow after Blanndynne backed up next to Diomedes.

Diomedes pulled out his canteen, his eyes focused on the rune he recognized for water. He splashed it. A bright cyan glow spread through the wavy lines, and he grinned.

"Looks like we're on a bit of a timer," Armannii said, making Diomedes frown.

"What do you mean?"

Armannii pointed to the air rune, which was beginning to dull.

"Refresh it," Diomedes said, shrugging off Armannii's concern. But when Armannii tried to blow on the rune again, it didn't get brighter. It continued to fade in front of their eyes.

"We better get the others finished fast," Armannii said, and Diomedes nodded.

"What's next?" Blanndynne asked.

Armannii directed her toward the fire rune. She created a flame in her hands and pressed it against the wall. It took a few seconds, but an orange light remained after she'd put out the fire.

"That leaves earth and life," Armannii said, his hands on his hips. "Maybe a bit of dirt for earth?"

Diomedes scanned the floor, but it was all stone. "Your boot, Armannii," Diomedes said, nodding to the elf. "Maybe there's some dry mud still inside it from when it got stuck." Before Diomedes had finished the sentence, Armannii was pulling his boot off his foot. Diomedes's pulse quickened as the glowing lights faded with each passing second.

Armannii tipped the shoe into Diomedes's waiting hands. A small pile of dirt sprinkled out, and Diomedes quickly transferred it to the wall. The rune glowed green.

"Quick thinking," Armannii said, slipping the boot back on. He stepped toward the final unlit rune. It was easier to see with the ambient light from the others. "I'm not sure what to do for the life one though." With a frown, Armannii pressed his hand against the life rune. Nothing happened. When Diomedes raised a questioning eyebrow, Armannii shrugged. "Thanks to you two, I'm alive. I thought it would work."

"Well, that apparently isn't it," Diomedes said, his attention on the wall. His gaze flicked to the side, where the other runes were fading in the order they had lit them.

"Any other thoughts?" Blanndynne asked after a couple more seconds of silence. "Because we're losing light."

"Let me see it." Diomedes took Armannii's spot near the unlit rune, running his fingers over it. "This one is different."

"Besides the fact that it's the only one not lit?" Armannii asked, his voice laden with sarcasm.

"It's carved deeper into the wall than the other five," Diomedes said, ignoring Armannii's comment. "Whatever it wants, it doesn't just want to be grazed with the element like the other five."

The center of the rune held a hole that went into the wall, and Diomedes ran his finger over the rim of it. The diameter was almost as wide as his pinky, and the closer Diomedes got, the more he could see a rust-colored stain near the hole.

"Sacrifice," he muttered, and Armannii stood up straighter.

"What do you mean?" the elf asked, glancing between Diomedes and the rune.

Diomedes didn't answer right away, pulling his knife out instead. He went to cut into his arm, but Blanndynne grabbed his wrist at the same time Armannii went for the knife.

"Explain before you slice, Didi," Armannii said, stepping back with the blade.

Blanndynne let go of Diomedes when he tried to pull away. Her eyes were wide, and her lips were pressed together in a straight line.

"Lifeblood," Diomedes said, gesturing toward the wall. "The wall demands a sacrifice."

"So you just open a vein?" Armannii asked, his forehead creasing as he narrowed his eyes at Diomedes.

"Well, we're running out of time, and—"

"Blanndynne, stop!" Armannii didn't have enough time to stop Blanndynne from using one of her throwing-knives to slice vertically down her forearm. Blood gushed right away.

Diomedes stumbled out of the way when she pushed past him and pressed her bleeding arm against the wall.

"What is wrong with you?" Armannii asked Blanndynne, trying to separate her from the wall, but Diomedes stepped between them. "Move!" Armannii growled, but Diomedes stayed where he was.

"No. She's finishing the puzzle," Diomedes said.

"She just slit her wrist! She's going to bleed out!" Armannii tried to get past Diomedes, but he shoved Armannii back.

"She's fine. Right, Blan—" Diomedes stopped short when he glanced over his shoulder to see Blanndynne using the wall to hold herself up. He spun and closed the space between them to catch her as her legs gave out.

Armannii helped him lower her to the ground. "Hold on, B," he said, pulling his rune pen out. "This is going to sting."

Diomedes kept her upper body propped up while Armannii drew the healing rune on her arm above the cut, which was still bleeding. However, Diomedes found it difficult to focus on Armannii when the wall behind him began lifting off the ground.

"Look," Diomedes said, nodding toward the opening. "It worked."

Instead of responding, Armannii leaned closer to Blanndynne, tracing each line of the rune with careful precision. After a few seconds, Blanndynne began moaning, and Armannii spoke gently to her.

"It's all right. I know it hurts, but it's a good thing. And—"

"We need to get inside," Diomedes said, jostling Blanndynne as he got to his knees.

"Wait for the rune to work and then—" Armannii started, but Diomedes shook his head.

"No, look. It's closing." Diomedes grunted as he slid his hand under Blanndynne's knees and stood up with her in his arms. Armannii stood up too, grabbing his bow and quiver, which he'd abandoned at the sight of Blanndynne bleeding out.

Diomedes passed through the opening first, and Armannii had to duck under when the wall descended above him. He barely made it through before it sealed with the floor again.

Chapter Twenty-Three

"Guess I didn't need to press so hard with the knife," Blanndynne mumbled after a few minutes of moaning and cringing at the pain from the healing rune. Diomedes glanced over his shoulder when she spoke.

Armannii straightened up against the wall where he sat, his ears perking up at Blanndynne's voice. "You think?" He crawled over to where she lay. Armannii had placed his bag under her head, and it rustled when she sat up.

They were in a cave room with a tunnel on the opposite end from where they'd entered. The room had taller ceilings than the tunnels they'd traveled through, but the thing that had caught Diomedes's eye the fastest was the skeletal bodies littering the floor. There must've been at least thirty. It was hard to tell, though, because some of the bones had been scattered around and were no longer connected.

"How's your arm?" Diomedes asked. He stood a bit farther away and had been exploring the immediate surroundings until he'd heard Blanndynne speak.

"That healing rune was worse than the cut itself," Blanndynne said, her eyes on Armannii as he ran his fingers over the healed cut. Her arm was still covered in blood, but a pink line traveled from her wrist halfway to her elbow.

"I find that hard to believe," Armannii said, letting go of her arm and sitting back on his heels. "You passed out in a matter of seconds. It was an idiotic thing to do."

"Not as much as standing around arguing about solving the puzzle," she said, moving her hair out of her face. "If I hadn't done something, you two would've argued until the runes were all out. Besides, we both want to help Diomedes find this thing." She spoke the last in a softer voice.

"It was foolish."

"Like running off to get stung by sand crawlers?" Blanndynne retorted, but Diomedes had stopped listening to their bickering.

"Where are you going?" Armannii asked, and Diomedes turned when he realized that Armannii was talking to him.

He was halfway across the room, distracted by the tunnel. "It's got to be through here," he muttered as he turned back to face the tunnel.

He wasn't sure when, but at some point in the last couple minutes, he'd felt a change inside him, like he could feel something calling him. Diomedes stepped over a body wearing the crest of Cyanthia on its chest, but the next body he came across was wearing something different.

The symbol on the armor was familiar, but he couldn't quite place where he'd seen it before. It was a tree lacking any foliage, and the roots grew below a horizontal line representing the ground. They tangled into the shape of a dragon with its wings stretched out wide.

"Diomedes?" Blanndynne called from behind him.

When he turned to glance at her, Armannii was helping her to her feet. Their gazes were on him. Armannii made sure Blanndynne was steady before letting go of her.

"What is it?" Blanndynne asked when she caught up with Diomedes. Color was returning to her cheeks.

"I think we're close," Diomedes said, pointing toward the tunnel. "It has to be through here."

"Well," Armannii said, patting the wall that had sealed behind them, "your way seems like the only direction to go. And here's a thought, let's try to keep the bloody messes to a minimum from here on out."

With his heart racing, Diomedes continued forward. It felt like he was in a dream as he neared the end.

"What is this place?" Armannii asked as soon as they reached the other side of the tunnel.

Diomedes paused at the entrance to a room that appeared to be the size of the underground marketplace in the desert town. But when he stepped in farther, it became clear that the room was at least twice the size. The floor they stood on was fractured, as if it had been broken with force, leaving a gaping hole in the center of the room.

"This has to be it," Diomedes said as he ventured near the hole in the floor. He peered over, but all he could see was darkness—no bottom in sight. "But how do I . . ." His voice trailed off as he pulled out the necklace with the mirror. He held it up with the light rune stone he'd fished out of his bag. His reflection nodded his head, but in a way that made Diomedes walk forward, following the subtle gestures of his twin. He began navigating the circumference of the chasm.

"Wait, wait, wait," Armannii said, jogging to catch up with him. "You're not going to try to go in there, are you? It looks like it's bottomless."

"I'm supposed to descend farther." Diomedes didn't pay much attention to Armannii, who kept pace with him as he continued around the hole. "To go to the deepest part of the cave."

"There's not a rope long enough to get us down there and back, and B can't fly right now."

"Yes I—"

"Let me rephrase," Armannii said, glancing at Blanndynne, who was trailing behind them. "You shouldn't fly right now. Especially when we don't know how deep this thing is or what's even at the bottom."

"That's why I'm looking for another way down..." Diomedes paused when his reflection nodded frantically. He paused, glancing over the edge. A dark shadow about ten feet below him caught his eye. "Is that a ledge?" He dropped to his hands and knees, leaning over the edge to get a better look. His glasses started slipping off his nose, and he caught them before they tumbled into the abyss.

Armannii held the strap to his bag as he looked down. "It looks like it, but I don't think—"

Diomedes didn't wait to hear what Armannii was thinking about. Something was calling him from the bottom of the pit. He needed to get down. With a grunt, Diomedes shimmied off the edge. Wind rushed by him, and he remembered to bend his knees right before the impact.

Blanndynne must've raced to the edge with Armannii because both of them peered down at him when he finally looked up.

"What's wrong with you?" Blanndynne shrieked. "You could've stumbled off the edge!"

"Not to mention you've got nowhere else to go," Armannii said, squinting down past the ledge Diomedes stood on. "I don't see another ledge for at least fifty feet."

Armannii was right. Diomedes stepped away from the drop, sighing as he approached the wall. Armannii and Blanndynne continued to chide him, but he blocked out their voices. Instead, he returned his attention to the necklace. His reflection nodded faster when he directed the mirror toward the wall of the pit, and Diomedes approached it with a frown. He ran his hand over the rough stone surface.

After a few seconds, he felt a cylindrical object protruding from the wall: a lever. It would've been easy to miss. It was the same dark color as the rest of the rock, and with only the light from his stone, it was difficult to see, even with the glasses on.

With a yank, Diomedes pulled it down. It screeched as whatever metal it was made of moved for the first time in years. But nothing happened.

"What was that?" Armannii asked. "What are you doing?"

"I'm trying something," Diomedes said, not fully paying attention to Armannii. He leaned forward, focusing on the lever and its surrounding area, only to be startled backward when the wall began to tremble. The shaking increased, rocking the ground. Diomedes scurried closer to the wall in case the ledge gave out, but there was nothing to hold on to.

The intense trembling stopped at the same time an overwhelming sound filled the chasm. It was rock scraping against rock, and movement to the left caught Diomedes's attention. Sprouting from the side of the wall was a descending set of stairs. Steps wrapped around and around the sides of the hole in a downward spiral until they disappeared in darkness below.

"How did you do that?" Blanndynne asked, her voice carrying more than its fair share of awe.

Diomedes didn't answer. Whatever was calling to him, ushering him forward, was at the bottom of the stairs. The mirror confirmed it. No trace of doubt lingered in his mind.

"Wait for us to get down there before you—of course he's not waiting," Armannii said as Diomedes toed the first step with his boot.

It remained sturdy as he increased his weight on it, and soon he found a steady pace down the stairs. He was over a quarter of the way around the hole when Armannii jumped down, and Blanndynne followed behind him, half floating and half falling to the ledge. Out of the corner of his eye, Diomedes watched Armannii lean over the edge to stare at the black abyss.

Around and around they went. Soon the darkness was above as well as below, but it did not deter him. Something in his gut pulled him, urged him to go faster until he was taking the steps down two at a time. He ignored Armannii's and Blanndynne's echoing complaints to slow down and be wary.

He was close.

Close to the object, the key to ending the war.

Close to one of his deepest desires.

It sent chills down his arms, making the hair stand on edge. Something in the darkness beckoned to him, and there was nothing to stop him from going to it.

The third time Diomedes paused to peer over the edge at the bottom, he stopped long enough for Armannii and Blanndynne to catch up with him.

"Is that—" Armannii's words must've gotten lost somewhere in his brain because after a few empty seconds, Blanndynne finished the thought for him.

"A dragon skeleton."

Diomedes took off down the stairs again, a new sense of curiosity over the dragon mixing with the excitement and anxiousness already brewing. Within another few minutes, he reached the bottom.

The dragon skull alone was at least ten feet tall, and Diomedes walked straight up to it, his eyes wide behind the runed glasses.

"Amazing," he breathed, running a hand over the jawbone. "Think of what it looked like when it was living. It must've been incredible."

"I think the word you're looking for is 'terrifying,'" Armannii said as he joined Diomedes by the skull.

"This must've been Mellacross's mother's dragon. The one that died in the final battle with the sorceress," Diomedes said.

"I wonder how it died," Blanndynne said, seeming a bit winded, but she didn't say anything in regard to how she was feeling.

Diomedes followed the spine all the way around the bottom of the pit. Distracted by the dragon, he stepped on a few bones. Human bones. He cringed back but was distracted once more by the remains of the great beast. The dragon bones got smaller until they ended in the point of a tail.

"Is this where we're supposed to be?" Armannii asked, still standing by the head.

"Yes," Diomedes said, not needing to refer to the mirror in his hand for confirmation. He could feel it. Diomedes slipped the necklace into his pocket.

Besides a pit full of bones, he didn't see much else. He crossed through the middle to get back to Armannii but paused when a metal item caught his eye.

Sticking straight out of a small crack in the ground was a dagger, its hilt standing up like it was demanding to be picked up. Diomedes cocked his head to the side, squatting down next to it.

It called to him.

Reaching out his hand, Diomedes grabbed the hilt.

Darkness.

Chapter Twenty-Four

Diomedes sat up, his mind spinning. He couldn't remember what had happened, and when he tried to remember, a stubborn fog covered his memories, hiding them from him. The room he sat in was dark, but he could make out four corners. No doors. No windows. The only source of light was a rune inscribed on the ceiling. It wasn't a rune he recognized.

"Hello, Diomedes. I've waited a very long time to see you again." A woman's voice echoed around him.

"What?" Diomedes jumped to his feet and reached to his hip for his sword. It wasn't there. "Who are you? Where am I?" He spun around in a circle twice but could not see anyone else. He was alone.

"No need to worry," the voice said in a silky tone. "I promise I'll explain everything in time. But for now, I need to see if you truly are worthy of receiving what you seek."

"You mean"—he straightened up, squinting as he searched for the woman speaking—"you mean magic?"

"Yes, and so much more."

Diomedes's heartbeat sped up, and he ran a shaky hand through his hair. "You'll give me what I need to end the war on magic? Just like that?"

"I want nothing more than to do just that. However," the voice said from behind him, and he turned again. "You must prove to me that you are strong enough to bear magic."

"I am." Diomedes tried to take a deep breath, but his nerves left him unable to do so.

"I don't doubt that you are physically strong enough. I'm well aware of your parentage. But I must test your mental strength."

"Do it," Diomedes said without hesitation. "Test me. I'll pass."

"Wonderful," the voice crooned, and it echoed in a way that made it sound like there were multiple voices saying the same thing all at once. "There will be six trials, each testing values that are pivotal for you to gain access to magic as one born without."

His hands shook, and he hoped whoever was speaking hadn't noticed. It wasn't the first time he had considered what would happen if he failed to obtain the object, but it was the first time he'd considered failing to *earn* the object.

"Enter through the door." At those words, a door appeared in front of him, light shining around the cracks. "Prove to me your motives are true."

Diomedes breathed out before opening the door and stepping through. Blinded by the light, it took him a few seconds before his eyes could adjust.

But a familiar voice told him exactly where he was before he could even see.

"Welcome, Son. We've been waiting for you." King Butch's voice carried with it an extreme sense of formality, and when Diomedes could finally see, it was clear why.

He had just entered into the middle of a council meeting, and all eyes were on him. A memory of a similar occurrence tickled the edge of Diomedes's mind, but the fog covered it as quickly as it had arisen.

"Father," Diomedes said, clearing his throat. "Council."

When was the last time he had seen his father? Had he always looked that old? The blond in the king's hair and beard was graying. Wrinkles had started to spiderweb across his face, especially on his forehead. But he still stood tall. His deep burgundy tunic had silver stitching along the collar and the sleeves. His surcoat was an even darker purple with a silver emblem of a dragon struck down.

King Butch stood at the head of the table, his hands resting on the edge. Next to him sat Evangeline. She wore a lavender dress with long sleeves. A thin crown rested over the top of her hair, which was an intricate nest of braids.

Each of the sixteen council members wore their sanctioned robes, which all bore the same emblem as the king's surcoat. Diomedes spotted Silas, who, as always, considered him with a soft smile. His brown hair was graying like Diomedes's father's, but on him, it softened his features; the king only appeared fiercer.

"We are so pleased you've come to your senses," King Butch said, stealing Diomedes's attention from the council members.

"Meaning?" Diomedes asked, clasping his hands behind his back.

"That you've decided to abandon your outrageous ideas and are willing to embrace the council's stance on the war," one of the councilmen, Clive, said. His scrawny figure irritated Diomedes just as much as it had before.

"Pardon me?" Diomedes said, his eyes narrowing at Clive. "What are you implying?"

"You stand with the court, with me, in regard to the Split," his father said, a forced smile crossing his lips. "You're going to join the council in planning out the next several years of the war on magic."

Diomedes's jaw dropped, and he couldn't help but scoff. "This is a joke, right?" He glanced at the faces of the council members, then at his father and Evangeline, but no one else seemed to find the notion entertaining. Diomedes cleared his throat. "Let me make this clear. I still have every intention of ending the war. To think I'd do the complete opposite is foolish, even for you, Father."

King Butch's face darkened. "You will be disowned. Disinherited."

"So you've said." Diomedes crossed his arms over his chest, planting his feet on the ground. "Let me assure you that the threat of disinheritance means nothing to me anymore." He stepped up to the council table and placed both hands on it, palms down. His stance matched his father's. "I will end this war, and you *will* watch. I'll make sure of it." Diomedes slammed his hands down, and the sound echoed around the meeting room.

Then, as if he'd closed his eyes for a prolonged amount of time, darkness swallowed the council and his father, whose face had morphed into one of rage.

"Well done, Diomedes. Your passion to end the war has led you one step closer to what you seek." The woman's voice returned, and Diomedes let out a breath he hadn't known he'd been holding.

The tremble in his hands had intensified at the sight of his father, and he hid them underneath his armpits. "I'm surprised that was ever a question. This war needs to end, and I fully intend to be the one who does it. No matter what."

"That's absolutely wonderful to hear."

Diomedes couldn't focus on the compliment, not when he was still trying to process what he'd just seen.

It had felt so real. Every detail of the room, of the council, of his father had been exactly how he remembered them to be. Every anxiety he'd ever had about facing his father's council had returned and vanished in mere minutes. And to have been pulled out of the test as quickly as he had . . . His head spun in circles. How had the test appeared so realistic?

"The scenery and the interaction with your father was fabricated from memories. Do you need a moment to catch your breath?"

Without hesitation, Diomedes shook his head. The point of the tests was to prove he was strong enough to bear magic. Any sign of weakness, even pausing between tests, could influence his outcome. And that was not something he was willing to risk.

"Excellent. Now, the next test will hopefully not take very long. I assume you are quick on your feet?"

Before he could ask for clarification, a door appeared once more. Diomedes approached it, hesitating for a second. If these tests were anything like the ones in his tutoring, he expected them to get increasingly difficult.

"They will," the voice said, startling him. "But I'm sure you'll pass this one with flying colors. You are a royal, after all."

Diomedes didn't try to break down what she had meant by that, instead turning the handle and entering into the next trial.

"Are you ready to address the people, Your Majesty?" a familiar yet forgettable male servant asked.

Diomedes's clothes had changed, and when he glanced at his reflection in the nearest mirror, his jaw tightened. He was wearing the same outfit he'd just seen on his father, except the color was blue rather than burgundy. The surcoat felt heavy on his shoulders, and he shifted it to the right. An ornate crown rested on top of Diomedes's black hair. Like the clothing, it too was uncomfortable. Too big. Too overbearing.

"Your Majesty?" the servant asked again, tilting his head as he tried to pull Diomedes's attention away from his reflection.

"Right, sorry, what?" Diomedes said, running his hands down the front of the jacket to smooth it out.

"The address to the people, Your Majesty." The servant gestured toward two large doors, which led to the balcony overlooking the castle courtyard.

"An address," Diomedes repeated, his brow furrowing.

"Yes, the one regarding the tax increase."

Diomedes did his best to hide his confusion. "Of course. Lead the way," he said, nodding.

Before the servant had even opened the doors, Diomedes could hear the ambient noise of people speaking over one another. It combined into a hum that sent chills up and down his back. As often as he'd been present for his father's speeches, he'd rarely had to do anything but stand stoically in the back.

His heart raced, and something in his stomach twisted. For a second, he thought he might vomit. To speak in front of his father's impudent council was difficult enough, but to give an address to the people? Diomedes pressed a hand against his stomach, pausing.

"Your Majesty? Are you all right?" The servant asked, but Diomedes straightened up, distracting himself with a loose button on his sleeve.

"Yes," he lied, straightening his sleeve cuffs.

The doors opened, and Diomedes walked out with his chin held high. The crowd roared for him, bringing an unexpected smile to his lips. Unlike with his father's council, the general public clearly wanted to hear whatever was about to come from his lips.

Diomedes raised his hand, silencing his audience. The roar faded to a murmur. When it was quiet enough that he could be heard, he projected his voice as best he could.

"Thank you all for being here today," he said, his voice carrying just as much power as he wanted to project. However, he'd barely had time to figure out what to say. He was unsure what the real reasons for the tax increase were, and as the people stared up at him, his hands began to sweat again.

"As I'm sure you've all heard, there's been an increase in taxes." He paused when many of the people below him started to grumble and mutter. His breaths came quicker, but he forced them to calm down, focusing on the opposite wall of the courtyard for a few seconds to regain his composure. "However, I wanted to make things clear for all of you. This increase is for your benefit and yours alone." Diomedes scanned the crowd, trying to make eye contact with those who would look at him.

"The money from this increase is designated to healing the damages left by the horrific war my forefathers began. We are going to fix Phildeterre, and this increase in taxes is just one small way you can play your part. As king, I personally want to thank each and every one of you for your support. Thank you."

As soon as he stepped off the balcony and back into the castle, the test faded away.

He could breathe again.

The filthy clothes he'd been in for far too many days returned.

He was not king of Phildeterre.

And the war was not over.

"You're quick on your feet," the woman said, and Diomedes could hear the smirk in her tone of voice.

Diomedes pressed his lips together, giving a brief nod. "Some matters, especially matters of state, are best kept to a small group of people." He stuck his hands in his trouser pockets, clenching them into fists when he realized who had taught him that. His father. The man keeping the war going.

Chapter Twenty-Five

ou must understand that if I am to give you your heart's desire, you must prove that you're willing to put yourself and the task of ending the war above all else. This trial will be more difficult than the first two combined. When you're ready, pass through the next door."

Just like before, another door appeared in front of Diomedes, and after the ease with which he'd passed the first two tests, he opened it and strolled through with an air of confidence making his steps lighter.

Blanndynne and Armannii met him on the other side. All three of them knelt in the throne room of the Cyanthian castle, and all three of them were cuffed behind their backs.

"How are we going to get out of this one?" Armannii asked, whispering in Diomedes's left ear.

Diomedes scanned the room, but it seemed empty apart from them. There weren't even royal guards at the doors. "Where is everyone?"

"Don't know, and right now, I can't say I care. We need a way out before we get put in the cells for the rest of our lives."

Armannii stood up, and to Diomedes's right, Blanndynne did the same.

"Can you get the cuffs off?" Diomedes asked Blanndynne as he rose to his feet.

Blanndynne frowned, but the metal chains binding her jingled, and within a few seconds, she held her hands out to either side, cuff free.

"Nice," Armannii said, a grin on his face. "You'd think they'd be smart enough to put on magic-dampening cuffs, but apparently not."

"It's strange," Diomedes muttered as Blanndynne removed his and Armannii's cuffs. He rubbed his wrists, frowning at the floor. "There should be people in here. They'd never leave convicted people alone in the throne room." His gaze traveled to the double doors, the only doors to freedom. There was no telling what or who was on the other side.

Armannii walked up to them, leaning his ear against a door. "I don't even hear someone breathing out there. So unless your father decided to add silencing runes to the hallway, I think we should try to get out."

"I don't know," Diomedes said, rubbing the back of his neck. "Something doesn't feel right."

"Come on." Armannii ignored Diomedes's hesitation, cracking one of the doors open and peeking his head out. "There's no one out here."

Blanndynne followed Armannii. Diomedes was the last to leave the room, and he paused, glancing over his shoulder before letting the door close behind him.

"Is the fastest way out still through the stables?" Blanndynne asked, glancing between Armannii and Diomedes.

"That was my thought," Armannii said, but Diomedes didn't respond.

A horde of royal guards stood like statues down the hall. How had they approached so quietly? How had Armannii not heard them?

Diomedes turned back to look at Armannii and Blanndynne only to find them unconscious at the feet of eight royal guards. His hand went to his hip, but his sword wasn't there. While reaching for it was instinct, he knew somewhere in the back of his mind that he could not wish to defeat the forty guards who filled the hallway. Not with Armannii and Blanndynne indisposed.

When one of the guards standing over Armannii and Blanndynne went to reach for him, Diomedes stumbled backward. Two guards grabbed his arms, forcing him to his knees.

"Get off me," Diomedes said, shoving to no avail. He continued to struggle until a familiar voice called his name.

"Prince Diomedes." When Diomedes looked back at the line of guards, Daven stood only a few feet away from him. "You have been offered a very generous choice. Have you made your decision?"

"What? What choice?" Diomedes asked, his gaze narrowing at Daven and the guards standing above Armannii's and Blanndynne's unconscious bodies. His heart raced, and he scanned his surroundings for a way out.

"You are freed from all charges against you if you agree to turn these two over." Daven nodded toward Armannii and Blanndynne.

Diomedes froze, tensing at Daven's words. He couldn't begin to process them as he shook his head. "That's ridiculous. Why would I do that?"

"Your freedom, of course," Daven said.

"What?" Diomedes's brows furrowed.

"Your father and his council have graciously offered you the chance to return to his good graces. You need only hand these two over." Daven cocked his head to the side. "Your father has even offered to discuss ending the war on magic should you agree."

Dread pooled inside Diomedes as he switched his gaze from his friends to Daven. The captain wore a smug grin on his face, as if he knew the chaos swirling around in Diomedes's mind. But despite the desire to fight Daven and the other guards, a new thought emerged. If he went free, there was still a chance to end the war. "And if I refuse?"

"All three of you will be charged and spend the rest of your lives in the dungeon."

The war would go on. None of them would be able to stop it from the cells. Diomedes struggled to find a way out, but there seemed to be only one way if he kept his focus on ending the war.

"I'm sorry," Diomedes mumbled to Armannii and Blanndynne, though they could not hear him. Somehow, that made the decision worse. They'd wake up in the dungeon without any clue that he had betrayed them. Or did they know about the deal? Would they find out that he had betrayed them in order to keep his position as heir? To end the war?

"Well?" Daven asked.

"I'll take it," Diomedes said through gritted teeth. Daven nodded.

Royal guards lined up to drag Armannii and Blanndynne down the hallway, and the two holding Diomedes let him go. Diomedes turned his back as he struggled to swallow. He felt sick to his stomach and had no desire to see the effects of his decision. His chest hurt, but before his guilt could swallow him whole, the hallway descended into darkness once again.

"Another test completed. I can see you will do what is necessary. Your determination is admirable." The female voice had returned. "I'm sure that was terribly difficult for you."

"What's next?" Diomedes asked, his jaw clenching. Uneasiness from the last trial still swirled in his gut. The sooner he was out of the trials, the sooner he'd be out of whatever world he'd found himself in and back to a reality where Armannii and Blanndynne were still free. But he couldn't help but recall the sight of his friends as they were taken away to be imprisoned forever. A choice he had made for them.

"Through this door, you will be tested on a skill that is important if you are to possess magic."

"And that would be?" Diomedes asked, looking up. He crossed his arms over his chest, trying to focus on the voice instead of the annoyance growing in him toward the trials.

"Finding your weaknesses and getting rid of them."

Diomedes frowned, then nodded. "All right. Let's get this over with."

As soon as he stepped through the door, Diomedes froze. Standing in front of him was a man with black hair, a black tunic, black trousers, and boots. A man who reached for the sword at his hip at the same time Diomedes did. A man who matched Diomedes's appearance perfectly.

"Well, this should be interesting," Diomedes said to his duplicate, who pulled out his sword when Diomedes did. The sword had appeared as soon as he'd stepped through the doorway, and it felt reassuring to hold the hilt in his hands once more.

The copy tilted his head, looking Diomedes up and down as they began circling each other. Out of the corner of his eye, Diomedes took in his surroundings. They were in one of the indoor training rooms at the castle, a place he had been many times.

"Your move," the doppelgänger said, and Diomedes cringed at his own voice. It sounded scratchier than he'd expected, like his opponent hadn't had a drink of water in days.

Diomedes took the opportunity to strike first, only managing to land a blow on the other's weapon. The sound reverberated around the room as Diomedes stepped back into his fighting stance.

The duplicate grinned, and just as Diomedes suspected, he struck shortly after. He moved out of the way, but before he could counterattack, his opponent returned to a ready position.

"This is definitely one of the more interesting duels I've—*we've*—been a part of, isn't it?" Diomedes asked, cocking his head to the side as he tried to watch for a recurring misstep. He didn't find any.

"It certainly is."

Diomedes swung to the left and then the right, but he was blocked on both accounts. The longer they fought, the more frustrated Diomedes became. His opponent knew each move he was going to make before he made it. How could he gain any sort of advantage when his copy already knew how he fought? Diomedes's stomach twisted when the doppelgänger once again parried his attack.

"Tired yet?" the copy asked, smirking at Diomedes.

"Not at all," Diomedes said through his clenched jaw. But it was a lie. The sword was heavier in his hands than when they'd first started, and sweat was creeping down the back of his head, sliding behind his ear. It was becoming more and more difficult to hold on to the hilt of the sword, as his hands were also covered in sweat. Diomedes rubbed the back of his forehead with his hand.

However, it appeared his opponent was in a similar position. His reactions, like Diomedes's, were getting slower. Taking advantage of his opponent's slower reflexes, Diomedes left himself partially open for the next strike, hoping to catch the other off guard. Instead, the doppelgänger caught his upper arm with the tip of his sword.

Diomedes hissed, expecting his opponent to take advantage of his weakened state by striking a second time. It didn't happen. Reaching up to grip his arm, Diomedes took several steps away. His opponent copied him, clutching his shoulder in the same way. And just like Diomedes, blood was beginning to drip from the doppelgänger's wound.

"What's this?" his copy asked, his voice a low growl as he inspected his arm. "How did you do that?"

Confusion mixed with the adrenaline and searing pain in his arm, caused Diomedes to furrow his brow. The woman's words came back to him.

"Find the weakness," he mumbled, trying to reach a solution he felt near enough to touch. But what was the weakness? His opponent matched him physically and mentally. How was he supposed to find a weakness when his doppelgänger could just as easily exploit the same ones?

With his eyes trained on the challenger, watching for any sudden movements, his gaze was drawn to the blood coming from beneath his fingers. A whisper of a thought echoed in Diomedes's mind, and he flinched as he lowered his hand from his injured arm. With a little finagling, Diomedes pulled his knife from his belt. He sucked in a deep breath. His body rejected his idea. He didn't let it stop him. Diomedes ran it along his lower arm, raising his gaze to rest on the doppelgänger as he gritted his teeth against the new pain. If he was wrong, then the only thing he was doing was giving his opponent an upper hand.

But if he was right . . .

"How are you doing that?" the man shouted through clenched teeth as he covered his bleeding lower arm. "Stop it."

An exhausted sneer crossed Diomedes's lips as he positioned the knife above his stomach. "I'm the weakness," he said, and before he could second-guess himself, he plunged the knife into his stomach.

Chapter Twenty-Six

iomedes entered the darkness panting, but there were no other signs of the fight. No sweat. No blood. No pain.

"Well done, Diomedes. I'm certainly impressed."

It took several seconds before Diomedes responded, finding the urge to check the places he'd been injured in the previous test to make sure he was whole again. "Only two more, right? Then magic?"

"Correct. Two more trials, and then I'll consider you worthy of possessing such a gift. But I must warn you. These next two tests are meant to be the most difficult. They require more sacrifice. What you're seeking will not come without a price, and you must be willing to pay it."

"I'm willing to do anything." Diomedes rolled his shoulders back, lifting his chin. "I *will* end this war."

"Then enter your next trial," the voice said, and when he turned around, the door appeared. "In this test, you will sacrifice something physical, not only to prove your loyalty to magic, but to be able to see the world in a new light, one that will give you access to more capacity for greatness than most born with magic could ever dream of."

Diomedes didn't have time to wrap his mind around what the voice had said before he passed through the door.

The room he entered was small and quite bare. On the wall in front of him hung a mirror with a small counter below it. Diomedes scanned the rest of the room but didn't find anything else.

Leaning forward against the counter, Diomedes peered into the mirror. His eyes had dark circles beneath them, and he rubbed his hands over his cheeks. He lowered his hands, gripping the narrow counter on either side. In the silence of the room, Diomedes allowed himself to breathe. He wasn't sure if the woman was still tracking his progress, and in the few seconds he closed his eyes, he didn't care. Though it was short, it was enough of a restful moment that he could reset his focus.

Two more trials. Then magic.

Diomedes opened his eyes, jumping backward when the reflection in the mirror was no longer his own. He spun around to see if the woman he saw in the mirror was in the room with him, but he remained alone.

"Hello, Diomedes," the woman said, and Diomedes instantly connected her voice to the one running the tests. "My name is Emmalee."

"You're her," Diomedes whispered as he tilted his head to the side, his eyes widening.

The sorceress, Emmalee Estrada, must've been only a few years older than Diomedes. She had curly brown-black hair that fell just past her shoulders, and the left side was braided tightly to her scalp in three horizontal braids. A faint scar traced down the right side of her face from her brow to her collarbone, visible because of the low neckline on the dress she wore. The garment was a burnt orange that faded into a deep maroon around the waistline.

"I'm honored to finally meet you like this, Diomedes. I've waited a long time." She smiled at him, revealing dimples on either side of her mouth. "Your mother spoke of you often during her time with me, and though it was only briefly, I did meet you when you were little."

"My mother," Diomedes repeated, his brows creasing. It was strange looking into a mirror and not seeing his reflection. Since she'd appeared, it felt like he was looking through a window instead. "You know what happened to her?"

Emmalee's smile disappeared, and her gaze dropped, as did her posture. "When the battle came to a climax, your dear mother and I were separated. Unfortunately, I never found out what became of her."

"Oh." It was all he could say without letting any extra emotion slip into his voice. Somewhere in the back of his mind, the sight of the sorceress had given him a false hope of learning what had become of his mother.

"I'm sorry to have taken her away from you at such a young age. It was wrong of me. A mother should never be separated from her child," Emmalee said, her voice low. A few strands of hair fell over her face as she tilted her chin down.

Diomedes nodded, struggling to swallow. "I understand. You tried to end the war. Sacrifices have to be—they must be made. I just . . . I was just curious." He stood taller, using the counter to make up for any strength he was lacking. "It was a long time ago." His voice faded away at the end.

"You're strong like her," Emmalee said, the smile returning to her face. "She was just as determined as you. A fighter. I was honored to have her join me."

"Thank you," Diomedes said, inclining his head. "What do I need to do to pass this test and finish what you and my mother started?"

"It requires an explanation, which is why I'm here." She stepped closer to the mirror separating them and blinked.

Diomedes stumbled back from the mirror when she opened her eyes. Only, her eyes were no longer there. They'd been replaced by two holes darker than anything he'd ever seen. They seemed to absorb all the light around them.

"What—"

"Don't be afraid," Emmalee said, and it almost sounded as if other voices whispered the same phrase from somewhere inside the room. In a second, her eyes and voice were back to normal. She had dark irises, but there were at least eyeballs in the sockets. "I told you earlier that this test would require a sacrifice. But there's meaning and purpose to it."

Diomedes tried to return his breathing to a normal state but struggled as he stepped back up to the counter. "What do I have to do?" He cringed at how feeble his voice sounded in his own ears.

"You see the world through a human lens. While you observe much, you do not truly see all the possibilities. Your humanity limits you, as it does those born with magic. To receive magic as one not naturally gifted, you must sacrifice part of your humanity so that I may replace it with something stronger—something superior. In doing so, you will see the world differently when you submit to the magic."

"Sacrifice my humanity? See the world differently? But how do I—"

"You're hesitant, but you have no need to worry. While there is a cost to what you seek, the reward in exchange for your compliance is complete power. But without this sacrifice, I'm afraid all of these tests and your journey here will have been in vain. I won't be able to pass the dark magic on to you."

Diomedes bit the inside of his cheek. Dark magic. His whole body vibrated at the mere thought of it—of possessing it. "What do I have to do?"

Emmalee reached down below where Diomedes could see, and when her hand came back up, she was holding a dagger made of black metal. It looked familiar, but a dark mist in his mind kept him from placing where he'd seen it before.

"You must sacrifice the way you see the world." She reached forward, and Diomedes's eyes widened when the dagger passed through the mirror. "Take it," she said, offering it to him.

The dagger was cold in his hand and heavier than he'd expected. He turned it over, admiring the craftmanship of the weapon. Runes had been carved into the blade near the handle, but they weren't any he recognized.

"If you are ready to submit to magic and allow it to show you how to view the world as the magic sees it, you must prove your loyalty by ridding yourself of your full humanity. Remove your sight."

Diomedes's head shot up, and he stared at Emmalee with a slack jaw. "What?" His body shivered at the thought of what she was asking him to do.

"I warned you the last two tests would be more difficult than all the previous," she said, her lips pressing together. "And I told you there's a cost to gaining magic as someone born from a magicless line."

"But how does cutting out my eyes have anything to do with trading some of my humanity for magic?" Diomedes's hand shook, and he placed the dagger on the counter, using both hands on the counter to steady himself.

"As I said, your sight represents the human way in which you navigate the world. If you desire to quit now, I—"

Diomedes stiffened, his jaw tightening as he glared down at the dagger. "This will help me get magic?"

Emmalee nodded.

With a deep breath, Diomedes grabbed the dagger and plunged it into his left eye.

Utter darkness. Diomedes couldn't feel any residual pain, but without much prodding, he could remember it. Pressure. Agony. Fire. Pain like he'd never felt before. It had taken his breath away. His own scream rang in his ears.

But it was over. Even the pain.

There was only one more test.

And he *would* finish it.

Something was different when the voice spoke next, but Diomedes couldn't tell if Emmalee was different or if the change had in fact been inside him. It felt louder, and when she first spoke, it almost sounded like a whisper of a voice echoed hers.

"You have continually exceeded my expectations, Diomedes. Lenora spoke proudly of you. Clearly, she had every reason to."

The mention of his mother should've elicited some reaction from him; however, he remained still. His only thoughts were of the last obstacle—the last test—separating him from magic.

And he needed the magic.

Whatever the last trial had done, it had left him with a growing hole, and he had an inkling of what would fill it. He needed to finish what he'd set out to do. No matter the cost.

"You have been prepared for the last step. Are you ready?"

Diomedes nodded curtly. "I am."

"Good. The previous test required a physical sacrifice, and this one requires a mental and emotional one. But be warned, your mind will fight against it. This will be the hardest test you've undergone, and it will be ongoing even if you should succeed. It's imperative you keep your mind focused on the task you set out to do. Only by sheer determination will you be successful."

Diomedes lifted his chin, surprised to see the last door appear in front of him. He flinched as he remembered the agony he'd experienced. Had he not just carved out his own eyes? How could he see?

As if reading his thoughts, Emmalee answered his unasked question. "Your tests have all taken place in your mind. However, when you awaken, you'll find there are permanent effects from these trials."

"I understand," Diomedes said, taking in the door. Something was different. The light beneath it was cherry red, and he blinked when it flickered.

Someone stood behind the door.

Diomedes placed his hand on the handle, pausing for less than a second to prepare himself for whatever was lurking. He pushed it open.

Diomedes came face-to-face with his father when he passed through.

King Butch was younger than Diomedes had seen him in years. His sandy-blond hair held only a few gray hairs, and a wide grin was plastered over his face. They were on horses, and Diomedes squinted up at the rising sun on the horizon.

"I told you it would be worth waking up for," King Butch said, holding the reins taut in his grasp. "Isn't it incredible?"

A memory.

He'd walked straight into a memory.

It had been a few years after his mother had left them—the most difficult years of his life. His father must've noticed the way he sulked around the halls, avoiding people like they held deadly diseases. It hadn't helped that Evangeline had entered the picture.

Diomedes had been frustrated, confused, and devastated when his father had told him he was planning to propose to Evangeline. To a woman not born of nobility. To a nobody.

The memory was one he'd almost forgotten. Only a week after King Butch had informed his son of his intentions to marry the woman who'd helped him bring down the sorceress, he'd invited Diomedes to go on an early morning ride with him.

Naturally, Diomedes had refused. He'd hated his father for trying to replace his mother with another lesser woman. But his father hadn't stopped asking. Diomedes eventually agreed only to get his father to stop.

On the morning of the ride, King Butch had entered his son's room quietly, waking Diomedes himself instead of sending a servant as Diomedes had expected. As busy as he was, his father had rarely spent any time in Diomedes's room; it was something Diomedes had appreciated the older he'd gotten.

With quiet whispers, they'd left the castle, and to Diomedes's surprise, they'd left alone, no guards scouting ahead or following behind. It had been pitch-black as they'd ridden through town, and Diomedes had been nervous. His father had trusted him to ride by himself, and it was the first time he'd gotten his horse to a full gallop.

But they'd made it to a hill near the north side of Cyanthia just as the sky was turning pink. The sun came over the edge of the horizon. He'd seen sunrises from his window, but they were never as vibrant as what lay before him.

Diomedes remained silent, but when he glanced over at his father, he found the king smiling at him.

"I know the last few years have been difficult, Dio, but I want you to remember something." King Butch pointed to the sun peeking over the edge of the horizon, lighting up the sky more and more every second. "There is a balance to darkness and light. When you're in the middle of darkness, light is right around the corner. The sunrise will come. Now I want you to close your eyes."

Diomedes obeyed, and in a second, there was only darkness. He couldn't see the sun rising or the night transitioning into day.

"Good, now open your eyes." His father beamed at him. "Dio, I'm proud of you, of how you've handled a dark situation. But I want you to realize that if you keep your eyes closed, if you don't look forward to the sunrise, then you're keeping yourself in the darkness. You can't expect things to get better—for day to come—when you're holding on to the night. To the pain of the past. To the darkness."

As young as he had been, Diomedes hadn't fully grasped what his father was saying. But he remembered feeling lighter after the conversation, even if it was only because his father had spent time with him and trusted him to ride the horse by himself.

A small grin crossed Diomedes's lips, and he glanced at his father. It was the first time in a while Diomedes had looked at him without regretting that they were related. He thought back on his father's words as he turned around to take in the glowing horizon. A feeling he'd not felt for a long time washed over him: peace. It lifted him and left him feeling light enough to float away.

But as Diomedes relived the memory, something tainted it. It wasn't until movement to his side caught his attention that he realized what felt wrong. Unlike years ago, it was no longer just Diomedes and his father on the hilltop.

Standing beside Diomedes, Emmalee stared out at the sunrise. The smile fell away from Diomedes's face, and he straightened up.

"You are content in this memory, are you not?" Emmalee said, clasping her hands in front of her.

"I am."

"Then you must destroy it, Diomedes. And many others like it. The happier the memory, the more power you will receive in relinquishing it to the darkness."

Diomedes's breath caught in his lungs, and he swallowed to try to hide it. "Why?"

"Contentedness will bring you nothing but the same. You will never achieve your aspirations if you're willing to remain content forever."

"But destroy it?" Diomedes flicked his gaze to the sunrise before returning it to Emmalee. "Is that necessary?"

"I told you this is the most difficult task. It's a great challenge for a person to give up the memories that make up their identity. However, what you seek is much greater than just you, Diomedes. Remember your purpose."

Diomedes frowned, turning back to look at his father. King Butch was still grinning at him. His gaze didn't waver once, not even when Emmalee stepped closer and placed her hand on the side of Diomedes's horse's neck.

"Are your memories worth more than freeing Phildeterre from the destructive grip of war? Are they more important than possessing magic?" Emmalee stroked the horse, her voice level and calm. But she glanced up at Diomedes with a dark eyebrow raised. "Or are you willing to give yourself up for something much more powerful than you could ever wish to be?"

Diomedes stared out over the land, watching the yellow rays of light coming up from the sun. He knew he needed to let go, to let the sun rise. And looking over the rolling land, it wasn't difficult to remember that he was there to save Phildeterre.

Yet the peace of the memory beckoned him to hold on. A tiny voice whispered to him, begging him not to forsake it. Diomedes struggled to swallow, a lump getting stuck in his throat. He had been so happy, and in that moment, in that memory, he had nothing but admiration and love for his father. The tranquility of the scene clung to him, and he longed to stay within it.

"Well?" Emmalee asked, stepping back from his horse. "What's your decision, Your Highness?"

Gripping the reins in his fists, he sighed, closing his eyes. Staying in a past memory would do nothing for his future. For the future of his country. "How do I do it? How do I destroy the memory?"

"All you have to do is let go. As soon as you do, you will invite the magic into you. You will have everything you've been searching for and more. You will possess the power needed to fight for the side of magic and end this war. Do you accept?"

There was no turning back, no matter the cost.

"Yes."

Chapter Twenty-Seven

Sweat covered Diomedes's forehead when he sat straight up on the floor of the chasm, surrounded by the bones of people and dragon alike. But he couldn't see them. He couldn't see anything.

"Hey, hey, hey," Armannii said, his voice near Diomedes's left. "Not so fast. Lie back down."

Blanndynne's voice rang out next to Armannii's, and Diomedes turned to face them. "You've been unconscious for a day from what we can gather." There was a tremor in her voice.

"What happened?" Diomedes's throat felt dry, and sitting up suddenly had left behind a headache the size of the mountain in which they sat. "Where are my glasses?"

"I-I don't think they'll be of much use," Armannii said, sighing after. "I'm not sure what happened, but . . ." He didn't finish his sentence, and his voice got a little farther away at the same time something crunched. A bone, most likely.

"Blanndynne, could you give me some light? I can't see two inches in front of my face," Diomedes said as he rubbed his temple with two fingers. The pounding had gotten increasingly worse with every second of consciousness.

"I-I am." Her voice was soft.

"Then why can't I—" Diomedes froze. He'd raised his hand to his eyes only to find nothing there. No eyeball nor lid. No trace of blood either.

A recent memory triggered. Emmalee's eyes, or lack thereof.

His heart raced, his hands trembled as he covered his face. He couldn't see. His eyes were gone. Diomedes shifted to his hands and knees when his stomach heaved. Nothing came out. His skin became clammy, and his breaths were short and quick. He rocked back on his heels, hanging his head low.

"She said there'd be a cost. She said—" He leaned forward as he ran his fingers through his hair. The volatile mixture of fear, panic, and confusion swirled again, and he tried to deepen his breathing as bile rose in his throat.

"She who?" Armannii asked, his steps silent enough that Diomedes startled when the elf laid a hand on his shoulder. He pressed something metal into Diomedes's hand: a canteen. "Drink," he ordered. "Then tell me who did this to you." Armannii's voice had an edge.

Diomedes's hands trembled as he raised the canteen. The metal edge bumped against his bottom lip, and he tilted it. The canteen was only a quarter full. A day. He'd been in the trials— wherever they had been—for a full day.

"What happened to you?" Armannii asked.

His question sparked something in Diomedes. Something unnatural. A cold calmness washed through him, spreading farther than the water from the canteen could reach.

"What did you see?" Diomedes asked after he'd taken a long sip.

"You collapsed," Blanndynne said, and Armannii grunted. "I tried everything I could—Armannii too—but we couldn't wake you. And then a few hours ago . . ." Her voice faded, and Diomedes could guess what had happened. "I looked away for one second, and they were gone."

Diomedes, still washed in the strange sea of calm, nodded. "Where's the dagger?"

Gravel shifted, and a hand with smooth skin pressed the handle into Diomedes's open palm. The dagger was heavier than his other knife, and as he ran his finger over the blade, he could sense a connection to it.

"Is it the object?" Blanndynne asked, and her voice moved back to where it had been before.

"I don't think that should be our biggest concern at the moment," Armannii said, his voice low. The sound of it was constricted, like he'd been clenching his jaw as he spoke. "We should be thinking of ways to reverse this. But in order to do that, we need to know what happened. Diomedes?"

"I did it. At least—" Diomedes paused, searching for the soothing coolness he'd felt earlier. It returned at the mere thought, lingering in his hands as he set the canteen on the ground. The refreshing sensation spread from his fingertips up through his arms, but he stopped reveling in it when Blanndynne gasped.

"Y-your arms." She must've shifted because something scraped against the ground.

"What?" Diomedes ran his right hand over his left arm, his chest tightening as the chill he'd called faded away with Blanndynne's distraction. It was clear now what the coolness reminded him of: Otto's dark magic.

Armannii took a deep breath next to him. "You did it all right. Your hands and arms were surrounded by a cloud of dark magic a few seconds ago."

So that was what the feeling was.

He'd done it.

His head was reeling, his heart pounding. And there was that feeling again. Starting in his fingers, the coolness—the *magic*—trickled up his arms in the silence of the room. It moved where he told it to go, but the longer he commanded it, the dizzier he got.

A voice echoed in his mind.

"*Easy now, Diomedes.*" Emmalee's silky voice swept over his thoughts as if she were sitting right next to him, only closer. "*You'll need to practice. That will come with time.*"

He'd tried not to react, but her first words had made him jolt.

"What's wrong?" Armannii asked, speaking at the same time as Emmalee.

Diomedes tuned him out, concentrating on Emmalee. His mind wandered through a few questions that'd been brewing since he'd woken from her tests, but her response left more to be desired.

"*I will teach you how to use the magic, but for now, you must once again prove to me that you are worthy of the gift I gave you.*"

His thoughts raced as he tried to understand what she meant. Hadn't he already proven himself? Why was he already tired from doing such little magic?

"Diomedes?" Armannii drew out his name.

Diomedes knew the elf well enough to tell from his voice that he was frowning at him. "I'm processing. I'll be fine."

"Tell us what really happened, Didi."

"*You must lie to them. They mustn't know the full truth. Not when the world thinks me the enemy.*"

Though he didn't understand why Emmalee was so concerned about Armannii and Blanndynne finding out she'd been the one to give him magic, he didn't argue with her disembodied voice.

"When I touched the dagger, I was tested to see if I was worthy of possessing magic. It wasn't easy, but I passed each trial." He paused, running through the memories of each test. "When I finished, I got what I needed to end the war," Diomedes said, his voice just as calm as Emmalee's. *Too calm*, a voice told him in the back of his mind. Too calm for the trials he'd just watered down in response to his best friend's questions.

"But what happened to—"

"There was a cost. I was willing to pay it." Diomedes's words came out sharp, and Armannii fell into silence again. Somewhere in the back of his mind, he questioned why he had snapped at Armannii when the only thing his friend was trying to do was protect him. But a pleasant surge of coldness removed the thought from his head. Armannii was clearly not focused on the task at hand. Diomedes's response had been appropriate.

"What's next then?" Blanndynne asked. Fabric rustled in a rhythmic pattern.

In theory, the answer was easy: end the war. But he knew better than that. They needed a plan to end the war, especially if it would take time like Emmalee had said. With the mere thought of the sorceress, her voice echoed in his head.

"*You must take the throne. Once you are king, you will have no problems ending the war.*" Emmalee paused, and Diomedes waited for a next step he could tell his friends—a closer one, preferably. "*While your powers develop over the next week or so, you must find a safe place to practice away from prying eyes.*"

"We need to find a way out of the caves," Diomedes said, his mind going to the map Amira had given him. Then they'd go to Raidah's. She was his ally, and he was sure she would extend a helping hand as he figured out what to do next. Diomedes attempted to stand. He wobbled, and a sturdy hand caught him under the elbow. "I'm fine."

"Yeah, clearly," Armannii muttered, waiting until Diomedes was steadier before letting him go.

Diomedes couldn't ignore the embarrassment of needing help. It was like in the maze when he'd needed a blindfold because of the dangerous runes. While he hadn't quite felt it sitting on the floor, the vulnerability returned as soon as he tried to take his first step and jumped when a bone crushed beneath his boot.

"Careful," Blanndynne said next to him. "Maybe you should eat something. You haven't in a full day."

Her suggestion left his stomach rumbling, and he held out a hand, waiting for something he could eat to be placed in it. After a bit of rustling, Diomedes took a bite of the item given to him, relying on his other senses—and his memory of the types of food they'd brought with them on the journey to the mountains—to figure out what it was. It was, he deduced, dried meat.

As he ate, Diomedes tried to remember how the pit at the bottom of the chasm was laid out, but there was no telling whether his companions had moved him after he'd begun the trials. "Here." He released the knife he kept in his belt and held it out until one of them took it. "I don't need it anymore."

It took two tries, but he got the dagger into the sheath his other knife had been in. The dagger was longer, and the handle stood out an inch more than the other one. He made a note to find another sheath for his new weapon when he had the chance.

"*Stay focused,*" Emmalee chided. "*You're not going to get out of here if you keep getting distracted.*"

"Help me to the bottom of the stairs," he said, and as the cold rush of magic swelled in his hands, he grinned. "It's about time we get out of this place."

Chapter Twenty-Eight

Diomedes kept his right hand on the wall as they walked up the spiraling staircase. Multiple times he didn't lift his boot high enough and had to catch himself before he fell. And while the chill of his new power was refreshing, it wasn't quite capable of extinguishing the growing annoyance at his lack of sight.

Armannii and Blanndynne walked behind him, and if he slowed his breathing down so it wasn't as loud, he could overhear what they were saying.

". . . just keep an eye on him," Armannii whispered. His footsteps were softer than Blanndynne's, as was his breathing. However, it was Diomedes who was nearly panting by the time they reached the top. He hid it as best he could.

"What's our best way out of here, do you think?" Armannii asked, and his footsteps led away from Diomedes.

Having been so focused on finding the object, Diomedes couldn't remember the exact layout of the room, and his muscles tensed. What if he accidentally walked over the edge and fell into the pit?

"*Here, let me help.*" Emmalee's voice echoed inside his mind, and Diomedes's breath hitched when he could see the room again.

Except, it was different.

Where he knew there to be a gaping hole leading to the pit, a solid floor stood. And as he stared at the room, he didn't see Armannii or Blanndynne. Instead, several people he didn't recognize stood in a huddled group. They didn't move, as if they had been painted there.

"It's from a memory of mine," Emmalee explained. *"I was standing where you are now."*

From what Diomedes could tell, Armannii had walked toward the tunnel they'd entered from. And sure enough, the elf spoke a few seconds later. "I don't remember seeing a way out after the door with the rune puzzle closed behind us."

"See where those people are? Walk straight forward to the wall and then follow it to the left."

"Where are you going?"

Diomedes ignored Armannii's question, following Emmalee's orders instead. He didn't stop, even when Blanndynne jogged over, calling his name. Astounded, Diomedes watched as the picture moved with him. It was as if he could see. That was, until he kicked a large rock that had apparently fallen from the ceiling sometime since Emmalee's memory.

"The images I show you are from the past. Things have changed," Emmalee said in response to the angry thoughts he'd directed at her. His toe throbbed.

"Do you want me to lead you somewhere?" Blanndynne asked, standing to the left of Diomedes. She touched his arm, her skin shifting from warm to cold and back again because of the light and dark magic she possessed. He shook her off.

"I'm fine. Just give me a second," he muttered.

"Good, now feel along the wall at hip height. There's a nook up ahead with a lever."

"What are you looking for?" Armannii asked as he joined them.

"I'm not 'looking' for anything," Diomedes said through gritted teeth. "I'm feeling for a lever."

"Why would there be a lever?" Armannii challenged, and Diomedes stopped and faced where he thought his friend was standing.

"A lever is what opened the stairs down to the pit."

"Right." Armannii smacked his lips together, and it sounded louder than it ever had before. "I guess we'll search for this lever too."

"*I want you to stop. Concentrate on the word 'find,' and hold your right hand out.*"

Diomedes obeyed, though a sense of vulnerability crept up on him when the image of the room Emmalee had shown him disappeared into darkness. Why did it have to be his sight? He removed his hand from the wall and held it out in front of him. He focused on the word, waiting for something to happen.

"*Try to imagine a lever in your mind. Direct the magic how you want it to react.*"

In the distance, he could hear Blanndynne and Armannii slowly making their way along the wall in front of and behind him in different directions.

"*Don't get distracted by them,*" Emmalee said, her voice stricter than it had been before. "*I want you to focus, Diomedes.*"

How was he supposed to picture something he'd never seen before? Diomedes growled when Emmalee answered his question by showing him another memory of hers. While it did not have the context of the rest of the room behind it, it did show him a lever that all but blended into the wall.

Diomedes's hand trembled in front of him, but as he pictured the lever in his mind, a tingling chill entered his fingers. Diomedes embraced the sensation as he concentrated on the word "find."

The magic in his fingertips responded, and he could feel it pouring out of him. Something pulled at him, compelling him to walk forward. He followed it, keeping his hand outstretched and his mind focused. With a few more steps, he reached the wall again.

His hand went straight to the lever.

"*Well done,*" Emmalee said as Diomedes pulled it down.

The wall near him trembled, and he kept his palm on it, feeling the vibrations course through him.

"How did you find this?" Armannii asked, his footsteps nearing the place Diomedes stood.

"How do you think?" Diomedes asked, raising his hand for Armannii to see. Residual coolness still rippled through his fingers.

"How?" Armannii asked, his bag rustling. "You've had magic for, what, twenty minutes?"

Diomedes noted the lack of congratulations in Armannii's voice. His hands tightened. "And?"

"And nothing. How are we going to get out of here? B and I can't use your magic mirror, and you . . ." Armannii's voice trailed off.

It was a fair question.

"*You can use the same spell to find your way out. Just focus on the entrance to the caves and let your power guide you.*"

Diomedes turned toward the wall. A breeze wafted from a direction, and he followed it. For a second, he wondered if it was something he would've noticed before. He doubted it.

Just as he'd done before, he pictured the thing he wanted to be led to: the mossy cave entrance. Diomedes imagined the fresh air and the change in temperature; though, after waking up from the trials, he had not felt as cold as he had before in the caves.

Diomedes held out his hand, concentrating as his magic reemerged. He paused, his stomach turning when he realized what he'd just thought.

His magic.

His.

He let the excitement fill him, twisting his nerves and increasing the magic that leaked out of his hands.

"That's incredible," Blanndynne said from beside him. "It took years for me to learn magic like that."

Her comment added to his sense of pride, and he let the supernatural pull lead him into the tunnel.

Unlike when they were in the enormous room, Diomedes did not rely on the walls to keep him from running into anything. Instead, he put full trust in the spell.

Armannii stayed quiet, walking several paces away from Diomedes. His friend's lack of excitement frustrated Diomedes. Blanndynne, however, kept up with him, commenting periodically about how what he was doing was impressive.

"You remember that finding spell I did on the pen a little while back?" she said after a while. "I had to practice it over and over to get it right. I just—I can't believe you're doing this right now."

"He could be leading us in circles," Armannii muttered in an almost inaudible voice.

"You're the one who can see," Diomedes said, pausing so Armannii had no choice but to catch up. "Have we passed through anything that looks like we're going in circles?"

"How should I know?" Armannii asked. "These tunnels are dark, and they all look the same."

Diomedes pressed his lips together, nodding. "And yet we made it to where we needed to go."

"With plenty of wrong turns along the way."

"Have we come to a dead end yet?"

Armannii remained silent.

"Then let's keep going." Diomedes spoke in a curt tone, turning back around and straining his mind to focus. But his hand trembled.

"You've lost your control, and you've already weakened your currently limited supply of magic. I suggest you find something to sacrifice or you may just be lost in my labyrinth forever."

Diomedes lifted his chin. Sacrifice. Had his sight not been enough?

"*I told you the final trial would continue after you received magic. I did not hide this from you.*" Emmalee's voice was matter-of-fact.

He knew he was meant to destroy another memory. The same resistance he'd felt in the final trial returned, and he hesitated. How many more? What would be left of him if he rid himself of all the things that made him *him*? How many more memories would perish to end the war?

"What's wrong?" Armannii asked, stepping closer. "*Are* we lost?"

Armannii's doubt was what Diomedes needed to make his decision. He pulled a memory from the back of his mind. As the darkness swallowed it, he watched one of his childhood friends run away from him as he chased the boy through the castle gardens. Then it was gone, and he couldn't remember which memory he'd given for the sake of his magic.

But the chill was back, and Diomedes continued with little regret at losing a memory he'd rarely visited in the first place.

When the moss from the cave entrance slid over Diomedes's face, he startled. He'd not been expecting it, and the sensation was unpleasant, like something had crawled over his skin, leaving a trail of moisture. It could've been avoided . . . if he'd been able to see.

"That was amazing, Diomedes," Blanndynne said, her voice carrying a rich sense of awe. "You didn't make a single mistake."

Armannii must've tossed his bag on the ground and sat down on the edge of the cliff. Something scratched against the stone ledge, and a rock could be heard tumbling down the face of the cliff, echoing as it pinged off the cliff below in its downward plummet.

Diomedes was surprised he'd been able to hear it over the deafening thunder of the waterfall. He'd heard the roar of the water long before he'd expected to, which had given him false hope that the uphill walk out of the caves was coming to an end sooner than it actually had. The sun warmed his skin as he stepped farther out from the cave. It was strange not to sense any light—almost as though his world were emptier than before.

What Blanndynne and Armannii didn't know—and would never know—was he had needed to give up two more memories to get them out of there, and the uphill climb had taxed him more than he wanted to admit. Several times Armannii had asked him if he needed to pause, but pride had kept Diomedes from relenting.

Maybe it was being in the dark caves too long or the new power coursing through him, but despite the outer warmth from the sun, Diomedes felt colder inside. It was strange, like he'd taken a sip from the Cyro Sea and the water was freezing him from within. But it didn't bother him.

"Careful," Blanndynne said, grazing Diomedes's arm as he walked toward where Armannii had sat down. "He's sitting on the edge."

"I won't walk over," Diomedes said, patting her hand before pulling away from her touch. "I'm going over that way." He pointed to the right of the mountain, where he remembered a path continuing. There hadn't been as steep of a drop-off, which made him feel safer. He needed a moment to be alone, to catch his breath away from prying eyes he himself couldn't see. "I need to relieve myself. I'll be back in a few minutes."

It was a lie, and it had come out as easily as he'd hoped. At the thought of her name, Emmalee spoke in his mind.

"You're quick, and you're already exceeding my expectations, Diomedes."

He lifted his chin, letting her compliment sink in.

"While you're at Raidah's, I will begin to teach you more. This is just the beginning. You have no idea what you are capable of—what lies within you."

Chapter Twenty-Nine

fter receiving further instructions from Emmalee in regard to keeping his friends from understanding what was happening in his head—something he had already decided upon—Diomedes turned to go back to where his companions were, then realized he could hear part of their conversation, even over the thundering waterfall. He wondered for a moment if his heightened hearing was part of "seeing the world differently," though he would've thought that'd have to do with "hearing the world differently." He remained still as he tried to make out their words, especially after he heard Armannii call him by his nickname.

"But that's the thing, B. I've never in my life heard of someone gaining magic, let alone magic as powerful as he clearly has. I mean, Didi led us back here as if he were navigating the halls of the castle, not a cave system with a million ways to get lost."

Blanndynne sighed, and Diomedes could hear her fiddling with her hair. "I mean, maybe he's acting a bit different, but wouldn't you if you woke up and couldn't see? And yes, maybe it's strange how he got the magic, but isn't that what we were hoping for? Something that would give us the edge on the war? I mean, you just said it yourself: with magic as powerful as he clearly has, we have even better odds at ending the war."

"But look at what it cost him." Armannii's voice got slightly louder, and Diomedes suspected he'd cast a glance in his direction.

"Wouldn't you be willing to give up whatever was necessary to get revenge for all the prejudice our kind has faced over the last century?"

Armannii scoffed. "Revenge? I'm not doing any of this for revenge. What's the point of focusing on the damage in the past if it's going to skew the way you see the future? I'm doing this *for* the future. For the generations that come after us. I don't want them to face persecution if I can have a say in it."

"And Diomedes is doing this for the future too. He's going to end the war, and our children's children will know his name."

Diomedes wanted to thank Blanndynne for coming to his defense, but the stronger emotion was his irritation. After all they'd done to get to where they were, to have Armannii begin to question everything he was doing for his sake and the sake of all those with magic was infuriating.

He forced himself to take a deep breath before returning. Hesitation grew in him as he neared where he'd heard his friends talking. One misstep and he'd fall over the edge of the cliff. His muscles tensed at the thought.

"Welcome back," Armannii said, his voice light, though Diomedes detected a lingering trace of the discussion he and Blanndynne had cut off, probably at the first sight of him. "Any more direction as to what we're doing next? I mean, as much as I love running around with no plans, shouldn't we think about our next move?"

Diomedes nodded curtly. "We're going to Raidah's. I believe it'd be wise to have some time to think and for me to . . . recover. Besides, I'm sure she'll be excited to know that her information was helpful."

"That's a great idea," Blanndynne said, and the lightness of her tone sounded like she was grinning. "How do we find her?"

He took off his bag, holding it out in front of him until either Blanndynne or Armannii took it. "Raidah is expecting us to seek her out. There's a map in my bag," Diomedes said, waiting for one of them to find it. "What?" Diomedes asked when Blanndynne groaned.

"The ink is all smudged because of the sea," Armannii said. Paper rustled. "I'm not exactly sure how usable it is."

"How much of it can you read?" Diomedes waited for a response. His impatience grew. If he could just see for himself . . .

"Maybe 30 percent," Blanndynne said, clearing her throat. "At best."

Though his frustration toward Emmalee for taking his sight was steadily growing, he turned to her for help.

"I can try to guide you there, but that depends on whether Raidah still resides in the same place."

"Does the 30 percent happen to hold the location of Raidah's home?" Diomedes asked.

The parchment rustled again. "Maybe? Can you make out that writing, B?" Armannii muttered.

"Um," Blanndynne said, drawing out the word. "Something about a tower in the sand. That's all."

"I know the place."

Blanndynne had taken Armannii down the cliffside first, and Diomedes let the breeze blowing over the ledge refresh him as he waited for her to return for him. But as he stood there, a question entered his mind. Emmalee was quick to answer it.

"You will have to travel as you did before, at least for now."

Diomedes bristled. He'd been slow before, unable to use speed runes or fly. How much worse would that be without his sight? The anger he'd felt building up exploded, and he found himself yelling at Emmalee in his mind.

"*Calm down, Diomedes.*" Emmalee spoke as if she were scolding a child. "*Your weaknesses will soon be strengths. And while it may take time, it will not take as long as you might think. The more you are willing to offer to your magic, the faster it will manifest.*"

He wanted to speak to Emmalee as he had during the trials, without fear of being overheard by his elf friend, but since he was unsure how much the waterfall would interfere with Armannii's hearing, Diomedes kept his rage contained within his mind.

How could she expect him to take Cyanthia by force if he could not take more than a few steps with confidence? He'd been clumsy before, but how much worse would it be now that he couldn't watch where he was going? He threw question after question at Emmalee until she'd clearly heard enough.

"*You chose this, Diomedes. You are more powerful now than you could've ever dreamed to be before. If you continue to submit memories in exchange for strength in magic, I will soon be able to show you ways in which you can use your magic to see. Remember what I told you in the fifth trial: you have not given up your sight. You have exchanged it to see the world differently, and you will only be able to do that when you submit and depend on your magic.*"

How long would he have to wait? Weeks? Months? Years?

"*That's up to you,*" she said, her voice lifting. "*Should you truly commit to this, it could be within a few short days.*"

"Ready?" Blanndynne asked, her voice stirring him out of his thoughts.

Diomedes nodded.

Blanndynne looped her arms under his armpits. He tried not to startle at her touch, but he twitched nonetheless. His stomach dropped when they flew off the edge. Wind rushed past, thundering in his ears. The mist from the waterfall blew over him as they descended. The motion mixed with the inability to fix his eyes on anything stable had him feeling sick once more. And then there was the lack of control. He couldn't determine where she flew.

Diomedes's stomach didn't feel quite right until both his feet had been on the ground for several minutes.

"Feeling better?" Armannii asked, joining Diomedes where he sat on a rock away from the waterfall.

"I'm fine," Diomedes said, his voice void of emotion. "From what I remember of the map, we need to go down to the start of the Albanistic Desert and go east." It was a lie. He hadn't touched the map since Amira had given it to him. But with Emmalee feeding him directions, it seemed easier to lie than to explain the voice in his head.

"We don't have a ton of food," Armannii said, and an air of hesitation filled his voice. "B and I rationed what we could in the caves, but we'll need to find something."

Diomedes nodded. "That's wise. We should start heading toward the desert, and when we set up camp, maybe you can go hunt something."

"All right. We'll set up camp once we get out of the canyon and farther south," Armannii said. He shifted next to Diomedes. "When you're ready, we can—"

"I'm ready," Diomedes said, standing up. His stomach felt better, but the unwavering sense of vulnerability climbed up through his body, seeping into his mind like a disease. It made him feel weak.

"*Patience, Diomedes,*" Emmalee whispered in the back of his head.

Diomedes held out his hand, and Blanndynne took it. Just as he'd expected, it took them longer to travel than when they'd first entered the mountain range. Much of what they traversed was downhill, and there were many times—though he did not vocalize it—when he felt like he was going too fast and would fall. Without being able to see the trees and scenery around him, Diomedes found their journey both more boring and more terrifying.

"The sun is starting to go down," Armannii said. The sound of the stream had lessened, though if Diomedes listened carefully, he could still hear it in the distance. "It's probably a good time to set up camp. I'd prefer to hunt with some light."

Diomedes thanked Blanndynne when she led him to an overturned log to sit on. He nodded in the direction Armannii's voice had come from. "Blanndynne and I will wait here for you."

"I'll be back," Armannii said, and Diomedes listened to the sound of leaves crunching beneath his boots as he walked away.

"How are you feeling?" Blanndynne asked after a few minutes. From the pops and crackles, it sounded like she'd created a fire, though with the direction the wind was blowing, he hadn't yet smelled it.

"I'm fine." Diomedes had taken out the dagger and was balancing it horizontally over his fingers. The balance wasn't quite as good as the knife he'd carried before, which he'd taken from a person who'd tried to mug him.

"What's it like? Is it what you thought it would be?" Blanndynne's voice was closer now, and he sat up straighter.

"It's different than I imagined," he said, pressing his lips together.

"In a good or bad way?"

He considered her question before responding. "It's just different. I don't know how best to describe it. I guess . . . I can feel the power from the magic, but at the same time, I've never felt weaker."

"Because you can't see?"

Diomedes nodded. A chill trickled into the palm of his hand as he tightened it into a fist, and he tried to imagine what the magic looked like. He remembered the way Otto's dark magic had spilled over the edge of the well when the man had performed a powerful spell. But what if it was different? He wouldn't be able to tell. His anger bubbled once more, and the magic in his hand swelled without him asking it to.

"Emotions make magic unpredictable," Emmalee explained as he loosened the fist. *"In order to remain effective and ready to end the war, I suggest you consider lessening your emotional reaction."*

Her suggestion was easier said than done. But Diomedes took a few intentional breaths, and the magic faded away.

"It's impressive," Blanndynne said, and she sat down on the same log as him, making it roll forward a bit.

Diomedes readjusted his seat. "I appreciate that."

"You know . . ." She chuckled, and he could hear the smile in her voice. "I already considered you strong. I mean, it takes a lot to stand up to the people who hold power over you." She paused, and Diomedes waited for her to continue. "Seeing Elias, seeing what happened to him. He got what he deserved."

"True. I mean, he betrayed you," Diomedes said, but she didn't respond right away.

"Who do you think cursed him?" Blanndynne asked.

"I'd guess his brother, but I don't know."

"You think Kylian hired someone to curse him?"

"So Kylian could inherit the throne." Diomedes nodded. "With Elias out of the way, forgotten, or whatever the curse did, Kylian could take the throne and start the war like he planned. At least, that's what I'd wager."

Blanndynne stayed silent. Her breathing was even, but she sighed after a few moments. "I guess the other option was to kill him. How else would he have taken the throne?"

Diomedes shrugged, his mind wandering elsewhere. He was about to take the throne. What options lay before him? Diomedes rubbed his temple, procrastinating that line of thought.

They continued to talk, though the subjects swayed to less intense conversation. By the time Armannii came back with two rabbits, they were speaking about the balls and ceremonies they'd taken part in at the Cyanthian castle. Apparently, Blanndynne had been present for her fair share when she'd served Elias.

Armannii was unnaturally silent as he went about preparing the rabbits for dinner, and Blanndynne kept most of the conversation going until it was time to sleep.

"We should probably rest a few hours. By the looks of the readable part of the map, we'll be in the northern part of the Albanistic Desert for the next part of our journey, and I'm not keen on sweating through every tunic I own," Armannii said, crunching leaves next to where Diomedes sat on the ground.

"Good idea," Diomedes said, remembering the heat of the desert. He was dreading the idea of traversing that much sand without his sight.

No one else spoke, and within half an hour, Armannii's and Blanndynne's breathing had evened out. They were both asleep. Diomedes was not.

"*You should try to sleep,*" Emmalee said softly. "*However, you won't have to rest as often the more powerful you grow.*"

Diomedes snorted. That was an unexpected perk. Less need for sleep meant more time to get things done. Like ending the war.

<hr/>

The sweat that'd been building up on Diomedes's forehead while he stood in the sun cooled him down when he called upon his magic. He summoned it to his hand, then ran it over the back of his neck and his forehead. The air was dry despite it only being an hour or two before dawn, according to Armannii.

Diomedes had only slept one or two hours, but it felt as though he'd gotten a full night's sleep. Emmalee had been relatively quiet all morning, only speaking when she had him ask his companions where they were in relation to certain areas.

"You must have a wonderful memory," Blanndynne said. "It's like you know exactly where we're going."

Emmalee warned him to lie, but he didn't even need the reminder. The partial lie slipped from his mouth as easily as the air he breathed.

"I'm using what I remember from the map as well as the tutoring I received." Diomedes rummaged around in his bag until he found his canteen. It was nearly empty, and he drank only as much as he needed to wet his mouth and throat. When Emmalee gave him more directions, he repeated them to Armannii and Blanndynne. "Keep an eye out for the remains of a castle. It will likely be on the left if we're as far into the desert as you say."

After they had all rested for several moments, they continued. Blanndynne guided him with her hand in his, though there were several times Diomedes still tripped in the sand. He had hated the way his boots had sunk in on the way to the mountain, and he hated it even more now that he couldn't see where he was going.

After a while, Blanndynne and Armannii stopped, and he stopped with them.

"That must be the castle you mentioned," Blanndynne said beside him. "It's definitely in ruins."

"I'm pretty sure wind erosion and sandstorms didn't take down that roof or that entire section of wall." Armannii's voice was farther away.

"*It was Raidah's parents' castle, and it was destroyed when their kingdom refused to join King Valryn in combining the five kingdoms under one throne,*" Emmalee whispered in his mind.

Diomedes straightened up, his shoulders rolling back. A trickle of ice traveled into his fingers at the mention of his grandfather. His skin crawled at the thought of being related to not two but three men who'd done more damage than good to Phildeterre.

One had started the war because of prejudice.

One had forced the unwanted uniting of kingdoms.

And one refused to put an end to the war.

He would not go down in history as the fourth Maudit to harm Phildeterre.

"Describe it to me," he said in a low voice edged with the fury he was trying to camouflage.

"It's made of sandstone bricks like the buildings in the town we went to when Armannii was hurt. It must be at least six stories tall, but most of the outer wall is rubble. I think I can see all the way into what must've been the throne room," Blanndynne said, and she pulled at his hand like she was leaning. "Yeah, I see two thrones sitting on an elevated platform, although one of them is broken in half and the other is flipped on its side."

Diomedes thought of Raidah and her children. His anger doubled, sending waves of dark magic to his hands. His grandfather had done this to them.

"What are you doing?" Blanndynne yelped, dropping his hand like it'd caught fire. "That burned!"

He couldn't respond. All he could do was stand there and imagine the castle from Blanndynne's vague description. But more than that, he pictured the sadness in Raidah's eyes when she'd spoken about her husband. A husband she'd lost in the war against King Butch. Against Diomedes's whole ancestry.

"Diomedes, calm down," Armannii said, his voice getting closer as he approached them. "You're kicking sand up everywhere." He raised his voice as the wind picked up.

It was swirling around him, a sandy vortex separating him from the rest of the world. The sand bit at him, but he didn't care. Even though he couldn't see it, he imagined a twister with him at the center. The wind howled, and beneath, he could hear Armannii and Blanndynne hollering at him to stop.

But the rush of dark magic flooding through him left him clenching his fists, watching in his mind's eye as the emptiness consumed a memory of his father from when he was younger. It disappeared fast enough that he'd barely registered it leaving.

"*That's enough, Diomedes.*" Emmalee's voice rang out above the sound of everything else. "*While your anger is rightly placed, there is no point in tiring yourself. You must continue to Raidah's home and develop a plan. One that will not fail.*"

The chill increased until Diomedes took a deep breath. Emmalee was right. He was wasting time. Nothing could be done about the past. The wind settled down as he relaxed his hands and took slow breaths.

"Are you all right?" Blanndynne asked, her voice drawing near as she rushed up to him.

"I'm fine," Diomedes responded, holding his hand out again. "We need to keep going."

But she didn't take his hand. Instead, Armannii spoke.

"You can't just throw a fit like that and expect us not to comment on it. You nearly started a natural disaster, not to mention you almost gave B frostbite on her hand. What's happening?" Armannii's feet shuffled through the sand until Diomedes could tell he was standing directly in front of him.

"We need to go," Diomedes said, his mind distracted as the chill returned with his annoyance.

"You're worrying us, Diomedes," Armannii said, his voice softer than it had been seconds earlier.

Diomedes took a step forward, crossing his arms over his chest. He could hear Armannii breathing right in front of him, and Diomedes turned his head to the side, tilting it as he listened. "My grandfather did this." He jutted his arm out, gesturing in the direction he assumed the castle was in. "He didn't get his way, so he destroyed those who stood against him."

Armannii remained quiet, but after many years of friendship, Diomedes could picture what he was doing. In his mind, he saw Armannii narrow his eyes, his hands positioned on his hips. He only had an inch or two on Diomedes, but he could make it feel like half a foot with one look.

"Yes, I got upset, but if you were me, you'd have done the same. Now can we please keep going?" Diomedes took a step to the right, hoping it was enough to pass by Armannii, but the elf caught him by the upper arm. "Get off." He emptied as much venom as he could into the words, and Armannii obeyed.

"You're going the wrong way," Armannii said, his voice flat.

Diomedes tightened his jaw, then held out his hand for Blanndynne to take. He waited several seconds before calling out for her. "I'm sorry for hurting you. I won't do it again."

Her fingers wrapped around his hand. "It's all right," she said in a low voice. "I get it. You just got your magic, and it takes a little getting used to. I'm all right."

"Look for a tower," Diomedes said before they continued in silence.

He'd hoped their resumed progress would help clear his head, but it didn't. Instead, he could only concentrate on Armannii's behavior.

"*You're letting your emotions overwhelm you,*" Emmalee said as an onslaught of sand flew into his face. "*While it's good to remember what you're fighting for, you must not let trivial things such as disagreements with your companions get in the way.*"

She had a point. As soon as he accepted what she'd said, all the frustration emptied out of him. It was like his dark magic swallowed the emotions, leaving him comfortably numb.

By the time Blanndynne stopped again, he felt nothing. Nothing except determination to find Raidah and ask for her help in ending the war.

"The tower is right in front of us, but I don't see a door," Armannii said. "Let me check it out."

Blanndynne let go of him while they waited for Armannii to walk around the span of the tower. Diomedes took a deep breath, noting the change in smell. While the desert had a salty taste and smell, something about their surroundings had a spicy odor.

"We're in the right place," Diomedes said, inhaling again. "I smell incense. Just like in the inn. We just need to figure out how to get inside."

"*Go to the tower and place your hand on the stone. There is a spell that will alert Raidah's men to your presence. Tell whoever answers who you are and request a presence with Raidah. I'm sure I don't need to be the one to inform you that you must present yourself with every air of royalty you can.*"

For the first time since he'd gotten magic, Diomedes almost laughed. He could perfectly remember his last meeting with Raidah.

Diomedes held a hand out in front of him, walking forward until he touched the side of the tower, which had been warmed by the sun. He waited.

Armannii walked up next to Diomedes. "Like I said, there are no doors. Not even a window. I doubt—"

A scraping sound resounded, and the tiniest of grins crossed Diomedes's lips at Armannii's sudden silence.

"You were saying?" Diomedes asked, clasping his hands behind his back.

"State your name and—" The unfamiliar voice paused, and there was a slight gasp from in front of Diomedes. The masculine voice continued after the man cleared his throat. "And your purpose."

"I'm Diomedes, prince of Phildeterre, and I would like an audience with Raidah immediately." Diomedes lifted his chin, using the sound of the man's voice to aim his face.

"And you are?" the stranger asked.

"We're with him," Armannii said.

The moment after the entrance had opened, the faint scent Diomedes had smelled earlier increased.

"My mistress has just now sat down for supper. You will have to wait, Your Highness."

"If your mistress requires that I wait until after she's finished dining, I will. But I suggest you ask for her opinion. I'd hate to think how she'd react if she found out you'd left her ally in a room to wait without her knowledge. Wouldn't you?"

Silence followed Diomedes's question, and he kept his smirk over his lips and his hands folded behind him.

"If you'll follow me," the man eventually said, and his tone held hints of irritation.

Armannii passed by Diomedes, who lifted his hand and placed it against the inside of the wall. With Armannii in front and Blanndynne behind him, Diomedes entered Raidah's home through a doorway to a winding staircase.

Chapter Thirty

was not expecting you to come so soon, Your Highness," Raidah said from across a table low to the floor. Raidah, Amira, Alphaeus, Diomedes, Blanndynne, and Armannii sat on pillows covered in silk fabric.

"Nor was I," Diomedes said, feeling around on the table for the goblet a servant had placed in front of him after refilling it. He couldn't stop the glass as it fell over, spilling its contents over the table.

Diomedes apologized, his muscles tightening as he listened to the sounds of at least two servants scurrying over to clean up the mess. He took a deep breath to calm down before he started another windstorm—or worse—inside Raidah's dining room.

"No apology necessary, Your Highness," Raidah said. "I'm sure it's been difficult to adjust."

"It's been challenging, yes." Diomedes cleared his throat, feeling all eyes on him. "Thank you for inviting us to dine with you." He wanted to change the subject, to feel the embarrassment of his mistake dissipate, but it lingered like the taste of something rotten.

"Well, I was eager to hear what you'd found out and whether my information had proved to be useful."

"Very useful," Diomedes said, nodding. The sounds of the others eating around him was rather distracting and difficult to block out. He'd always hated mouth noises, and it felt like they were amplified with the lack of visual distractions. He also had to force himself to concentrate on the words of whoever was speaking as well as how they sounded since he couldn't read their body language. It didn't help that a few musicians sat somewhere in the room, filling it with more things Diomedes had to listen over.

"What did you find in the caves?" Raidah asked. Silverware clinked nearby.

Diomedes unlatched the dagger from his belt and held it up. "This."

Raidah, or it could've been Amira, gasped.

"That was Emmalee's. Was it the object you were searching for?" Raidah's voice was low.

"Yes. I found it in the bottom of one of the mountains." Diomedes rubbed his thumb along the hilt, enjoying the coolness of the metal. "It's what I need to end the war. Well, this and your assistance."

"I'm assuming you mean my men?" Raidah said, swallowing as some ring or piece of metal chimed against her goblet.

"Yes." Diomedes nodded. "Soon enough, we'll take back Phildeterre for magic folk."

"Wonderful," Raidah said. "I'm more than willing to set up an army to march on Cyanthia. Send word when you decide upon a day, and I'll send my men. In the meantime, let us celebrate your success in your search and the upcoming strike on our collective opponent."

Diomedes raised his goblet, which a servant had needed to refill once more, in a salute, and Amira, who sat to his left, knocked hers against his. He heard goblets clunk together and the sounds of others drinking, and he joined them.

"Your mother has been very generous in letting us stay," Diomedes said as Alphaeus led him to the room he would be staying in. The younger man had not spoken much.

"She wants this war over as much as the next person," Alphaeus responded, his voice soft yet confident.

"And you?"

Alphaeus paused in the hallway. Diomedes found he could tell the difference in the flooring; the hallway was not covered in a carpet as was the room they'd eaten dinner in. Diomedes could tell when his young host moved and when he stopped; however, twice Diomedes had run into a table on the side of the hallway. Each time, he missed Blanndynne's gentle guidance.

Amira had shown Armannii and Blanndynne to their quarters. Diomedes had been surprised at how spacious the underground home was. It was most definitely a castle in both design and size. The hallways went on for long distances, and Alphaeus had needed to slow his pace for Diomedes.

"I want what my mother wants," he said, but something about the way he'd said it, maybe his hesitant tone, made it sound like there was more. Diomedes waited for him to continue, and the young man eventually did. "However, I'm less likely, I suppose, to trust the son of my mother's adversary when he comes knocking on our door."

"That's understandable," Diomedes said, a genuine smile on his face. "And wise. I would do the same if I were you." He tilted his head down. "You are, after all, the man of the house."

"I am. And you should know that I take my mother's and older sister's safety as of highest importance."

Diomedes chuckled, knowing from experience that Amira, like his own sister, did not need her brother's protection. He kept the thought to himself. "It's admirable. And I don't ask that you trust me. I'm a stranger, after all. But," Diomedes said, lifting his chin back up, "what I'm doing—what your mother is doing—will change the future of this country, and I invite you to join."

For the first time in what felt like a lifetime, Diomedes bathed. Raidah had set each of them up in their own room and had sent servants to prepare a bath before Diomedes had finished his plate.

With his stomach full and with the feeling of clean skin and hair, he felt his way to the bed with a grin. The mattress welcomed him with its softness, and he let out a sigh. His aching muscles relaxed, but just as the last time he'd tried to sleep, it didn't arrive right away.

As he lay there, the only thing he could think about was the embarrassment he'd felt after he'd knocked over the goblet. Or when he'd bumped into the third table on the way to the room. He cringed even at the memories.

"I need to learn how to see the world differently, or whatever you mentioned earlier," he muttered, rubbing his hand over his forehead.

As expected, Emmalee responded to him. *"You're willing to sacrifice more memories for it?"*

Diomedes frowned, sighing. He wondered if he'd always have to sacrifice memories in order to use the magic he'd earned.

"After a certain point, the power inside you will reach a peak. At that point, your sacrifices will no longer be needed. But until you cross that threshold, you must continue to provide for the magic inside you," Emmalee answered.

Another question emerged regarding others with magic, and he waited to hear Emmalee's response. She didn't speak right away.

"No," she finally said. *"Those of us who are naturally born with magic do not require such a sacrifice with every use of magic. But dark magic, as I'm sure you know, does not show without the*

person's heart breaking. Often, that in itself is a sacrifice that sets the entirety of a person's magic in motion." Emmalee paused. *"As for light magic, it doesn't seem to require a sacrifice or a tragedy. At least, that's my own observation. Both are pure magics passed down bloodlines, although light magic has solely taken on the name of pure magic."*

Diomedes rubbed his jaw, no longer as comforted by the soft bed or the state of his cleanliness. If he didn't sacrifice to learn the spell, he'd continue to make a fool of himself. A horrifying image crossed his mind of him tripping into a council meeting. Even with his magic, he could imagine his father and the council laughing at him. The embarrassment over the imaginary scenario had his skin crawling, and he made his decision.

"I'll do it. Just tell me how."

"First you must sacrifice a memory, and it must be a strong one. If you cannot find one with enough power, you may need to sacrifice more than one."

It took a few moments to sort through his memories, but he eventually landed on one of his first training sessions with the royal guard. He'd been waiting since he'd been a little boy, watching his father's men duel in the courtyard or in the training rooms. The adrenaline had left him shaking during his first lesson, and since he had secretly been practicing in the privacy of his room, he had surprised his teacher—a guard who had since retired. He remembered the excitement and pride he'd felt when the guard had given him nothing but praise.

Despite the resistance Diomedes still felt every time he willingly relinquished a memory to the dark mist—fighting the desire to hold on to the memory—he watched it fade in his mind's eye.

"That was good, but not enough. Find another. It must be a powerful memory. One that has defined who you are."

Diomedes racked his brain, and one came to mind. He'd been in his early teen years, and it was the first time he'd snuck to the lower town, even before he met Armannii. Diomedes had run into a young beggar woman and her four-year-old daughter. He'd handed her his entire coin purse. When he'd returned to the castle, he'd spoken to his father about creating a relief effort for the poor in the lower town. It had been the first project his father had let him lead alone.

"*That's good,*" Emmalee said without Diomedes speaking a single word. "*Now let go of it.*"

Diomedes bit the inside of his cheek, then sighed, releasing the memory. It faded to black, and a coolness washed over him. A numb sensation followed.

Whatever memory he'd given left him vibrating with power. It coursed through him, and he couldn't help but grin. He could feel the dark magic stronger than he'd felt it before.

"Amazing," he said, and though he couldn't see the magic, he could sense it spreading through his body. "I can feel it. The power you were talking about."

"*This isn't even a fraction of what you can do. The more you are willing to sacrifice, the more powerful you will be. Now sleep, Diomedes. I will teach you the spell in your dreams.*" It was as if her permission was what he needed, and soon he was sound asleep.

Emmalee came to him in a dream dressed in the same orange-and-maroon dress. They stood in what looked like a part of the Black Forest, only there was a break in the leafy roof above them, letting light shine down on the valley of purple flowers surrounding them.

"You did very well today, Diomedes," she said, a wide grin on her face. "If it wasn't clear enough from your tests, you are certainly the perfect person to bear this gift of magic."

"Thank you," Diomedes said, nodding.

"Before I teach you the spell, tomorrow morning I want you to meet with Raidah. If you are to send word to her later that you are in need of assistance in taking the throne, she will need some instruction to give her men."

"What instruction?" Diomedes asked, his mind hyperfocused on the spell rather than the directions Emmalee was giving him.

Still, he tried to pay attention since he'd need to repeat the information to Raidah the next day.

"When the day comes, her men will serve as the distraction while you and your companions enter the castle unnoticed. If she is hesitant about the role her men will play, you may need to pull her aside and *privately* tell her that I have been the one giving you instructions. I have no doubt she will comply when she learns this information. She was a loyal friend when I was leading the rebellion."

Diomedes stood straighter, looking down at Emmalee from several inches. It was strange. The dream felt so real, yet he was oddly aware that in reality, he'd never see again. It almost made him cling to the dream, to the ability to see.

Somehow, Emmalee picked up on his line of thought. "Although it may be difficult to understand, your sacrifice was worth it. Remember, the power inside you is more than you could ever imagine. It just needs you to listen to it, to feed it. To comply. Then we will achieve everything we've ever dreamed of."

"Teach me the spell," Diomedes said, sticking his hands in his pockets. "I'm tired of relying on everyone else. I'd rather rely on magic."

"Very well. While this spell may take a few days to reach full effect, it should begin to work as soon as tomorrow, though it may be tiring at first."

"Teach me."

"I will, but first I want to show you what you're capable of." Emmalee held out her hands, and Diomedes took a step back when darkness surrounded them. She closed her eyes, and as she raised her hands, the darkness shot up through the break in the trees. The blue sky above them lost its color, and darkness spread over it.

"That's incredible," Diomedes said when she stopped and the darkness dissipated. "I want to learn that one too."

"In good time." She tucked a piece of hair behind her ear and then crossed her arms over her chest. "Shall we begin?"

Chapter Thirty-One

I assume you rested well, Your Highness?" Raidah asked when Amira escorted him to her study. It smelled strongly of some sort of wood, maybe sandalwood. But there was something else, something bitter hiding beneath it. Diomedes tried to hide his reaction to the strong scent by nodding.

"Of course, and I'm sure my companions did as well." Diomedes listened to the sound of Amira departing from the room, and she closed the door behind her.

"Tell me something, Diomedes," Raidah said, her voice getting closer until she was right in front of him. Her hand was gentle as she touched his wrist, pulling him until she lowered his hand to the arm of a chair. He sat down, and she must've done the same in front of him. "What was it like? The caves."

"It was a labyrinth. Easy to get lost." Diomedes crossed one leg over the other, leaning back against the chair. The padding on the arms and the seat itself was made of silk, and having seen Raidah before, he didn't doubt that the chairs were probably some shade of red. Though maybe she decorated her house differently from the way she dressed.

"But you navigated it just fine?"

Diomedes shook his head. "Not at first. I had all but forgotten the gift you gave me. It was very useful."

"It belonged to my husband," Raidah said, and while he couldn't see it, he could almost feel her gauging his reaction. "The sorceress—Emmalee—gave them to her commanders. When my husband passed, she asked me to give it to the person who would come seeking to end the war next. Someone who sought power. Magic."

Smiling, Diomedes leaned forward, summoning the dark magic to his fingertips with a mere thought. "I seem to fit that description quite well."

Raidah chuckled. "You do. Though I must say it surprised me when I realized it was the prince of Phildeterre she was referring to. After your ancestors, I . . . Let's just say I've been waiting for someone from the Maudit line to have a correct way of thinking for a long time."

"I appreciate that," Diomedes said, sitting back again as his magic left his hand. He relished the coolness as it trickled away. "Now, I was hoping we might discuss the plans to infiltrate Cyanthia. I think it wise to have a plan so that when you receive word, you and your men are prepared."

"Of course." Raidah shifted, clearing her throat. "What will you need from me?"

"I will need your men to serve as a distraction, a cover if you will, so that my companions and I may enter the castle without being seen." He had spent the time before this meeting devising a more detailed plan and was grateful in the moment for the forethought.

Raidah was silent, and Diomedes wished for the ability to read her body language.

"Emmalee said you are someone who can be trusted," Diomedes said, testing Emmalee's suggestion from the night before. It at least sparked a reaction from Raidah.

"Emmalee?"

Diomedes nodded. "She's been speaking to me, in my head, since I received my magic. She wanted me to tell you she's the one providing guidance to me."

"And she wants my men to serve as a distraction against the royal guards?" Raidah's voice was hesitant.

"Yes." Diomedes waited to hear her response. When she didn't give one, he continued with the plan he'd thought up. "There are a series of tunnels leading in from the catacombs to the castle. Some of your men may enter from there. The others should dress in inconspicuous clothing and blend in with the people in town. When a signal is given, they can swarm from the outside."

"And you?"

With a sneer, Diomedes stroked his jawline. "I'll be paying my father a little visit."

The morning passed by faster than Diomedes realized. He'd spent multiple hours in a private room with Raidah planning out the best line of attack on the castle.

"My men will get in position when you send word, and when they see your signal, they will move in," she said as someone opened the door to the dining room for them. They had finished their planning before lunch. Prior to entering the room, Diomedes could hear Armannii and Blanndynne speaking with Amira and her brother around the table.

Armannii fell silent as soon as they entered, but Blanndynne approached them.

"We were beginning to wonder where you were."

Diomedes could tell from Blanndynne's voice that she was beaming, probably at Raidah rather than him.

"How did it go?" Alphaeus asked, his footsteps nearing before he stopped and gave his mother a kiss on each cheek.

"Our prince here has a quick mind," Raidah said, grazing her hand on Diomedes's arm to lead him to the table, where Amira took his hand and sat down next to him. "We have our plans, and if all goes well, soon the war will be over."

"I'll drink to that," Amira said, sliding Diomedes's goblet into his hand as Blanndynne sat down next to him on his other side.

Armannii stayed quiet, but with a note from Emmalee to ignore it, Diomedes joined the others in a toast. Still, the elf remained silent for the entirety of lunch and barely said a word as Alphaeus, Amira, and Raidah left the three of them alone in the room after a while.

It was only when Blanndynne moved beside Diomedes that he noticed something he hadn't before. He could sense the table near his knee, though it was still a few inches from it. And when Blanndynne adjusted her hair, some part of her drew near enough that he felt as though something had touched him on the side of the arm.

"It's the beginning of the spell you started last night," Emmalee explained as Diomedes rubbed his hand along his arm. *"While it'll start with sensing nearby objects, it'll grow stronger until you can sense everything within a room—everything around you. Almost like a phantom image. No color. No change in lighting. But it will aid you in simple tasks."*

Diomedes had to remind himself not to react to Emmalee's words, though he desired to smile. The fact that he could sense his goblet before he actually touched it meant he had done the spell correctly.

"Well?" Armannii said, and while his voice was light, there was an edge to it. "Care to fill us in on your conversation with Raidah, or maybe what our next step is?"

"Of course," Diomedes said, lowering the goblet back to the table after he'd finished with it. He shared with them some of the matters he'd discussed with Raidah, but he did not share all of it. He gave them the big picture, keeping details like Emmalee and his plan to take the throne closer to his chest. It wasn't that he didn't trust Armannii and Blanndynne, but the way Armannii had reacted to his magic had been less than satisfactory, and he didn't want the disappointment of disagreeing with his friends distracting him from his goals.

"Then what are we going to do in the meantime?" Blanndynne asked.

It was the question he did not yet have an answer to. He knew his end goal, which would end with him in Cyanthia taking the crown. He did not, however, know what steps he'd have to follow to get there.

"I'm not sure," Diomedes said when Emmalee didn't offer any sort of answer either. It was as if she'd all but abandoned him.

"*I haven't abandoned you. I'm simply thinking.*"

"How long are you thinking we'll stay here?" Armannii asked.

Diomedes pondered the question. "I suppose until I decide where we need to go next. In the meantime, enjoy the baths and beds."

That evening, Emmalee visited him in his dreams once more. They stood at the top of a hill in a boulder field southeast of Cyanthia. At least, that was where Diomedes thought it was.

"You're correct," Emmalee said, standing on one of the boulders. "Did you know this boulder field lies over top of the remains of the Cyanthian portal to the Dark?"

"I-I didn't," Diomedes said, shaking his head. The nonchalant way in which she spoke of the destroyed portal unnerved Diomedes, but a soothing coolness soon eased any concerns he may have had.

"It's also the first place your father and one of his marshals almost managed to kill me. I narrowly escaped," Emmalee said, and the way her voice trailed off had Diomedes wondering if there was more to the story.

"Always." Emmalee's voice was clipped. "But that does not matter in this moment. For now, I want you to focus on what steps you plan to take in order to ascend to the throne."

Diomedes sighed as he sat down on a flat boulder, which was split down the middle by a giant crack.

"I don't know what to do next. I never . . . I never pictured what would happen if I got this far." Embarrassment clouded his mind, and he fell silent.

Despite this only being a dream, the ambience of the world around him seemed louder when he allowed his mind to focus on it. Birds and small mammals skittered through the branches of the trees surrounding the boulder field. Mainly, though, he heard the gentle breeze that blew around him.

"It's unwise to rush into anything, especially something as important as what you're doing, without a plan." Emmalee stood behind him, and her shadow blocked the warmth of the sun.

"Well," Diomedes said, tilting his head as he looked out at the horizon of trees surrounding the boulder field. "What did you do when you were planning something as big as this?"

Emmalee chuckled, though it lacked an ounce of humor. "I went to the Dark to find a seer."

Diomedes spun around and looked up at her. "Oh?" He rubbed the back of his neck. "That could be helpful. I mean, it would at least be a chance of some direction." He frowned, remembering how he'd said something similar over and over again when searching for information on how to find the dagger in the mountains.

"It's not a bad idea, but it will take time to get there. Even if Raidah can offer transportation over the desert and men to accompany you, it may take six days just to get to the portal you entered through last time."

It was still unnerving to know she could fish around in his mind, searching through his memories and thoughts. Again, the coolness he'd felt before filled him, and he easily returned to Emmalee's response.

"You think it would be worth it to go?" Diomedes asked, standing up to face her.

"I believe so, but I suppose only time will tell."

"I thought this might come in handy," Amira said the next morning. Her breath tickled the back of Diomedes's neck, and he squirmed as he waited for her to finish tying the silk scarf around where his eyes should have been. "I don't mind it," she said in reference to Diomedes's lack of eyes, "but you did give a few of the servants a good scare, and since you'll be out and about . . ."

"It's a great idea. Thank you, Amira," Diomedes said, moving several steps away as soon as she was finished. She had met him in a small room with a few bookshelves and recliners. Diomedes had asked her to take him to Armannii and Blanndynne—he wanted to share his new plan with them—but she had wanted to give him the scarf for his eyes first.

"Of course," she said. Something in her voice led Diomedes to believe she had something else to say, and he waited several seconds before asking. "I have a request." Her voice was not nearly as bold as he had heard it in the past, and Diomedes's old friend curiosity snuck in.

"I'm listening."

"When you become king, I want to be on your council. And I know that's presumptuous, but I want to make a difference. I have studied like I would still inherit a throne. I know about politics, and I know what it takes to run a country, even if I've never had one of my own. It would mean a lot if you would just—"

"I'll consider it," Diomedes said, nodding.

"You'll . . . oh, thanks." Amira let out a short laugh. "I didn't think you'd agree that quickly."

Diomedes shrugged, clasping his hands behind his back. "I know I'll need to replace a few people on my father's council when I become king." His mind went to the sniveling council member by the name of Clive. He would be the first to go. "You'll be one of the first I'll consider. And your brother, if he so desires."

"I'm sure he would appreciate that," Amira said, and she led him out of the small study—at least, that was what she had called it. The sensing spell had not yet gotten strong enough that Diomedes could tell where things were until he got within six inches of them.

"Your brother is quiet," Diomedes said, moving to the side when he sensed a table near his hip. He questioned why Raidah had so much furniture in her halls; it clogged them and made them difficult to navigate. "Has he always been that way?"

"Al studies people—the way they act, speak, and work. It's easiest to do that when listening and watching. He'll give his input when he thinks it's required or necessary, otherwise he remains caught up in his mind as he studies." Amira held a door open for Diomedes—he could hear the hinges creak—and he thanked her. "And if he's not studying people, he's studying books."

Diomedes chuckled. "I can think of someone I know who's very similar in that regard." He thought of his sister, who wandered around the castle with her nose in a book.

"Nice scarf, Didi," Armannii said from inside the room. "It's probably a good idea."

Blanndynne moved to the doorway, greeting Amira. "Thanks for accompanying him," she said.

"Thank you for your time, Amira," Diomedes said, nodding in the direction she stood, or at least he thought she stood. She had moved back and out of reach of his sensing spell.

"Of course," Amira said before the door closed.

Diomedes's hand tingled a second before Blanndynne reached for it. She led him to a pillow on the floor and sat down next to him. It didn't take long before Diomedes shared his new plan with his friends.

"We're going to the Dark. There's someone there I need to speak to."

"Seriously?" Armannii asked, shock filling his voice. "The last time we were there, the Dark Soldiers—"

"We'll be fine," Diomedes said, his voice unrelenting.

"But you can't see, and—"

"Which means it will hardly be different from the last time. It's called the Dark for a reason. Besides, there's someone there I need to speak to."

"Don't tell me we're going back to Otto," Blanndynne said, a hint of a whine lining her voice. "He was awful."

"It's one of his defining qualities," Armannii muttered. "Who do you need to find, and why is this person so important?"

"There's a seer," Diomedes said, noticing when Armannii's breathing hitched. Both of his companions shifted where they sat.

"Why?" Armannii asked.

"Why do you think? To tell us the future. To provide some reassurance. Need I go on?"

Armannii grunted but didn't argue further.

An hour or two later, Alphaeus and Amira led them out of the underground home—although, by the size of it, Diomedes had decided upon calling it a subterranean castle.

Just as Emmalee had predicted, Raidah offered to have a few men escort them out of the desert, even providing Albanistic camels for them to travel on. The beasts had been born and raised in the desert, and they could travel for weeks without needing water. They stood ten feet tall, and they blended in with the white sand—at least, that was what Diomedes had been taught. He'd never seen one, and with his sight gone, he never would.

"Thank your mother again for letting us stay here," Blanndynne said, and it sounded like she hugged Amira.

"We will. Hopefully we will see you soon, when you send my mother word to move on Cyanthia," Amira said, and after she'd said goodbye to Blanndynne, her steps moved toward Diomedes.

The spell had been growing stronger with each passing hour. As Amira approached him, a tingling sensation began in his arm right before she touched him there. He placed his hand on hers and guided it to his mouth, where he pressed it gently to his lips.

"A pleasure, Amira," he said, a small grin lifting his cheek. Another tingling sensation occurred on his left after he let go of Amira's hand, and he turned to face whoever had approached him.

"Your Highness," Alphaeus said, clearing his throat. "I wish you well on your journey."

Diomedes held out his hand, and Alphaeus shook it. "Thank you for your hospitality. I hope you join us when the day comes."

"I'll be there."

"Travel safely," Amira added as she and her brother returned to the coolness of the tower. Though the sun had set and nighttime was approaching, the heat from the day still radiated through the air.

Somewhere to Diomedes's left, one of the camels snorted, and the sound of one of the men scolding the beast brought a grin to Diomedes's lips. He was already excited to ride one, and it also meant less walking on his part. His leg had been rewrapped multiple times since arriving at Raidah's, and it had started to look better according to one of her healers. Still, riding a camel through the desert would be a welcome change to their typical way of travel.

The sound of stone scraping stone resounded as the opening disappeared, startling Diomedes from his thoughts. Then it was just Armannii, Blanndynne, Diomedes, four of Raidah's men, and four camels outside.

"This way," Blanndynne said, guiding Diomedes by the hand.

The camel she brought him to smelled like hay and something musty, and Diomedes flinched when a wave of hot air blew over him.

"He likes you," one of Raidah's men said with a heavy northern accent. "He's sniffing you."

Diomedes smiled, following the man's guidance to climb onto the saddle, which had a small awning tucked into the back for travel during the day. Each saddle, according to the man, held two passengers. Diomedes settled back into his seat, gripping whatever he could around him when the camel shifted to its feet, making the saddle wobble from side to side.

They traveled all night, and Diomedes found himself wishing he could sleep just to make the time go faster. At one point, he could hear Armannii talking to the man directing the camel he sat on. But besides Diomedes's own camel wrangler humming, most of the journey was filled with the sound of the camels' giant hooves pounding the sand on the ground below them.

They stopped three times to eat and for various members of the traveling party to relieve themselves, but otherwise they stayed on the camels. The temperature had dipped until it was almost cold, but it rose later when the night faded into early morning.

"We must stop to make camp, Your Highness," the man who had directed the camel said, and Diomedes nodded.

Diomedes stretched his legs, which had cramped, waiting for Raidah's men to finish setting up tents for them to rest. Blanndynne and Armannii joined him, both talking about their impressions of the camels—apparently, none of the trio had ever ridden one—while the men spoke in their native tongue, Bysha.

Before long, the tents were set up, and Armannii, Blanndynne, and Diomedes shared one with three cots. According to one of the men, they would sleep until dusk, pack up, and leave. Diomedes found it difficult to fall asleep, especially with the heat outside sneaking its way into the tent, though the tent did help quite a bit.

The second night, Diomedes asked the man directing his camel when they would start to have to worry about sand crawlers.

"The crawlers don't like the camels. They will leave us alone." The man went back to humming soon after without offering an explanation, and Diomedes didn't bother to ask, as he started to get motion sickness around that time. He spent most of the second night concentrating on anything but the nausea creeping up inside him.

Two more days passed; the caravan set up camp and slept each day. Though Diomedes was grateful not to have to walk, and even more grateful—though not as much as Armannii—for the lack of venomous crawlers, he was sick of traveling by camel by the fourth day. There wasn't much to practice sensing, and Emmalee had been all but silent in his head.

Thankfully, the weather started to get more temperate, and soon enough, they slowed down.

"We cannot go any farther, Your Highness," the man directing his camel said in his thick accent. "The beasts must stay in the desert, and we are nearing the Glass Fields." He stopped the camel, and the others behind him followed suit.

"Thank you for taking us this far," Diomedes said, his voice hitching slightly as the camel began to kneel down. The motion of the saddle moving back and forth for hours had left Diomedes a little unsteady on his feet, but he regained his balance as his companions joined him on the ground.

"Safe travels to you," one of the men said, and Diomedes, Blanndynne, and Armannii echoed a similar goodbye.

When they had walked far enough away that Diomedes couldn't hear the men talking to one another in Bysha, he paused. Armannii spoke before he could.

"I'm assuming you want to go to Hess's portal instead of risking going through the main portal?" Armannii asked to the right of Diomedes.

"Yes." Diomedes adjusted the strap of his bag so it wasn't rubbing against his collarbone, then held out his hand in the direction he knew Blanndynne was standing. As much as he wished the sensing spell were strong enough to help him navigate the forest, he had a feeling he'd need more time before he could comfortably walk without the risk of tripping over roots and smacking into tree trunks, not to mention the small section of the Glass Fields they needed to cross to get to the Black Forest.

"Then let's go before the sun comes all the way out and roasts us alive," Armannii said.

Chapter Thirty-Two

Careful," Armannii said once they reached the boulder that protected the entrance to the guardian's home. "I'm about to draw the levitation rune. B, I suggest you and Didi go at the same time since you can fly down. I'll climb down the ladder."

Despite Diomedes's protests, they had stopped at an inn twice since they'd reached the Black Forest. While he had felt no need to rest—another effect Emmalee had prepared him for—Armannii had. Diomedes had spent his time practicing sensing the objects around him while Armannii and Blanndynne slept. Each time, it had been more than a few hours before everyone was up and ready to go. More hours lost to sleep. The fact that he didn't need to sleep as much was one of the things he was appreciating more and more.

Their journey through the Black Forest to Hess's had been exactly what Diomedes had expected: painstakingly slow. However, the additional practice time seemed to be paying off because during one moment of absolute concentration, Diomedes thought he saw a shadow form in his mind of a tree right before Blanndynne pulled him around it.

"All right." Blanndynne moved to stand behind Diomedes, and the tingling sensation began right before she looped her arms under his armpits. "Ready."

"Three, two, one, go," Armannii said at the same time a crunching noise sounded.

Blanndynne lifted Diomedes off the ground, and the musty air from the underground tunnel met them as she flew him to the bottom. The moment Diomedes's feet hit the ground, a thudding noise echoed down the tunnel.

"You'd think I could make that rune last a little longer with how often I've drawn it," Armannii muttered from the top of the ladder.

Diomedes doubted he'd intended anyone to hear him, but his comment left a little grin on Diomedes's face.

Blanndynne and Diomedes waited for Armannii to reach them at the bottom, and as soon as Diomedes heard the sound of the elf's feet hitting the ground, he started down the tunnel. His arm tingled, and Diomedes stepped to the side to avoid clipping the wall when he entered the tunnel.

"How'd you know to move just now?" Blanndynne asked as she caught up to him.

Diomedes shrugged. "Call it intuition." He had no desire to give a full explanation, nor did he think Emmalee would allow him to do so.

"*You're correct,*" Emmalee said, speaking for the first time in a while. "*It's wise to give your companions vague answers for now.*"

Since Emmalee was already present in his mind, Diomedes posed a question he'd briefly thought about on the way to the portal. Her response did little to block out the monotonous sound of footsteps as they marched through the tunnels. The stone around them echoed every sound even more than the cave system in the Elemental Mountains.

"*It's a fair question, and I'm glad to see you're thinking ahead. Very wise,*" Emmalee said. "*Unfortunately, the spell you did in the caves will not work to find people. Tracking people is more difficult and usually requires the blood of the person you seek. As you don't have the seer's blood, I can't walk you through any of those spells. However, I know that when I went to visit him many years ago, he was set up in the northern part of the Western Cliffs near the upper uncharted areas.*"

Although it was good information, it wasn't as specific an answer as Diomedes had hoped for. He posed another question to her, and she reluctantly agreed.

"*I suppose having your elf find out where the seer resides will be useful information, but be careful how much you share,*" Emmalee said in response to his thoughts.

Diomedes didn't pose any more questions, and Emmalee remained silent in his mind. Clearing his throat, Diomedes slowed down a second to let Armannii walk closer to him.

"Once we're in the Dark, I need you to figure out where the seer lives," Diomedes said, forcing his tone to be light.

"What, you don't magically know that information already?" Armannii asked, but before Diomedes could respond, Armannii continued. "I'll find him. I doubt he's in hiding, and even if he is, someone in the mycelium grid will know something. It's not easy to hide in the Dark. Believe me," he muttered, falling back again in a clear move to end the conversation.

"Do you want to stop and rest here?" Blanndynne asked near Diomedes's left. "Or to go straight in?"

"I'd prefer the latter," Diomedes said, shrugging to hide how much he didn't want to waste more time resting when there was no need.

"We're going straight in." Armannii's voice was bold. "Staying isn't an option. Not after last time."

Beside him, Blanndynne paused, but she caught up with Armannii. When she spoke, her voice carried resentment. "I thought we were past this. I messed up. I fixed it. Leave it alone."

Diomedes didn't intercede, content to listen, as their argument served as a break from the never-ending tunnel. When Blanndynne had made a mistake in enchanting the guardian the last time they were here, Armannii had nearly lost his mind and had certainly lost his temper. For that reason, Diomedes and Blanndynne had kept her enchantment practice an intentional secret from Armannii.

"I am leaving it alone. I'm just saying there's no way we're staying here to rest." Armannii's tone was defensive.

Blanndynne scoffed but didn't argue.

On and on they walked, and Diomedes wondered how long the entrance tunnel could go on. He could almost taste the moisture in the air, and more so than before, he could hear little creatures scurrying about. Those he was grateful to not see.

"I was not expecting you back so soon, Your Highness." Hessland's voice was distant since they hadn't exited the tunnel. "I'm assuming the war has not ended. Am I correct?" His gravelly voice increased in volume the closer Diomedes got.

"Not yet," Diomedes said, moving to avoid the wall when the right half of his body tingled. "But we're close, and I need to return to the Dark before I return to the Cyanthian castle to end the war."

"How do you—you have magic now? How is that possible?" Hessland must've only been a few feet away. He didn't know how, but the old man had sensed it. That was not typical. Not between rune magic and the pure magics, as rune magic was not volatile toward light or dark magic like both were to each other. But he too could feel the magic radiating both off the guardian and the rooms behind him, primarily from the tunnel he knew led to the portal.

Diomedes tried to remember what the old guardian looked like. The old man's pure white eyes—which lacked irises and pupils—were of course the first thing Diomedes remembered. Hessland had been shorter than Diomedes, his skin equally as pale. And if Hess hadn't suddenly changed his hair, it was probably still gray with a long braid at the nape of his neck. He at least sounded the same; his voice still carried the disdain he had for Diomedes.

"Good observation." Diomedes clasped his wrist behind his back, puffing out his chest.

Several seconds passed before Hessland spoke again. "All right, you may go through the portal."

"Just like that?" Blanndynne asked.

The guardian's immediate acceptance of Diomedes was out of place and shocking given the resistance both he and his brother had given him the first time around.

"Follow me, and I'll explain." Hessland grunted, and the sound of him shuffling away reached Diomedes's ears. He fell in step behind him. "My role is to vet those who go in and out of the Dark, as is my brother's. Zephrium and I both have a method of doing so, and when you passed through the last time, you proved your noble goals, though I would not have even considered letting you be tested had you not convinced me beforehand."

"Tested?" Diomedes asked, trying to think of any test the guardian had given him besides testing his patience.

Armannii walked with Blanndynne while Diomedes followed behind Hessland, whose footsteps echoed even more in the second tunnel. Neither of them spoke.

"Other guardians use other methods. My brother and I—" He paused, and Diomedes knew why. They had entered the room with the portal. Energy filled the room and coursed through Diomedes, mixing with the magic within him. "My brother and I prefer a more passive test."

Diomedes could feel the source of the energy—the portal in the middle of the room—pulling him toward it, but he resisted. The magic that formed it was just as hypnotizing as it had been the first time, even without his sight. Something buzzed, and he was unsure if it was from the portal or from the flora he knew lined the room. Either way, it was distracting as he tried to focus on Hessland's speech.

"I'm sure you remember this room?" Hessland asked, and Diomedes nodded. "It is the test."

"How so?" Armannii asked, his voice more distant than Diomedes had expected.

"Should anyone enter with ulterior motives, the flora would react. Then I could do my job," the guardian said.

"How would it react?" Diomedes asked, thinking of the leaves and vegetation that came in every color imaginable. He had contemplated their purpose upon first entering the portal months earlier.

"These plants are protective of the portal, as am I. They would protect."

"How?" Diomedes asked again.

"Each in its own way. Some are poisonous, others simply subdue." Hessland's voice had continued toward the portal, and Diomedes followed behind.

Though he knew Hessland bore no nefarious schemes, that his intentions were good, the knowledge the guardian had given him made him hesitant as he followed the pull of the portal to the staircase. He didn't want to accidentally tread on one of the plants and end up paralyzed or worse.

"When you passed through this room before, you unwittingly proved that you were in fact on the side of magic. I was hesitant to let you this close, though, and for that I apologize. You continue to challenge my understanding of the Maudit royal line."

"I appreciate that, Hessland. And your willingness to help," Diomedes said as he took the first step toward the portal. Footsteps followed him, and Armannii spoke from somewhere near Diomedes.

"Thank you, Hess," Armannii said. "And I'll lead." Armannii reached for Diomedes's wrist, causing it to tingle just before he grabbed it.

Blanndynne grabbed Diomedes's other hand, and after Blanndynne reiterated Armannii's gratitude, the elf pulled them through the portal.

Without the nauseating sight of light and dark magic merging together, Diomedes was pleased to find he had a better reaction to the travel than he had the first two times.

"I'd hoped I wouldn't have to see you three again," Zephrium, Hessland's twin brother, said as they passed through the connecting portal into the Dark.

Diomedes let a smirk cross his lips. He turned in the direction of Zephrium's voice. "Do you remember what you said to me the first time you allowed us into the Dark, Zephrium?" Diomedes cocked his head to the side, wiping his hands off on his trousers.

"I don't recall the particulars." Zephrium's voice wavered, and Diomedes wondered if it had to do with the scarf tied around his lack of eyes. He assumed Hessland's twin brother could tell he had magic just as the first guardian had.

"If I remember correctly, you told me the future was unclear, even for seers." Diomedes paused, but no one spoke, so he continued. "We've come to test your theory."

"You're here for the seer?" Zephrium said, and Diomedes pictured the old man's opal eyes widening in surprise. He got the slightest bit of enjoyment in using his words to garner similar reactions; it made him feel like he had control even over the emotions of others. It felt like the power swirling inside him.

"We are." Diomedes stepped forward, using the sensing spell to move in the room until he had descended from the platform the portal stood on and was nearer to Zephrium. The spell was progressing faster every hour, and Diomedes could picture a blurry shadow in his mind where he assumed Zephrium stood; no color and no differences in lighting, yet still somehow sight.

Diomedes faced the amorphous shadow. "We really should be going. Would you mind leading us out?"

"You've clearly changed, Your Highness."

"You've noticed?" Diomedes grinned. "I've changed in some ways, but not all. I'm just as determined to end the war on magic as I was before, if not more. And each step we take is one closer."

Zephrium shifted in front of Diomedes. "How close, Your Highness?"

Diomedes let his grin slink farther across his lips as he took another step, feeling the tingling in his shoulder as he leaned forward. "Very," he whispered in Zephrium's ear. The guardian smelled musky, though beneath it was a hint of something sweet. The juice they drank in the Dark smelled similarly.

The old man's breathing only gave him away for a second when it hitched, but he cleared his throat and took a step back. "Well then, I won't stand in your way. Follow me."

By the time they entered the Dark, the sensing spell had strengthened enough that Diomedes rarely needed Blanndynne's help. He navigated around branches and trees, only getting scratched a few times when he lost focus. He followed the sound of Armannii's footsteps as they journeyed toward Bayan Village, where they would stop and stay in an inn per Armannii's and Blanndynne's request. While it felt like a waste of time, he knew Armannii would want to seek out the seer's location alone; it was easier than needing to keep track of him and Blanndynne.

"Did you know about the guardians' tests?" Diomedes asked Armannii as he prepared to leave their room at the inn. It smelled of old socks and lavender incense, an overwhelming combination that had Diomedes wishing there were a window to crack.

"I didn't. But I knew most guardians in the past had some way of testing the people who passed through, so I figured there must've been something." Armannii's quiver clacked, and Diomedes tilted his head in his friend's direction.

"How long do you think it'll take you to find the seer?" Blanndynne asked. She sat across the room from Diomedes, and while he couldn't quite sense how large the room was, he could see a shadow in the shape of a boot-covered foot move out of his spell range when he focused on it. The room was bigger than he'd thought.

"Not sure. Depends on whether he cares about being found or not." Armannii breathed deeply. "Not all seers are open to welcoming people in for quick reads of their future. Some have been known to be more . . . reclusive. And I'm pretty sure most of this generation of seers have died At least, that's what I've heard. Never met one if I'm honest."

"Let's hope that changes today," Diomedes said, and with a quick goodbye from Armannii, he and Blanndynne were left alone. After a few minutes, Diomedes felt it was safe to say what he had wanted to say when they'd first reached the portal. "Whatever you did to Hessland seems to have worked well over time. He didn't remember what you did."

Blanndynne hesitated before thanking him. "It felt weird returning, like I was waiting for him to remember every second we were around him. My magic is strong, but to go against a guardian?" She snorted. "That would be unwise. Their rune magic is unmatched."

"Don't tell Armannii that," Diomedes said, a smirk crossing his lips. He ran a hand through his hair. "If the guardian hadn't let us through, I was going to find a way to distract Armannii so you could have a second try at Hess."

"I would've taken it. Each time I practice, I can feel myself getting a better grasp of it."

Emmalee's voice startled Diomedes since she had been silent for so long, lingering in the depths as a passive onlooker.

"*You should tell her that if she continues to practice and adds runes to her magic, she'll make it stronger, allowing her to command more at once and for longer spans. It will take time though,*" Emmalee said, and Diomedes communicated what the sorceress had told him.

"I guess that's something I'll have to try after all of this is over." Blanndynne paused, and Diomedes thought he saw her shadow shift at the same time the cot she sat on creaked. "I have a question."

Diomedes motioned for her to ask it, but it took several seconds before she spoke.

"When you're king, can I be on your council?"

While the question was unexpected, it made him chuckle since Amira had asked the same thing of him. However, while he had delayed giving Raidah's daughter a straight answer, his response to Blanndynne was immediate. "Of course. You'll be one of my highest members."

"Really?" The excitement in her voice was tangible. "That would be incredible."

"You'll have all the control you want," Diomedes said, letting his mind wander to the freedoms he'd have when he was king.

"Stay focused, Diomedes," Emmalee whispered in his mind. *"You must take the throne before it becomes yours, and for that, you can't get distracted by daydreams."*

Armannii returned several hours later without having been followed by the Dark Soldiers he'd run into.

"Thankfully, they can't run as fast as me in those suits of armor," Armannii said, taking off his bag and plopping it on the ground. There was something unsettled in his voice, but Diomedes doubted Blanndynne had picked up on it.

"What did you find?" Diomedes asked, splitting his focus between sensing the shadow of the dagger, which he was spinning on his hands, and his friend, who sat down on the cot across from him with a sigh.

"The Western Cliffs seems to be the best lead. That's where most people last saw him, and from the sound of it, some of the encounters were recent," Armannii said.

Somewhere in the back of his mind, Emmalee was already trying to instruct Diomedes how to get to the cliffs. But he told her to be quiet.

"How recent?" Diomedes asked, tucking the dagger away.

"A few months ago," Armannii said, metal clinking and liquid sloshing as he took a drink from his canteen.

"Good enough for me," Diomedes said, rising to his feet. "How soon can we leave?"

"We have no idea where we're supposed to look for him," Armannii said. "The Western Cliffs go on for miles, even into uncharted territory. How do you expect to find him?"

Diomedes should've known one or both of his companions would question his directions, yet he hadn't planned a response. The anxiety he'd felt in the trial where he'd given an unprepared speech returned until he pushed the feelings down, reaching out for help where he knew he'd find it.

When Diomedes turned his focus to Emmalee, she seemed reluctant to speak to him, likely because he'd snapped at her to be quiet. But she eventually answered his question.

"*Yes, I can lead you. But you can't tell your friends that,*" she said, her voice dry and void of emotion.

"I have an idea," Diomedes said, and with a simple thought, his hand radiated the chill from his dark magic.

"What?" Armannii scoffed. "You're going to find him with magic?" The elf snorted. "That's not possible without blood."

"You said it yourself. My magic is stronger than most you've ever seen. Let's test that theory." Diomedes released his magic, letting it dissipate as his skin warmed back up.

"It's impossible," Armannii countered.

"Maybe for you," Diomedes said, clasping his hands behind his back. "But we may as well try."

It, of course, was a lie, and Diomedes relied heavily on Emmalee's instructions, which he verbalized to Armannii in a whispered voice once they started on their way to the Western Cliffs. When Emmalee wasn't speaking to him and he was simply following Armannii, Diomedes realized that if he concentrated, Armannii's shadow moved in his mind, walking as his friend did, almost as if he were seeing it. Almost.

Just like when she'd given Mellacross the directions to the caves, Emmalee had not given specific instructions for how to find the seer's home. But unlike before, Diomedes trusted he would find it just as he had the pit.

Armannii, however, wasn't as certain.

"And you're sure this spell is working? I mean, we're headed toward the cliffs, but . . ."

"But what?" Blanndynne asked before Diomedes could respond. "That's where we're supposed to be going. Just let him concentrate."

They resumed walking without further conversation. Diomedes's fist clenched as he considered Armannii's never-ending questions and the conversation he'd overheard between his companions on the top of the mountain after they'd first emerged from the cave. Armannii was having trouble adjusting, and Diomedes doubted he had the elf's unconditional trust, as he'd had in the past. But that was not something Armannii needed to know at the moment.

"That's true." Emmalee's voice startled Diomedes, but he avoided the next branch without much of a problem even with the break in his concentration. Soon, he figured, he wouldn't need to focus so much on trying to sense the things around him.

They continued their walk with only the ambient sounds of the Dark playing around them. Tree branches snapped, and leaves rustled on the ground. Something chittered overhead—some small animal, Diomedes assumed.

The smell of moisture and rotting leaves hung in every breath of air, and a soft breeze whistled around them, whispering through the branches. And amidst all the sounds were the constant steps of Diomedes and his companions.

A bird cawed, and the sound bounced off something large in front of them.

"You're getting close," Emmalee said, her voice light. *"Follow the edge of the cliffs south a ways."* A flash of an image

appeared in Diomedes's mind, and he frowned because it distracted him from the sensing spell, and he kicked a branch that could've been otherwise avoided.

But before he could snap at Emmalee, he realized what she was showing him. It was the Dark. A wall of rock went far past the intertwining branches of the trees. On the cliff wall, which looked very similar to where Armannii had taken him to meet Otto at a pub in the south of the Dark, a rune was inscribed. Diomedes didn't recognize it.

"It's from when I visited the seer," Emmalee explained as Diomedes studied the memory. *"And it's what your friends are looking for."*

After a few minutes of studying the image while trying to regain focus on his sensing spell, Diomedes decided upon how he was going to tell his companions what to look for. "We're close to the Western Cliffs, aren't we?" Diomedes asked, avoiding an object hanging in front of his face by ducking around it.

"We are, but how do you—"

"Magic," Diomedes said, answering Armannii's question before he'd even completed it. Diomedes began describing the image Emmalee had shown him, using the spell as a scapegoat.

"So we're supposed to do what exactly?" Armannii asked, his voice skeptical. "Follow the cliffs for miles until we come across a bare spot with a rune? You *do* realize that nearly everyone in the Dark can write runes. I can't even tell which one you're trying to describe because there are so many variations of the sight rune that it could be any number of—"

"I'll keep an eye out for it," Blanndynne said, speaking over Armannii, who grunted.

They kept walking.

Every once in a while, a branch would crack in the distance, and they would fall silent. Only when Armannii muttered that it was safe to move would they continue along the side of the cliff face.

Armannii stopped walking, causing Diomedes to nearly stumble into his back. For the first time in his life, Diomedes did not wonder what the elf could hear that he couldn't. He heard the approaching set of footsteps too. Another sound accompanied it: a male voice humming.

"*Do not draw your weapon,*" Emmalee said when Diomedes's hand dropped to the hilt of his sword. "*I recognize the voice. The man coming toward you is the one you seek.*"

"What is it?" Blanndynne whispered, and although Diomedes was sure she'd directed the question at Armannii, he was the one who answered.

"It's the person we've been looking for," Diomedes said, relaxing the muscles in his shoulders, which had tensed when he'd heard the humming. "Put your arrow away," he said at the sound of Armannii prepping his bow. "We have no reason to attack him."

"How can you possibly know who those footsteps belong to?" Armannii asked. He hadn't unloaded his bow yet.

"Because His Highness possesses more than just his own knowledge." The humming had stopped, and a man's voice called out from in front of Diomedes. "Isn't that right, Prince Diomedes?"

"You're the seer?" Diomedes asked, and when the man confirmed he was, Diomedes continued. "What's your name?"

"Reymond, and I do believe you and I have a meeting we should be getting to."

Diomedes's cheek pulled up in a half smile. "Lead the way."

Chapter Thirty-Three

t would be wise to send your companions off," Emmalee said at the same time Reymond stopped walking. Diomedes questioned Emmalee's secrecy for a second but submitted before she could chide him.

"We're here," the seer said. His voice was deeper than Armannii's, and he spoke with a lisp. When Diomedes stood downwind from him, he caught hints of cinnamon and cloves.

"Wonderful." Diomedes turned to where Armannii's and Blanndynne's footsteps had stopped. "Go to the nearest market and restock our supplies."

"What?" Blanndynne asked, shock filling her voice. The shadow, which he assumed was her since it was smaller than the one beside it, stepped toward him.

"No," Armannii said in a low voice. "We aren't leaving you here with some stranger."

"I assure you, he'll be perfectly safe," Reymond said, but he must've been facing the wall because his voice was not as clear.

"A word?" Armannii asked, and Diomedes's shoulder tingled before Armannii pulled him away from Blanndynne and the seer.

"Why are you sending us away again? I'd think by now we've proven that we can be trusted."

Diomedes pulled his shoulder out of Armannii's grip. He needed a lie or a change of subject to serve as a distraction. "A more appropriate question is why you're questioning me. Again." Diomedes stood tall, his hands clenching at his sides. He could feel the cool trickle of magic collecting in his fingertips.

"I—"

"You say in words that you trust me, but I need you to show me. Don't ask questions. Just go." Without another word, Diomedes turned on his heels and returned to where Blanndynne and Reymond waited.

"Where's Armannii?" Blanndynne asked when Diomedes approached them.

It hadn't taken long for Diomedes to realize Armannii hadn't followed him. "He's waiting for you. I'll be here when you two return."

"All right," she said without arguing. Her hand grazed his shoulder as she passed. "We'll be back."

When her footsteps faded, Reymond spoke.

"Follow me, Your Highness. My home is in here." Reymond's clothing rustled, and after hearing a few scratches of something against rock, Diomedes entered Reymond's home in the side of the Western Cliffs.

"I suppose I should not be as impressed as I am that you knew I was coming," Diomedes said, holding back a repressed choke. The air was thick with incense smoke. It was a wonder Reymond only slightly smelled of it.

"I've been a seer for a long time, Your Highness. One hundred and seventy-three years to be exact. I've been expecting this day since I had my first vision."

Diomedes's brow furrowed. "Really? And why is that?"

"All in good time, Your Highness. Please, come sit." Their footsteps, which had been echoing as if they were passing through a tunnel, faded, and thick rugs silenced them. "There's a chair to your left."

Diomedes didn't need to be told. He could see the vague shadow of a chair next to him using the sensing spell. Diomedes sat down, his knee bumping against a table. Reymond sat across from him, and fabric moved, making Diomedes think he'd removed a cloak.

"Do you know why I'm here? Is that something you've . . . seen?" Diomedes asked, leaning against the back of the chair. He crossed one leg over the other and rested his arms on the armrests.

"That's the thing about my gift," Reymond said. "It's not always clear. It can be rather frustrating at times. But I have something that might help you."

"Help me? With what exactly?"

"I've heard a rumor about you trying to end the war, so that assumption is not based on my gift." Reymond was quiet for a moment, and his chair creaked. "Are you aware what happens when a seer gives a prophecy?"

Diomedes nodded once. "It's written down in a book that cannot be altered or destroyed."

A thud resounded around them. Reymond had dropped something heavy on the table; Diomedes had felt the vibrations through his knee, which was pressed against the wooden frame.

"This is my book," Reymond said. The chair squeaked again, and Diomedes assumed he'd sat back down. "When a seer receives a prophecy, it comes in the form of poetry, images, or both. It depends on the strength of the prophecy. My book is over 6,500 pages long and weighs as much as a small child. I've given tens of thousands of prophecies. But despite that, only two stand out in my mind."

"Is this going to help me?" Diomedes asked, his stomach tightening. "I need a prophecy that will help me take the throne and end the war."

"What you make of it is entirely up to you," Reymond said, his voice airy. "I'm simply the messenger."

"Well then, please do share," Diomedes said, rubbing his thumb beneath his chin.

A gentle swishing noise sounded as the seer flipped through the book. The rustling stopped. Reymond cleared his throat and began reading aloud from the page at which he'd arrived. His tone and cadence were rhythmic, almost musical.

> *A nest with two eggs—divergent, opposed;*
> *An egg breaks open, an infant exposed.*
> *One bird without feathers—jealous and flightless;*
> *Another born colorful, scared of bias.*
> *Steal feathers from others—a price is paid;*
> *How to open the eyes, a life slayed.*
> *No longer bare, but worthy, powerful;*
> *Feathers of one are natural, bountiful.*
> *A crack in the ground, opening wider;*
> *A clash of feathers, one survivor.*

Halfway through, Diomedes had stopped moving. Had stopped breathing. But his magic, dormant at the beginning, was swirling around his fingertips. He clenched his hands into fists as he tried to process the prophecy. "This . . . this is about me?"

"Not just you, Your Highness," Reymond said, flipping through the pages of the book, the parchment shuffling lightly. "There were two birds mentioned."

"Who is the other?"

Reymond did not answer.

Emmalee did.

"*Isn't it obvious?*" she said, her voice trilling. "*Who is the only other person, besides your father, who poses a threat to the crown?*"

A threat? Diomedes tried to think of someone besides the current king but came up empty. He could see no threats.

"*What if you were disinherited?*"

Diomedes sat up straighter. "Is this . . . is this about my sister?"

"It is," Reymond said, his voice calm. But over the sound of the seer riffling through the book again, Diomedes could hear his own heartbeat as it sped up.

"What does it mean?" Diomedes uncrossed his legs and planted his feet firmly on the ground. Reymond didn't respond right away, and frustration bubbled up in Diomedes. Why was Ellayne part of his prophecy?

"*She's a threat, Diomedes,*" Emmalee said, her voice carrying a warning behind it. "*To successfully become king, you must remove all obstacles, and she—*"

"Why is my sister in this prophecy?" Diomedes interrupted the woman in his head, posing the question to the seer.

Reymond remained quiet.

The cryptic nature of the prophecy left magic gathering in Diomedes's hands as he slammed them down on the arms of the chair. "Tell me what this means!" He wasn't sure if he was shouting at Reymond, or just in frustration over his own befuddlement. Or both.

"I'm only the vessel through which the future reveals itself. I'm not here to decipher its mysteries."

"Why would you tell me and not give an explanation?" Diomedes asked, fighting for control over his emotions as they tried to stir his magic.

"I am unbiased, Your Highness. It is my role in things to share the future with those who seek it. Not all seers of the past shared my sentiment, but I will not abandon it to tip the scale in a certain direction. Many have come to me with that very request, and I have refused each one."

"What does that even mean?" Diomedes asked, his hands clenching and unclenching.

"My purpose, my desire in all of this, is to keep those who seek to meddle with destiny from accomplishing their schemes." Reymond's vague and lofty responses grated on Diomedes, twisting his stomach in anger.

Diomedes lowered his voice, hoping Reymond would need to lean forward to hear him. "Tell me. What. The prophecy. Means."

"He's lying to you. Reymond is far from unbiased. He's hiding the truth. Reymond knows that your sister is your only threat. He's doing it to protect her. He wants you to fail, just as he wanted me to fail." Emmalee's voice was a whisper echoing through Diomedes's mind, and he clenched his jaw at her words.

"You know, Your Highness, I did say there were two prophecies I remember above all else," Reymond said as he shut the book.

"I don't care about the other prophecy unless it's about—"

"You. It *is* about you." The shadow representing Reymond in Diomedes's mind stood, and his chair made another creaking noise. But with the rug on the floor, the sounds faded away, and Reymond was too far for the sensing spell to track his shadow.

Diomedes stood up too, tilting his head at every sound he heard. It was faint, but he could hear Reymond breathing softly to his left. Diomedes turned his body, angling it toward the sound.

"What did it say?" Diomedes asked, refraining from reaching for his sword. The hair on the back of his neck stood up, and though he was thankful for the ability to sense what was near him, his frustration—his vulnerability—at not being able to see still ate at him from the inside.

"Calm down and focus. You are not helpless. Let your magic take control."

"Before I tell you, let me ask you this." Reymond's voice came from the direction Diomedes was facing. "How did you get dark magic? I know well that the Maudit line before you was completely human. Not a drop of magic in your veins. How did you steal it?"

The magic Reymond referenced filled Diomedes, and he wiggled his fingers by his side. "I didn't steal it. I earned it. I sacrificed for it."

"She gave it to you. The sorceress. Didn't she?" The old seer's voice betrayed him, breaking and trembling as it shifted away from its calm and steady nature. "Emmalee visited me many years ago, but my prophecies were not what she wanted to hear. She wanted me to give her an edge that would help her in the battles she faced against your father. She knocked me unconscious for a while to try to read my book. I'm still unsure as to what she found, but it clearly didn't help her." A trace of venom lined his voice. "People act in rash ways when they hear a future they want no part in. But that's what people don't understand. You can't move off the path that destiny lays before you. You can try, but no matter what you do, you'll end up in the room with the man destined to kill you."

Diomedes's posture went rigid. "What?"

"I knew you were going to be in the Dark today. I knew you were searching for me. I knew the information you wanted. I knew that a great darkness lay within you. And I knew that as soon as you found out that your sister is going to be your biggest enemy, you'd kill the messenger. You'd kill me." Reymond didn't trip over a single word, and if Diomedes hadn't been paying such close attention to what he was saying, he might've been able to avoid the seer's book flying through the air before it hit him in the gut.

"*He's right, Diomedes.*"

"The first prophecy I ever heard was of my own death. I've dealt with that fear every day, come to terms with it. Made my peace. But that does not mean I have any desire to make it easy."

Diomedes gripped his stomach, leaning over as he coughed. The book's impact had almost knocked him off his feet, and he'd grabbed the back of the chair to steady himself.

"*You must kill him, Diomedes.*" Emmalee spoke in an even tone, but it did nothing to calm the panic rising in Diomedes. "*If he lives, he might go to your sister, aid her in defeating you. In ruining every hope you've ever had for ending the war.*"

"I've never killed anyone," Diomedes said, both to the seer and to the disembodied voice in his head. He grimaced.

"I can see the darkness in you. It's eating you alive. You're an abomination."

Diomedes shook his head. "I'm . . . I'm not. I'm here to end the war."

"Whether you believe that to be true or not, I know you are not going about it the right way."

"Right way?" Diomedes straightened up, still gripping his stomach. "You believe there's a right way to end the war? It's war."

Reymond scoffed from a different part of the room. "Your father is trying to end the war in the right way. He's trying to end it so that prejudices don't follow either side into the next generation. He's doing it in a way that will last."

Dark magic flooded through Diomedes at the mention of his father. "My father is a coward. If you think he'll end the war, then maybe you don't see as much of the future as I thought you did. His council is doing everything *but* ending the war. I'm going to stop it, and no one is going to stand in my way."

"*Give control to your magic, Diomedes. Let it sense him. Find where he is, and let the magic seize him.*" Emmalee's orders were easier said than done, and time slowed down as Diomedes tried to get a grip on the storm raging in his mind.

Writhing beneath his skin, his magic wriggled around like snakes waiting to strike. Diomedes lowered his head, his skull pounding as he raised a hand bathed in dark magic to his temple. His own touch was cold, and he rubbed his fingers in circles. He didn't want to lose control. The thought of it scared him, and he clenched his hands even tighter until his nails dug deep into the skin of his palms.

Even if he did obey Emmalee, her instructions were too much. There was no way he could pull enough magic to do what Emmalee had suggested.

"Then give up another memory. You mustn't let Reymond go."

But the resistance returned in full force. He knew himself. He wasn't a murderer, and his stomach turned at the thought of taking the seer's life. He couldn't do it. Not when people like Reymond were the very ones he was trying to save by ending the war.

Emmalee's voice continued to rage in his head, getting louder and louder until he gripped his forehead and bent over in pain. Her voice warped as it had when she'd revealed her lack of eyes in the mirror—a multitude of voices whispering behind hers.

"Not only is it your destiny to kill him, but if you don't, he will find a way to disrupt your plans to lay siege to Cyanthia and your father's castle. He is standing against you—against us. He doesn't want the war to end. Remember your trials, Diomedes. Do not put anything above ending the war. Not even this man. You must—" Before she could keep screaming at him, Diomedes lost control, digging deep into his mind. A memory emerged.

He'd snuck Ellayne into their father's office, and they'd sat for hours reading the books on magic he kept hidden in a secret shelf behind a map on the wall. Diomedes could picture little Ellayne, wide-eyed as he explained what a seer was. She'd curled up next to him on the small couch, and he'd answered all of her questions as best he could.

The memory disappeared, replaced by darkness and a sense of emptiness. For a second, his concerns dissipated. He carried no more qualms about murdering Reymond. Diomedes's blood was filled with ice, and he could feel the power rippling just below the surface, waiting to be used—waiting to obey his every command.

But was he there? Was he the one taking slow, menacing steps in the direction he heard Reymond's breathing? Why was he raising a hand—a hand filled with overflowing dark magic? Darkness fogged his brain, stifling the questions with a heavy mist.

A numbing mist.

With a deep breath, Diomedes sent a wisp of magic into the room, and it felt like he was moving with it, though his feet remained firmly planted on the rug.

"You cannot stop what has been set in motion," Reymond said, his voice cracking. He bumped into something that hit the stone wall, and something, maybe a smaller table or a stool, crunched.

Diomedes could feel his control over Reymond. Could feel the seer's heart pulsing in the palm of his hand. Could feel his lungs pumping air in and out as he panicked. Could feel his shivering body.

"Take control. Tell it to stop moving."

Obeying, Diomedes tightened the hand that had sent out the magic into a fist, and Reymond made a gurgling noise.

"Good. Very good. Now kill him before you lose control over his body. Shut down his organs."

Diomedes hesitated.

It felt wrong. In that second, it felt like *he* was the one not in control of his body. Almost like someone—no, something—was pulling his hand into a tighter fist, forcing the life out of the seer. And the more he thought about it, the harder he tried to stop.

The panic he'd felt before began to reemerge, but it didn't matter.

He couldn't stop.

Chapter Thirty-Four

Diomedes stood still, letting his magic fade away after hearing Reymond breathe his last breath. The moment it was over, Diomedes choked. His hands trembled as he took a shaky seat in the nearest chair. The sensing spell had grown too strong, and for the first time, he wished he couldn't make out the shape of Reymond's crumpled body before him.

He'd killed a man. Of all the injuries he'd given others, he'd never once stopped a man's heart.

Reymond was dead, and he'd been the one to do it.

His heart raced, beating like a drum in his chest, echoing in his ears. He tensed, concerned he would be sick. He raised shaky hands to his forehead, wiping his sweaty face. Despite the scarf, it was unsettling to feel the gaping holes where his eyes had been. Diomedes rocked forward and backward, trying to calm himself.

His head spun. At what point had he decided he would kill the seer? He couldn't remember—couldn't remember anything but the sputters of the dying man. The man he had murdered. *That* he remembered too clearly.

"*We must discuss your sister.*" Emmalee's voice trickled into his panicked thoughts, and he shook his head.

"No. No, that's not going to happen," Diomedes said, rubbing his hands over his face. The scarf around his head went askew, and he fixed it as he directed his fear and confusion at the sorceress. "Tell me what just happened. Why did I kill him? I didn't want—I didn't—"

"*That's enough, Diomedes,*" Emmalee said, her voice getting louder. "*Reymond stood in the way of ending the war, stood against you becoming king.*"

"But he never said—"

"*He was a threat, and you handled him thusly.*"

"Handled him?" Diomedes let out an exasperated breath. "He was innocent, and now he's dead. What am I going to tell Armannii?" A sinking feeling filled Diomedes's stomach, and he rested his head on his hand.

Armannii wouldn't understand. He had been furious when Blanndynne had enchanted Hessland. But this wasn't just enchantment. Reymond was dead.

"He'll leave. He won't understand, and he'll leave," Diomedes muttered, his jaw tightening.

"*And would that be the worst thing? You yourself have questioned the elf's loyalties since you received magic. Why not let him depart?*"

Diomedes bristled. "Armannii is my closest friend. My brother."

"*Then I suggest you come up with a lie. And make sure you take Reymond's book. It may be of use later.*"

By the time Blanndynne and Armannii entered Reymond's home, Diomedes sat with the prophecy book in front of him on the table. He leaned forward, resting his face in his hands until they walked in, at which point he raised his head. Reymond's body was still against the wall; Emmalee had told him to leave it, and he had not fought her.

"What happened?" Armannii asked, speeding across the room. The shadow of the elf dropped to the floor next to the seer to check for a pulse. "He's dead. How did this—are you okay?"

Diomedes used the arms of the chair to push himself up. His voice trembled, but he tried to hide it by standing up straighter. He *needed* Armannii to believe his lie. "I'm okay." He kept one hand on the enormous book. "Reymond had all but sat down when he started choking. I didn't know what was happening. When I— when I made it across the room to where he'd collapsed, his heart had already stopped. There was nothing I could've done."

"But you're okay?" Blanndynne asked beside Diomedes.

"Shaken up. I've never . . . This is the first time someone has died in front of me." Diomedes stiffened when she placed a hand on his arm.

"So you didn't get to hear the prophecy?"

"Are you serious, B? A man is dead, and you're concerned about that?" Armannii asked, joining them at the front of the room.

Blanndynne made a sound like she was about to speak, but Diomedes stepped in front of her to face Armannii. In the time he'd had alone since he'd killed Reymond, his mind had settled on one thing—one single thing that was keeping him together. If Reymond had been standing against him, if he had been a threat to Diomedes ending the war, then Emmalee had been right. He'd been an obstacle. His death, though sudden and unsettling, had, in a way, been necessary.

If it hadn't been . . . Diomedes shoved the thought away, clinging to what he needed to be true.

"It's terrible, and believe me, I-I'm still trying to process it. But we have to keep going. Even without his prophecy, we have a war to end."

"I thought he was the reason we're ending the war? Or did you forget about the people you're trying to free from prejudice and persecution?" Armannii's vest rustled, and Diomedes could almost make out the shadow's blurry arms crossing over its chest.

"I'm doing this *for* the people."

"Really?" Armannii scoffed. "Then let's give Reymond a proper burial."

"*It'd be wasting time,*" Emmalee muttered.

"Armannii," Blanndynne cut in, speaking before Emmalee had finished in Diomedes's head. "Calm down. He's still doing this for those with magic. And—"

"Let's bury him," Diomedes said, and he wasn't sure if it was because he fully agreed with Armannii, or if it was from the guilt of knowing he'd ended the man's life, or if it was simply to spite Emmalee, who was getting on his nerves the more she ordered him about. Whatever the reason, his response seemed to have surprised both Armannii and Blanndynne, and they went to work digging a shallow grave outside Reymond's home with a shovel Blanndynne had lying around in her magic depository. Armannii did most of the work, and while he was outside, Diomedes had Blanndynne place Reymond's book in her magic storehouse. Unlike Armannii, she didn't ask questions, just obeyed.

When the grave was finished, they stood next to it in silence.

Only Diomedes, though, felt the full weight of the moment bearing down on him.

They traveled back to Bayan in relative quiet, and Armannii rented a room at the same inn they'd stayed in on the way to Reymond's. Blanndynne tried to offer some small talk over dinner, but neither Diomedes nor Armannii contributed, and eventually they all fell asleep.

For the first time, Diomedes wished he wouldn't see Emmalee as soon as he began to dream. But his wish was not granted.

"You're upset," she said, tilting her head. They stood in the middle of what appeared to be a village in the Black Forest, what with the giant trees sprouting around the outskirts. Around them, buildings rose on platforms, and from what Diomedes could tell, they were in the middle of a village square.

It was just the two of them.

"Of course I'm upset," Diomedes muttered, directing his attention anywhere but toward Emmalee. "You made me kill an innocent man."

"Reymond was far from innocent, and I thought you'd come to terms with the fact that his death was necessary to end the war."

"Whatever," Diomedes said, finally facing her. "What do you want?"

"Do you know where we are?"

"Black Forest." Diomedes shoved his hands in his pockets.

"Shongbay, to be exact," Emmalee said, her gaze scanning the area around them. Something heavy lingered behind her eyes, and she wrapped her arms around herself. "This was where I lived with my husband and daughter until they were murdered by royal guards."

Diomedes straightened up, glancing around at the empty buildings, flicking his gaze to Emmalee every few seconds. "Why are you showing me this?"

"You need to remember what you're fighting for, Diomedes. I'd like to believe that every choice I made was for my family. They were innocent casualties in this war. Hazel, my daughter, was barely two. I fought for them, Diomedes. I lived for them, and I died for them. Anyone"—her voice darkened as she glowered at the ground—"who did not side with me was against me, and it is the same for you. You must understand, Diomedes," she said, taking a step toward him. "What I've given you is a gift, and you must eliminate all those who oppose you, those who are obstacles to your ultimate goal."

Diomedes lifted his chin, glancing away from her. "We're not discussing this. My sister is not a threat."

"She isn't?" Emmalee asked, though her voice was soft, pensive. "Even if your father were to act on his word and disown you? Disinherit you as an heir?" Emmalee cocked her head to the side. "You're close to her. I understand. Your stepmother was my closest friend, like a sister to me. But what you don't yet understand is that those closest to you are the ones who are capable of hurting you the most. Whether she is a threat now or will be later, Ellayne is an obstacle, and the way to ensure your victory is to eliminate her."

"You didn't eliminate Evangeline," Diomedes said, crossing his arms over his chest.

"And I *lost*, Diomedes," Emmalee said, jutting her chin out. "At least, I lost that battle. But now you're here, and you're finishing the work I began. You'll do better because you're stronger than I was. As long as you don't let an obstacle overtake you. I'm trying to help you."

Diomedes frowned. "If you could've, would you have killed Evangeline?"

"I would now," Emmalee said, lifting her chin. "It doesn't matter what I would've done. What matters is this moment. You have a chance to make a decision I didn't make."

"I'm *not* killing Ellayne," Diomedes said, shaking his head. The relational connection between Evangeline and Ellayne did not escape his attention, and before he could put his question into words, Emmalee answered it.

"No," she said, pressing her lips together. "I don't want you to kill Ellayne just because she's Evie's daughter."

"I don't believe you."

"If you come up with a way to remove your sister's threat without killing her, I'll stand behind it. But I know you'd be hard pressed to find something like that, and you must take the throne soon, or I fear your father will disinherit you. I only say this because you're blinded by your relationship with your sister."

Diomedes shook his head. "I'm not killing her."

"Very well. If you're willing to risk everything for one person, then I have nothing left to say to you."

"Thank you for letting us pass through, Zephrium," Blanndynne said as she grasped Diomedes's hand and followed Armannii through the portal.

Emmalee hadn't spoken to Diomedes since his dream, and for the first time since he'd gotten his magic, it felt like he had only one voice in his head: his own.

The portal was even less of an event than before, and Diomedes cracked his neck on the other side.

"I think that's one of the fastest trips someone has ever made into the Dark," Hessland said when they came out the other side.

Diomedes chuckled. "I suppose it was, though we stopped twice to rest."

"And did you find what you were searching for?" Hessland asked, guiding them out through the flora to the main room.

"Unfortunately, there were some complications," Diomedes said before Armannii or Blanndynne had a chance to speak.

"I'm sorry to hear that. Will it impact your plan to end the war?"

"I hope not, but I suppose we'll have to wait and see. In the meantime, we should be going." Diomedes paused near the exit to tunnel. "Thank you again, Hessland, and I hope we meet again soon."

"Your Highness," Hessland said, and his shadow bowed its head.

All three said goodbye and left out the long exit tunnel. Diomedes didn't miss a single turn as the sensing spell guided him.

"We should head south. There's a village about half a day's walk from here that has an inn," Armannii said as they reached the ladder leading to the surface.

"Sounds like as good a place as any to stop and regroup," Diomedes said.

But all the way from the guardian's portal to the inn, the only thing Diomedes could think about was his conversation with Emmalee from the previous night. He needed a way to get his sister out of the line of inheritance without killing her. Some way for the world to forget who she was—for Ellayne to forget who she was—but for her to be safe, out of harm's way.

When Blanndynne bumped into him while walking, the answer became clearer than he'd thought possible.

Though it wasn't going to be easy.

It wasn't until Armannii stopped short of the inn, pausing at the notice board for the town, that Diomedes snapped out of his thoughts.

"Um, Didi, we may have a problem," Armannii said, clearing his throat. "There's a new notice here that the king will be giving a speech in less than a week. Four days from now, actually."

"Does it say what it's in regard to?" Diomedes asked, hoping it was one of his father's typical speeches he gave every so often to boost morale during the war.

"You," Armannii said, his voice low. "It's about you."

Diomedes tensed, his magic swirling in his hands, which he hid within his cloak. "Does it—"

"No. It doesn't say what it's about, but I'd wager—"

"He's going to disinherit me," Diomedes muttered, subduing the panic rising inside by clamping one hand over the dagger at his hip and clenching the other into a fist at his side. "We need a plan. Let's get to the inn," Diomedes said, his voice low when he heard other people walking by. "It'll be safer to talk there."

Chapter Thirty-Five

Diomedes paced the room Armannii had rented, trying to get Emmalee to respond to him to no avail. He had sent Blanndynne and Armannii out for supplies and more information and hoped Emmalee would speak to him before they returned. He wanted a solid plan before his friends began to pester him about it.

Rubbing his hands over his face, he finally switched to speaking out loud. "Emmalee, I know you can hear me. Just speak to me already." He paused in the middle of the room, hoping to hear her respond. She remained silent. "I have an idea for what to do with Ellayne, but I need your help. I need your input, and now with my father's speech planned, I'm—"

"*Running out of time,*" Emmalee finally said. "*It would be in your best interest if you just—*"

"What if I curse her?" Instead of telling Emmalee about Elias, he focused on his memories with his ancestor, collecting the information he knew about the curse and organizing it before her. "If I can figure out what curse was put on Elias, I might be able to find a way to remove Ellayne from the picture. I mean, Elias didn't know who he was, and no one else remembers him. And he's still alive after all these years. He's safe and not dead. Do you think it could work?"

Emmalee fell quiet, and Diomedes thought she was giving him the silent treatment again until she spoke. "*Many years ago, I was searching for a similar curse, and I studied many. They're difficult, and few who set them survive. It would be a gamble, and you don't have time to waste.*"

Diomedes began pacing again, irritation at Emmalee rising with each step. "I'm willing to risk it if she's safe and I'm king."

"*You'd be risking your life should you not be strong enough. Are you willing to do that?*"

"Yes."

"*You do not know the curse set on your ancestor, correct?*" she asked, and Diomedes muttered his answer. "*So you would need to return to the desert to fetch this book you found and put into place all of the parts before the end of the week? Do you have a backup plan?*"

"No." Diomedes sighed, rubbing the back of his neck. He probably sounded insane talking to himself in the room. "Well, maybe. But it depends on if you can find me a faster way to Elias's."

"*What is your alternate plan?*"

The ideas in his mind hadn't completely formed until Diomedes was speaking them out loud. "I'll send Armannii to Raidah to have him help her prepare. Whether I figure out how to curse my sister or not, we will move on Cyanthia the day before my father's speech. We don't have a choice."

"*You could strike earlier. Raidah will be quick to prepare. And you could just—*"

"I won't. If I can't get the curse ready in time, I'll figure out what to do with Ellayne after we've taken the castle."

"*And your father? I suppose you'll simply ask him to step aside?*" The spite in Emmalee's voice was evident, and Diomedes wondered if it was directed at him or his father. "*And Evangeline? What of her? Do not underestimate her.*"

"I want my father to stay alive." Diomedes bristled. "I want him to bear witness to everything I do after I take his crown. I want him to see that he has been wrong to ignore my suggestions. He needs to be there when I end the war and change Phildeterre forever. I want him to watch as I change the country in ways he was too afraid to attempt. Is there a spell that can do that?"

Emmalee remained silent, and Diomedes waited for her response. "*There is a spell that could subdue him while allowing him to remain aware of all that is going on. All you need is a mirror, preferably one small enough to keep with you.*"

Diomedes raised a hand to the chain around his throat, which held his medallion and the small mirror Emmalee had left him. He'd added it to the same chain his medallion was on after they'd left the cave. Something of a keepsake.

"*It will work,*" Emmalee said, answering the question Diomedes had not voiced aloud. He could hear a bit of a grin in her voice.

"How difficult is it?"

"*It's not. And while I agree that it is just to have your father watch from a place of powerlessness, you must also consider Evangeline. She will fight, and she is stronger than you think.*"

Diomedes tried to reconcile his stepmother with strength but could not combine them into a single thought. Still, Emmalee knew her better than he did, and he had not come up with a plan for her yet. The thought of Evangeline left a tinge of anger within him that he did not recognize as his own.

"*She will be an obstacle. Bear that in mind, Diomedes.*"

"I will," he muttered, his attention on planning his next steps before Armannii and Blanndynne returned.

"*You're probably right to send the elf to Raidah before you.*" Emmalee eventually joined him in planning, though her unfeeling tone did not go unnoticed by Diomedes. "*I've seen from one of your memories that he was a soldier to Darrick.*"

"Who?"

"*You know him as the Dark King,*" Emmalee said, an audible smirk resounding in her voice. "*If your friend was a Dark Soldier, he would do well helping to organize Raidah's men, especially if you can tell him the way in through the tunnels beneath Cyanthia.*"

Diomedes's mind was still wrapped up in hearing the Dark King's real name for the first time, but he nodded. "I'll tell him to set off for Raidah's tomorrow morning."

"*And if you have your heart set on protecting your sister by placing this curse on her, then you must be prepared tomorrow to release many memories.*"

"How come?" Diomedes asked, sitting on one of the cots.

"*You asked if there was a faster way to travel. There is.*"

He found his bag and took out his canteen. "What, a horse? Or are you going to teach me to fly or something?"

"*Yes.*"

Diomedes spit out the water he'd just taken into his mouth, choking. He clapped his hand on his chest several times before he was able to speak without coughing. "Flying? Seriously?"

"*Despite your occasional outbursts and the way you've brushed several of my suggestions aside, I do see quite a bit of potential in you, just as I did when you found my dagger in the caves. I believe that with more of your humanity exchanged for magic, I could teach you how to fly.*" Emmalee's words sucked the air out of Diomedes's lungs for a second time, and he coughed.

He couldn't keep the excitement from covering his face. Flying. Now that was worth losing his sight for.

"*You continue to impress me, Diomedes. As a reward, I will teach you one of the most difficult things I ever learned. Most people with magic, light or dark, can't fly. But since you hold such great power within you—more than is natural for one born with magic—I believe it is possible. And it will help you get to your ancestor's home faster. I just hope you haven't made a mistake in not removing your sister's threat entirely."*

"I want you to go prepare Raidah's men. You'll have to go alone since you can use speed runes. Raidah knows the initial plans, but I'm trusting you to lead them to the northeast part of Cyanthia," Diomedes said to Armannii the next day, handing him a piece of parchment on which he'd done his best, using arrows and numbers, to outline the directions of the tunnels beneath Cyanthia. If he had been able to see, he would've drawn it out. But he'd made do with what he could, using one finger to keep track of where he was on the page so he didn't end up writing over the same space multiple times.

"They must be ready to lay siege the day before my father's speech. Blanndynne and I will make our way in that direction, but you must prepare for Raidah's men." Diomedes adjusted the cloth covering where his eyes should've been.

"You'll stay with him?" Armannii asked, and in what Diomedes was now calling the shadow world in his mind, he watched Armannii cross his arms over his chest. It was strange to see a shadow version of his friend, and while the sensing spell was clearer than it had been even the night before, he still missed the details that came with being able to see light and color.

It had not escaped Armannii's attention that Diomedes could somehow sense the things around him, and he'd commented on it previously.

"She will," Diomedes said, waving the question off. "You should go."

"All right. You sure you can make it without me?" While he'd said it as a joke, Diomedes could sense the genuine query beneath it. Armannii was still concerned for him.

Blanndynne moved next to Diomedes in the room. Before Diomedes could respond, she did. "I think we'll manage."

Diomedes nodded.

"Okay, I guess I'm off then," Armannii said, his voice skeptical.

Armannii left, and they waited several moments before speaking. Blanndynne had apparently caught on to Armannii's tendency to eavesdrop because she checked the hallway for him.

"He's gone."

"I don't hear him," Diomedes said, keeping his voice low. "Still, speak softly."

"What are we actually going to do?"

"You're not going to like it," Diomedes said, looping his bag over his head. "At least, not the second part."

"Then tell me that part first," Blanndynne said, holding the door open for him. Together, they left the inn.

"We need to go to Elias."

"What?" Exasperation filled her voice. "What part of 'I never want to speak to him again' was lost on you?"

They stepped out onto the street. A fresh breeze welcomed Diomedes, making the loose ends of the cloth tied around his head flap gently. He hadn't realized how stale the air was in the inn until he left. A couple of people milled about in the narrow streets of the village, and Diomedes pulled his cloak hood all the way down over his face. He had no need to leave any room to see, and while he was growing more confident with the sensing spell, he had yet to test it in a fighting situation. "Lower your voice," Diomedes said.

She didn't. "And it'll take days to get there. Days we don't have. What exactly do you—"

"I said quiet, Blanndynne," Diomedes snapped, his whisper harsh as he pulled her away from the village. After days of being guided by her, it was strange to be confident enough with the sensing spell to lead her where he wanted to go.

"I'm sorry," she said, lowering her voice. "I just don't understand why we need to go back there."

"I need the book I got for him." Diomedes continued to lead her farther from the village, searching for a relatively open spot in the trees while he explained.

"A book? You're going to make me face Elias again because of a book?" Her volume started to rise again, but she caught it. Her voice was a hoarse whisper the next time she spoke. "Go to a library," she said, turning around to stalk away.

"Blanndynne, wait," Diomedes said, not turning in her direction. "You need to come with me."

"Why?" she asked, her voice biting. "You're doing just fine on your own."

"You want to feel powerful? In control? Then you need to face this fear and—"

"I'm not scared of Elias."

"That's not what I'm saying. I wouldn't expect you to be scared of him. He's a scraggly bookworm and likely a shell of the man he once was. Your fear is not in the man but in what he represents."

Blanndynne didn't respond, but her shadow counterpart took a step toward him, cracking a branch.

"Come with me to get the book from Elias, and prove to yourself once and for all that you are no longer bound by any master. That you're truly in control."

"I don't need to . . . I know I'm in control."

"Oh?" Diomedes said, crossing his arms over his chest. "So you don't feel insignificant and subservient at the mention of his name? You didn't feel like you'd been knocked down from the hill you'd finally been free to climb when you saw him? Elias has no power over you?"

"No!" Blanndynne snapped, but her breath hitched in her throat.

"Then prove it." Diomedes cocked his head to the side.

"Fine," she said, stomping toward him. "Let's go."

Diomedes pressed his lips together, hiding the grin he'd felt pop up at Blanndynne's agreement to accompany him. "First, there's something I need to learn to do."

"What are you—"

Blanndynne's question became significantly less important the moment Emmalee spoke in his mind. He had followed the sorceress's instructions, finding a more secluded place that was open.

"The ability to fly will require more memories, more than you've given thus far. But I doubt that will be a problem for you. It's getting easier to embrace the magic, isn't it?"

She spoke the truth. As much as it surprised him, the power he felt after giving up a memory was addicting, and he had to remind himself that the memories held great importance. Otherwise, he could've easily given them all away for the power he could get his hands on. If that was the cost, he was more and more willing to pay it, though the resistance within his mind continued to fight with every sacrificed memory.

One by one, Diomedes pulled memories from his mind, trying to ignore the distraction Blanndynne posed as she questioned him. He focused on the images of many happy memories before allowing the dark magic to absorb them. Each offering to the dark magic filled him with a surge of strength like none he'd known before. He breathed heavily, his hands clenching into fists as they filled with the excess power. It was like a door was opening inch by inch inside him, and with every wisp of dark magic he let in, he lost his weaknesses and everything that made him feel powerless.

"What are you doing?" Blanndynne asked, but he ignored her when Emmalee started talking again.

"It's exhilarating, right?" Emmalee asked, and he could hear a smile in the way she spoke, almost like she was reminiscing.

"Incredible," he whispered, his heart pounding in his chest at the magic, adrenaline, and energy pulsing through every vein.

Blanndynne shifted next to him, and her voice was hesitant when she spoke. "That's a lot of magic. How are you . . ." Her words trailed off.

Diomedes couldn't remember a time when he'd felt this powerful—like nothing could stand against him and survive.

"For now, this should do. I want you to focus on being lifted into the air. Imagine being weightless. Remember the feeling when the genie flew you to the top of the cliff or over the desert. Let it fill you."

He did as she said, positioning his feet shoulder distance apart. He could almost feel the cool air whipping past his face, the feeling of his stomach rising and falling with each change in elevation. He could hear the deafening sound of the wind, could taste the crispness and smell the freshness surrounding him.

Diomedes could no longer feel the ground beneath his boots.

"Diomedes!" Blanndynne shrieked, and her piercing voice broke through his concentration, sending a quick wave of panic through his body. He collapsed to the ground on his hands and knees. Though his magic was still there, it was fainter than it had been a second before.

"You need to focus. If you get distracted when you're hundreds of feet in the air, you will *die."*

He didn't bother to point out that it wasn't his fault his concentration had broken. Blanndynne rushed to his side.

"Are you okay? What are—are you trying to fly?"

"I'd figured that was obvious," Diomedes said, grunting as he pushed himself to his feet. He brushed his hands, which he could feel were covered in dirt, on the front of his trousers. He questioned whether he was actually capable, and Emmalee was quick to respond to his thought.

"I am sure you are. You just need to focus. Empty your mind and let your magic guide you. It knows what it's doing. Tell the genie to be quiet while you practice."

"I didn't learn to fly for years, and—"

"I know I can do it, Blanndynne. I just need to focus. So if you could just . . ." He held a finger up to his lips, and she didn't say a word after that.

Diomedes took a deep breath, adjusting his bag strap before focusing on lifting off the ground. After only a few seconds, he was up again.

Over and over he tried to get more than a few feet off the ground. And he would, but then he'd come back down, some landings harder than others. Frustration began to fill him, and Blanndynne's constant questioning as to whether he was all right irked him.

Diomedes moved away from her when she bent down to help him up. He ignored her extended hand. "I'm fine, Blanndynne, just—"

"*Don't worry about her. As soon as you get this down, you'll travel just as fast as she does. Just focus.*"

Diomedes asked Emmalee how long it had taken her to fly, hoping to use the moment to take a break from the strain flying was putting on his mind.

"*Weeks, maybe months. But you have more power in you than I did.*"

He questioned the statement, knowing the magic he had was the sorceress's. Diomedes's lips pressed together at the same time as his brows.

"*It is, and much more. You hold the power of many who perished with dark magic. It may have taken me weeks to learn to fly. But I believe in your ability to do so faster. Now keep trying.*"

More than one person's magic? That explained how quickly he'd picked up on all she was teaching him. Blanndynne and Armannii had both noticed how powerful he was from the start. It sent a thrill through him.

Within another half hour, he was consistently staying twenty feet or so off the ground. It was far enough that he could no longer get a good reading of the world beneath him in the shadow realm his mind created. Blanndynne rose with him and had caught him twice when he'd fallen from that height.

Between the voice in his head and the voice next to him, Diomedes was surprised he'd even managed to float an inch off the ground, let alone high enough to reach the first layer of intertwining branches.

"*Good. Very good,*" Emmalee said, her voice filled with enthusiasm. "*It took me weeks to do what you just did! Now when you get above the roof of the forest, you'll want to give directions to your magic. You remember the spell to find things?*"

Though he was sweating, Diomedes grinned, and he answered her question positively. Keeping his breathing steady, he directed his magic to take him upward, and in his mind, the shadows of branches and leaves got larger. Blanndynne kept up with him, and he was doing what he could to keep his attention on his direction rather than the genie. While his concentration was focused on upward motion, he couldn't focus on avoiding the branches and leaves. They scratched at his face, attacking him from all sides. Diomedes covered his head with his arms as best as he could, but then he started to fall.

Blanndynne shrieked his name, but she wasn't close enough to grab him immediately.

"*Focus!*" Emmalee shouted so loudly that he cringed.

Light. He needed to remember to be light, weightless. He clenched his hands into fists, repeating the word "light" over and over in his head, accompanying it with consistent breaths.

His stomach wobbled in his gut, and he could sense the ground fast approaching. The air whooshed around him, deafening his sensitive hearing.

But he never hit the ground.

On his way down, he'd twisted his body so that he floated horizontally in the air. He remained there for several seconds, catching his breath. Then, with another order to his magic, Diomedes righted himself.

"Are you all right?" Blanndynne asked, hovering next to him. "I tried to grab you, but—"

"Everything's fine. I'm closer. I won't be long now," he said, and he resumed his ascent.

Diomedes prepared for the roof of the forest this time, covering his face as he continued to keep his mind focused on flying. Maybe one day he'd be strong enough to focus on both. But for the time being, he could handle the stinging in his arms if it meant not breaking every bone in his body.

Blanndynne congratulated Diomedes when he broke through the top of the forest, but he was already focused on Emmalee's next instructions.

"All right. You've been to your ancestor's house. Picture it in your mind. Ask the power inside you to guide you to it. The more vividly you can picture it, can remember it, the stronger the connection you'll make and the easier it will be to follow it."

Diomedes tried to remember Elias's house on the outskirts of the desert, but the moment he pulled it up, he could feel the darkness eager to consume it as it had other memories he'd focused on for extended amounts of time.

"Don't submit it just yet." Emmalee's warning tone echoed in his mind as Blanndynne spoke about directions at the same time.

"I'll use a spell. Just give me a second," Diomedes said to Blanndynne, who continued to gush over Diomedes's quick learning of a skill she was still trying to remaster.

Returning his thoughts to Elias's house, Diomedes remembered the heat of the desert and the uncomfortable feeling of sand in his shoes, the panic rising in his stomach at the thought of Armannii sick in the cot. Diomedes pictured the lanterns that lined the corners of Elias's main room and the writing he'd glimpsed on the walls of the room in the back. With each memory, he felt a tug.

"Good," Emmalee said, interrupting his memory. *"Now send your magic to that place. Anchor yourself to it and then follow the path you've created."*

It happened just as she said. He made the connection.

"Follow me," Diomedes said, soaring in the direction in which his spell was calling him, pulling him. After what felt like half an hour, Diomedes felt himself losing altitude, and he sacrificed the first memory that came to mind: his memory of when Armannii had gotten sick years earlier—a memory he had visited all too recently. As soon as it was gone, Diomedes lifted back into the air.

Though he could feel the spell pulling him, he couldn't tell exactly where they were. Several times he asked Blanndynne, and she would describe the ground beneath them. When the heat from the sun became more intense, he was not surprised to hear her say they'd managed to reach the desert. It was hard to tell how long it took them to get to Elias's village, but for as fast as they were flying, Diomedes wouldn't have guessed more than three or four hours. They stopped twice, not because Diomedes needed a breather but because Blanndynne did.

But soon, as they soared over the Albanistic Desert, Diomedes felt the spell call him downward.

"I see it," Blanndynne said soon after Diomedes had begun his descent.

"*Bend your knees,*" Emmalee said only a few seconds before the shadow of the ground filled most of his mind. He felt the tingle of the ground near his feet.

He bent them at the last second and took a few wobbly steps forward after landing. But he didn't fall. For some reason, that filled him with pride, and he stood up taller as he ran a hand through his windswept hair.

He'd landed near the front door to Elias's house, and Blanndynne touched down not far from him.

"You landed like you've been doing this for years, not hours. I'm extremely impressed," Blanndynne said, and Diomedes couldn't hide the smile her words brought to his face.

"Are you ready?" Diomedes asked, nodding toward the house.

"I am. I guess." Blanndynne hesitated, but she followed as Diomedes walked up to the front door.

After Diomedes knocked a second time, Elias opened the door. Blanndynne's breath caught in her throat, though Diomedes could decipher no reason for it.

"What do you want? What are you . . . Your Highness?" Elias said, taking a step back. "Come in."

The cool air from inside Elias's house refreshed Diomedes as he entered the main room.

"Is everything all right? Why are you wearing a blindfold? And where's your other friend?" Elias did not invite them to sit, nor did he offer them anything to drink. Not that Diomedes had expected it.

Before Diomedes could answer, Blanndynne spoke, and while there was no kindness in her voice, there was an air of concern. "What happened to your hand?"

In the shadow world Diomedes could sense, nothing appeared to be wrong with either of Elias's hands, and he waited for an explanation to be given.

"It's the curse. It's progressed," Elias muttered, shoving his hands in his pockets and out of sight.

Instead of asking more questions about what Blanndynne seen—he'd ask later—Diomedes put forth his request.

"I need the book I got from the merchant for you. It—"

"No." Elias shook his head. "I'm sorry, but no."

"Why not?" Blanndynne snapped, crossing her arms and popping out her hip. "You've got a perfect memory of everything you've read thanks to me. I'm assuming you've finished it." She waited until Elias nodded. "Then hand it over."

"I might need it still," Elias said, and it did not escape Diomedes's attention that Elias had positioned himself between

Diomedes and Blanndynne and the door to his bedroom. "I still haven't figured out how to break the curse, and—"

"Give us the book, Elias," Blanndynne said, her voice strict. "I won't ask nicely again."

"That was nicely?" Elias scoffed.

"Convince him," Diomedes said, his voice low. While he would've preferred the man give them the book willingly, he could feel the weight of his father's impending deadline approaching. He needed to make sure he ended up with the book.

When Blanndynne glanced at Diomedes, he gave her a brief nod.

"You're not going to convince me to . . ." Elias's words trailed off as Blanndynne's shadow counterpart raised a hand.

"Give Diomedes the book, Elias," Blanndynne said, though her voice was softer, gentler.

Elias stood still for a moment. "I can't. It was stolen." When he spoke, his voice was flat and emotionless. It made sense, though, because Blanndynne was most certainly already worn out from the flight into the desert and couldn't put as much energy into the enchantment as she had when she'd enchanted Mellacross right in front of Armannii.

"By who?" Diomedes asked, his stomach sinking. He needed the book in order to keep his sister from being a threat.

"I wasn't around when it happened."

"Now what?" Blanndynne asked, massaging her temple.

"Did you really read all of the book, Elias?" Diomedes asked, an idea forming in his mind.

Elias didn't respond until Blanndynne told him to answer Diomedes's questions. "I did."

"Tell me what the curse on you is called," Diomedes said, his hands clenching as he waited with bated breath.

"The Curse of Infiniti," Elias said. He stood still, his shoulders hunched forward.

"Do you have parchment and a pen?" Diomedes asked, and Elias nodded. "Go get it. I want you to write down what you remember about this curse."

Blanndynne sat down on the bed when Elias left to the bedroom to gather the supplies Diomedes had requested.

"Smart thinking," Blanndynne said, but she paused. "What's so important about the curse though? I'd think you'd be a little more focused on the timeline your father has shoved down your throat." In a moment of silence, Blanndynne took a deep breath. "Who—who are you planning on cursing?"

Diomedes wondered if he should tell her. Without Emmalee chiming in and with Elias under the enchantment, he decided to fill Blanndynne in.

"My sister. With my father's plans to disinherit me, my sister will be next in line and is therefore a threat to the throne and our plan to end the war. I don't want her to get hurt, and I decided this curse is the best way to keep her alive and still remove the threat."

Blanndynne rubbed the side of her face before speaking. "How difficult is it to set the Curse of Infiniti, Elias?" she asked when he reentered the room with several sheets of parchment and a pen.

"The amount of magic required to set this curse is typically fatal," Elias responded dully.

Diomedes bristled at the thought that the curse would likely kill him. Emmalee had said the same thing when he'd brought up the idea. But something else Emmalee had said rang louder. He didn't just have one person's magic in him—he had a multitude.

"That's true," Emmalee said, making Diomedes straighten up. *"I've had some time to think on it, and I doubt the curse would kill you. It may weaken you for a spell, but I believe you will live. And your sister will too, just as you hope."*

"This sounds dangerous," Blanndynne said, her voice wavering. "Isn't there something else you could do to your sister? Something that won't end in your inevitable death?"

"I won't die," Diomedes said, choosing to put his trust in Emmalee.

"You're sure about this?" Blanndynne asked. She sounded distracted, and one glance at her shadow counterpart gave an explanation as to why. She was looking over Elias's shoulder. "It sounds dangerous, and I know you can't see it, but the curse has spread down into his hands. They're completely covered in the same black veins, like he dipped them into an inkwell. It's . . . it's unnatural."

Diomedes ignored her question, asking Elias one of his own as the man continued to write. "Elias, do you forget your identity every time it resets?"

"Yes," Elias answered in an unfeeling tone. Though, having been under Blanndynne's enchantment, Diomedes knew it was quite the opposite. Elias was likely madly in love with Blanndynne in that moment. Poor man.

"Who else forgets you?" Diomedes asked.

"Anyone who was not present in the room when the curse was set," Elias responded without having to be prompted by Blanndynne.

Diomedes frowned. "Then why does Blanndynne remember you?"

"The book said there are certain spells that might counteract that part of the Curse of Infiniti, but they are rare and powerful. I suppose Blanndynne's vessel protected her when the curse was set."

"Hmm," Diomedes muttered, pressing his lips together. "So I'll forget who you are again when it resets?"

Elias nodded.

"And were there instructions in the book on how to set the curse?"

Elias nodded again.

"Can you read me some of what he's written?" Diomedes asked Blanndynne after a few minutes.

"The Curse of Infiniti is a high-tiered curse and should not be performed under any circumstances." Blanndynne's voice was hesitant as she kept reading. "Should you forgo this warning, please note that the possibility of anyone breaking the curse except the person setting it is nearly impossible, and it is permanent after the death of the person who set it."

"Tell me what I need to do."

Blanndynne kept reading.

"A vessel must be prepared with these runes." She paused, tilting her head. "He's copied them onto the parchment."

"Good," Diomedes said, nodding for her to continue.

"These runes are of the highest level and require a sacrifice. Within the vessel, combine the blood of both the victim and the individual setting the curse. Then . . ."

On and on she read as Elias wrote silently. Diomedes listened, and the more he learned of the Curse of Infiniti, the more he was certain Ellayne's future would be better if she were under the curse and well out of his way.

Chapter Thirty-Six

iomedes wasn't sure how long he'd been flying, but it couldn't have been more than two hours. Each minute seemed more precious as the clock counting down until his father's speech ticked in his head. He had less than two and a half days to collect all he needed for the Curse of Infiniti and still meet Armannii and Raidah's men for the siege.

After making sure Blanndynne promised to keep what they'd discussed private for the time being, Diomedes sent her to meet with Armannii and Raidah's men, telling her to assure Armannii that Diomedes was all right. She knew before she left that the elf would be furious with her for abandoning him, but she hadn't shown any ounce of worry.

"I can handle Armannii," Blanndynne had said, making sure the papers Elias had filled out were in a neat stack in Diomedes's bag. "The one with the runes is the one folded on the corner. And here," she had said, pushing something cold into his hands. "You can use this jar as the vessel."

"Thank you for your help," Diomedes had said, tucking the jar into his bag before they flew in separate directions.

He had not told her where he was planning to go. The moment she had mentioned the runed vessel, his mind had gone to the memories he had of the portal room at Hessland's. It had been filled with powerful runes, more so than other portals because, according to the guardian, the portal had required it for balance with the light and dark magic that formed the doorway to the Dark. And then there were Hessland's robes, which had been marked all over with runes that radiated the same power needed to enact the curse.

As Diomedes pondered Hessland's powerful rune magic, he traveled with the breeze blowing through his hair. It was hard to believe that not a week ago it would have taken him four days to travel what he'd managed to cover in about two hours.

By the time his spell guiding him to Hessland's began to pull him down, Diomedes was already realizing a flaw in his plan.

"*It's a boulder, Diomedes,*" Emmalee said in response to what he was referring to as an obstacle. "*Concentrate on your magic and move it.*"

Diomedes couldn't help but notice the lack of compassion in Emmalee's voice as he landed.

"*You've done much more difficult things,*" Emmalee countered.

It was more difficult than he'd expected, but soon Diomedes had shifted the boulder far enough to the left by lifting it with his magic that he could descend into the tunnels. Diomedes didn't bother with the ladder, jumping in and letting the wind rush by him until he landed gently on the ground. Before he entered the main tunnel, Diomedes rested his hand against the side of his bag, making sure the jar Blanndynne had given him was still in place.

The tunnels felt shorter compared to the distance it'd felt like he'd crossed the last four times.

In no time at all, Hessland's voice called out.

"Your Highness? You've returned?"

"I did say we'd meet again soon." Diomedes put a smile on his lips.

"Where are your companions?" Hessland asked. He stood nearby, and his shadow counterpart crossed his arms over his chest.

"They're preparing for the siege on Cyanthia. I wanted to not only bring the good news but to ask a favor of you," Diomedes said, pulling out the empty jar. He held it in one hand, tilting it back and forth. It had some weight to it, though it was empty and made of glass. "I need your help."

"With?"

"In order to enact my plan to take the castle and the throne from my father, I am in need of a spell. A curse, really. And while I do have great power now, I'm no expert in runes."

"If I recall, your friend Ovair is one of the best when it comes to rune magic. Why haven't you asked him?" There was a hint of suspicion in Hessland's voice, and the guardian took a step back.

It was as though Diomedes could feel what little trust Hessland had in him slipping away by the second. He was losing him.

Diomedes matched the guardian's step, advancing forward. "Armannii is talented, but I remembered the powerful runes you have here. While I'm sure Armannii could manage, I need someone who is well versed in complicated and ancient runes. Here." He held out the jar and waited for Hessland to take it. "You'll need to inscribe them on here."

"And what exactly are these runes?"

Diomedes pulled the parchment on which Elias had drawn the runes out of his bag and handed it to Hessland.

"What—what kind of runes are these? I've never seen anything like them before."

"Nor would I have expected you to," Diomedes said, crossing his arms over his chest.

"The level of magic these runes require . . . it's impossible."

"I'm sure you can manage," Diomedes said, his patience slipping at the same time his magic swirled within him. Its cold tendrils snaked toward his hands, but he held back. "Draw the runes, Hessland." The kindness emptied from his voice.

"No." The guardian shoved the jar and paper into Diomedes's chest. Diomedes managed to grab them before they fell.

The sound of Hessland's footsteps sprinting off toward the portal room had Diomedes frowning. It could've been so easy. If he had just obeyed . . .

"*You must get him to write them,*" Emmalee said in Diomedes's mind, her voice carrying with it an urgency that spread into a physical reaction within his body. His heart began to beat faster, and tension rose in the back of his head. "*If you must, you should—*"

He didn't wait to hear the rest of her instructions. Diomedes had already straightened up and was pursuing the guardian toward the portal room. As he had when facing Reymond, Diomedes felt the magic within him swelling and waiting to be released, and as before, he held on, doing what he could to subdue it.

"Leave now, Maudit." Hessland's voice boomed through the tunnel Diomedes had entered. "You are no longer welcome here."

Before Diomedes reached the portal room, the sound of something slithering against a stone surface resounded. In the shadows of his sensing spell, Diomedes could see the once still plants thriving with life. Vines slithered along the walls and floor toward him, and a few bushes almost seemed to be leaning into the path, blocking it and separating him from Hessland, who stood by the portal.

Standing in the entryway, taking in his surroundings, Diomedes did not notice the vine that had snuck down the wall behind him until it wrapped around his midsection and yanked him into the air.

Diomedes shouted in surprise, his fingers slipping on the jar. Before it could hit the ground, Diomedes extended his hand and reached out to the vessel with his magic. It stopped in midair.

Another vine snaked out and latched around both of his wrists, and the jar dropped, clinking against the floor, though it did not shatter. Diomedes struggled against the vines, gasping when one wrapped around his neck and closed his airway as it constricted.

"I was wrong to trust you," Hessland said, his voice too loud in the room. "I will not make that mistake again."

"*Focus.*" Emmalee's voice felt more distant the longer the vicious plants choked the life out of Diomedes.

He was too far past panic to focus, his mind a chaotic mess as he opened his mouth and no words came out. Somewhere deep inside his mind, he could hear Emmalee shouting at him to fight back, but he couldn't. He wasn't strong enough.

"*You will not die.*" Emmalee's voice was distorted, sounding like many voices screaming at him from all angles.

A river of ice traveled from Diomedes's core to his fingers in an instant, and then he was falling. Diomedes hit the ground on his hands and knees. His lungs sucked in air, leaving him gasping.

No longer in control of his body, Diomedes felt himself stand up. A thought entered his mind, but it wasn't his. He hadn't thought to brush off his clothes. But there he was, smacking at the dirt that had inevitably covered him when he'd fallen.

"Enough." Had that been his voice? He didn't remember thinking the words.

Dark magic swirled in his hands, and as he directed them toward the attacking flora, one word echoed in his head. *Burn*. But he hadn't come up with the word—hadn't even considered setting the flammable plants ablaze. Whose idea had it been? Why couldn't he control his body?

"Hessland!" Diomedes's voice reverberated around the burning inferno as he took slow steps into the room. Was that what he sounded like? Diomedes couldn't remember. And though he could smell the smoke and knew he was walking through the flames he'd set, he didn't feel a thing—no heat, no burns, just a coolness that licked at his skin. Not a single plant attacked him as he made his way to the platform.

But when he climbed the stairs, Hessland was no longer there.

Find him. The thought wasn't his, nor was it his decision to raise his hand and send a wisp of magic in search of the elusive guardian. Though he didn't think he was controlling it—didn't know who was controlling it—Diomedes could feel the wisp of magic searching the burning plants for Hessland.

A growl escaped Diomedes's lips. Had that been him? It could've been. The frustration felt like his. But was it? Was it real? Diomedes struggled against the mist holding him hostage, and he bent over to grip his head, which felt like it was about to explode.

"*Find him,*" Emmalee ordered, once again echoed by other voices. Whose voices? "*Go, Diomedes. Now.*"

The mist in his mind thickened, yanking him out of control once again. His feet moved without him asking them to, and the wisp of magic he'd sent after Hessland traveled back down the tunnel he'd come from. He stopped only for a second to pick up the jar on the way out.

It was only when Diomedes had gotten far enough from the cracks and pops of the roaring fire that he could hear the panicked shuffling of the guardian's footsteps. Diomedes's hand rose, and he pushed the dark magic deeper into the caves. When he felt Hessland's presence near his magic, he reached out and snatched him.

The magic, his magic, held the guardian still while Diomedes caught up with him.

"All you had to do was write the runes, Hessland." Diomedes's voice sounded silky to his own ears. "You've made this infinitely more difficult than you needed to."

Diomedes gritted his teeth as he approached Hessland. The protective runes he wore were at war with the magic holding the guardian still. Sweat lined Diomedes's neck, and he rubbed it with the back of his hand.

"Write the runes," Diomedes repeated, using his magic to force Hessland's hand out. He placed the jar in the man's grasp, ready to catch it should it drop again.

"I won't."

"Your brother is inches from death on the other side of your portal." The lie had formed in his mind fast enough that Diomedes barely had time to process it before it escaped from his lips.

Hessland's heartbeat quickened, but his voice remained calm. "That's a lie."

Diomedes shrugged, cocking his head to the side. He took a few steps, then paused. "I had a feeling you'd be resistant, so I set up a backup plan. If you don't write these runes on this jar and I don't cross through that portal in two minutes, your brother will die. You have my word."

"Your word means nothing."

"You're welcome to think that. But you've got about a minute and a half until Zephrium is dead. It would've been more, but you decided to make this all more complicated than it needed to be." Diomedes rubbed his neck where the plant had strangled him. It would bruise, and it would be difficult to hide from his comrades.

A problem for a later time.

"If I were you, I'd start writing."

Hessland huffed. "Give me the parchment."

The sound of something scratching glass filled the room, and a smile snuck across Diomedes's lips.

"Wh-what are these runes?" Hessland asked, panting after a minute.

Diomedes didn't answer, but he wondered the same thing. He had not seen them, nor did he have any idea what each did, but by the sound of it, Hessland had collapsed against the wall. Thankfully, there was no sound of broken glass.

"Keep drawing," Diomedes said, his voice gruff. Once again, he couldn't remember thinking the words. What was happening with his magic?

"I-I can't." Hessland's voice was weak. "I've drawn four. That has to be enough. I-I can't do any more."

"Keep going." Diomedes stepped forward, standing over Hessland. "Your brother's life depends on it."

"But I—"

"You have fifteen seconds."

After a few more moments of heavy breathing, Hessland coughed below Diomedes.

Diomedes's brow furrowed. *Thud. Clink.* Glass landed on stone, and the heavy breathing stopped.

As Diomedes bent down, the sensing spell outlined the shadow form of the jar in Diomedes's mind. When he picked it up, the glass was hot in some places and cold in others. He traced over the inscriptions with his fingers.

"*It appears he wrote them correctly,*" Emmalee said, her voice void of any others.

"And Hessland?" Diomedes asked, not needing the sensing spell to tell him that Hessland wasn't moving. Squatting down, Diomedes placed two fingers against Hessland's neck. He received his answer.

"*The instructions from your ancestor were clear. The final rune was meant to take his life as part of the curse. His brother will die now too.*"

"Why?" Diomedes asked, his hands beginning to tremble again, just as they had after he'd killed Reymond. For the first time since Hessland had run from him, he felt like he was fully in control of his actions again. And with that came the guilt.

Another man was dead because of him.

"Why does Zephrium have to die too?"

"*It's part of the spell that binds them to the portal.*"

Diomedes struggled to swallow, his breath catching in his throat. His knees felt unstable, and he collapsed against the floor from his squatting position. Similar to the first time Diomedes had ever traveled through the portal, he felt nauseated, and he gripped his stomach with one hand.

"Why did you make me do this?"

"*Make you?*" Emmalee scoffed. "*Need I remind you that this curse was your idea? That man is dead because you want to keep the only real threat to the crown alive.*"

Stowing the jar in his bag, Diomedes rubbed his face with both hands. His head still throbbed, and it didn't help that Emmalee's words felt louder than usual.

"*You should go before the magic in the portal implodes.*" Emmalee's voice was too calm for what she'd just said. "*But before you go, take the guardian's rune pen. If you remember, you'll need it for the next part of the curse.*"

Diomedes hesitated for a second, not wanting to mess with Hessland's body. It felt wrong. But with the threat of the portal imploding, Diomedes reached down and picked up Hessland's pen, which had still been grasped in his hand. Tucking the pen and the parchment with the runes, which had been in Hessland's other hand, into his bag, Diomedes rose to his feet and followed the tunnel out.

Just as he reached the small room with the ladder, a wave of energy surged through the tunnel and smacked into him, slamming him against the wall. His shoulder ached where he'd hit it, but he was otherwise unharmed.

Except for his mind, which repeated the same question over and over again.

Had it been necessary?

It had to have been.

It had to.

Diomedes stayed the night in an inn, though he did not sleep. His mind was too busy reliving the deaths of the two men he'd killed—three if he considered that Zephrium had died because of him too. He paced up and down the room, rubbing the back of his neck and his shoulders until Emmalee told him to stop.

"Tell me what happened back there," Diomedes said, sitting on the edge of the single cot. "I was dying. That vine, it was choking the life out of me, and then I was free. But then I—it was like—I wasn't in control. What did you do?"

"I waited too long for you to find me to allow you to die when you could've easily gotten free."

"What. Did. You. Do?" Diomedes took off the scarf covering his eye sockets, placing it to his side.

"I took control. I saved you. And I got you what you needed for this curse you're so eager to enact." Emmalee's voice got louder each second, and Diomedes cringed. *"The only thing you should be saying to me is thank you."*

"Thank you?" Diomedes said, scoffing. "You stole control over my body. Over my mind. How could I trust you after that?"

Emmalee was silent for a moment, and when she spoke again, her voice was softer. *"You're strong, Diomedes. Strong like your mother. It's why I chose you. And you're too important to let die. Our plans are too great, to allow them to fade away because you haven't fully grasped how and when to use your magic. But you'll learn. It's why I'm here. To teach you how to work with and submit to the dark magic you've been given."*

Diomedes stiffened at Emmalee's mention of his mother. He had strived to live in a way that would've made her proud had she still been in his life. But now . . .

"She would *be proud, Diomedes,"* Emmalee whispered.

Instead of responding to Emmalee or dwelling on his mother and the past, Diomedes set his jaw, preparing himself for the next step of the curse—a step he would take in only a few short hours.

A place to reset. That was the last part of the curse he needed to prepare before they marched on Cyanthia in a day and a half. Diomedes had been flying over what he assumed was the Black Forest for a few hours. Emmalee had offered a place to allow

Ellayne to reset, and she had given Diomedes the direction to fly east.

"*I need you to find this house,*" Emmalee said after a while.

An image appeared in Diomedes's mind of a tiny house in the middle of a clearing amongst the trees. It was only one story. There was a small farm peeking out from the back, and the house itself looked old and worn down.

"That's where you think my sister should be brought back to every time she's reset?" Diomedes asked, his muscles tensing as he hovered he didn't know how high above the ground. It had to be over 150 feet at least since that was how tall most of the trees were.

"*It's better than the middle of the Albanistic Desert.*"

Diomedes pressed his lips together and nodded. He took in the image she'd left in his mind and focused on the way the tall grass moved and how the rays from the sun had lightened the dark wood making up the tiny house. With each thing he noticed, he felt something to the right pulling him, the same tug he'd felt in the cave.

With an inward direction his magic could follow, Diomedes continued to balance his thoughts between navigating toward the clearing with the abandoned-looking structure and staying in the air. His mind felt increasingly drained with every second that went by, and it was a bit disconcerting that he had no idea which direction he was headed in or even what part of Phildeterre he was in. At least with the last two times he'd flown, he'd visited the places before and had been able to visualize them for himself.

"*It's located in the eastern part of the Black Forest near Cyanthia.*" Emmalee's voice almost broke Diomedes's concentration, but he regained it as he felt himself lose a bit of altitude. "*I grew up there and stayed in the house for a time after I discovered I possessed dark magic. I couldn't return to my home. Not when—not when the village held so many tragic memories. So*

I returned to this place and began practicing my magic. At first, I didn't have anyone to teach me like I'm doing for you."

Diomedes furrowed his brow. He couldn't begin to imagine what that would've been like, to be alone and confused. Then again, at least he wouldn't have had to be concerned about the voice in his head taking control of his body.

"*I came here for safety,*" Emmalee said.

"When was this?" Diomedes asked out loud, though his words got lost in the wind.

"*After your father and his council ordered the raid that killed my family.*" She was quiet for a moment. "*I never forgave him for that. And I never will.*"

The magic pulled him, leading him in the direction of the tiny house from Emmalee's past. Wind blew around him, and though he knew he should've been shivering, he wasn't. Something about his magic was protecting him from the cold—not keeping him warm, but almost taking away the sensation of being chilled.

Before long, he landed with some air of grace in the middle of the clearing. Though his journey through the air had ended, the spell pulling him toward the tiny house had not, and he continued walking until he reached one of the outer walls of the house. The wood on the outside was rough enough that Diomedes considered he might get splinters if he pressed too hard on it.

"*Go to the front door. The part of the curse your ancestor mentioned in regard to setting the reset point of the curse must take place inside,*" Emmalee reminded him. It had not been difficult to organize all the things he had needed to do for the Curse of Infiniti, but it did help to have an extra mind keeping him on track and remembering details he might not.

The house appeared small according to the sensing spell—he could almost see its entire shadow in his mind—but at least it wasn't in the desert. His sister would not have to deal with the terrible heat and the poisonous creatures. Diomedes supposed, in that way, he was doing her a kindness.

Working his way around the tiny house, Diomedes found the front porch with three steps leading up to it. The door was unlocked, and it creaked as Diomedes entered. A musty smell wafted out, and Diomedes turned up his nose.

"I don't think anyone has been here in a while," he said, his forehead creasing. An idea emerged, and no sooner had he thought it than Emmalee responded by bringing memories of the house to the forefront of his mind as she had in the caves.

When he combined them with the shadow image from the sensing spell, it was almost like he could see again.

But not quite.

The memory Emmalee showed Diomedes was of a small kitchen with a counter and two cabinets. A single chair sat at a table pressed up against the wall under a window. Toward the back was a door and a hallway.

"*There are two bedrooms and a washroom. The back bedroom would be best. There should be a mirror against the wall.*"

Diomedes followed her directions to the bedroom door, which was closed. The musty smell was much stronger, and Diomedes shrank back when he first opened the door.

"So this is where she'll be every time she's reset?" Diomedes asked when he ran his fingers over the mirror at the back of the room. It was about four feet tall and a foot and a half wide, and according to Emmalee's memory of it, the frame was made from the black wood of the trees outside.

"*She'll need a place out of the way to return to. Somewhere nearby where you, or maybe someone you trust, can keep an eye on her.*"

Diomedes leaned against the wall, tilting his head down. "At least it's not the desert."

"*She will be safe here, and if she is harmed during the thirty days, all her injuries will be healed and she will be returned to perfect health when she wakes up. At least, that's what I remember the genie saying when she read from your ancestor's notes. And your sister will never die.*"

Diomedes straightened up. "Unharmed and not a threat. Sounds to me like a perfect compromise."

Emmalee's laugh was light, though her next words were quite the opposite. "*Ellayne Maudit will cease to exist.*"

"And only I and those in the room will remember her," Diomedes said, tucking one of the ends of his scarf back around the band.

"*When the time comes to set the curse, choose your company carefully.*" Emmalee's warning did not go unnoticed, and neither did her abrupt change in subject. "*Now, I know you have not done any runes before, but I figured you might like a way to keep track of your sister. I will show you a series of runes that you should trace onto the lower frame of the mirror. They are not nearly as powerful as the ones on the jar, so you shouldn't have much trouble drawing them.*"

"What will they do exactly?"

"*When you inscribe matching ones on a different mirror, you will be able to see into this mirror and keep an eye on your sister.*"

"I doubt I need to remind you that I can't see," Diomedes muttered.

"*I'm well aware, Diomedes,*" she retorted, her voice carrying as much attitude as he'd given her. "*I trust you'll find someone who can be your eyes for you. Maybe your genie. If you trust her enough, she could watch over your sister and make sure she doesn't get too close to the truth.*"

As Emmalee showed him image after image of runes, sweat collected on the back of his neck and his forehead. They were not as simple as she'd made them sound, and halfway through tracing them, he had to give up another memory; he and Ellayne had used all of the linens from one of the upstairs closets to build a massive fort in one of the third-floor family studies. But Ellayne and everything in the memory disappeared as he regained power and enough energy to complete the runes.

"*Well done,*" Emmalee said as Diomedes ran his fingers over the inscriptions to check his handiwork.

"I suppose it's wise to keep her close, but not too close," Diomedes said, running a hand through the top of his hair. He remembered Elias's explanation of how the Curse of Infiniti could be broken—and why Elias would never be free. In order for his sister to be set free once placed under the curse, she would need to get close enough to Diomedes and convince him to say that he released her. Only the person who'd set the curse could free the victim.

"*It's not that simple, thankfully. You must bleed, as will she, and there must be some part of you that wants to release her. While it's never been done before—not that I've heard at least—it's wise to keep her away.*"

"And I'm sure it helps that pretty much everyone else who has set the curse has died doing so, meaning there's no one to break it," Diomedes muttered, and to his surprise, Emmalee agreed.

"*You will likely be one of the first to set the Curse of Infiniti and witness it in action. It's an honor. Now, you need to do the part of the spell that will actually tie your sister to this place. This will require your blood.*"

Without hesitation, Diomedes pulled out the dagger. "Tell me what I need to do."

As powerful as Diomedes felt an hour later, he had lost track of how many memories he'd given up to complete the part of the curse that linked the victim to the location. Diomedes's hands trembled with the dark magic surging through them as he slid the final floorboard back into place. Diomedes stood up, brushing the dust off his pants.

The emptiness he felt inside mixed with the refreshing coolness of his magic, and he found himself grinning as he pushed his hair back from his face. His arm was still bleeding from where he'd sliced it open, but after following Emmalee's directions to the kitchen, he wrapped it in a towel. The pain in his arm was no match for the absolute bliss of power coursing through him. He could barely feel any resistance in that moment, almost as if his mind was finally beginning to submit to the magic within.

"*That was marvelous, Diomedes. And now the final steps are all you have left. Once you combine your blood and your sister's blood in the jar, paint the rune I've shown you on her forehead.*"

Diomedes paused, thinking over what she'd just said. He cocked his head to the side while he applied more pressure to his wrist and the towel covering it. "How do you know what the rune looks like? I didn't see it, which means you couldn't have."

"*I told you before, when you first started looking for a way to remove the threat of your sister with a curse, that I had researched similar curses. In fact, I came across the Curse of Infiniti in my research, though I ran into complications.*"

"Who were you going to use it on?" Diomedes asked, though he could've guessed the answer before she said it.

"*Your father. However, Evangeline caught wind of what I was trying to do, and she put an end to it,*" Emmalee said, her voice lined with razors.

"You were willing to die to—"

"*Yes,*" Emmalee said, cutting him off.

Diomedes cleared his throat when Emmalee didn't speak again right away. "After I draw the rune, I have to break Ellayne's heart, right?"

"*Correct.*"

"How do you suggest I do that?" Diomedes asked, leaning against the kitchen counter. It was strange to hear his own voice speak so lightly over something as dark as breaking his sister's heart. But as he felt a mist of coolness trickle through his brain, he found no conflict or guilt over the topic. Voices whispered in his head. He wasn't killing her. That seemed noble enough, especially since he was doing it all to end the war.

"*What are you planning to do with Evangeline?*" Something in her voice lent itself to the idea that her question was a test.

"Why?"

"*I told you she's not to be underestimated, and I was telling the truth. But in regard to your question about the final step, you might consider your sister's relationship to her mother. It could provide an answer to your problem.*"

Diomedes wasn't fooled by Emmalee's smooth talk, but he didn't challenge her any further on it. He could feel the same thread of anger burrowing deep within him, though the thread was not his. It belonged to Emmalee.

Chapter Thirty-Seven

The temperature of the air warmed as Diomedes traveled north toward where he'd told Blanndynne to meet Armannii and Raidah's men. He hadn't realized it was nighttime until the sun's rays peeked over the horizon and poured warmth on his skin. One more sunrise and they'd march on Cyanthia. The thought made him grin.

It was not difficult to sense the army of men preparing to infiltrate the castle. They made enough noise. Diomedes began his descent, and when he was close enough to the ground, he heard Armannii's voice first.

"Make sure this group has your strongest fighters. It's imperative they hold the line. We don't want any fighting to cause unnecessary casualties in this part of town. And—" Armannii paused his instructions as Diomedes landed nearby.

Though it was difficult to read facial expressions in the shadow realm of his sensing spell, he could tell that Armannii and the five men surrounding him were all looking at him.

"I'll be back in a moment," Armannii muttered, and the sound of his footsteps grew louder. "Did I just see you fly?" Armannii's voice was low as he placed his hand on Diomedes's shoulder and guided him away from the others. "Since when can you do that?"

"Blanndynne didn't tell you?" Diomedes asked, a smirk on his lips. "After you left," he said when Armannii shook his head. Diomedes was thankful Emmalee had shown him how to drawn the healing rune because he was sure the bruising around his neck from the vine at Hesslands's would've sparked Armannii's questions otherwise. The blasted rune had burned like the desert sun though. "How are things going here?"

Armannii glanced over his shoulder. "Well, I think." He scratched the side of his jaw. "Why did you send Blanndynne out here without you? You could've been hurt or—"

"I'm fine." Diomedes stopped, forcing Armannii to pause as well. "Now my question for you."

"But you never answered—"

"Are we still on the same page about what lies before us?" Diomedes asked, lifting his chin.

"What do you mean?" Armannii asked, confusion clouding his voice as he moved his hands to his hips.

Diomedes clasped his hands behind his back. "Is your heart still set on ending the war?"

Armannii was silent, but his foot began to tap. "Really, Didi? I can't believe you just asked that. I've been beside you for the past, what, seven years? And you think I'd turn away now?"

"You've been questioning me nonstop since I left the castle. I don't know if that is some sort of sign that you want out. If it is, then now is the time to do so."

The elf took a deep breath, and Diomedes prepared for him to argue—to get mad. Instead, his voice was soft. "I want the war to be over. I do. But I've always considered my loyalty to you as *most* important." His voice was low. "I've blindly followed people before, and the only thing it ended in was hurt and death. I just . . . I don't want that to happen again. I want the war over, but I don't want to see valuable lives lost. And *every* life is valuable, Diomedes. Every single one."

Diomedes pressed his lips together but didn't respond. He could hear the hurt in his friend's words, and somewhere in the back of his mind, it made sense.

"I want this war over. I've wanted it over for a *very* long time. I just—I don't think shedding blood is going to be the best way to win people's support, whether that's royal guards' or your father's. There's already been enough blood shed." Armannii shifted, and his clothing rustled.

"I have no intention of killing my father," Diomedes said, his facial expression remaining neutral. "Unfortunately, we must risk some lives in order to get into the castle. My father won't make it easy."

"I know." Armannii sighed. "I do, I just—if that's what it takes to end the war . . . I'm with you, brother. I am."

Diomedes's cheek pulled up in a half grin. "I'm glad to hear that. We should finish planning. We'll move in tomorrow morning. If my guess is correct, we should be able to catch my father in the middle of his midmorning meeting."

Diomedes was not tired. Whether it was from excitement, nerves, or magic, he wasn't sure. But when everyone else was waking up in their tents the next morning, Diomedes was already waiting. Raidah's men packed up within half an hour after breakfast, and after a few words from Diomedes, which had come more easily than he'd expected, they set out for Cyanthia. According to Armannii, Raidah had sent over four hundred men, and while that wouldn't even make up a battalion under one commander, let alone a captain, Diomedes had a feeling his father had dispatched many of his own men to search for him. He also knew that his father kept only seven to eight hundred guards present within the upper town of Cyanthia, including the castle. There was a chance that his father had upped the number of guards in Cyanthia since his speech was the next day and many people would travel to see it, so Diomedes prepared Raidah's men just in case that happened.

If they were lucky, the castle would be unprepared and scrambling.

But even if they'd been tipped off, Raidah's men—though they didn't know it—were just a distraction. The real battle would begin as soon as Diomedes and his companions were inside. And Diomedes knew exactly where to enter.

"Once we get to my balcony, we'll be able to give the signal to begin the siege and head to the council room. We should be able to make it there before the royal guards arrive to get my father to a safe room," Diomedes said to Blanndynne and Armannii. "Go make sure the group coming through the tunnels reaches the entrance, and then meet Blanndynne and me near Camile and Forrest's old shop." Diomedes waited for Armannii's shadow counterpart to nod. He left soon after.

When Blanndynne and Diomedes were alone, he spoke to her in a quiet voice. "After we enter the castle, you may need to enchant some of the royal guards. Do you think you'll be able to?"

He could sense the smile on her face as well as hear it in her voice. "I was already practicing on a couple of Raidah's men for fun. I definitely can." She paused, tilting her head. "Do you have everything you need for your sister?"

Diomedes nodded, a grin on his face. "Shall we?" he asked, lifting a few inches off the ground. Blanndynne snorted, joining him in the air.

While the rest of Raidah's men split up to go to their appropriate locations to attack, Diomedes and Blanndynne slipped into the lower town unnoticed. Armannii met them at Camile and Forrest's old shop, bringing with him the news that Raidah's men had reached and entered the tunnels. Diomedes left the shop with them and they entered the street.

With a reminder from Diomedes, Blanndynne and Armannii pulled their hoods on their cloaks as far down as his was. They were hidden in an alley, and Diomedes was making last-minute adjustments to the plan.

"Now that I can fly, you can take Armannii up, Blanndynne. I'll follow. You will stay and send the signal thirty seconds after Armannii and I have left my room. Then I need you to find the queen and take her to the throne room. Armannii and I will take care of the council. Is that understood?"

"What are your plans for the council?" Armannii asked. "We'll definitely be outnumbered."

"I'll take care of the council. You just concern yourself with subduing my father."

"Great," Armannii muttered. "I'll just assault the king of the country. I'm sure that won't end horribly."

"After I'm done with the council, I will fetch my sister. I only want my family in the throne room with us."

"What do you need with Ellayne?" Armannii asked, his voice filled with confusion.

Blanndynne remained silent, for which Diomedes was grateful. The bag with the runed jar hung by Diomedes's side, and though he thought about grabbing it and holding it tighter, he refrained. Instead, he crossed his arms over his chest.

"I believe it's time we have a family meeting. Now, shall we go? I think we've given Raidah's men enough time to get to their positions."

The air swept around Diomedes as he pictured his balcony and felt the pull of his magic directing him to it. He sensed Blanndynne and Armannii land first, and he followed behind them.

"It's locked," Armannii said, jiggling the door that led inside.

"So use the opening rune," Diomedes said, wishing he had eyes to roll in that moment. "And make it quick. If any of the guards in the gardens look up, they'll be able to see us easily. Keep an eye down below, Blanndynne."

Diomedes waited several seconds, balancing his listening between Armannii's rune pen scratching on the lock and

Blanndynne running her fingers over the rough surface of the balcony railing.

"There," Armannii said, and the lock clicked. He pushed the door open, and the hinges gave a slight creak.

"Give us thirty seconds and then—"

"Send out the beam of light, I know. Now go," Blanndynne said, nudging Diomedes inside.

Armannii had already made it to the door leading to the hallway when Diomedes entered his old room. It was strange to walk into a place that smelled familiar and that he had many memories of yet could no longer see.

It smelled musty, as though no one had bothered to go in since the night Blanndynne had flown him off the balcony. Images of the room returned to the front of his mind, but for the first time, he didn't want to see them.

"You're going to need more power to take down the council," Emmalee said in his mind. She'd been quiet for a while, and her sudden presence startled Diomedes. *"You could release some of those memories to begin building up the strength you'll need."*

With the nerves building up inside him, he felt a desire for a new hit of power. She didn't have to ask twice.

By the time Diomedes stood next to the door, his magic was already flooding through his veins.

"What's with the temperature drop?" Armannii whispered next to him. "You're going to alert everyone in the castle to our presence if you keep leaking cold air like that."

Diomedes fought for control over the magic as it strained against him. The power almost had a mind of its own, and a thin layer of sweat lined the back of Diomedes's neck before he was able to bring it back under control. He promised to call it again when it was needed.

"Better. And I just heard the—"

"Guards. I know. We should have plenty of time to get to the servants' staircase in the left hallway." Diomedes's ear was tingling from the sensing spell, only a foot or so away from the door. He'd heard the patrolling guards' footsteps as well.

"Ready when you are," Armannii said, a slight grin hidden in his words.

Whether he was having doubts or not, Diomedes knew Armannii was taking some pleasure in the action and adventure of the siege.

Diomedes gripped the handle. With one more moment of silence, he turned his hand and pushed the door open. It didn't even make a noise.

Instead of letting his magic lead him to the council room, he let his memories. They guided him around every corner, his hand always on the hilt of his sword. When they reached the servants' stairs, they waited a few seconds to listen for anyone traveling up or down. It was silent.

"Let's go," Armannii said, taking the lead.

Following behind him, Diomedes kept his right hand against the wall as they spiraled down. The temperature of the stone bricks matched the coolness from his magic, and with the reminder of what he was about to do, Diomedes dug into the depths of his mind to find even more memories to rid himself of. Each step down, he gave a little piece of himself up for the dark magic.

He would not fail.

Not with the power radiating out from him.

They reached the bottom of the stairs, and Diomedes, feeling the boldness spurred on by the magic, pushed past Armannii and led the rest of the way to the council room.

Diomedes stood taller when he heard the first shouts of the two royal guards stationed outside the meeting room. A sneer crossed Diomedes's lips as he cracked his neck from side to side.

"*You're strong enough to throw them, just like you moved the boulder at Hessland's. Push your hand out and send them flying down the hallway.*" Emmalee's instructions came just in time; the guards' stampeding footsteps echoed down the hallway at the same moment Diomedes heard Armannii nock an arrow.

Raising both hands horizontally in front of him, Diomedes pushed his magic in the direction of the oncoming guards. A wave of energy spread down the corridor, and Diomedes ran a hand through his hair to fix it after he heard the grunts and crashes of the guards landing against the opposite wall at least twenty yards away.

"That was—" Armannii's grip on the bow loosened slowly so that it wouldn't make a noise as it returned to a resting state. His voice was filled with awe.

"Let's go." Diomedes strolled to the double doors of the meeting room. Filled with energy, he pushed them open with nothing but his magic. "Hello, Father. I heard a rumor you were looking for me."

The muffled voices of the council members silenced as soon as the doors slammed open. A chair scratched against the floor, and someone stood up.

"Diomedes." King Butch's voice rang out, filling the room with a boom. "What is the meaning of this?"

"*Show your new strength. Close the doors. Flick your hand, and pull them with your magic.*"

Many gasps resounded throughout the room as the doors closed behind Armannii and Diomedes.

"*Seal them,*" Emmalee ordered, her voice ringing in Diomedes's mind. She gave further directions, and as Diomedes obeyed her, a surge of cold air filled the room. Barriers of dark magic blocked the entrance.

Diomedes's ears perked up when he heard the sound of weapons being drawn; he could sense each council member—a shadow in his mind—as they rose to their feet. It sparked a smirk. Could they not see what they were up against?

Had that been his thought? Diomedes cringed when his temple began to throb, but he tried to hide it with grand, sweeping gestures.

"I've decided we need to return to the topic of the war, but only if you have time in your meeting, of course," Diomedes said, waving his hand off to the side as his voice dripped with sarcasm.

"What have you done, Diomedes?" King Butch's voice wavered for only a second.

"Oh, nothing much." Diomedes raised an eyebrow, clasping his hands as he moved around the edge of the room. Nearby, he heard one of the members shift their weight toward him. Diomedes paused, ready to protect himself. In a split second, he heard Armannii draw his bow.

"*Don't* move," Armannii said, his voice low.

Diomedes chuckled as he resumed his steady pace. "I came to you several months ago with the truth about the war you've continued participating in. I told you how it was built on lies and the untimely death of two of our ancestors. You didn't believe me."

"That's because what you proposed was ridiculous. Absolute rubbish," said a familiar voice. Diomedes recognized it as Clive, and he cocked his head as he listened to the brave council member continue. "To think that King Kylian would kill his own—"

"That's enough," King Butch said in an even tone.

However, Diomedes's magic was already pooling in his fingers. Ice ran through his veins, and he turned in the direction of Clive's voice. Raising one hand, Diomedes tilted his chin up, clenching his fist. He locked his magic around Clive's throat—just as he had with Reymond—and as he tightened his fingers, a gurgling sound echoed in the room. It bounced off the walls, and as it grew louder, Diomedes's sneer spread.

"Enough!" King Butch slammed his fist on the table. "Release him!"

Diomedes scoffed, but with a sigh, he let go of Clive and slipped his hand behind his back.

"Armannii," he said, his voice filled with false levity. He nodded toward his father, but before Armannii could take two steps, more chairs screeched against the floor. "All right," Diomedes said, shrugging. "We'll do this the difficult way."

"You need to give more, Diomedes. You're no match for every council member. But if you find more strong memories, you can use the paralyzing spell you used on Reymond to hold back all of the council members while the elf removes your father from the room."

It was a good idea. Wasn't it? As quickly as he could, he pulled out memories he'd returned to frequently: training with his father in sword fighting, stealing fresh bread from the kitchen to bring to some of his friends in the lower town, escaping from boring lessons with Ellayne, and going to his first pub with Armannii. Each one was zapped out of existence and replaced with a darkness he could barely control, a darkness so powerful it overwhelmed any other emotion in conflict with his desire. Take the throne. Ensure he would be king. End the war. Each whispered over and over by many voices in his head.

Diomedes gritted his teeth, and with a deep breath, he held out his hands and let his magic snake out, finding targets all around the room. With his magic taking control, he could sense Armannii as the spell spread around the room, and he avoided the elf. But everyone else was not as lucky.

Weapons clattered to the ground as the council members and his father were forced to their knees. There were shouts of confusion and pain, which Diomedes silenced with a wave of his hand, stealing control of even their vocal cords. It was thrilling. Invigorating.

He laughed, his lip pulling up as he sneered.

"Diomedes." Armannii's voice was low as he took a few steps toward Diomedes. "This is—"

"My father, Armannii," Diomedes ordered, one hand still raised, keeping control over the people in the room. "Now."

In the silence, Armannii's footsteps echoed. Diomedes's hand shook, but the spell held. From somewhere in the hallway, he could hear hollering from the remaining royal guard, most likely because Raidah's men had begun to breach the castle from the tunnels.

"I will be along shortly," Diomedes said as Armannii dragged King Butch toward the exit. He wondered how long the spell would last after Armannii and his father left the room. However, he wasn't worried. Armannii was more than capable of fighting the king, especially with the advantage of starting in control.

"Uh-huh," Armannii muttered.

Diomedes lowered the magic barrier blocking the exit. The doors to the meeting room opened and closed. He raised the barriers once more.

Diomedes faced the council members, and before Emmalee could prompt him, he flew up and landed in the middle of the table. With every passing second, his power grew as more of his memories slipped into the silent darkness inside. It was a whirlpool, and his memories sank down and disappeared into the sea of magic. Was he still in control?

"I have a proposition, and I suggest you consider it." Diomedes, still with his hands holding everyone frozen, paced up and down the table, sensing and turning at the end every time. "In less than an hour, I will be king. You have two options: you pledge your allegiance to me here and now, or you die. There is no in-between." His mind scrambled to remember if he'd come up with those words or if something, maybe his magic, had suggested them. He couldn't remember.

Diomedes tried to frown, but his face remained in a wicked grin. His mind became fuzzier and fuzzier. The voices in his head were getting louder, just as they had when he'd killed Hessland, when he'd lost control. Had he lost it already? When? Had it been the voices in his head who had slipped words from his lips? He didn't want to kill anyone. Did he? No, he hadn't wanted to kill Reymond or the guardians. He didn't want to kill the council members either. Did he? Diomedes hesitated but did not lose control of the spell. Something, the darkness, had stolen control. All he could do was listen as he gave the power of speech back to each council member.

"What is your decision?" It was his voice, but he hadn't thought the words. He tried to reel the magic back in as panic seeped through the numbness.

"I stand with the true king," the first council member said, voice trembling as Diomedes towered above him. Diomedes tried to cringe as his hand clenched, suffocating the life out of the man. Four. He'd killed four. He hadn't wanted to. He wanted to stop.

The councilmen had been in the wrong, but did they deserve to die?

"*Yes*." The chorus of responses in his head was overwhelming. He wanted to grip his head and stop, but his body kept moving without his permission.

Diomedes couldn't cower, couldn't quit as he stopped the hearts and suffocated the lungs of each council member who sided with his father. He hadn't intended to kill them, only scare them. When had he lost control? These were people, faces, he recognized.

No. He wanted to say the word—wanted the magic to stop. Diomedes tried to plant his feet on the ground when he saw who was next. It was no use. His stomach twisted when his mouth opened, spouting the same question.

"Silas, what's your decision?" Diomedes heard his own voice say, and it felt like he was only an observer to what was happening around him. Silas, the man who had felt like his only comrade, his only friend, one of his only allies in the council room. Silas, who had been one of the first to advocate for Diomedes to start training with the royal guards. Silas, the man whose brilliant blue eyes lit up a room as much as his rolling laughter.

Stop. He wanted to stop.

"Don't do this, son. This isn't you." Silas wheezed when the magic tightened its grip around his neck.

He was right. But Diomedes couldn't listen, couldn't obey. "Your decision?"

"I have always and will always stand by your father."

Diomedes tried to shout, to fight, to pull away. But he couldn't. He wanted to be sick when the sound of Silas's neck snapping filled the room. Diomedes tried to get Emmalee to respond, but she seemed lost in the voices committing mass murder.

Even Clive's death brought a sharp pain to Diomedes's heart. When only three members remained—the three who had submitted—Diomedes regained some control of his body. Diomedes jumped down from the table, his breath heavy. He leaned against the table, head hung low. He felt sick, like he was going to pass out. Not from exhaustion, but from horror. Bodies lay around him. Lives he had taken. He needed to get out, to breathe fresh air, to—

"*Calm down, Diomedes*," Emmalee said in a soothing voice as Diomedes lowered the barrier in the meeting room. "*Remember why you're doing this. They never would've ended the war. You are so close to accomplishing what you came here to do. Don't give up now.*"

Diomedes closed the meeting room behind him, pressing his hand against the lock to keep the last three council members trapped inside. He'd deal with them later.

Deal with them?

What had he meant by that? Those hadn't been his words.

He ran his hands through his hair, cringing at the sweat dripping from his forehead and the back of his neck. Guilt was destroying him, and he felt like crying out as he clenched his jaw shut. "What did you do?" His entire body shook. "Why did you—all of them—they're all—"

Something snapped. Diomedes leaned against the wall as a swell of magic surged through him, just as it had when the vine was choking him to death.

Every feeling but determination fell away.

He needed to find and curse his sister.

He needed to deal with his stepmother.

He needed to put his father in a place of powerlessness.

He needed to end the war.

He *would* end the war.

His magic set his mind back in the right place. *Right place?* Diomedes straightened his tunic and made his way upstairs as numbness filled every part of him. If his guess was correct, his sister would be in her room with her nose in a book.

Run. Ellayne needs to run.

The sound of pounding footsteps flooded the stairway. It was not Raidah's men. A swarm of royal guards rushed to where they thought the king was.

Diomedes didn't even turn when he flicked his hand out to the side and threw the first line of men down the stairs into the guards behind them. He continued striding through the hallway as though nothing were wrong. Mechanically, Diomedes rolled up the sleeves to his tunic, biting the side of his cheek.

"When you begin the curse, you're going to need to give all you have. If you cling to any part of your humanity, there's a good chance you might die. Any person with lesser magic would. But I believe in you."

"All of it?" Diomedes asked.

No. Don't do it. A faint voice whispered in his mind.

His thoughts almost turned to where he kept his special memories: Ellayne being born, sneaking into the kitchen for her, spending time on the roof with her at sunset. However, he knew what happened to memories he thought about for too long, and he quickly went to others, hoping the magic inside him hadn't seen the precious ones.

"Yes. You must give this ultimate sacrifice for the power needed to complete the takeover."

Diomedes paused when he rounded the corner to Ellayne's room. A tiny voice in the back of his head murmured something, but the darkness drowned it out, and after the moment of hesitation, he resumed his wide stride to the door.

He didn't knock.

"What are you—Dio?" Ellayne's voice was breathy, and he could hear as she rose to her feet in the corner of the room. "You're back! But what . . . what happened to you?"

"What, no hug?" Diomedes held out his arms, but Ellayne didn't move. "Fine then. Straight to business. You're coming with me. We're having a family meeting in the throne room."

"I don't think so," Ellayne said, and her hair swished against her clothing as she shook her head. "I think I'd rather stay here." She sat down in her chair again and shrieked when Diomedes sent a wisp of dark magic in the direction of her shadow counterpart. Her breathing sped up.

"It isn't optional," Diomedes said, his sneer returning to his face as he wrapped the magic around her wrist and yanked her across the room.

Stop, the resistance whispered, but as soon as it appeared, magic swept through and erased the thought. He needed to keep going. Needed to take her to the throne room and remove the threat.

Ellayne struggled against the magic latched around her, but Diomedes didn't budge as he pulled her toward the door.

"Dio, stop this. Whatever you're doing, stop. Dio!" Ellayne yelped when he slammed the door behind them with his magic.

Ignoring her pleas, he led her down the servants' stairs, knowing it'd be easier to avoid the royal guards prowling the hallways. Somewhere deep in his mind, the tiny voice returned.

He ignored it again.

Chapter Thirty-Eight

Any guard who approached him while he forced his sister to the throne room got blasted into a wall with Diomedes's magic. And when they got to the enormous double doors of the throne room, a few of Raidah's men met them.

"Your Highness," one man said with a low grunt.

Diomedes didn't wait for them to open the doors, doubting they even would. They weren't royal guards, after all. Instead, he flicked the doors open with his magic and shoved Ellayne in.

The spell on King Butch had worn off. That was clear as soon as Diomedes stepped into the room.

"I don't know what you think you're accomplishing by doing this, Son, but you're terribly mistaken. You're not going to get anything done right by forcing those around you to comply to your will." King Butch continued to speak as Diomedes forced Ellayne to the front of the room, where the staircase led up to the two thrones.

"Is that so, *Father*?" Diomedes asked, spitting out his last word like it was rancid. "Because I wholeheartedly disagree. Sit down," he said, pushing Ellayne toward the thrones. She continued to struggle against him. "And that's enough out of you." He flicked his hand toward his father to silence him as he passed by.

"Your father's right, Diomedes."

His body tensed at the sound of his stepmother's voice. But it wasn't his reaction; it was Emmalee's. He pressed his palm to the side of his head when her anger and hurt saturated his mind. Her emotions were attached to images that flashed by so quickly they made him feel sick for a moment.

In every image Emmalee forced upon him, Evangeline was there. A few images repeated over and over again. Evangeline as a young woman in a bookstore Diomedes didn't recognize. Evangeline embracing Emmalee as the latter sobbed. Evangeline facing Emmalee in a familiar field of purple flowers, a pained expression on the queen's face. Evangeline standing in the cave where Diomedes had found the dagger, bloody and bruised as the floor fell out from beneath her. Evangeline holding Emmalee's head in her lap, tears leaving streaks through the dirt, blood, and grime on her cheeks.

Diomedes staggered to the side, begging Emmalee to stop. After being increasingly numbed by the dark magic since the council, the sudden influx of emotion disoriented him. He lost grip on the thin line of magic holding Ellayne's wrists, and she kicked him in the chest, sending him back down the stairs they'd been climbing toward the raised dais the thrones sat on.

He grunted as he pushed himself to his feet, rubbing the side of his head, which ached like he'd been clobbered with a blunt object.

"That's enough," Diomedes said, both to his sister and to Emmalee. Rubbing his chest to soothe the pain where Ellayne had kicked him, he turned to face her. "I said *sit*." He pointed toward her shadow counterpart, where he could hear her heavy breathing, and forced her body into the throne. "And stay put. I'll deal with you when I'm ready."

"*Tenebrous Thorns,*" Emmalee said, her voice calm despite the outburst she'd had only moments earlier. "*The vine from the Dark. You can summon it and keep your sister in place while you prepare for the curse.*" She continued to give him instructions, and after a second of raising both hands, Diomedes could sense the vines as they snaked out of the floor and wrapped around his sister, digging their three-inch thorns into her skin. She cried out, but with the emptiness filling him, he didn't hesitate.

"Dio, stop this," Ellayne said, her voice laden with emotion. For a moment, he thought she might cry. He ignored her.

The wall of darkness protecting his present actions and words struck down every thought which longed to go to Ellayne's aid.

"Now for the interesting part," he said, pulling the runed jar out of his bag. "I'm sure this is clear, but I will be taking my place on the throne a bit earlier than everyone expected." He climbed back up the stairs and knelt down near the throne. With nimble fingers, he removed his dagger—Emmalee's dagger.

"Where did you get that?" Evangeline asked, her voice sending the same reaction through Diomedes's body. But he clenched his jaw and kept working, using the dagger to reopen the wound in his wrist he'd used to tie the curse to the tiny house earlier.

The blood dripped into the jar quickly at first but slowed down a few seconds after he took away the pressure he'd placed on it. Shadow Armannii shifted, but he did not speak.

"This little old thing?" He waved the dagger off to the side, shrugging with a grin. "Found it at the bottom of some deep dark pit. Around the same time this happened, actually." He pulled off the scarf covering where his eyes should've been and heard at least two gasps.

"You don't know what you're doing," Evangeline said, her voice filled with anxiety. He could hear her straining against Blanndynne, who snorted from behind the queen. "That thing, it's dangerous."

"It is quite sharp," Diomedes said, rising to his feet with the jar in one hand and the dagger in the other.

Ellayne hissed as she tried to squirm away. "Don't. Dio, don't!" She let out an ear-piercing scream when Diomedes felt through the vines and found where her arm was pinned down. With careful precision, he pressed the tip into her skin and sliced it open.

Once again, blood trickled into the jar.

"Diomedes, please. I know what you're doing. I know Emmalee has something to do with it. But please, please don't." The queen let out a sob, and her bracelets jingled as she struggled against Blanndynne. "Not to her. Please, not Ellayne."

"You know what I'm doing?" Diomedes straightened up and angled his head in Evangeline's direction. Somewhere in the back of his mind, he could feel Emmalee's presence perk up at the mention of her name. "If you do know what I'm about to do, you know I'm doing her a favor." He flicked the dagger out to the side again as he spoke, gesturing with both his hands. "Because this way, she stays alive. She has to be out of the picture though. She's the only other threat to the throne, and we all know she'd be no different than my father, spending entirely too much time worrying over tiny matters while a war rips the country to shreds. So as unfortunate as it is, Ellayne's got to go."

Stop. The resistance was demolished the second it appeared.

"If you do this, you're a monster. I don't know what Em—"

"And that's enough out of you too," Diomedes muttered, silencing his stepmother as well. Emmalee seemed to approve.

"Dio, please." Ellayne's voice was strained, and he could hear the terror in her words. "I'm your sister. This isn't you."

"Oh, but it is now." He grinned at her. "And you should be thanking me. I'm doing you a favor here. You'll be safe and sound, out of the way with no memory of any of this ever happening. Beats being dead, right?" He tucked his dagger back into its place on his belt and then reached into the jar, coating his fingertips in their mixed blood. "Now hold still."

Emmalee had already called the intricate rune needed for the curse to the forefront of Diomedes's mind, and he used the image to trace the rune on Ellayne's forehead. She shifted and tried to lean away from him, but in a huff of frustration, Diomedes grabbed hold of her throat, slamming her head against the back of the throne with one hand while he completed the rune.

She sputtered into a cough when he finished and released her. He didn't care.

"Diomedes, what are you doing? When did this become part of the—"

"Hush, Armannii." Diomedes's voice boomed, filling the throne room. The elf fell silent, but Diomedes could sense his growing restlessness.

There were two more steps: another rune, which he painted over her left wrist—the one he'd sliced open—and then the moment he had not thought out all the way.

"*I all but told you what to do. I told you how to break your sister's heart,*" Emmalee said, her voice too loud in his mind—too crisp. "*Kill Evangeline.*"

The resistance returned, weaker but still present. For as long as he could remember, he'd resented his stepmother—the woman who'd replaced his mother on the throne and in his father's heart. But to kill her? That was cruel, wasn't it?

"*No, it's justice. Revenge for your mother.*" Emmalee's voice was warped with voices again, and Diomedes cringed.

He could sense Emmalee somewhere in his mind and struggled to separate her anticipation from what he felt. He wanted to kill her. No, *she* wanted to kill her. The noise in his head was overwhelming. But as he put the jar by the bottom of the throne and pulled his dagger back out, he knew what he needed to do.

"Now what?" Ellayne asked, anger filling her voice and replacing her meekness. "You're a monster, you know that? How could you betray your own family? Dio, please! You don't have to do this. I'm your sister, Dio!"

Diomedes could hear his father and stepmother struggling against Armannii and Blanndynne, but the only thing it did was bring a grin to his face as he marched down the stairs toward Evangeline. Was he grinning? What control did he still have? What was real and what wasn't? The dark magic within him swelled with anticipation—like it knew the role it would play in laying the curse and wanted nothing more than to do its part.

"Submit it all. Everything. You mustn't hold on to a single memory. Hand everything over before you complete the curse, Diomedes. Do it now." With her command, the resistance retreated, hiding in the depths of his mind somewhere behind a sealed door. Diomedes began emptying every memory that came to mind into the hungry dark void swirling inside him. The power was instantaneous, and so was the emptiness. No emotions. No feelings. No guilt. Just magic.

Just power.

"Hand her over," Diomedes said to Blanndynne, and Evangeline made a noise as Blanndynne shoved her toward Diomedes. Her shadow counterpart fell on her knees in front of Diomedes, and she leaned over, struggling to take off one of her bracelets until he reached down, catching a fistful of her hair.

"Diomedes, you need to stop," Armannii said, his voice taut. "You need to calm down and—"

"Quiet," Diomedes said, snapping his head in Armannii's direction. "Don't speak again."

Those weren't his words. The voices had spoken for him. Moved for him. Against him.

Diomedes yanked Evangeline to her feet. She brought both hands up to try to release his grip from the back of her head, but he was stronger. Diomedes walked her a few feet back toward the bottom of the steps leading to the thrones. He pushed her down to her knees again.

"You know"—Diomedes tilted his head to the side—"I've resented my father for a long time. I blame him for my mother

376

leaving me. For his constant disappearances to private meetings around the country. For his indecision about ending the war. But most of all, I hate him for marrying you." He pulled her hair, tilting her chin and face up. "You were a nobody who had no right becoming queen. You became a distraction for my father." He gestured toward Ellayne before angling the dagger against Evangeline's exposed throat. Was this his anger or Emmalee's?

Diomedes's hand, which rested on Evangeline's shoulder, warmed up from the touch of her skin, but he didn't have time to process it because Butch shoved against Armannii. But the elf did something to make him fall silent again.

"Diomedes, wait! What are you planning on—"

"Quiet," Diomedes barked at Armannii, cutting off the elf's question before he could finish.

"But she's not—"

Turning his head, Diomedes caught a glimpse of Armannii's shadow counterpart taking a step around the king. "I said *quiet*." Diomedes's whisper was deadly. "Speak again and you'll regret it."

He refocused on his stepmother.

"You, Evangeline, are the voice whispering in his ear for the war to continue. You're the one who fought the sorceress in the final battle. You took away magic's best shot at overcoming the Split. You've been an unwelcome guest in this place for too long. But not now. Now there's a promise of hope for those with magic. I will end this war and make sure everyone sees magic for what it is. Power."

Inside his mind, he could hear the expectancy in Emmalee's words. "*Let her speak.*"

Curious as to what his stepmother had to say—and slightly hoping she would beg for her life—Diomedes lifted the spell keeping her mute. To his disappointment, and Emmalee's, her words had nothing to do with the dagger to her neck.

"Ellayne, don't watch, love."

"Diomedes, Dio, please," Ellayne begged, her voice cracking. "Please."

Evangeline didn't stop talking, her attention only on speaking to her daughter. "You must be strong. I love you. Honey, I love—"

"*Do it.*"

Diomedes pressed down, raking the blade over Evangeline's throat. The queen made a guttural gurgling sound and thudded on the floor when Diomedes let go of the back of her head.

"No!" Ellayne's scream permeated every inch of the room.

Then came silence.

Chapter Thirty-Nine

When the Curse of Infiniti took effect and whisked his sister away to the house he'd prepared, it drained Dio of a majority of his magic, and he stumbled forward before catching himself. In that second, he couldn't breathe. Couldn't speak. Couldn't do anything but feel guilt, pain, and confusion over what he'd just done. Crippling self-reproach swallowed every accessible part of his mind.

How could he have taken yet another life without hesitation? How could he have cursed his own sister, his only ally in the castle? The scent of the blood on his hands burned his nostrils, and he wanted to retch. How could this have happened? When had he lost control? He tried to breathe, tried to calm down, but the resistance he'd felt to giving up his memories wouldn't relent. He was a monster, just as Evangeline had said. A monster. A murderer. A traitor. Was there a way to undo it all? To get his sister back? To apologize and be forgiven? To go back in time and never pick up that dagger?

He felt alone, like he was suffocating in the room by himself. It kept getting smaller by the second.

"What was that?" Armannii's voice was harsh, and without his magic, Dio relied on his words to figure out where he was in the room. Footsteps clicked toward him, but he staggered away.

"Stay back. Keep your distance," Dio said, struggling to get the words out. It felt like his windpipe was closing in on itself, and a pain formed somewhere in the back of his throat.

"Diomedes, are you okay?" Blanndynne asked, her voice soft. It was her footsteps he had heard.

He was sweating, and it dripped down the side of his neck, absorbing into the collar of his shirt. His chest felt tight, and he gripped it as he leaned forward, resting one hand on his knee to keep himself steady. He was terrified, the same way he had been when he'd woken up with nightmares as a little boy.

He wanted to apologize. To take it all back. To make it right.

"That's enough, Diomedes. You have done everything as I planned, and now you will deal with your father."

At Emmalee's return, darkness began to fill him, albeit slowly. Slow enough that the agony of his guilt continued to tear him in two.

"What have you done?" Butch cried, and Diomedes stepped out of the way as his father broke free from Armannii and sprinted to the place where his dead wife's body lay.

The voices were returning, one by one, trying to force control back into their hands. But Dio rebelled. The resistance joined him, fighting for Dio to keep control. But the darkness was stronger, and the more it built up, the less Dio could control his words and actions.

On the outside, Diomedes shrugged as he wiped the bloody dagger on the front of his trousers. On the inside, Dio tried to claw his way out. To be seen. To be noticed.

Instead, he heard his own voice speaking words he had not chosen to say. "Simple. I've secured my place as king."

His father didn't respond. King Butch's sobs were muffled, and Diomedes could hear him rocking back and forth, holding Evangeline's limp figure.

He'd killed her. Another one. He wanted to be sick, but his body wouldn't obey. A prisoner. He was a prisoner in his own mind.

"Now there's only one more thing to do." Diomedes tilted his head, a smile on his face as he angled his body toward his father. Inside, Dio feared the words he'd speak next. Was it still him if he was not in control? Was it real? Which one was truly him?

"To be the new king, I've got to get rid of the old one." Diomedes twirled the dagger around his fingers. "Don't worry, I intend on giving you a front row seat to all the changes I'm going to make."

"That's enough, Diomedes!" Armannii snapped, crossing the space between him and Diomedes.

He stopped right in front of Butch. He had put himself in the cross fire, and Dio wordlessly begged for him to move, to stay out of the way. He'd get hurt. Dio didn't want him to get hurt.

"What was that?" Armannii flung his arm toward the empty thrones. "What are you doing? This wasn't the plan."

"Get out of my way, Armannii," Diomedes said, his teeth clenching as he spat out the elf's name. "Not the time."

"Armannii, he's right. Just let him—"

"You think this is right, B? He just killed the queen and did goodness knows what to his sister out of, what, spite? How is that right? I thought it before, but now I know you've gone too far. Diomedes, you've got to stop." Armannii lifted a hand to place it on Diomedes's shoulder, but Diomedes caught it with his magic in midair. Diomedes pushed him backward a few inches with a flick of his wrist.

Dio cringed, though his outside appearance did not change.

"If you know what's good for you, you'll stand down." Diomedes's clutch on the dagger tightened, and his lip pulled up in a sneer. "I will not ask again."

Blanndynne's voice was dipped in concern. "Armannii, just listen to him."

"Are you kidding me? Am I the only one who hasn't lost their mind? You're making history repeat itself. How is this any different than what your grandfather or your great-grandfather did? Huh?" Armannii moved to block Diomedes when he tried to step around him, placing a warning hand against Diomedes's chest to keep him from getting any closer. "You aren't getting your way, so you're throwing a temper tantrum and hurting everyone who stands against you. Well, now I'm standing in your way. So what are you going to do to me? Kill me like you did the queen? And I bet that seer didn't just keel over. You killed him too, didn't you?" Armannii paused, and he must've been studying Diomedes's reaction because the next thing he said was in a low, cautious voice. "What have you done? How many have you killed?"

Too many. He'd killed too many.

"Do you want me to answer that honestly?" Diomedes cocked his head to the side, twirling the dagger in his fingers. He grinned. Dio's fear for his friend doubled each time the elf opposed him. "Because I doubt you'll like the answer."

Armannii shook his head. "This isn't—I didn't—I never wanted this. I wanted the end of the war. I wanted peace. I wanted freedom. Not . . . not this though." Armannii's voice was quiet, and he sighed. "Not this way."

Dio tried to shout that it was not the way he wanted either, but the words were lost in a void of darkness, a void that was growing larger every second.

"This is the only way, Armannii. I *will* become king, and I *will* end the war." Diomedes planted his feet. "The question is, will you be with me when I do?"

Besides the sound of Butch still crying over his wife's body, silence permeated the air. Diomedes waited, his chin held high. In his mind, Dio stood with Armannii.

"It's an easy enough question. Join or not." Diomedes cocked his head to the side. "In fact, it's the same option I gave the council members, come to think of it."

So many bodies. So many deaths. Dio trembled. He didn't want Armannii to be next on the growing list.

Armannii's shadow counterpart tensed. "No." The elf shook his head again. "No. You've made a mess where there was none. Ellayne was your little sister. You were meant to protect her. She wasn't a threat. And the queen shouldn't have died. I won't help you take more lives. I won't."

"Unfortunate, but I can't say I'm surprised." Diomedes gripped Armannii around the throat, and with a boost from his magic, he tossed the elf across the room. A crack resounded.

Dio had tried to stop it. He had pushed and pushed against the darkness when he'd seen its plan, but he hadn't been strong enough. He couldn't take back control—not fully.

To Diomedes's left, Blanndynne gasped, but she didn't move.

"So you're going to kill your best friend?" Armannii asked, coughing as he shifted on the ground. "Is that the cost?"

"No," Diomedes said, his voice light. "No, this is because you're in my way. An obstacle."

"Well, someone's got to tell you that you're being insane." Armannii let out a choked sound when Diomedes gripped him with his magic, lifting him several feet into the air.

"*Kill the elf and be done.*" Emmalee sounded bored.

But he couldn't—wouldn't—kill his best friend. Dio blocked the order from Emmalee, rejecting the idea.

Diomedes hesitated, losing focus on his magic when the war in his head raged louder.

Armannii shouted in pain when Diomedes dropped him to the tile floor. The sound of his friend in pain stirred more strength within Dio, and he pushed back against the darkness. It was cold, unmoving. Then, for a brief moment, he felt a sliver of control enter his possession.

"Leave. Now," Diomedes said through gritted teeth.

"*Do not let him go, Diomedes. He saw what happened with your sister. He knows about the curse.*" Emmalee's voice was terse, and she raised her voice when he didn't obey. Her voice was terrifying, and Dio cowered, losing control again. "*Kill. Him.*"

"You should kill me." Armannii's voice was low, and he let out a hiss as he got to his feet. He took a couple steps toward Diomedes but stopped when Diomedes raised his hand again. "You kill me now, or so help me I *will* come back and make everything right."

He didn't want to kill him, and the thought strengthened Dio, shoving him through the wall of darkness for another brief moment.

"Leave," Diomedes barked, cringing as he fought back Emmalee's shouts in his head. "And if you ever return to Cyanthia or any of my men catch you, I will not be so merciful."

Because he couldn't. Dio felt his strength fading every time he fought against the darkness. He wouldn't last. Not when the darkness was so much more powerful. But if he could just hold on long enough to get Armannii out safely . . .

"Blanndynne, come with me," Armannii said, his voice cracking. "You'll be better off if you just—"

"No." Blanndynne's voice was soft, but it wasn't weak. "How dare you make me choose? What gives you the right to put me in that place?"

Armannii was breathing heavily, but he stood straighter. "You can't be telling me you'd rather stay here?" The pain and shock was audible in the way Armannii's voice trembled.

"I am. I want to stay here with him." Blanndynne glanced back at Diomedes, though he did not move.

"What?" Armannii took a step forward, gesturing toward Diomedes. "Why? You see what he's become?"

"Yes." Blanndynne stepped back from Armannii when he advanced toward her. "He's powerful. He's in control. And he freed me."

"Every step of the way, I've been there for you," Armannii said, his voice dropping.

Blanndynne snorted. "Seriously? Between the two of you, Diomedes has been encouraging me to grow and gain my own sense of control. You would be perfectly content to see me stagnant, with the same amount of strength and ability as when I first came out of that vessel. But Diomedes has helped me grow stronger every day. He trusts me. And you've been jealous of that since the beginning."

"That's not—please, Blanndynne. You need to come with me."

Blanndynne rolled her shoulders back, lifting her chin. "No. I'm staying with Diomedes."

"Very well," Diomedes said, nodding. "You've both made your choice. And you have ten seconds to get out of here before I take back my generous offer and kill you on the spot."

"Fine," Armannii said, and his footsteps were uneven as he limped toward the double doors. He grabbed his bow and quiver off the floor, scraping one end against the tile. "But I *will* be back. I will make this right."

Dio begged him not to return as he held back the wall of voices screaming for him to kill the elf. He wouldn't. No. Not his best friend. Dio wished he could regain control one more time. To say goodbye to his friend. To tell him that he wouldn't be able to stop the darkness should Armannii ever return. It would kill him. And worse yet, Dio could tell it would enjoy it.

Every second, Dio grew weaker.

But he held the darkness back while Armannii's footsteps retreated. He was leaving. He would be safe.

"You better hope for your sake that your eyes are gold."

Chapter Forty

When the double doors closed behind Armannii, the emptiness swallowed Diomedes. The skirmish in his head was over. Armannii was gone, and Dio's will to fight the darkness had gone with him.

But right before it overwhelmed him, the resistance ran, almost as if it were a separate entity inside him, a separate consciousness. It locked itself away, keeping what little pieces of his memory he had left concealed, inaccessible to him and to the magic. It hid them in a corner of his mind it would protect with whatever remained of his humanity.

The darkness didn't seem to notice. Diomedes spun on his heels and directed his attention to where his father's breathing was still laden with sorrow.

"Blanndynne, send for Amira, Al, and all the remaining council members. I believe my father and I need a little bonding time together."

"Where do you want me to gather them?" Blanndynne took a few steps toward the doors and paused.

"Wherever you think is best." He gestured toward the doors, keeping his head angled toward his father below him.

The click of Blanndynne's footsteps faded as soon as one of the double doors closed behind her.

Diomedes cracked his fingers. With one swish of his dagger, he cut his father on the shoulder, using his shadow counterpart as a guide. It didn't matter as long as his father's blood was on the knife.

King Butch cried out, but he didn't move from his dead wife.

"And to think, all of this could've been avoided if you'd just listened, just taken a moment to hear what your only son had to say." He ran his thumb along the dagger's handle.

"I warned you." His father's voice was low, and he shifted on the floor. "This was the last thing I wanted for you. I—"

"You didn't want me to feel powerful. Is that it? Because that's what this is, Father. Power. Ultimate power."

"With the ultimate cost, Son. How do you not understand that?"

"Oh, I understand. I understand that I was willing to pay it. That I was willing to risk everything to end this war. To fight for people persecuted because of their heritage." Diomedes stood taller.

Now that it was only him and his father—and his stepmother's body—the room felt smaller. He knew the ceilings went three stories up; he could even picture the mural of purple flowers painted on the ceiling.

"I never wanted this war to continue for as long as it has. I didn't. I know you don't believe me. But I've been trying to end it since I took my father's crown. It takes time though. There are things that need to happen to end a war in a way that doesn't create more problems. And—"

Diomedes scoffed. "And to think I'm going to take your crown and do in a month or less what you've been unable to do." He let out a laugh, shaking his head. "Do you realize what a failure that makes you?"

"It may have been slow, but we were changing things. If you would just take the time to let me show you."

"That time is up," Diomedes said, reaching down the neck of his tunic to pull up the chain that held his royal medallion. The tiny rectangular mirror tinkled against it. "Instead, you'll get to see all the changes I'm going to make as soon as you're gone."

"The people will never stand for it. I already signed the disinheritance papers. They'll be announced tomorrow. Ellayne is the next to inherit the throne. You won't be the heir after this betrayal, after this tragedy. As soon as word gets out—"

"That's the beauty of what I did to Ellayne. No one outside of those of us present for the curse will remember her. In the eyes of the people, I will be the only option for king. And you'll be missing your speech."

King Butch moved again, grunting as he stood up. Diomedes and his father had been similar heights for many years. Maybe it was the grief weighing his father's shoulders down, or maybe it came from the magic making Diomedes stand up straighter, but Diomedes felt taller and stronger.

"The people will never stand for this hostile takeover you've plotted."

"And they'll never know about that either." Diomedes took a step to the side, walking until his back was toward the thrones and he was facing his father head-on. "You see, with a little lying and manipulation, I'll have the whole country believing a mystery group of disgruntled citizens banded together and swarmed the castle because they were tired of the war. In the process, the king and queen were killed, and their only son was blinded. But he fought back and won." Diomedes spoke through a sneer, opening his arms out wide. "I'll be a hero."

"So that's it? You're going to kill your own father?"

Diomedes shook his head. "No, no, no. Have you already forgotten what I told you?" He held up the mirror that dangled around his neck. "I plan to keep you close to my heart forever."

"What?"

"Don't worry." His voice was light and airy as he pulled the chain off and wiped the dagger, which had blood from both him and his father on it, across the mirror. He held the small mirror out in front of him with one hand while facing the palm of his other hand toward his father. "I'll show you."

Diomedes took a deep breath, recalling the instructions Emmalee had given him the night before while Amira, Al, and the rest of Raidah's forces had been sleeping. He had what he needed: a reflective surface, the blood of both the captor and the victim, and the magic necessary to cast the spell.

Picturing his father's face—the blond hair that had turned gray, the wrinkles on the sides of his eyes and on his forehead, the straight-edged jaw Diomedes himself had inherited—Diomedes drew on the dark magic. It grew stronger the harder he concentrated, and he could feel as it rushed into his hands. With a single tug of his mind, he felt his magic reach out and snatch his father, sucking him into the mirror he'd prepared with the blood.

A clatter resounded after Diomedes had completed the spell, and a slow grin spread over his lips. He knew what the sound was: the crown his father had worn almost every single day.

And now it was his.

With a hand raised, Diomedes pictured the crown flying into his hand, and he caught it instinctively when it flew across the room into his waiting fingers. The metal cooled down at his touch, his hand still vibrated with humming magic waiting to be used.

His magic.

His crown.

And after he sauntered up the stairs and sent the Tenebrous Thorns back to the place from whence they'd come, he sat on *his* throne.

Epilogue

The declaration has spread throughout the country, and word has been sent to those in the Dark as well. Soon everyone will know that the war is over," Blanndynne reported from the seat next to the king.

Diomedes stroked his chin as he leaned against the arm of his chair at the head of the meeting table. His council was less than half the size of his father's, though he had intentions to grow it soon. It had, of course, only been a week. With the three council members who'd pledged their allegiance to him, along with Amira, Al, and Blanndynne, his council was made up of six people.

"I'm pleased to hear that. And how have the people been reacting to the news?" Diomedes asked, reaching up to adjust the silk scarf that covered his absent eyes. Emmalee had suggested that his magic remain hidden from those who did not already know. He agreed—for the time being, at least.

"There has been rejoicing all over Phildeterre," Amira said, an audible smile in her voice.

Diomedes was well aware of the celebrating. He'd heard the sounds of magic explosions filling the air at night and could only imagine the colorful bursts they'd created.

"Very good. Well," he said as he sat up straight. "If that's all, I—"

"Pardon, Your Majesty, but we've only just begun," one of the council members who'd worked for his father said, not backing down when Diomedes furrowed his brow at him.

"Yes," said another. "The tunnels that led to the castle caved in and sank a few houses when they collapsed during the siege. Shouldn't the tunnels be rebuilt or the ground at least reinforced?"

"Seal the ground, but don't rebuild the tunnels. They're clearly a liability," Diomedes said, waving his hand to the side. "And now—"

"And what about the changes now that the war is over?" the first council member said. "While people seem to be rejoicing over the end of the war, many are asking about the social and economic changes that'll result. They want to prepare for—"

Diomedes cut him off with a flick of his hand, sending out silencing magic.

"I said"—Diomedes gritted his teeth—"if that's all. But I suppose I should've clarified that this meeting is over." He stood up, his chair scratching against the floor. "Blanndynne," he said, nodding to her. "Walk with me."

Other chairs moved as people stood up to give respect as he left, Blanndynne's hurried footsteps trailing behind him. Neither of them spoke until the door closed behind them in his father's old office, which was now his.

"I have a special task for you," Diomedes said, sitting down in the chair behind the desk. He straightened the dragon figurine he'd purchased in the underground market in the Albanistic Desert. Considering it was made from crystal, he was surprised it hadn't chipped on the journey.

Blanndynne came to a stop in front of him and waited for him to continue. Reaching inside the top drawer, he pulled out a hand mirror, upon which he'd inscribed the same runes as the mirror from the tiny house. It was wrapped in a soft fabric, and Blanndynne breathed out an audible sigh when she unwrapped it.

"It's beautiful, but what—" Her words fell short, and Diomedes grinned, knowing exactly why. "That's your sister."

"Good observation." Diomedes leaned against the chair, looping his fingers together to cradle the back of his head. "I want you to keep an eye on her. You read the book and understand the curse. She'll have no memory of who she is. You're free to tell her whatever you so desire as long as it doesn't lead her back here. Her curse is, well, it's permanent for the most part. There's only one way out of it."

"You," she said, and the fabric rustled as she wrapped the mirror back up.

"Right you are. She's free to run around all of Phildeterre. Let's just keep her out of the castle until we see the true extent of this curse, shall we? Could even be fun. You spent plenty of your life under the control of others. How would you like to give the forgotten princess of Phildeterre a never-ending list of tasks for infinity?"

Diomedes grinned, but somewhere in a hidden corner of his mind lay his last remaining memories. The resistance. And from somewhere in there, a tiny voice repeated the only words that could free her. *Ellayne, I release you.*

* * *

Turn the page to get a sneak peek of the first chapter in

Curse of Infiniti!

Available Now!

Chapter One

From the first moment of cognition, a heavy mist muddled her mind, and emptiness echoed like the silence that rang in her ears. With her eyes still closed, she opened up her mind to her other senses, inhaling an odor of mildew that left her forehead wrinkling. Her tongue stuck to the roof of her mouth, drawn there by the moisture it lacked. Her lips cracked as she pressed them together. As she thought about the lack of taste in her mouth, her stomach rumbled, vibrating through her core.

Lying on her back, she placed a hand over her abdomen, and the scratchy wool from a blanket tickled her fingers in response. In the stillness, she could feel her pulse beating beneath the blanket. Focusing on the steady rhythm, she inhaled deeply and let it out, feeling her limbs come to awareness in a slow ripple from the epicenter of her torso down to her toes.

Her eyes flitted open, adjusting to the light coming in from a small window with burlap curtains covering it. *Where am I?* Whispers of questions began swirling in the recesses of her mind. She straightened her head from where it had tilted to the side on a thin pillow. The gray wool blanket that covered her from the chest down rustled as she pushed herself up, resting on her elbows.

Not an ounce of familiarity came to her as she took in the small room. Besides the bed she was perched on, there was a chair by the window and a body-length mirror hanging on the wall opposite the single door. A skeleton of a room.

What is this place? Even her thoughts dripped with drowsiness, slurring in her mind. She sat all the way up. Her legs swung over the edge of the bed in one swift motion as she pushed the blanket off. The clothing the blanket revealed caused her muscles to tense. Like the room, they were foreign to her: a pale green dress with a cream apron tied around the front covered her torso and legs down past her knees. Her hand shook as she smoothed the fabric of the apron.

The scuffed floorboards had seen better days, and were rough and cold on her bare feet as she rose from the bed and stepped to the center of the room. Her breathing hitched and her heartbeat fluttered in a rapid tempo as soon as she laid eyes on her reflection.

A young woman with long, wavy blond hair stared back at her, brown eyes wide and growing mistier the longer she gaped into them. The reflection copied her actions as she raised a hand to her head, feeling the shape of her face from the temple down to the jawline in a slow trail. Every inch she touched seemed to place a heavier weight on her chest.

As her fingertips traced down the curve of her neck, she watched her hand stop at a thin silver line—a necklace glimmering in the light. Her fingers caressed the cool metal.

She examined the necklace up close. It was a medallion the size of a small coin. The side that looked up at her had a crest carved into it and at the center was what looked like a dragon with a sword through its heart. The image sent a shiver down to her toes, and she flipped it over to inspect the back. There was something inscribed in minuscule, scrawling lines, but she couldn't decipher what it was. After a minute of staring at it, all she could see were interlacing curves without much of a pattern.

She lifted her chin to look back into the mirror, letting the necklace return to its resting place above the neckline of her dress.

Taking a step closer, she stared straight into her own eyes, searching them for answers to the questions that continued to grow louder in her head.

What happened to me? There was no controlling the heat pooling in the corners of her eyes as frustration replaced the numbness she'd felt up to that point. The first droplet traveled down her cheek, and when it stopped momentarily in the corner of her nostril, she watched until another tear followed its trail and moved it farther down her face. It dropped off her chin, and she squeezed her eyes closed.

Emptiness dug sharp claws into the crevices of her mind, refusing to budge as she pulled at it. She raced to recall what had happened before she woke up, but she hit a dark wall in the center of her brain. The paths she tried to follow ended abruptly, and soon her thoughts were dripping in a swirling black mist.

The battle in her mind crippled her.

Her legs buckled, and she hit her knees. Covering her face, the real tears began as her shoulders heaved. Frustration clashed with fear, and despair bit sharply back. Together they mingled in her mind, controlling her as she pushed against her eye sockets until bright shapes danced just behind her lids. Her breaths ripped through her chest, leaving it in tatters.

Name.

She searched and searched, but couldn't find a single sign that revealed her name. *How can I not have a name?*

Moving her hands from her face, she opened her eyes. The room closed in around her—a cage. It squeezed more air out of her than she had to give.

"Who am I?" she whimpered, her voice reverberating off the empty walls and bouncing back to her ears. It too was unfamiliar. "Who am I?" she repeated over and over. The woman in the mirror mouthed the same question with her. Her violent sobs turned to weeping, with hitched breaths and hiccups. But she didn't stop asking the question. *Who am I? Who am I? Who am I?* She didn't notice she was rocking back and forth with her knees to her chest until she saw the other woman doing it in the mirror.

Time ticked away while she moaned. *Why can't I recognize my own face?* She wiped at her eyes, carrying away some of the salty wetness. She stopped rocking. Caught in the hypnotic pull of rediscovering her own features—the now puffy eyes, crooked red nose, flushed cheeks—her breathing leveled out, hitching less and less. Her body stopped shuddering while she sat there, transfixed once again by her mirror image.

The silence returned, pushing down on her as she straightened up. Behind her in the mirror, the door caught her attention. She sniffled and rubbed her nose with the back of her hand. Pressing off the floor, she stood and turned her back on her reflection. The mirror had made the door seem farther away, but it now stood a few feet in front of her.

Another step carried her closer, and she found herself rubbing the back of the necklace with her thumb as she considered whether to turn the handle or not. Making her decision, the floorboard creaked once more as she leaned forward and placed her hand on the worn metal handle. With a quick exhale, she pressed it down and pulled the door open.

READ ELLAYNE'S STORY IN

THE INFINITI TRILOGY!

Can Ellayne collect enough fragments of her past before the nightmarish figure from her dreams catches up with her?

Find out in **Curse of Infiniti**!

How much is Ellayne willing to risk to free her father from the spell laid on him by the same person who cursed her all those years ago? Will she risk it all?

Don't miss the thrilling sequel, **Defying Infiniti**!

It all comes down to this. Who will win the war? Who will end up sitting on the throne of Phildeterre victorious?

Ellayne's story comes to an end in the suspenseful finale, **Infinit**!

SIGN UP FOR MY AUTHOR NEWSLETTER

Enjoy interactive maps, character art, short stories, and other exclusives from this series and others by subscribing to my newsletter and visiting my website at:

www.rachelhetrickwrites.com

Acknowledgments

Another series complete! It's hard to believe that I've published five books in less than two years. The Lord is good. His creativity is what gives me the ability to do all of this. He should receive all glory!

Of course, I want to thank my parents, Marc and Beth, who play numerous roles within my publishing journey. From beta readers to biggest fans, their encouragement is endless. I'm so extremely thankful for them. Thank you Mom and Dad!

I also want to thank my sister, Becca, who covers me in words of affirmation whether I want them or not. And then there's my Syra, who is the best fur baby to exist. I'm not biased at all.

Thank you to the world's best editor, Natalia Leigh, who fit me into her tight schedule and has wonderfully edited all five of my books. I'm so grateful for her, and am always excited to send her my new projects. I will continue to sing the praises of Enchanted Ink Publishing all my author days! Thank you Natalia!

Miblart has also been a staple within my publishing journey. They've given me nothing but BEAUTIFUL covers since I first started working with them in 2020. I highly recommend Miblart to any indie author looking for amazing art. A huge thank you to the team for working with me again on this book!

This book was rough when I sent it to my beta readers, and I need to thank each and every one of them for helping me piece it together to make it into the exciting story in front of you. I am so thankful for both rounds of beta readers. Thank you to Zoey B., Kaisa Burnett, Sydney Fowler, Rhoni Goslin, Marc H. Hetrick, Elizabeth Hetrick, Rachael Huszar, Cydney Knight-Pinneo, and Sarah Orr. Thank you all so much! I couldn't have finished this series without you!

My mom is the only other person to have read my books almost as much as I have, so I want to give her extra thanks.

Proofreading isn't the easiest, especially on a short time span. She's also a genius when it comes to formatting, and has kept me from chucking my laptop across the room on multiple occasions. Thanks Mom!

It wouldn't be a complete acknowledgments section without me thanking YOU! It's an incredible feeling to have people reading the stories that have been in my head since high school. Thank you for picking up my book, and I hope you enjoyed Dio's side of the story. Thank you for sharing in these adventures!

I hope you enjoyed The Fallen Heir Series! If you did, **please consider sharing it, writing a review, or telling your neighbor**. One of the best things you can do for an author is leave a review and a rating!

I hope you know how much you are loved and appreciated!

SCAN THE QR CODE BELOW TO GO

DIRECTLY TO THE GOODREADS PAGE

FOR *THE HEIR'S BETRAYAL!*

DON'T FORGET TO LEAVE A RATING AND REVIEW!

About the Author

Rachel Hetrick has now published five books (*Curse of Infiniti, Defying Infiniti, Infinit, The Heir's Descent,* and *The Heir's Betrayal*), and is excited to release many more. She was born in Colorado, and graduated from the University of Colorado Colorado Springs in 2017 with a Bachelor of Arts degree in English Literature and a Creative Writing minor. Soon after she graduated, she moved to the opposite side of the world and taught English in Asia for a year and a half. However, when the world went nuts at the beginning of 2020, God made it clear that the time had come to pursue her childhood dream of becoming a published author. With the inspiration of many incredible authors on Youtube, Rachel grew as a writer, editor, and now publisher. She has since moved back to Colorado and lives with her Siamese cat, Syra (who kicked Feline Infectious Peritonitis, FIP, in the rear end). She looks forward to hearing from her readers!

YOU CAN CONNECT WITH RACHEL THROUGH:

WEBSITE: www.rachelhetrickwrites.com
INSTAGRAM: @rachel_hetrick_writes